Joy Takes Flight

Other Books by Bonnie Leon

SYDNEY COVE SERIES

To Love Anew
Longings of the Heart
Enduring Love

ALASKAN SKIES SERIES

Touching the Clouds
Wings of Promise
Joy Takes Flight

ALASKAN SKIES · BOOK THREE

JOY TAKES FLIGHT

A NOVEL

BONNIE LEON

a division of Baker Publishing Group
Grand Rapids, Michigan

© 2012 by Bonnie Leon

Published by Revell
a division of Baker Publishing Group
P.O. Box 6287, Grand Rapids, MI 49516-6287
www.revellbooks.com

Printed in the United States of America

Library of Congress Cataloging-in-Publication Data
Leon, Bonnie.
    Joy takes flight : a novel / Bonnie Leon.
        p.   cm. — (Alaskan skies ; bk. 3)
    ISBN 978-0-8007-3361-2 (pbk.)
    1. Women air pilots—Fiction. 2. Alaska—Fiction. I. Title.
PS3562.E533J69 2012
813'.54—dc23   2012006215

Scripture used in this book, whether quoted or paraphrased by the characters, is taken from the King James Version of the Bible.

Published in association with the Books & Such Literary Agency, 52 Mission Circle, Suite 122, PMB 170, Santa Rosa, CA 95409-5370, www.booksandsuch.biz.

The internet addresses, email addresses, and phone numbers in this book are accurate at the time of publication. They are provided as a resource. Baker Publishing Group does not endorse them or vouch for their content or permanence.

12   13   14   15   16   17   18   7   6   5   4   3   2   1

To my brother, Bruce, an Alaskan
who may have been born 100 years too late.

— 1 —

Kate stared into the church mirror and recited the name once more. "Mrs. Paul Anderson." She'd tried on the name many times, and in less than an hour it would truly be hers. This all felt like a dream. She'd thought she'd lost him. And now she was about to become Paul's wife.

She turned to the side and smoothed her floor-length gown. Her dear friend, Muriel Stevens, had convinced her to use a little extra makeup, and she'd made sure her hair was perfectly coiffed. Still, she looked like Kate Evans—tall and athletic, her auburn hair peeking out from beneath a veil and hazel eyes vibrant with anticipation. "Kate Anderson. Mrs. Paul Anderson."

February 26, 1938, would draw a line in Kate's history, one that stated she'd never be the same. She'd still be Kate the bush pilot who loved a challenge, but she'd also be Paul's wife . . . She'd be better because he shared her life, but she was a little frightened. She didn't know how to be someone's wife. Kate smiled at her image and almost giggled. Poor Paul. It wouldn't be easy on him while she learned to relinquish some of her independence.

Kate glanced at the clock—thirty minutes. Nerves skittered

up and down her spine, tickled her arms, and made her stomach flip. What kind of wife *would* she be? Kate thought of her mother. She was strong and supportive, always thinking of others. She knew how to do all the wifely things. She could sew up a dress in a day if needed and the food on her table was always delicious. Kate knew she'd never be that kind of wife. She barely knew how to cook and Paul was better at sewing than she was. Plus being submissive wasn't something that came naturally. Paul knew that and he wanted to marry her anyway. A swell of joy rose up inside Kate. It wouldn't be long now.

She let out a sigh. If only her parents could be here. Over the years she and her mother had talked about what her wedding would be like. Kate had always imagined that her parents would be part of this momentous day. Poor apple sales had put a stranglehold on their budget and drained most of their savings. There was no extra money for a trip to Alaska. Albert Towns, one of her first friends in the territory, would walk her down the aisle. He was as close to a father as she had here in Alaska.

The bangs Muriel had carefully combed to the side fell into Kate's eyes. She pushed them back in place and considered using one of the pins that held the tiny flowers in her veil to clip them.

She folded her arms over her chest. No. She was still plain Kate, a pilot who didn't care about what her bangs were doing.

She envisioned Paul—tall and broad shouldered, with coffee-colored hair and serious brown eyes. When he laughed, they'd brighten, and when he looked at her, they gentled. She loved to hear him laugh. Wonder engulfed her. She was about to marry the most amazing man in the world. But he was a man with a secret. She felt a quiver of uncertainty, but brushed it aside. She loved him. Questions and answers were for another day.

She turned her back to the mirror so she could see if the ribbon hung properly. The gown swept slightly longer in back than the front. She smoothed the soft peach lace that lay over the satin taffeta slip lining. Muriel and Helen had tried to talk her into a white gown, but Kate wanted something different. She'd never considered herself beautiful, but this gown made the most of her features and her figure. She imagined Paul's expression when he saw her and a breath caught in her throat.

"Oh, how I love you," she whispered, feeling happiness she'd never known. They would work out their differences. It might not be easy but they'd find a way. He was still afraid of losing her in a flying accident, but he'd said she could fly when and where she wanted, no strings. Kate knew she'd have to make some compromises. After today she'd never be just Kate, a woman who made her own choices and didn't answer to anyone, except God. She and Paul would be forever bonded and what affected one would affect the other.

Again, her bangs dropped into her eyes. She removed a pin from her veil and secured them. She picked up her bouquet made of daisies, white asters, and tiny pink roses, then stepped back and studied herself in the full-length mirror. Today she *was* beautiful.

She glanced at the clock. It was nearly time.

The door opened and Muriel stepped in. She beamed. "You look absolutely stunning."

Kate made a small twirl. "You think so?"

"Absolutely." She smiled, but there was hesitation in her blue eyes.

"Is everything all right?" Kate asked.

"Of course." Muriel compressed her lips.

"How is Paul? Is he nervous?"

Muriel glanced at the door. With a small shrug, she said, "I'm . . . not sure. I mean, how can you tell, really?"

Kate knew Muriel was keeping something from her. Apprehension stirred in her heart. "You haven't talked to him?"

Muriel moved to Kate and placed her hands on Kate's shoulders. "Now, don't get upset, I'm sure there's an explanation."

"Upset about what? An explanation for what?" Apprehension exploded into fear.

"Well . . . Paul's not here yet."

"What? But the ceremony begins in a few minutes. He has to be here. Are you sure?"

"Yes." Again Muriel's eyes wandered toward the door. "It's snowing hard. I'm sure he's on his way. It's the weather. That's all."

"He's only coming from the hotel. That's not more than fifteen minutes' drive."

Muriel pressed her hands together and changed the subject. "Everything else is ready. The church looks absolutely gorgeous. Mrs. Simpson did a wonderful job with the flowers. Bless her for donating flowers from her hothouse." She lifted her brows and smiled playfully. "And in spite of my mother and Sassa's differences about decorating the reception room, they managed to come to agreement and everything looks lovely."

Kate didn't care about the decorations. She needed to know what had happened to Paul. Where was he?

"Wait until you see the cake. It's gorgeous. The church is packed—"

"Paul should be here." Kate moved to the door, opened it slightly, and looked down the short hallway that led to the church foyer. The murmur of voices carried from the vestibule. "Did he call?"

"Not that I know of." Muriel's hand fluttered over her lace collar. "Don't worry, Kate. He'll be here."

Not worry? How could she not worry? "What if something happened?"

"I'm sure we would have heard."

If he was safe, then what had happened? As long as Kate had known Paul he'd been afraid to love anyone. It had been nearly seven years since his wife's death, and since then he'd held his heart in check . . . until now. Maybe he'd changed his mind. Kate turned and looked at Muriel. Her voice tight, she asked, "What if he doesn't want to get married?"

"Of course he does," Muriel twittered. "He loves you."

"I know . . . but he's had trouble . . . you know, with my flying and the loss of his wife."

"That's all behind him." Muriel sounded too cheerful. "I'm sure it's this terrible weather. Why, it's nearly a blizzard out there."

"You said the church is full. Everyone else managed to get here." Kate paced. "A little wind and snow wouldn't keep him away."

"Well, whatever it is, I'm sure he has a good reason." Muriel glanced at the clock. "It's not quite time yet."

"He should have been here thirty minutes ago." Kate could hear the strident tone in her voice and hated that she'd allowed her distress to show. She pressed her hands together and took a deep breath. Instead of achieving calm, her mind returned to how she'd called off her wedding to Richard three years ago, one week before they were to be married. If she'd done it, Paul might. People changed their minds about things every day. *But he loves me. I know it.*

The door opened and Muriel's mother, Helen, and Paul's native neighbor, Sassa, stepped into the room. Sassa ambled across the floor, her face aglow. She pressed chubby hands on Kate's cheeks. "You are beautiful!"

Helen gazed at her. "You're stunning, dear."

11

"Thank you. Is Paul here yet?"

The two women glanced at each other. "No. Not yet. But I'm sure he's on his way," Helen said.

Kate walked to the door, opened it, and looked out. "He's not coming. I know it. He's changed his mind."

Helen stepped up to Kate, encircled an arm around her waist, and closed the door. Her voice calm, she said, "You wouldn't want him to see you before the wedding. He'll be here. I'm certain of it. He'd never change his mind." She took Kate's hands. "He loves you."

"He does, but you know how hard he's struggled to allow himself to care. Ever since his wife—"

Helen put a finger to Kate's lips. "Now, no more of that. You're about to marry Paul. You've got to have faith in him. He'll do the right thing. He'd never desert you. Never." She led Kate to the mirror. "How could he resist you?" She smiled, her eyes alight.

Kate wished she possessed Helen's serenity. "What if something's happened to him? What if he's been in an accident?"

"Albert and Patrick have gone out to check the roads, but I'm sure he's fine."

Sassa picked up Kate's bouquet and handed it to her. "Let's see how you look." She stepped back. "Perfect." She smiled.

Kate fought tears. No matter how much her friends tried to encourage her, she knew—Paul had changed his mind.

───────

Bundled deep inside his coat, Paul paced the train station platform. Although his hood was pulled snugly around his face, icy wind swept down his neck. He kept his eyes on the track to the south. The train was late. He glanced at his watch. He was supposed to be at the church. He imagined Kate, waiting and distressed. The thought made him sick to his stomach. When he'd insisted on everyone keeping the secret, he never meant to hurt her. He'd been foolish. As soon as he knew there was a delay, he should have told her about the surprise. This was the day they'd waited for, dreamed about. And now he'd ruined it.

He strode inside the depot and to the ticket window. "Any word on the train from Seward?"

The clerk shrugged. "In weather like this, ya never know. She'll get here when she gets here."

She'll get here when she gets here? Paul's frustration nearly boiled over, but he clamped his mouth shut and walked away from the counter. He glanced at the clock. The ceremony was supposed to begin now. He stormed out to the platform and resumed pacing. He had envisioned Kate in her bridal gown, her eyes aglow with love and expectation. Tall and graceful, she'd look stunning as she walked down the aisle. He'd imagined it, dreamed of it. And now everything had gone wrong. Instead of anticipation, she must be feeling abandoned, afraid, angry. The last thing he wanted was to hurt her. *I'm sorry, Katie. So sorry.*

Wind whipped at his hood. This was intolerable. He'd have to leave. And then a train whistle echoed. He stared down the tracks, standing on the edge of the platform, willing the train to appear. And then he saw it, belching steam and chugging toward the station. Paul's tense muscles released.

The train rolled into the station. He watched the windows, searching for Kate's parents, but he didn't see either one. They'd sent a wire. They were supposed to be on this train.

The engine clanked to a stop with a loud whoosh. Steam billowed, swirling around the train. Paul stepped down from the platform and walked alongside the cars, watching the faces of passengers as they disembarked. And then he saw them.

Bill waved and Joan clutched her husband's arm. *Thank you, Lord*. Paul strode toward them.

Bill held out his hand. "Thought we'd never make it." He clapped Paul on the back. "I've never seen so much snow in all my life."

Joan gave Paul a quick hug. "We're late, aren't we? I can't believe we held up your wedding. Kate must be beside herself."

"She doesn't even know you're coming."

"You didn't tell her we'd been delayed?"

"I wanted it to be a surprise. I was sure you'd make it on time."

Joan clasped her hands together and pressed them to her chest. "She doesn't know where you are?"

"No. She doesn't."

Joan shook her head side to side. "Oh my. She must be in an absolute fret. Her groom hasn't shown up."

"I should have told her. I feel awful. But I thought it would work out. We better get a move on."

After getting the luggage, Paul loaded the bags into the trunk of the Towns' car while Joan and Bill climbed in.

Kate sat on a chair, her bouquet in her lap. How could Paul do this to her? Tears slid down her cheeks. They'd talked and talked about their future and dreamed of what could be. She sniffled into a handkerchief. Now none of it mattered. *He just couldn't do it*. Kate's heart squeezed painfully. She doubted it would ever mend.

Helen and Sassa had gone to speak to the guests. Kate couldn't bear to do it. Muriel knelt beside her and rested a hand on her arm. "Don't give up hope."

"If he wants to be here and can't make it, then something terrible has happened. Maybe someone should call the hospital."

Muriel looked stricken, but she smiled and managed to speak calmly. "I'm sure there's an explanation. One day, when you look back on your wedding, you two will laugh about this."

Kate compressed her lips. "What explanation can there be?" She knew. Love was just too great a risk. Whatever secret he'd left behind in San Francisco still had ahold of him. If only he would tell her, maybe she could help.

Sassa's laughter echoed from the church entrance. Kate stood, hope stirring. Was it Paul? Was he here? She headed for the door, but before she could grasp the knob, the door swung open.

"Katharine!" her mother said, swooping in and catching her daughter in her arms. She held her tightly. "I'm so sorry we're late. We almost didn't make it."

"Mom! What are you doing here?" Kate hugged her mother, joy and surprise bubbling up inside.

"That wonderful husband, almost husband, of yours insisted we come. He paid our passage. He wanted it to be a surprise, but not like this. The weather kept us in Seward for two days. We were supposed to surprise you at the rehearsal dinner." She stepped back and gazed at her daughter. "Oh my goodness. You are a picture of beauty. Absolutely stunning."

"There's my Katie girl," Kate heard her father say. He walked in, wearing a broad smile. "You surprised?"

Tears of joy streaming down her cheeks, Kate stepped into her father's embrace. "I had no idea." Kate wanted to run to Paul and throw herself into his arms. He truly was the most wonderful man. And he loved her. He loved her!

Sassa, Helen, and Muriel all stood watching, their eyes shimmering. "You knew. All this time you knew!" Kate exclaimed.

"Paul made us vow to keep the secret," Helen said. "I nearly told you. It was so hard to watch you suffer." She smiled sheepishly. "But now he's here and he's ready to get married."

Everyone, except for Joan and Kate, filed out of the room. "I'm a mess," Kate said.

"All you need is a little touch-up." Joan tidied Kate's hair a bit and her veil. Kate applied fresh lipstick and freshened her makeup, then stood back and looked in the mirror. "Do I look all right?"

"I've never seen a prettier bride." Joan hugged her daughter, then looking at herself in the mirror, said, "I'm a sight." She took off her coat and smoothed her dress. "I changed on the train so I'd be dressed appropriately, but my hair is a mess." Kate handed her the brush and watched while her mother smartened up her hair.

"I still can't believe you're here. Now everything is perfect."

Joan turned and looked at her. "Perfect." She rested her hands on Kate's arms. "This is the wedding God meant for you, sweetheart. Paul's the man the Lord chose." She smiled gently. "You're both blessed. You'll be a good wife, I have no doubt."

"I don't know much about being a wife. I need to learn to cook." Kate giggled.

"I doubt Paul cares much about any of that." Joan gave Kate a kiss on the cheek. "I'd better go in. I love you, Katharine." With one more hug, she left the room.

Kate stood in front of the mirror and stared at herself. Her life was about to change forever. She pressed a hand against her stomach. "It's time for me to become Mrs. Paul Anderson."

— 2 —

Muriel opened the dressing room door and peeked in. "It's time."

Kate's heartbeat picked up. Holding her bouquet, she stared at her reflection in the mirror.

Muriel stepped in. Circling an arm around Kate's shoulders, she said, "You ready?"

Kate glanced down at the quaking bouquet in her hands. "I guess." She laughed.

"We better go. Your father's waiting. He's actually pacing." She tucked an arm into Kate's and the two walked out of the room.

The sounds of a hymn being played on a piano drifted through the church. All of a sudden, Kate didn't feel ready for this and wished the short hallway were longer. Everything seemed to be happening too fast. *You're being silly. You've been waiting and praying for this day.*

She'd given up on Alaska, on flying, and on Paul. When she'd moved back to Yakima, Washington, she was certain her adventure was over. She'd decided to live an ordinary life— work in a store, be a clerk or . . . something commonplace. Maybe one day get married and have a family.

And then everything had changed. She'd returned to Rimrock Lake and an encounter with God had given her back her life. She remembered looking out over the lake, the whisper of wind in the pines and the presence of her friend Alison. Years before, Alison had died there in a plane Kate had been flying. But on the day Kate had returned, when she gazed at the lake, it felt as if her friend had spoken to her straight from heaven. Kate knew she had to return to Alaska. Her eyes teared at the memory and she felt washed anew in forgiveness and hope. If only Alison were here. She'd be so happy for Kate.

Maybe Alison is here. Maybe God gives people glimpses of the special days. She smiled at the idea.

Helen stood in the sanctuary doorway with Grace, one of Sidney's nieces who'd agreed to be the flower girl. The youngster twirled, and the skirt of her frilly pink frock stood straight out. Flower petals flew out of her wicker basket.

Helen placed a hand on the little girl's shoulder. "That's enough, Grace. You don't want to fall." She picked up the petals and dropped them into the basket.

Helen spotted Kate and smiled. "Oh my, you look lovely!" She captured Kate in a quick embrace, then moved to the sanctuary entrance and nodded at a pianist, who immediately changed from a hymn to the melodic tune of Bach's "Arioso."

Prickles of excitement moved up Kate's arms. This was it.

With a pat to Grace's bottom, Helen sent the child down the aisle. The little girl walked slowly, just as she'd been taught, and tossed flower petals along the way. Muriel stepped to the entrance, holding her small bouquet of asters and daisies in front of her. When Grace was halfway down the aisle, Muriel stepped out and gracefully walked toward the front of the church.

Kate's father approached his daughter. Eyes brimming, his

salt-and-pepper hair looking slightly disheveled, he stood in front of his daughter.

She tamed a cowlick in his hair. "There—you look perfect."

"I got ready in a hurry." He chuckled, then reached out and gently took hold of Kate's arms. "It seems like yesterday you were my little Katie romping about the farm and begging me for rides in the plane." His voice broke. "And now . . . you're all grown up—a gifted and intelligent young woman." His smile was tremulous. "I'm so proud of you."

Kate hugged him. "Thank you, Daddy. But I'm me only because of you and Mom. You're the best. I love you both so much." She kissed him on the cheek. "I'm so thankful you're here."

Her father linked Kate's arm with his and he led her to the doorway. They stood side by side and waited until Muriel had made her way to the front of the church.

Kate's gaze moved to Paul. He stood at the front with his neighbor and friend, Patrick. *Lord, thank you for Paul.* The quiet notes of "I Love You Truly" filled the sanctuary and the guests stood. The music swelled and so did Kate's nerves. When her eyes met Paul's, her stomach did a little flip. His look was ardent.

Unable to hold his gaze, she glanced at her bouquet trembling in her hands. She was about to become Mrs. Paul Anderson.

"You ready, Katie?" her father asked, giving her arm a squeeze.

She took a deep breath, gave a nod, and then stepped into the sanctuary beside her father. Everyone's eyes were on her, but all she could see was Paul. Dressed in a gray wool worsted suit with a burgundy tie, he'd never looked more handsome. His shoulders seemed broader and his dark looks more captivating.

Paul's gaze followed her as she walked down the aisle. A smile played at his lips. Love was in his eyes. This was just how she had imagined it would be.

The words of the song played through Kate's mind. They were part of the reason she'd chosen it. When she was with Paul, life's sorrows, its doubts and fears, faded. When he held her hand, she could feel his strength and she felt stronger. Together, they would face life's challenges. And they'd never be alone.

The music stopped. Father and daughter stood before Reverend Stephens. Kate liked the minister. He'd always been kind and seemed to genuinely care for the people in the community. Although she missed a lot of Sundays because of work, when she did make services, his messages were always uplifting and enlightening.

He smiled and quietly asked Kate, "You ready?"

She glanced at Paul, then with a deep sigh of release, said, "Yes. For a very long time."

The reverend chuckled, then cleared his throat and looked about the sanctuary. Kate glanced at the front row on the groom's side and felt a prick of sadness. None of his family was here. He hadn't invited them. She still didn't know what terrible thing from his past plagued him and kept him estranged from his family. Maybe she'd never know.

"Dearly beloved," began Reverend Stephens. "We are gathered here in the sight of God—and in the face of this company—to join together this man and this woman."

Kate looked at Paul. He was staring at her, his eyes filled with devotion. Kate's heart skipped a beat. He smiled and she wished the reverend would hurry so they could begin their new life.

The minister seemed to talk for an awfully long time before he finally asked, "Who gives this woman in marriage to this man?"

"Her mother and I do," said Kate's father. He turned to her and dropped a kiss on her cheek. "We love you, Katie." He placed her hand in Paul's, and then walked to the front pew and sat beside Kate's mother. Dabbing at tears, Joan leaned against him. He took her hand.

Kate's heart warmed. She and Paul would be like that. They'd grow old together and their love would become stronger.

"Please step forward," Reverend Stephens said.

Clutching Paul's hand, her legs trembling, Kate took two steps toward the minister. Paul's hand was strong and calloused. She could feel his depth of character and the strength built of hard work. She was proud of him. She felt a gentle squeeze and answered back with one of her own.

As the pastor spoke about what it meant to be husband and wife, how they were to honor and respect one another, and to be a help to the other, Kate tried to listen. She knew it was important, but all she could think about was the tall, broad-shouldered man beside her and how good his hand felt in hers. She forced herself to keep her eyes on the minister, but she wanted to look at Paul. She could feel his pulse, strong and steady—his matched hers, as though they were already one.

She envisioned what life would be like for them. They'd stand together against the world, work together, make love whenever they liked, and they'd raise a family. She hoped their children looked like him. She loved his dark hair and eyes and his stalwart nature. She'd never liked how tall she was. At five foot ten, she towered over most other women. She hoped that if they had a daughter, she'd be a more suitable height.

She considered what their life would look like. She knew there would be troubles, but she was certain that together she and Paul could work them out. And he'd always stand by her.

In everything? The words flung themselves through her mind. Would he be able to support her job? She'd be away a lot, and every moment in the air held danger. He'd said he supported her, but once married he might change his mind. And what if he did?

Kate didn't know the answer and she didn't want to think about it, not today. In a few minutes she'd be Paul's wife—that's all that mattered.

"Face one another," the minister instructed. He smiled down on them. Kate felt a pang of guilt. She hadn't heard anything he'd said.

"Do you, Paul Anderson, take Kate Evans to be your wife—to live together after God's ordinance—in the holy state of matrimony? Will you love her, comfort her, honor and keep her in sickness and in health, for richer or poorer, for better or worse, in sadness and in joy, to cherish and continually bestow upon her your heart's deepest devotion, forsaking all others, keep yourself only unto her as long as you both shall live?"

Paul didn't answer right away. Instead he seemed to breathe in Kate's presence and the momentous occasion. And then in his deep steady voice, he said, "I will."

Kate felt her legs grow weak. He meant it. He was hers for all time.

Reverend Stephens turned to Kate and repeated the vows. Kate gazed at Paul, her heart swelling with devotion. "I will."

After the exchange of rings, Kate and Paul held one another's hands, delighting in the moment and in one another.

"Be one in heart and in mind," the minister said.

We are. Always and forever, Kate thought, wanting to hurry the minister along. She wanted to be Paul's wife.

"Inasmuch as Paul and Kate have consented together in marriage before this company of friends and family and have pledged their faith—"

"I love you," Kate whispered. Oh how she wanted to kiss him. She didn't hear anything else the reverend said—all she knew was that Paul was her husband, or would be if only the minster would hurry and make the pronouncement. And then she heard the words she'd been waiting for.

"By the power vested in me I now pronounce you husband and wife."

Relief and joy spilled over Kate. And all of a sudden she didn't know what to do.

"Paul, you may kiss your bride."

There was a twitter of laughter and then Paul took a step closer to Kate, pulled her into his arms, and their lips met. His lips captured hers. Unaware of onlookers, Paul and Kate sealed their vows with a kiss that left Kate weak. Paul folded her in his arms, and Kate didn't want the moment to end.

Clapping and cheers of congratulations erupted from the guests. Reluctantly, Kate and Paul parted and faced the room, their hands clasped.

Paul leaned toward her and whispered, "I love you, Katie. You can't know how much."

"I know," she said.

All of a sudden the sound of the recessional blasted its way into their brand-new union. They walked down the aisle and into the foyer. Paul immediately scooped Kate into his arms and twirled her around. And then he laughed and pulled her close. "I was beginning to think it would never end. All I wanted was to kiss those luscious lips of yours."

Kate felt herself blush, but before she could say anything, he held her face in his hands and kissed her tenderly. "I promise to take care of you always, Katie."

Her breath caught in her throat. "And I'll love you forever." She caught a glimpse of her wedding ring—the symbol of their eternal commitment to one another.

Sassa and Patrick walked out of the sanctuary.

"Fine job, there, Paul," Patrick said, clapping Paul on the back. "You two make a striking couple. And Kate, it will be an honor to have you as a neighbor."

"Thank you, Patrick. I'm looking forward to being there more."

"You're not living in the cabin?" he asked.

"Well . . ." She glanced at Paul, feeling uneasy. "Not right away. I have a house here in town and the airport is here in town. It'll be easier if I stay in Anchorage part of the time."

"We're trying to decide just what to do about that," Paul said, his voice slightly stiff.

Kate knew he wanted her out on the homestead all of the time, but it didn't make sense, so they'd agreed on a compromise, which meant she'd be staying in both places. "Sometimes Paul will be in town too. That way we can go to church together more often." She glanced at him. "We'll work it out," she said, her confidence fading slightly.

Muriel stepped into the foyer. "Oh Kate! It was perfect!" She hugged Kate and then Paul.

People filed out of the doorway. They greeted and congratulated Paul and Kate, and when everyone had offered their good wishes, Patrick said, "Come on. We've got a party to get to. This way." He headed toward the reception hall.

The evening felt like a dream to Kate. There was music, dancing, good food, toasts, and lots of well-wishes. Kate danced with Paul. They'd never danced before and she was surprised at how good he was. She felt as if she were gliding across the floor.

When it was time for them to leave, the single women gathered and Kate threw her bouquet. Lily caught it and her cheeks flushed pink. There were shouts of jubilation. Kate said a silent prayer that Lily would meet the right man. She and little Teddy needed someone to share their lives with.

Finally, in a flurry of congratulation and a shower of confetti, Kate and Paul ran for their car. Paul opened the door for Kate and she slid in, then he hurried around to the driver's side and climbed behind the wheel.

He leaned across the seat and kissed his bride. "So, how does it feel to be Mrs. Anderson?"

"Good," she said. "The name suits me." She put her arm around his neck and pulled him closer. "Kate Anderson." She giggled. "I like the sound of it."

The newlyweds headed for the Anchorage Hotel. When they pulled up, Kate remembered her first visit here. She'd just arrived in Anchorage and didn't know where to stay. This had been the only place she'd found. It had been too expensive, but she'd stayed anyway.

When Paul and Kate walked up to the desk, the young man, Bill, who'd been a bellboy on Kate's first visit, stood at the desk. "Hi, Kate. Paul. Congratulations to you."

"Thank you," Paul said. He smiled and lifted his eyebrows. "I believe we have a reservation under the name of Mr. and Mrs. Anderson."

"You do—our nicest suite. It's all ready for you." He touched a bell and a young man appeared. "Ted, can you show Mr. and Mrs. Anderson to their room—suite 332." He handed the bellboy the keys, then turned to Paul and Kate. "Enjoy your stay."

Kate suddenly felt nervous. She hadn't thought much about her wedding night. She wasn't sure what was expected of her. She worried over it as they followed the bellboy up the stairs and down a carpeted hallway. By the time they reached room 332, her stomach was churning. The bellboy opened the door, walked in, and set their luggage inside.

Paul dropped a generous tip into his hand and Kate moved toward the doorway.

"Oh no you don't," Paul said.

Before she could protest, he picked her up and cradled her against him. Kate laughed. "You don't have to do this."

"Of course I do. A new husband has an obligation to carry his bride over the threshold." He kissed her briefly, and then stepped inside. "And besides, it gives me a reason to hold you." He pushed the door closed with his foot.

Still cradling Kate, he kissed her again—only this time it was long and deep. Kate could feel the heat of passion. Her nerves fell away. "I love you."

She circled his neck with her arms. "I'll love you forever."

The ghost of a memory touched Paul's eyes, but only for a moment. "And I'm yours, always."

3

When Kate woke, her first thoughts were of Paul . . . her husband. The idea of it made her feel warm inside. She ran a hand over the finely woven sheets, then rolled onto her back, her head sinking into a plush pillow. She opened her eyes and looked at the other side of the bed, expecting to see Paul. He wasn't there.

She pushed up on one elbow and looked around the room. "Paul?" No answer. Kate climbed out of bed and glanced in the bathroom. He wasn't there—where was he? She moved to the window. The frozen white street below was empty. Her gaze moved to the Chugach Mountains shimmering pink and white in the distance. Resting her cheek against the cold window, she smiled, her heart and thoughts swelled with love. Everything was different now—it was better.

Stretching her arms above her, and then letting them rest on her head, she wondered where Paul had gone. When in town, he always seemed a little unsettled. Maybe he'd decided to take a walk.

With a yawn, Kate wandered back to bed and dropped onto the cushioned mattress. It was much softer than what she was used to. She pulled the plush spread up under her chin and closed her eyes, her mind returning to the previous evening.

When she and Paul left their guests and headed for the hotel, her nerves had set in. She knew what went on between men and women, but she'd never experienced anything more than a passionate kiss. A soft smile touched her lips. She loved Paul's kisses. He'd been gentle and tender, touching her as if he were caressing a priceless treasure. He'd raised passions in her she didn't know existed. They'd fallen asleep in each other's arms, knowing they belonged to one another forever.

She heard a key in the lock and the door opened. Through half-opened lids, she gazed at her handsome husband.

Paul stepped into the room, carrying a tray laden with Danish, coffee, and cream. He caught sight of Kate lying on the bed, her expression passionate. He wished breakfast could wait. He pushed the door closed with his foot. "Good morning. Don't you think it's time you were up?" He grinned. "The day's half over."

Kate fluffed her pillows and sat up. "Sorry, but I didn't get much sleep last night." She chuckled, the tone in her voice reminding him of wind chimes ringing in a breeze.

"And you're blaming me for that?" He raised his brows and smiled.

Kate bent her legs and pulled her knees up against her chest, where she rested her chin on them. "I'm not complaining."

Paul sat on the edge of the bed, unable to ignore how alluring Kate looked. "Thought you might be hungry." He set the tray on a bureau next to the bed, then bent and kissed her. "You know you're beautiful when you sleep."

"Oh?" Kate's face flushed. "I never thought of myself as

beautiful. When I was a kid, I was just tall and gangly, and my hair was red." She put on a crooked smile.

"Now you're willowy and your hair is a gorgeous auburn." He lifted her hair off her cheek and brushed it back, wishing they had more time before they needed to catch the train. He straightened. "You like cream in your coffee, right?"

"Uh-huh."

Paul poured cream into one of the cups and stirred it into the coffee, then handed it to Kate. Using a fork, he cut off a bite of apple Danish and held it out to her.

Kate accepted the offering. "Mmm. Delicious." She sipped her coffee, desire in her eyes.

Paul handed her the Danish and then settled on the bed beside her.

Kate set the coffee on the bedstand and took a bite of Danish. She leaned against him. "I love you."

He pressed a kiss to her tousled hair. "Will you still love me when mornings are about getting up to a freezing house and trying to get a fire going before your fingers freeze, then making a batch of flapjacks instead of enjoying pastries in bed?"

"Always," she said softly and snuggled closer.

Paul couldn't imagine life being any better than this. He kissed her hair again, then downed his coffee and ate his roll. "I wish we could stay here all day, but we've got to get moving. We have a train to catch."

"A train? Where are we going? I thought we were staying here in town and then heading out to the creek."

"I have a surprise for you." He rolled off the bed.

"What?"

He smiled slyly. "Do you ski?"

"A little. Why? Are we going skiing?"

"Maybe," Paul said, wearing a smug grin.

The train wheels clacked over the tracks while Kate watched the passing forests of spruce and fir laden with snow. They were traveling south, but Paul wouldn't say where exactly. Their hands clasped, the two rested against each other, both wearing smiles they couldn't erase.

Kate looked up at her husband. "I didn't know I could feel this happy."

Paul squeezed her hand and then pressed it against his cheek. "After Susan . . . I thought I'd never love anyone again." His eyes glistened with unshed tears. "Then I found you." His voice caught. "I tried not to love you, but when something's meant to be . . . it can't be stopped." He let out a puff of breath. "When I think of how foolish I've been." He shook his head. "Well, I'm glad God's overruled my stubbornness."

Kate rested her cheek against his shoulder and closed her eyes. They'd nearly lost each other. A whisper of a sigh escaped her lips.

The next thing Kate knew the train whistle blew. She opened her eyes. The couplings clanked and the engines ground to a stop. "Where are we?" she asked, gazing out at wilderness.

"This is where we get off." Paul stood and helped Kate up.

"But . . . there's nothing here."

"There's a depot." Paul nodded at a small building.

The porter carried their bags out and set them on the depot steps. The place looked deserted. Paul tipped the man, then watched him climb aboard the train.

Kate had a sense of being abandoned as the train headed down the tracks and disappeared. She glanced at the tiny shack. "Doesn't look like anyone's here." Ice-cold air chilled her face.

Paul glanced at his pocket watch. "Someone will be here soon." He took in a breath and blew out a puff of frosty air. "We better wait inside."

He ushered Kate through the door. It wasn't any warmer indoors, but a barrel stove and a stack of wood and tinder took up one corner of the room. Kate hoped they wouldn't have to wait long.

"I'll get a fire going. At least that way we'll be warm until our ride gets here."

Kate gazed out the window and wondered what kind of ride. She couldn't imagine anything other than a dogsled. "So, are you going to tell me where we're going?"

Paul stuffed paper and kindling into the stove and glanced at Kate. "Nope." He smiled devilishly as he took a match from a can and lit it.

"You're going to leave me in suspense?"

"That's right." He held the tiny flame to paper, which flared to life.

Soon the wood popped and crackled and the aroma of burning birch filled the room. Just the sound of it made Kate feel warmer. She sat on a wooden chair and bundled deeper into her coat. "It'll be dark soon. Are you sure whoever's coming has the right date?"

"As sure as I can be." Paul bent over her from behind and wrapped his arms around her. "Don't worry. They'll be here. They were highly recommended." He nuzzled her neck, then walked to the window and looked out.

Kate thought his shoulders looked a bit tight. He was worried too. What if no one came? *We'll be fine*, she told herself. *We'll just wait for the train to come through tomorrow.*

Something like the rumble of an engine growled from within the forest. "What's that?" she asked.

"I expect it's our ride." Paul grinned. "Have you ever ridden in a weasel?"

"A what?"

"It's a cat made for the snow. It has tracks like a tractor.

I'm pretty sure that's what they use to carry passengers out here in the winter." He straightened. "Yep. There it is."

What looked like a combination tractor and truck rolled toward them, its tracks digging into the snow. Kate hoped it had a heater. "Paul, I don't have anything to ski with."

"That's okay. Everything's been taken care of." He steered her toward the door, then picked up the bags and followed her down the steps.

The weasel crunched through deep snow and stopped alongside the depot. A man wearing a heavy parka opened the driver's side door and climbed out. "Howdy. You Mr. and Mrs. Anderson?"

"That's us." Paul extended a hand. "I'm Paul and this is Kate."

She shook the man's hand.

"I'm Levi. Good to meet you folks." He looked at the smoke rising from the chimney. "Sorry I'm late. I meant to be here early enough to have the place warmed up for you. But Ole Sadie here had other ideas. She decided she wasn't runnin' today. Took some doing to get her to turn over. For a while I was afraid I'd have to hitch up the dogs." He laid a hand on the cat. "But she came through." He smiled, then stepped inside the depot and picked up Paul and Kate's suitcases. "I've got hot coffee. Climb on in and I'll get you a cup."

He stood to the side and gave Kate a hand up. She sat in one of two seats in the rear of the rig. Paul took the other.

Levi handed up the bags and then climbed in. He rummaged through a duffel bag, then pulled out cups and a vacuum bottle. After unscrewing the lid, he poured steaming hot coffee into a cup and handed it to Kate.

"Thank you." She took a sip. It was strong, but good. And it felt warm going down. "That's just what I needed."

Levi handed a cup to Paul. "My wife's got supper waiting

for us at the house. She told me to give you a nice easy ride up the mountain." He chuckled. "I'll do my best. But either way, it's worth the trip. My wife's the best cook in all the territory." He ground the gears and then turned the vehicle back the way he'd come.

The mention of food reminded Kate how her empty her stomach felt. It had been a long time since her morning Danish.

"How far is it to the lodge?" Paul asked.

"'Bout forty minutes. This contraption doesn't move very fast."

"So, we're going to a lodge?" Kate asked.

"Yeah. I thought it might be fun to do something different. I used to ski when I lived down south. Me and my family would head up to the Sierras every winter."

Kate's excitement grew. "I'm not very good. But it sounds like fun." She pressed her hands between her knees and peered up front as Levi ground the way upward, following a trail between the trees.

Levi glanced back at them. "We have a batch of youngsters at the place right now, but that's all. It'd be pretty quiet, but those young bucks believe in having a good time. They hit the trails first thing and ski like they *want* to break their necks." He shook his head. "Hope no one gets hurt."

"My husband's a doctor," Kate said proudly. "If there's a problem he'll know what to do."

Levi glanced at Paul. "Glad to have you."

By the time they reached the lodge, it was dark. Levi stopped in front of a large cabin. "Go on in. Make yourselves comfortable. My wife will see to you."

Paul and Kate climbed out, and Levi headed Sadie up the hill.

Kate looked out at the white world falling away from them.

In the light of a rising moon, the snow looked like rivers of white weaving their way down the mountain between batches of evergreens. "It's beautiful." She hugged Paul. "Thank you for bringing me here. How did you know about it?"

"Patrick knew a fella who stayed here once. He said the skiing is good. And there's a pond for skating too."

"Oh, I can't wait. I haven't skated since I first left Yakima. I'm a pretty good skater. There were lots of ponds in the valley where I lived." Kate moved to the door.

"I was told the accommodations are fine, but nothing like what we had last night." Paul sounded apologetic as he opened the door for Kate. They stepped into an overly large room. The first thing Kate noticed was the smell of fresh-baked bread and roasting meat.

"Evening," said a stout, friendly looking woman as she stepped into the room from the back of the cabin. "You must be the Andersons. I'm Mary Jo Connolly." She shook both Kate's and Paul's hands. "Congratulations. Heard you're newly married."

"We are. I'm Kate and this is my husband, Paul." She glanced around the room where mounted trophies of caribou, mountain sheep, and moose stared at them. A large brown bear rug hung on a wall at the foot of a staircase. "This is a nice place. I didn't even know it was here."

"We're not a big outfit, don't wanna be. We mostly like small groups. Makes things more friendly." She moved to a desk and turned a registry toward Kate. "I do like to keep a record of our guests, though." She handed Kate a pen.

Kate wrote Kate Evans and then realized she'd written the wrong name. "Oh my gosh." She looked up in embarrassment. "I'm not used to writing Anderson yet." She corrected the mistake, then handed the pen to Paul, who wrote in his name.

He threw an arm around Kate. "We could have just written Mr. and Mrs. Paul Anderson."

"I didn't think of that," Kate said, feeling a flash of irritation. She had a name—Kate. She might be married to Paul, but she was still her own woman.

"Well now, let me show you to your room." Mary Jo led the way to a corridor directly off the main room. There were four doorways. She stopped at the third, and grabbing a wad of keys out of her apron pocket, she stuck one into the door and opened it. "It's not fancy, but it'll give you some privacy. We make sure to keep the pitcher filled and there's a bureau for your things. The barrel stove will keep the cold out."

Kate followed the woman into a small room, which was just big enough for the stove, bureau, and bunk beds. A tiny window framed by plain cotton curtains allowed in the subtle light of the winter moon. She hadn't expected anything fancy, but this was so far from what one might expect on a honeymoon that she had to hold back a chuckle. Her eyes met Paul's and she could see his disappointment.

"Dinner's at 7:00." Mary Jo handed Paul a room key and moved back into the hallway. "After your long day you might like to take a rest. The dining hall's through that door you saw me come out of when you first arrived. If you need anything, just holler. There's a bathing room, but no running water, so let me know in plenty of time if you want a bath. That way we can heat up enough water for you." She smirked. "Levi promises we'll have indoor plumbing by the end of next summer. We'll see. Sometimes things take longer than planned." She turned to go, then stopped. "Oh. The outhouse is on the west side of the building, just go out the front door and follow the path." She headed down the hallway.

Paul closed the door and looked at Kate. They both laughed. He circled his arm around her waist and they turned to look at the bunk bed. "Do you think we'll both fit on that bottom bunk?"

"We'll manage, one way or the other," Kate said, leaning against him.

After a meal of roasted moose, potatoes, and carrots along with freshly baked sourdough bread and crowberry cobbler for dessert, Kate and Paul sat over steaming cups of coffee at a long table with benches for seats. Kate was feeling the fatigue of the busyness leading up to the wedding, lack of sleep, and the long day. Her lids felt heavy and she longed for bed. However, it didn't seem proper to eat and then leave without some conversation. She did her best to look interested as the three young men talked about their adventures.

They were all from Palmer. Charles was tall and thin and had a big toothy smile. And there was Fred who liked to talk. He was a big man. Sam was smaller and quieter than the other two, but he seemed friendly enough. All three were red-cheeked and looked tousled, as if they hadn't taken any time to clean up before dinner. They were full of stories. Hours of skiing hadn't seemed to have worn them out at all.

Paul was full of questions about the slopes and was obviously eager to set off on his own skiing adventure. Kate sipped her coffee and thought of bed. She tried to focus on what Fred was saying . . . something about a jump he'd made. The room felt overly warm and seemed to swim in front of her.

Paul draped an arm around her. "You ready for bed? You're looking worn out."

Kate leaned into him, loving the feel of his strength. "It has been a long day."

"So, the two of you just got hitched, huh?" Fred said.

Paul gave Kate a little squeeze. "Yesterday."

Fred's smile turned into a lopsided grin. Kate knew what he was thinking and felt a blush heat up her face.

Paul stood. "It's been a pleasure. Thanks for all your tips. We'll try out some of the hills you mentioned." He helped Kate to her feet. "And thank you for the delicious meal, Mrs. Connolly."

"Yes. Thank you. It was wonderful," Kate added.

"We've got a pond up on the flat. We make sure to keep it cleared of snow so folks can skate. And we've got skates if you want to give the ice a try."

"That sounds like fun," Kate said, thinking about laying her head on her pillow. "Good night."

Paul looped Kate's arm into his and they strolled to their room. Kate felt as if she'd been tucked into a warm cocoon of contentment. Paul opened the door and stepped back, allowing Kate to step inside.

He stood with his arms folded over his chest and studied the bed. "You want the top or the bottom bunk?"

"The bottom. And we can both fit." Kate climbed onto the narrow mattress and scrunched up against the wall. "See, there's plenty of room." No longer sleepy, she smiled up at her husband provocatively.

Paul climbed onto the bunk and lay on his side, facing her. He gently swept a strand of hair off Kate's face and then traced a line down her cheek and jaw line. "We just fit," he said and kissed her.

"I love it here. It's the perfect place for us."

Paul's dark brown eyes gazed at her. They blazed with desire. "I feel more alive today than I have in years." His voice was deep and heavy with emotion. "I have a reason to live again, and I can't wait for all the days ahead." He cupped her cheek in his hand.

"I've no doubt our life will be full of thrills, but we can count on troubles too."

"Good days are all I'll allow," Paul said, grazing his lips over hers.

After a breakfast of flapjacks, bacon, and eggs, Paul and Kate headed outdoors. Levi followed.

"I think I've got just the thing for you," he said, as he inspected several sets of skis leaning against the side of the building. "Here we go." He picked up a pair. "These have Dovre bindings. They'll hold your boot in so your skis won't come off." He handed the skis to Kate, then moved down the row until he came across another set. "These ought to work for you, Paul. They're a little heavier and they've got the same kind of bindings. Have you used them before?"

"No. Never even heard of them."

"I'll give you a hand and show you how to strap them on." Levi helped them get their boots secured in the bindings, then with a salute said, "Have fun. The rope tow is already running. Things are pretty quiet this morning. Seems the lads are sleeping in. We're expecting a few more guests later today, though." He headed toward the snow cat.

Paul snugged his hat over his ears. "Ready?" he asked Kate.

Kate shrugged. "It's been awhile." She struggled to keep the skis parallel. "Which way to the tow rope?"

"Just follow me." Paul headed away from the lodge.

Kate pushed off with her poles, working hard to catch up.

They were soon at the bottom of a steep hill where the sound of the tow's engine disrupted the morning quiet as it wound its way through the pulley and up the hill. "Just grab hold and it'll carry you all the way up." Paul waited for Kate. "Don't let go until you get to the top."

"I know. I've skied before," Kate sniped. She hadn't meant to sound so sharp, but she hated to be incompetent at anything.

"Okay. Let's go. I'll follow you."

Kate grabbed hold of the tow and nearly lost her balance as it dragged her uphill. She wasn't about to fall, not after what Paul had said. She had to prove she was capable. Soon she was gliding along smoothly and feeling ashamed of herself for her competitiveness. By the time she'd reached the top she felt exhilarated.

Paul skied up beside her. They looked out over a valley of white, glistening in the sunlight. Evergreens looked like shrubbery in the deep snow. Craggy peaks, reaching through white mountains, surrounded the high valley.

Kate took in a breath of icy air. "I feel as if I'm standing on top of the world. It's so beautiful."

Paul was silent as he gazed at the view. "It reminds me of the old days back in California when my family used to go skiing." A tone of longing touched his voice. "It was a long time ago."

"Maybe you should visit?"

Paul didn't answer right away, then said, "Maybe." He glanced at her. "Ready?"

She peered down the slope. It looked steep. She stuck her poles in the snow on either side of her, feeling a shiver of fear. "I'll give it a try. Besides, there's no other way down." She chuckled, but her muscles felt tight and prickles of anxiety moved up and down her body. Still, she pushed off and picked up speed, too much speed. If she didn't slow down, she'd end up in a heap. Cautiously she turned her skis so she moved across the hill, then she made another turn and swooshed downward.

"Hey, this isn't as hard as I thought," she called as Paul caught up with her.

He grinned and, with a wave, passed her, cutting a fine edge in the snow.

Not to be outdone, Kate turned her skis so they pointed down the hill. She'd catch him and then slow down. By the time she reached Paul she was out of control and going too fast. She turned, trying to slow down, but as she did, one foot slid too far to the left and she caught the edge of the ski.

With a yell she plunged sideways and her legs went in opposite directions. The left ski dug in and her knee exploded with pain. She plunged forward and tumbled downward. With a jolt she stopped, her face planted in the snow.

She turned her head to the side to breathe, but with the wind knocked out of her she could barely get a breath. And she hurt everywhere, but mostly her left knee. She was afraid to move.

Kate tried to call for Paul, but all that came out was a weak, feeble sound that barely resembled her voice.

4

Kate!" Paul hollered as he skied across the face of the hill. She wasn't moving. *God, please, not Kate.* It felt as if he were slogging through mud.

When he finally reached her, Paul freed his boots from his skis and dropped to his knees beside her. His hands trembled. "Kate? Are you all right?" He thought he heard a mumble as he tore off his gloves and felt for a pulse. It was strong, but too fast.

"Kate. Can you hear me?"

She nodded and, in a voice that sounded like she was short of breath, she said, "I hurt my leg."

Relief washed over Paul, and he carefully removed one of her skis, then started to unhook the other when Kate cried, "Stop! It hurts! "

Paul stopped immediately. "What—your foot? Your ankle?"

"No. My knee. But my whole leg aches. I don't think I can move it."

"I need to get the ski off, honey. I'll be careful."

Cautious not to move her knee, Paul untied the leather lacings and slipped off the ski boot. Kate groaned. Paul won-

41

dered if she'd torn a ligament. Or if she'd broken the tibia, pain could be radiating to her knee.

He rested a hand on her back. "Take some deep breaths. Everything's going to be fine. We'll get you back to the lodge where I can have a look at your injury."

"How am I going to get there?" Kate looked down the hill, trepidation in her eyes.

Paul glanced around to see if there was anyone who could help. The slopes were empty. "I'll have to get a sled." He took her hand. "We've got to get you on your back. Try to relax and let me do the work." He grasped her arm and hip and rolled her onto her side.

Kate let out a gasp, then said, "I feel sick."

"That's normal." Paul made sure his voice remained calm. She might be going into shock. "Ready?"

She nodded, and he turned her over the rest of the way. She stared up at him, pain dulling the vivid color in her hazel eyes. He'd have to leave her. His stomach clenched at the thought. He stripped off his coat and covered her with it.

"I'll be back as quickly as I can. Okay?"

"I'll just wait here," Kate said, managing a small grin.

That's my Kate. Always courageous. He loved her more, if that were possible. He held her face in his hands and kissed her "I love you. Hang on." After quickly lacing on his skis, he pushed himself upright. "I won't be gone long." Reluctant to leave her, he headed down the hill.

The trip to the lodge seemed to take forever, and when he finally approached the building, there didn't seem to be anyone about. What would he do if there was no one to help? He unlaced his skis and ran inside. "Hello. Anyone here?"

Mary Jo emerged from the kitchen. "Hi. Didn't expect—" Concern touched her eyes. "Something's happened. What is it? Where's Kate?"

"She took a bad fall. I need a sled and someone to help me. I had to leave her up there."

"Oh dear. Levi's not here. He went to pick up guests." She headed for the hallway and Paul followed. "I saw Fred come in a while ago." She stopped at a door and knocked.

"Yeah, just a minute," he called from inside. A few moments later, the door opened. He looked at Mary Jo, then Paul. "Everything all right?"

"Kate's been hurt," Paul said. "I need your help to get her off the mountain."

"Sure thing." Fred grabbed his coat and gloves, then followed Paul and Mary Jo down the hallway. "What happened?"

"She fell and wrenched a knee pretty badly. I won't know how serious it is until I can examine her. We need to hurry— she's up on the slope alone." Driven by urgency, Paul strode out the front door.

Mary Jo grabbed a quilt off the back of the sofa and followed them out. "Here. You'll need this." She handed it to Fred. "There's a sled in the barn that Levi uses when things like this happen. I'll make some tea so she'll have something hot to drink when she gets back."

"Thanks." Paul headed toward the barn.

The sled was easy to find, but Paul fought panic as he pulled it outside. Kate was alone and vulnerable. He had to get to her. He and Fred grabbed hold of the tow and headed up the mountain. She could go into shock or the wolves he'd heard the night before might find her. He shut off the thoughts and turned to prayer, begging God to protect her.

When he reached the general area where she'd fallen, Paul called over his shoulder to Fred, "This is far enough." He let go of the tow. "She's over this way somewhere. He headed down a steep hill. Pulling the sled made skiing more difficult, but he pushed himself to keep up a fast pace.

It didn't take long for Paul to realize he'd made a terrible error. He hadn't marked the area or been careful to remember landmarks. Everything looked the same. Searching the landscape, he tried to find anything that looked familiar. Nothing. Where was she? Snow had started falling, along with the temperature. What if he couldn't find her? He stopped and scanned the slope. "I don't see her."

"You don't know where she is?"

"I thought I did. She's got to be close by. Kate!" he yelled, the rising wind carrying away his voice. "Kate!" He tried to quiet his drumming heart and listen.

He thought he heard something. "Did you hear that?"

"Yeah. I think it came from over there." Fred pointed toward the south side of the hill.

"We're coming," Paul yelled and hurried across the face of the slope. And then he spotted her. "Thank God." He skied as fast as he could manage. "Kate, we're here," he hollered.

When he reached her, he pulled off his skis and knelt beside her. "You all right?"

Kate nodded, but she was shivering.

"We've got a sled." He pressed his cheek to hers. She was badly chilled.

"I'm glad to see you." She managed a trembling smile. "It's cold."

He gently kissed her. "We'll be at the lodge in no time. Fred's here to help." He maneuvered the sled alongside Kate. "Are you having pain any place besides your knee and leg?"

"Yeah, just about everywhere, but I think it's mostly bruising and sore muscles."

"Okay. Fred, can you lift her under the arms, and I'll get her legs."

Careful to keep his hold on her thighs and away from her

44

knees, Paul slid his arms under her. "Ready? On three—one, two, three."

They hefted Kate onto the sled and she let out a yelp of pain. Once settled, Paul covered her with the quilt. "Mary Jo sent this along."

Kate only managed to nod. She was shaking uncontrollably.

Paul tucked in the sides. "We'll have you warmed up soon. Just hang on." He took her pulse. It was too fast. And her skin looked pasty white. He had to hurry. She might be going into shock.

By the time they reached the lodge, Kate looked better and she was in good spirits. "I'm sure it's just a strain," she said. "I feel silly over all this fuss."

"No reason to feel silly. And I'll decide whether it's a strain or something more." Paul's voice was stern. They pulled the sled to a stop at the lodge's front porch. Kate immediately sat up. "Stay put," Paul ordered.

"I'm not a child. I can—"

"I'm the doctor and you're the patient. So, do as you're told." He tried to sound as if he were teasing, but he was serious. At this point there was no way to know how serious Kate's injuries were. He leaned over her and checked the pupils of her eyes. They looked normal. Her skin color was good. He picked up her hand and pressed his fingers to her wrist. Her pulse was slightly elevated but much better than it had been. "Do you have any pain in your neck?"

"No."

"Okay. You can sit up, and then we'll carry you in."

Kate pulled the blanket back and gingerly sat up. She groaned when she tried to bend her leg.

Paul leaned down and caught her under her right arm. "I'll lift and you push up with your good leg." Kate stood and leaned against Paul, careful not to move the injured left limb.

"Fred, you and I can make a chair for her with our hands," Paul said. "It'll be easier to carry her."

Putting her weight on Paul, Kate stood on her right leg while the two men clasped hands and made a seat for her.

The front door opened and Mary Jo stepped onto the porch. "My goodness. You poor thing."

Kate draped her arms over the men's shoulders and cautiously lowered herself onto their locked arms.

Mary Jo backed into the house. "I have the sofa all ready."

Paul and Fred moved slowly across the room, and when they reached the davenport, they carefully lowered Kate onto it. She propped herself against a pile of pillows at one end and Paul placed a pillow under her injured knee.

After removing her coat and gloves, he did a quick check of her arms and shoulders, feet and ankles. Kate wasn't just another patient. He hated to see her like this. Paul rechecked everything to make sure she was okay before saying, "Everything seems all right. But if I'm going to look at that knee, you'll have to remove your pants."

Fred ducked his head slightly. "Well, I'm hungry. I'll see if I can find something to eat." He headed for the kitchen.

Kate unbuckled her belt and unbuttoned her pants, then Paul gingerly slipped off the pants, careful not to move Kate's left leg.

"Oh, my word." Mary Jo covered her mouth with her hands. "That's a terrible-looking knee."

"It's already swollen and black and blue," Kate said. "And it's throbbing. Do you think I broke it?"

"Lay back, Katie," Paul said as he gently palpated the knee. It looked bad. He hoped she hadn't broken it. Kate groaned. Paul didn't feel anything out of place. "This is going to hurt. Take deep slow breaths."

Kate nodded and closed her eyes. Paul bent the leg and Kate let out a moan. He rotated it to the inside, then out.

Beads of sweat appeared on Kate's forehead and she grabbed hold of one of the sofa cushions. "Is it broken?"

"I don't think so. But you've got a bad sprain." He straightened the leg and rotated it away from her body. "The hip seems okay." He smiled. "You're lucky. It'll probably only take a few weeks and you'll be back to normal. But, you'll have to stay off of it."

"That's not hard to do," she said with a smirk.

He looked at Mary Jo. "We'll need some ice."

"We've got plenty of that."

"Do you, by chance, have a pair of crutches too?"

"I do." She smiled and lifted her brows. "Never know when you're going to need them." She chuckled. "This isn't the first time we've had an injury."

"I'll wrap the knee. It'll help support it and should decrease the pain. I'll need my bag."

"I'll get it and the crutches too." Mary Jo hurried off toward Paul and Kate's room.

Kate ran a hand over her forehead. "I'm so sorry. I've ruined everything." She looked dejected. "Our honeymoon."

Paul was disappointed, but he wasn't about to let Kate know that. And at this moment, he cared more about her than their honeymoon. "It's all right. I just wish you weren't hurting." Paul's mouth tipped into a sideways smile. "'Course, you might not be laid out on this couch if you could rein in your competitive nature just a little."

"I wasn't being competitive . . ." Her voice slid to a stop. "Well, maybe I was . . . a little. But so were you."

"Yeah, but I didn't fall." He chuckled.

After three days' rest at the lodge, Paul and Kate headed back to Anchorage. Kate's knee was still swollen and bruised, but it felt better. Kate kept her leg elevated on the seat next to her. She already felt the humiliation of meeting her parents at the depot. Once again she'd run into trouble.

Bill and Joan had stayed at Kate's home in town while she and Paul had been away. Kate could see them on the platform as the train pulled into the station. Using her crutches, Kate managed to hobble down the aisle and to the steps. Paul lifted her down and she made her way toward her parents.

"Oh Kate, are you all right?" her mother asked.

"I'm fine. Just sore," she said with a sigh. "I got too bold and ruined everything."

Paul came up behind her. "You didn't ruin anything." He leaned close to Kate and whispered in her ear. "We didn't get to do a lot of outside activities, but I did like the inside activities."

"Paul," Kate said as if shocked, but she smiled.

He kissed her cheek and then loaded the bags in the trunk of the car.

"Glad it wasn't anything too serious, Katie," her father said. "You'll be good as new before you know it." He walked alongside her as she crutched to the car. He opened the door and helped Kate lower herself onto the backseat, then her father handed her the crutches. She set them on the floor.

Paul climbed in on the other side. "You doing all right?"

"Yes—for the hundredth time." Kate loved that Paul cared about her, but since she'd been hurt, he'd been hovering. She'd never seen him so concerned for a patient.

Once on their way, Joan looked at Kate. "So, what happened?"

"We were skiing and I hit a rut or something and went tumbling. My knee went one way and my ski the other. It's just a sprain."

"You were always too gutsy for your own good," Joan said.

"When you were a girl and we'd go skiing, I was forever telling you to slow down. Of course, you never listened."

"Some things never change," Paul said with a grin.

"I was just trying to catch up to you. I wasn't being foolhardy."

No one said anything. Kate knew they didn't believe her. She slumped into the seat and crossed her arms over her chest. Why was she considered a daredevil when Paul had been just as aggressive on the hill? He didn't believe in doing things halfway any more than she did.

After getting Kate settled at home, Bill drove Paul to the airport. He had a medical run and would be gone for a couple of days. Kate rested on the davenport with a pile of magazines and books piled on the side table. Her mother seemed to take great pleasure in caring for Kate's every need, while Kate hated depending on her or on anyone else.

Her mother walked into the room carrying a cup of tea. "I'm wondering if your father and I should delay our departure. How are you going to get along when we leave?" She set the tea on the table beside Kate.

"I'll be fine. I'm getting up and around on my own more. And I have Muriel and Helen. They've been here almost as much as you."

Joan walked into the kitchen and returned with another cup of tea and a plate of cookies. She set the dessert on the coffee table and then sat on a cushioned chair across from the davenport. "I wish you were a little less daring." She took a sip of tea. "Have you considered what you'll do about your flying if you have a child?"

Why can't I be who I am without having to answer for it? she thought, but said, "I don't know for sure. It's not something I have to think about today." She was weary of the topic and didn't want to discuss it.

"Yes, but one day you will. You do want children, don't you?"

Kate's irritation intensified. "Of course we do. But whether I work or not is something Paul and I will decide together—at the right time." Kate couldn't imagine not flying.

Joan set her cup on the table. "I've always worried about you. If you weren't up a tree, you were walking the top of a fence line or begging your father for another ride in his plane." She shook her head. "You can't possibly be a mother and a pilot."

Kate was getting angry. She sat up straighter and jarred her leg. Pain shot through her knee. She bit back a howl and instead demanded, "Why not?"

Joan compressed her lips as if trying to hold back a response. "Well . . . you're not a girl anymore. You're a grown woman with womanly responsibilities and a husband to take care of."

Kate gritted her teeth. She knew she ought to let this go, but she couldn't. "What do you think my womanly responsibilities are?" she snipped.

"When you married Paul, you made a promise—to love, honor, and obey. And part of that means keeping a home for him and being here when he needs you and one day taking care of his children."

"I do love him. And what is it that you think I'm doing that doesn't honor him?"

Joan took a slow breath and picked up her cup. Her hands trembled slightly. "You need to put him first."

"He is first. I don't know why you don't see that."

"How can you be a full-time wife if you're off flying and leaving him to fend for himself?"

"That's not how it is." The volume of Kate's voice rose. "We work together a lot of the time. And when I'm not home, Paul's quite capable of taking care of himself."

Joan massaged her temples as if to soothe away tension. "Kate, are you sure your job isn't first?"

Kate wanted to scream. Why couldn't she make people understand? "Mom—Paul and I agreed that I should keep flying. He said if I'm happy, he's happy."

"But you could injure yourself or be killed—you know how much that possibility tortures him."

"He's come to accept the danger of my job. And there's no way to live a life of absolute safety anyway." She clasped her hands tightly. "I could have broken my neck while I was skiing." Kate sat up as straight as she could. "I refuse to lock myself in my house and spend my days dusting and baking and praying for a baby."

"You know I didn't mean that."

"Then, what *did* you mean?" Kate was beyond caring whether she was angry or not.

Her mother crossed her legs and seemed to consciously relax her muscles. "I'm just thinking about your future. A man wants a woman who will make his home a haven, a place where he can come home and know there will be a hot meal and loving arms to hold him."

Kate studied her hands and lowered her tone. "Okay, so I don't cook so well. But I'm learning, and my arms are open to him." Some of what her mother had said penetrated Kate's uncertainty. Was her mother right, at least partially? Did she need to make a better home for Paul? Be here for him more? "Mom, Paul and I can't be a replica of you and Dad. We've got to find our own way."

"I don't expect you to be like me and your father." Joan brushed a loose strand of hair off her face. "I just want the best for you. I want you safe." Tears pooled in her eyes. "And if there are babies, they'll need you."

"I plan to be here for them. And they can come with Paul and me some of the time."

Joan's eyes widened. "You can't possibly take them with you."

"When I was a girl, I went with Dad all the time." Kate wished she could stand and walk. She wanted to get out of the house, away from the convicting words, the uncertainty.

"Flying in the Yakima valley is not the same as flying the Alaskan wilderness. You know that."

Kate did know, and when there was a child, she wasn't sure what she'd do, but today wasn't the time to solve the question. "Paul and I will make our own decisions about all of that when and if the time comes. I don't want to talk about it anymore."

"I'm sorry. I never meant to bring it up. It just slipped out." Joan leaned forward, resting her arms on her thighs. "And you're right—you and Paul need to make your own choices." She stood and moved toward the kitchen. "I was just trying to help."

Kate could hear the hurt in her voice. "I know. And I'm thankful that you care."

Joan managed a small smile. "Would you like some soup? I can warm up some from yesterday."

"Thank you. That sounds good," Kate said, thinking about anything but soup. She knew her life would change, that it would be complicated, but she didn't want to think about it. Not yet.

— 5 —

Heavyhearted, Kate leaned against Paul as she watched her parents' train pull out of the station. Yakima was a long ways away even for a pilot.

"I wish they'd move up here," she said, blinking back tears.

"Maybe they will . . . someday."

"I think Mom would, but my father's married to his orchards. I don't think he'll ever leave them." Transferring her weight to her crutches, she straightened. "It's probably for the best."

Paul placed an arm around her waist. "Why do you say that?"

Kate hadn't shared the conversation she'd had with her mother about her continuing to work. "I think it would be hard on Mom. She's old-fashioned." Kate glanced at Paul. She didn't want to bring up the topic of her flying, even though he'd told her he understood her passion for it.

"Old-fashioned? How so?"

"You know . . . she thinks a woman's place is at home, taking care of her husband and family."

"It's not?" Paul grinned and gave her a squeeze.

"You're teasing, right?"

"Mostly."

Not the response Kate wanted. "I thought you understood."

"I do. But how can a man not want to have a beautiful woman like you waiting for him at home?" He kissed her.

Kate relaxed into him, hoping that's all he'd really meant.

"So, what do you want to do with the rest of the day?" he asked.

Lifting one of her crutches, Kate said, "I'm feeling pretty spry." She smiled up at him and felt her heart swell at the light of love in his brown eyes.

"I was invited to go ice fishing. You think you're up to it?"

"Sure. Who invited you?"

"Actually us—and it was Sidney."

"I didn't even know he was in town. I'd love to see him."

"Ran into him at the mercantile yesterday. He plans on staying."

"What do you mean?"

"He moved back."

"But what about—"

"His father died." Paul's tone turned leaden.

"Oh. I didn't know."

"Yeah. About a month ago. The family's able to watch over his mother so he decided he belonged here. In fact, he's back at the airfield, only as a pilot this time. Jack hired him."

"Can't imagine Sidney working for Jack. Jack's not an easy man to work for, and he doesn't run things like Sidney used to." Kate moved toward the car. "Are we supposed to meet him at the airfield?"

"Uh-huh. They're probably already out on the ice."

"This should be fun." Wielding her crutches like a pro, Kate picked up her pace. "Let's go."

When Paul pulled up to the airfield, Kate saw Sidney's plane right off. Memories of their first meeting tumbled through her mind. He'd looked nothing like other Alaskans. He was clean shaven, wore cowboy boots and an oversized cowboy hat, and looked too young to own an airfield. He was tougher than he looked. It had taken all Kate had to convince him to give her a chance. After a nerve-racking flight, she had a job.

Kate didn't wait for Paul to open her car door. She was in a hurry and got her crutches set in calf-deep snow and maneuvered herself out of the car.

Paul managed to get there just in time to close the door behind her. "You don't have to be in such a hurry."

"Sidney's a good friend." She tossed Paul a smile, then as fast as she could manage, she moved toward the shop door.

Paul opened it for her and she swung herself over the threshold and inside.

Kenny and Alan were sitting across from each other at a small table, playing a game of checkers. They barely looked up. Sidney leaned against the wall near the woodstove, his well-worn cowboy hat sitting at an angle on his head and a cigarette resting between his lips. He looked older, but his blue eyes lit up at the sight of her.

He removed the cigarette. "Heard you were laid up." His gaze moved to her crutches. He shook his head. "Nothin' keeps you down."

She chuckled. "Why didn't you tell me you were here?" She crutched her way across the room toward him.

He met her halfway. "Only been here two days." He pulled Kate into a bear hug. When he released her, he glanced at Paul. "Wish I could have made the wedding."

"I thought we were going ice fishing." Jack grabbed his fishing gear and moved to the door.

"What, no work?" Kate asked, following him.

"Not today." Jack took in a deep breath and gazed out over the frozen lake. "Some days aren't meant for working."

Kate wasn't sure she'd heard correctly. Jack was always set on making money, which meant working.

Sidney chuckled. "We all know what's really up."

"What d'ya mean?" Jack snarled.

"I heard the scuttlebutt about you and your lady friend." Sidney grinned. "What's her name . . . Linda, right?"

Kate pressed her lips tight, forcing back a sarcastic comment. She couldn't imagine Jack with anyone. Who'd be interested?

"Linda's just a friend." The sound of a car approaching caught everyone's attention. Jack removed his cigar from his full lips, dropped it on the ground, and stepped on it.

A sparkling clean, green Plymouth pulled up in front of the shop. Jack hurried to open the door and a petite woman stepped out. The wind caught her short blonde hair and she pulled up the hood of her parka.

She smiled at Jack. "I'm sorry I'm late. I got held up at the hospital."

"No problem. We were just about to head out." Jack closed the car door and turned to the group. "This is Linda Carson. She's a nurse over at the hospital. Linda, these are the pilots who work for me." His tone was authoritative.

Kate was sure he wanted to look like a big shot in front of his new girlfriend.

His short-cropped black hair looked almost frosted in the cold air. "This is Alan, Kenny, Sidney, and Kate." He gave Paul a nod. "And Paul's our bush doctor."

"It's very nice to meet you all." Linda's voice was sweet and so was her smile.

"Good to meet you," Sidney said. The rest murmured their agreement.

Kate wondered how Jack had managed to attract someone so nice and pretty. She wouldn't last.

"Well, let's get moving. The fish are waiting," Jack said, then turned his dark eyes on Kate. "In your condition I doubt you'll be able to navigate the snow and ice."

"I'll do just fine." Kate held up one crutch. "I'm much better. I'll be ready for a flight by next week."

"It's up to you." Jack headed toward the lake, then slowed down and walked alongside Linda. He turned to Alan. "Can you get the saw and axe?"

"Sure." Alan hurried back inside the shop.

Fishing gear in hand, the men hurried onto the ice to their fishing spot. Kate followed along behind, but kept slipping. Finally Paul and Sidney made a chair with their hands and carried her.

Embarrassed, Kate started a conversation. "Glad we've got clear skies. Seeing the sun almost makes me feel warm."

Sidney snorted. "Sunshine or not, it's freezing out here. But Jack's got everything ready, including wood for a fire. Figured I couldn't back out. Don't like fishing much." He studied the men who had already reached their fishing spot. "He seems a little softer around the edges these days."

"A woman can do that for you," Paul said with a smile for Kate.

"We'll see how long she lasts," Kate said. Paul and Sidney set her on her feet. "Thanks for the ride."

Alan and Kenny were clearing new ice from the hole while Jack built a fire. Linda huddled near the fledgling flames.

"Sidney, it's good to have you back. But I'm sorry about your dad," Paul said.

Sidney nodded. "After the stroke, he never really came back. His going was God's mercy."

Kate's mind went to her parents. Death was inevitable, but she couldn't imagine life without them.

"I'd probably still be there, but my family convinced me that this is where I belong." He turned and looked at the airfield. "It feels good to be back."

"How do you think it's going to work out—you being Jack's employee instead of his employer?"

"It'll be all right. Jack'll give me a hard time, but I'm just glad to be flying again. Figure I'll like it better, just being a pilot—more time in the air that way." He chuckled. "I wouldn't be surprised if Jack's sorry he bought me out."

"Yeah, some days I'm sure he wishes he was just a hotshot pilot again. But I think it's been good for him. Sometimes I'm almost convinced he actually cares about his pilots, even me." Kate smiled.

Sidney chuckled. "Jack's always been full of himself, but I figure he's got a good soul he keeps hidden from the world. Looks like Linda might've found it." Sidney pulled a hat with ear flaps out of his pocket, braced his cowboy hat under one arm, and pulled on the cap, tugging down the ear flaps. He planted the cowboy hat on top. He looked silly, but warmer. "The new fella . . . Alan, what's he like?"

"Quiet. He keeps to himself mostly, but he's dependable and from what I've seen he's a good pilot."

"With my being back we've got a full crew again. That'll take some of the heat off Jack. He might be able to fit in a few extra runs."

"Maybe," Kate said.

Paul slipped and nearly took a tumble, almost falling into Sidney.

"Hey, watch it," Sidney said. "Hate to have us all go down." He sucked in a breath.

"It hasn't been that long." Sidney straightened slightly.

"Sorry to hear about Mike. Doesn't seem right—his not being here."

"It's never been the same since he was killed." Kate's heart squeezed. She leaned against Paul, thankful for him. "He was a good pilot and a good friend to everyone."

Squinting, Sidney looked at the men settling around the fishing hole. "Over the years, we've lost a lot of good pilots. Sometimes I wonder if we're all just a bunch of nitwits."

"I don't understand the appeal," Paul said. "Long hours, and sometimes the work is rough, and pilots never know if their present flight will be their last."

Kate could see worry in his eyes and so she said, "Today we're fishing, not flying."

Kate couldn't bear to lie around any longer, so although her knee was still painful she returned to work.

"You sure you're ready?" Jack asked, eyeing her.

"My doctor, who happens to be my husband, says I'm good as new. My knee's just a little stiff." She lifted the leg and bent her knee to prove her point, making sure not to cringe at the tenderness. "I'm dying to get back to work."

"Bad choice of words," Jack said dryly. "Okay. I've got a couple of miners up at Talkeetna who need a lift into town." He handed Kate a flight chart. "They'll meet you at the airfield."

Kate took the chart and tucked it inside her flight jacket. "Thanks." This was a good first run—a short trip. She'd be out on the homestead in time for dinner.

"You staying in town?"

"Not tonight. But when I am, I'll let you know."

"It'll be harder to get you runs—living all the way out there."

"We've got a radio, so call me anytime. It's not that far."

"You plan on living at the cabin?"

"We haven't made up our minds yet." Kate didn't want to think about it. She wasn't sure what to do. Paul loved the homestead—so did she. But it didn't make sense to live all the way out there when her home base was in town.

Jack shook his head. "Don't make sense."

"I admit, it would be easier if we were in town, but Paul built that cabin and all the outbuildings. He's got a good garden. He has a lot of time and sweat invested in the place. It means a great deal to him."

"You'll get less work."

"I know." Kate hated the idea of losing business, but how could she ask Paul to give up his home? Not to mention that the house in town had been Mike's—it still felt like his.

"You better get a move on if you want to get back here and then out to the homestead before dark."

"I'm on it."

Carrying a pan of warm oil, Kate walked toward her plane, careful not to limp. She removed the canvas cover from the engine, thankful the temperature was moderate, which meant she wouldn't need to heat the engine before starting the Bellanca. She added the oil and then cranked the flywheel. When it was singing along, she tugged the crank loose, climbed inside, and started the engine. The roar set her pulse flying. She'd been grounded too long.

After checking her instruments to make sure the readings were accurate, moving the controls, and doing a mag check, Kate gave the hefty ski-plane enough throttle to begin taxiing to the snow-packed strip, then eased back on the power. The skis ratttled over ruts and she gave it a quick burst of power, enough to slide around the final turn for takeoff. Sunlight glistened off the Chugach Mountains, making them look like an endless shimmering castle. Winds were calm, skies clear, and the white frozen world sparkled. It was a perfect day to fly. She gradually increased to full power and gently lifted off, exhilarated at the freedom of flight.

A white patchwork world of open fields and forests stretched out below Kate as she approached Talkeetna. In the distance, Mount McKinley stood like a gigantic white gem. She wondered what it would be like to land on a high mountain glacier. As much as she admired her Bellanca, it didn't have the power to work at McKinley's high altitudes.

She spotted the airfield. Two men stood nearby with their gear. She did a flyover to check for obstacles on the snow-covered landing strip. It looked clear. Turning, she set up for her approach, then descended until she was just above the trees. When she reached the airstrip, she dropped down until she was flying only feet above the white ground. Her skis touched and a small shudder moved through the plane. By the time she'd come to a stop, her passengers had already grabbed their packs and stood alongside the plane. They must be in a hurry. Kate opened the door and was immediately hit by a barrage of questions from a dark-haired man who looked like he hadn't shaved in months.

"What took you so long? We were wondering if you'd ever get here. We've got plans."

He had blue eyes just like Mike's, and Kate sucked in a startled breath. Would she ever stop missing him? "Sorry. I got a late start." It wasn't true, but Kate wasn't about to get the men riled. Better to apologize and keep them happy. "I'm Kate Anderson." She held out a hand.

"Norman," the man said, shaking her hand. "And this is John."

John grasped her hand. "Glad to meet you."

"Let's get your gear loaded, and we'll be on our way."

"This is all we got," Norman said, holding up a duffel bag and glancing at John's. "We're only spending a few days."

Soon Kate was back in the air. "I heard you're miners," she hollered over the thrum of the engine.

"Yep," Norman said. "We got a stake way up on the Talkeetna River. Found a little color, but figure there's a lot more to be had."

Kate had heard it before—men panning for gold, certain they'd hit it big one day. "So, you have family in town?"

"Nope. Been working long and hard. It's time for some fun—might even find us each a dame." John grinned.

Not without a bath and shave, Kate thought.

The engine sputtered. Oh no. Not again. Kate checked the mixture—it seemed fine. The engine gasped and paused. *This can't be happening—not my first trip*. Kate fought rising panic.

"What's wrong?" John nearly screeched.

"I'm sure it's nothing. We'll be fine." The engine coughed and hesitated again. Kate needed to find a place to land. "I'm going to set us down." Could she make it back to the airfield? "Stay in your seats!"

She scanned the fields. There was another airfield to the south—if she could make it. The plane bucked and sputtered so badly that it bounced and felt more like a ship on a rough sea. Kate looked for the field. There wasn't time. She needed any open ground. And then she spotted it—the grass strip. "We're gonna be fine." She pushed the wheel forward and headed down. She dropped too quickly. There wasn't enough airspeed.

"We gonna crash?" Norman shouted. "I paid good fare for this ride and I expect you to get us to Anchorage in one piece."

Thinking what an idiotic statement that was, Kate didn't answer but kept her concentration on getting them safely on the ground. The engine sputtered and was barely running. She'd been so excited to get back in the air she'd skipped completing a thorough preflight inspection. How could she have been so careless?

"Hang on!" Kate came back on the throttle, holding enough pressure on the elevator to slow down. She pushed the nose forward. Even with the engine limping along, she managed a nearly perfect landing. When they stopped, the men clambered out.

Pale and looking angry, John demanded, "Now what do we do?"

"I'll radio in to the airfield and then I'll have a look to see what's wrong. We'll be on our way in no time." She tried to keep her voice light and cheery, hoping it turned out to be as simple as she'd made it sound.

If she was late, Paul would worry. And if he knew what had happened, he'd be upset. She'd had too many close calls. Maybe she could come up with a story. He didn't need to know. As soon as she considered the idea, she knew it was wrong. She couldn't lie to him. Besides, she'd never been very good at it and he'd know right off. She'd have to tell the truth.

— 6 —

With a glance at John and Norman, who stood huddled against a cold March breeze, Kate reluctantly put in a call to Jack. The radio crackled to life. "Anchorage airport, this is Pacemaker 221. Over."

"Two-twenty-one, this is Anchorage. Go ahead. Over."

"Jack, I had engine trouble and put down just out of Talkeetna."

"What's the problem?"

"Loss of engine power."

"What the heck happened?"

"I don't know yet. I'll check the engine and get back to you."

"Crud, Kate, will it never end? You're always in some kind of trouble." There was a long pause. "You all right?"

"Yes. No injuries."

"Do you need assistance?"

"I'll let you know."

"I'll be here."

Kate smiled. Maybe she was mistaken, but she thought she'd heard concern in Jack's voice. "Copy. Over and out."

The radio went dead. Kate stared at it. First time out since her injury and she'd muffed up. At this rate, she'd have trouble maintaining a good reputation as a pilot. She glanced up to see Norman and John climbing inside the plane. "Too cold for you?" she asked, trying to keep a happy lilt to her voice. She didn't want them upset.

"It's freezin' out there," John said, dropping into a seat and huddling deeper into his coat. "Sure could use some heat."

"With any luck we'll be back in the air soon," Kate said, her mind going to the plane. What had gone wrong? She went to work while the two men ate biscuits and jerky. They offered her some, but she wasn't hungry. She needed to get her plane back in the air.

She lifted the engine cowling and searched for mechanical clues.

There'd been no odor of oil or smoke. And she couldn't see any sign of an oil leak. Methodically she examined the engine. And then when she touched one of the ignition wires, it fell free. It had barely been attached. How had she missed it?

You didn't even check—that's how. She thought back to her preflight check. Her mind had been on Paul and her new status as a married woman. This was nothing more than carelessness. And her negligence could have cost her life and that of her passengers. They'd want to know what had gone wrong. What should she say?

Norman climbed out of the plane and called up to Kate, "So, you find the trouble?"

"Sure did. And it's an easy fix. We'll be in Anchorage before you know it."

"What was wrong?"

"Just a loose wire," Kate said, reattaching it and making sure it was snug. She closed the engine hood.

"You know what you're doing?" Norman eyed her suspiciously.

Kate blew out an exasperated breath. Why was it that men never trusted a woman to do anything mechanical? "I've been working on planes since I was a kid."

Norman nodded but didn't look completely convinced. He climbed back inside the plane.

Once they were in the air, Kate tried to figure out what she'd say to Jack. He'd have her hide when he found out what had gone wrong. She'd radioed him with a brief message that she'd corrected the problem and was on her way. He'd want more when she reached the airfield. She'd just have to be honest with him. People make mistakes.

Her stomach tumbling, Kate brought the plane into the field. It pitched from side to side and the skis shuddered over scars in the snow. She couldn't concentrate. Once on the ground, she opened the door and climbed down. Pasting on a smile, she shook John and Norman's hands as they left the plane. "Have a good time."

"Thanks for getting us here in one piece," Norman said.

"You're welcome." She turned to see Jack standing in the doorway of the shop, arms folded over his chest, cigar stub clenched between his teeth. There was no avoiding him. She headed for the shop.

"One of these days you're not going to make it back." Jack took the stogie out of his mouth and studied it, then looked at her from beneath his heavy brows. "What happened?"

"A loose ignition wire. Nothing I couldn't take care of," Kate said, concentrating on keeping her tone casual.

"How'd you miss it?" His voice was heavy with accusation.

"I . . . I don't know." Kate hedged.

"Did you do a thorough inspection before takeoff?"

Watching her feet, Kate tapped the heel of one boot against the toe of the other. She licked dry lips. "I guess I forgot. It won't happen again."

"You bet it won't." He puffed on the cigar and the stink drifted into Kate's nostrils. "If it does, you're out—fired. You could have gone down. Pilots don't always get a second chance. You of all people should know that."

Beneath his ire, Kate heard concern. He was afraid . . . for her. The thought made her dislike him a little less.

Jack stuck his cigar back in his mouth, turned on his heel, and marched into the shop, slamming the door behind him.

Kate stared at the building. She didn't want to go inside, but she had to sign in. If she didn't, Jack might use it as an excuse to fire her. With determination, she walked into the shop. Jack sat at the desk, studying a map. He didn't look up.

Kate crossed to the ledger and signed it. "I'll be at the homestead. You can contact me on the house radio if you have a run for me."

Jack acted as if he hadn't heard. Kate wasn't about to defend herself—there was nothing she could say.

Now, she'd have to face Paul.

Letting out a sigh of relief, Paul watched Kate's Bellanca touch down on the frozen creek. She'd radioed and told him she'd be late, explaining she'd had engine trouble. His stomach turned at the thought. Would her life end like so many others—one fatal mistake, one last flight?

When he'd married Kate, he thought he would be able to deal with the dangers she faced. Now he wasn't so sure. Every time she went out, he couldn't stop thinking about her and worrying whether she'd make it home.

He walked down the path toward the creek, Angel at his side. The malamute/husky mix had her tail flagging. When she spotted Kate, she dashed across the frozen stream toward her. Paul watched Kate kneel and pull the dog into her arms.

When Kate stood, she gazed at Paul, then with a wave she moved toward him.

Paul's heart skipped a beat as he watched the long-legged beauty. He doubted he'd ever get used to how beautiful she was—not just how she looked, but the way she moved and the way she loved him. He stepped onto the ice and met her.

"Kate," he said, opening his arms and gathering her against him. He held her tightly, almost afraid to release her. "Thank God you're all right."

Kate snuggled closer. "It wasn't bad. I even had a landing strip to set down on. And the problem was easy to fix."

"What was it?"

"A loose wire. I should have spotted it." Kate stepped back with a shrug and smiled at him with a glint of mischief in her eyes. "I guess my mind was on something else."

"Oh? What?"

"It's more like *who*." She grinned and hugged him again. "I couldn't wait to get home to you."

Paul held her more tightly. Oh how he loved her. He dropped a kiss on her forehead, then hefted her pack and circled an arm around her as they walked toward the trail that led to the house. "I have dinner ready. How does roast with carrots and fresh bread sound?"

"Delicious. I'm starved."

Jasper sat on his perch near the back door. "Hello there, Jasper. Good to see you." Kate reached out to the raven. He pecked at her finger and flittered away. "I don't think he'll ever get used to me."

"He's never taken to anyone except me. I don't know why."

"Maybe he understands you saved his life."

"I doubt birds comprehend things like that." Paul opened the door and held it for Kate.

She stepped inside. "It's good to be here. I've been thinking about it all day. I'd like to have enough time off to just laze around for a few days."

"You have a run again tomorrow?" Paul could hear the defensiveness in his voice and wished he'd curbed it.

"I don't know. Jack's supposed to radio me if he has a run. But, living out here means I'll work less—it's easier to call in one of the pilots who are close by."

Paul shut the door and carried Kate's bag into the bedroom. "It's worth it, though—having you here." He peeked out of the door and winked at her.

Kate smiled, but Paul thought he saw discontent in her eyes.

The meal was good, but the conversation stilted. Kate didn't say much and Paul couldn't stop thinking about what had happened to her. It could have been so much worse.

"I missed having Angel with me today," Kate said, taking a drink of coffee.

"She had a good time with the other dogs, but I think she missed you too."

Kate looked at Angel, who lay on the rug in the front room. "She loves to fly almost as much as I do."

Paul didn't respond. He cut into his meat, forked it into his mouth, and chewed, his mind brooding over Kate's close call. He wanted to say something, but wasn't sure it would do any good. He set down his knife and fork. "When you were late today, I called the airfield. Jack told me what happened. Why didn't you radio me sooner?"

"It didn't take more than a few minutes to fix the problem so I figured I could let you know after I had things straightened out with Jack. He was mad, really mad—even threatened to fire me."

Paul placed his forearms on the edge of the table. "Maybe that wouldn't be so bad," he said before he could capture the thought and keep it to himself.

"What do you mean?" Kate set down her fork and knife and stared at Paul.

"Just that you'd be here more and we could spend time together, working on the place. Might even be able to run a trapline this year." Paul didn't want her to know how much he worried.

She buttered a piece of bread. "I'd love to have more time with you, but we'll have that when we make your medical runs. And there's lots of time to get the work done around here. 'Course I don't know about trapping—it's kind of disgusting. I hate killing animals."

Paul nodded. The room turned quiet. He was afraid for Kate. Yet her tenacity and courage were part of what made her special—they were two of the things he loved about her. When she agreed to marry him, he'd promised her she could fly without restrictions—that she'd be free to make her own choices. He couldn't go back on that.

Kate reached across the table and rested a hand on his. "I know you worry about me. And I'm sorry that you do. But hazards are part of the job." She squeezed his hand. "You know I'm a good pilot. I can get out of just about any scrape, but I can't guarantee something bad won't happen."

Paul lifted her hand to his lips and kissed it, then pressed it to his cheek. "I know. I just can't stand the thought of losing you." He barely managed to choke out the words. He gazed into her hazel eyes. "I'm so proud of you. I won't ask you to quit."

The gold in Kate's eyes intensified. "I love you. And I swear not to take foolish chances. Today I got careless, but it won't happen again."

Kate cleaned up after dinner, while Paul fed and cared for the dogs. When he stepped into the house, Kate asked,

"Would you like a cup of coffee? I thought we might sit on the porch."

"Yeah, I'd like that. It's cold, but clear and really beautiful."

Kate poured them each a cup and Paul grabbed the wool blanket off the back of the sofa and followed her out. They sat on the top step. Kate handed him his coffee and snuggled beneath the blanket with him. She leaned against him, peering up at a sky splashed with shimmering stars and touched by the glow of the moon peeking over the treetops.

Paul loved these moments with Kate. She was independent and courageous, but she needed him. And he needed her.

"I think I love this more than anything else about Alaska—enjoying God's beauty with you—being here with you." Kate kissed him.

The dogs started barking and tugging on their leads. Angel stood on the porch and growled. Paul's protective alarm went off when he heard the crunch of snow.

"Quiet down, dogs," Lily called. "It's just me." She appeared on the trail, carrying a lantern. A tall native man was with her.

The two of them walked up to the porch steps. Paul and Kate stood.

"I heard your plane come in," Lily said, "and thought you two might want to meet our new neighbor." She turned to the man standing beside her. "This is Clint Tucker. He took over the homestead that belonged to Klaus." She smiled up at the big man in a way that made Paul wonder if she might have found the man of her dreams.

Paul reached out a hand. "Good to meet you, Clint."

"Nice to meet you." Clint's grasp was firm.

"Paul's a doctor and Kate's a pilot," Lily said. "We're all set for a ride or medical help if we need it."

"I like that." His smile was quiet, but friendly. "I was lucky to find this place. It's exactly what I've been looking for."

71

"Do you have family around here?" Kate asked.

"Not exactly. My parents and two brothers live up near Palmer—not too far."

"You've got yourself a fine place. Klaus put a lot of work into it." Paul draped the blanket around Kate. "The cabin's solid and there's a large garden patch. And in all the years Klaus lived here I don't think he ever had an animal break into his cache." Memories of old Klaus ignited in Paul's mind. He was a fine man and Paul missed him.

"I heard he was a good man."

"True. And a good neighbor. He's buried on the rise overlooking the river."

"Yeah. I saw that. I figure I'll keep up his grave." Clint's dark eyes were warm.

"So, what are you two doing out here in the cold?" Lily asked.

"Stargazing," Kate glanced at Paul. "And dreaming a little."

"They just got married," Lily explained.

"Ah." Clint grinned, showing off large white teeth. "Congratulations."

"We'll leave you to your stargazing," Lily said.

"Glad to meet you." Clint tossed a black braid off his shoulder. "It'll take me awhile to get the feel for the place. You mind if I ask you a question now and then?"

"Anytime." Paul liked Clint and looked forward to getting to know him. "You ever run a team of dogs?"

"Sure. I want to get some dogs and I plan to make a sled."

"Let me know if you need a hand. And you might check down at Susitna Station if you're looking for dogs or pups. They have some from time to time."

"Okay. I'll do that."

"Bye," Lily said, and then she and Clint headed toward Lily's place.

Kate and Paul returned to their porch step. Kate chuckled. "I think Lily likes him."

"I think you're right. And who knows—maybe he's the one for her."

"I hope so. It would be nice for her and the baby. Being married makes life better."

Paul gave Kate a lingering kiss. Then speaking against her lips, he said, "You make life better."

She kissed him and giggled.

He draped an arm over her shoulders and looked out over the property. "Do you think we ought to expand the garden? There's just two of us now, but who knows . . . maybe one day there'll be more."

"Maybe." Kate smiled at him. "Only God knows about that." She looked at the garden area. "Will we be here enough to take care of a large garden?"

Paul shoved down frustration. Kate hadn't heard him. He slid his arm off her shoulders and leaned forward on his thighs. "I don't think it'll be a problem. If we need to, we can hire Patrick's boys. They helped out last summer. So did Lily. But with two of us to work, it might be easier. And we won't be gone all the time."

"You know how it is in the summer," Kate said, glancing into her empty cup. "I'll be gone a lot and so will you. The days are long and so are the flights. Plus you'll be needed more. There are a lot of folks who wait until summer to see a doctor."

Paul let his gaze roam over the forest and across his property. "I was hoping you'd work less . . . now that we're married. I have plenty of money and you don't need to save up for a house. In fact, you could sell the place in town."

"Sell it?"

Kate's strident tone took Paul by surprise. "Well . . . having two houses doesn't really make sense."

"It belonged to Mike. He wanted me to have it."

"I know, but that was when you needed a house."

Kate shoved her fingers through her short hair. "If I sell it, I feel like I'm giving away part of him." Her voice wobbled. "I loved him." She swiped away tears. "Not the way I love you, but he was my best friend for a long time."

Paul felt like he'd stepped into a minefield and wasn't sure how to find a safe way out. "I just thought—"

"I'm not selling it. Maybe we could sell this place. I work out of Anchorage and being in town makes sense. It would be easier for you too—to get your supplies and work with patients that need hospitalization."

"No. I'm not moving." Paul stood and walked to the bottom step, looking out over his property. How could she even suggest he sell his home? "I've put endless hours into this place. I built this cabin, the workshed, the cache, and I put in the garden. And what about the dogs? There's no place for them in town. And no room for a garden."

"We can use the store . . . like other people do. That's what you did when you lived in San Francisco."

"That was different. I'm not the same man I was when I lived there." He shoved his hands into his coat pockets. "I've spent the last six years here, and I'm not moving."

"You sure you're not just trying to keep me safely on the ground?" Kate couldn't keep the accusation out of her voice. "If I'm out here, Jack's not going to use me nearly as much. And eventually he could drop me altogether."

"He wouldn't do that."

"Jack can do anything he wants and he does."

Paul looked at the cabin. "I love this place. I envision us living here, raising a family, fishing the river, and mushing the dogs." He gazed at her in the light of the rising moon. "I thought you felt the same."

74

"I do. I love it here." Kate moved down the steps to Paul. "Town just seems more reasonable." The combativeness seemed to have gone out of her. She tucked an arm into Paul's. "We don't have to decide right away. We can take as long as we need." She leaned against him. "Let's not fight."

"Yeah. I don't want to fight," Paul said, but he knew he wouldn't change his mind. This was home. It was a friend—the place that had sheltered him from the world when he'd needed it.

Kate would get used to it. She'd agree with him . . . eventually.

K ate held a stick up out of the dogs' reach. They danced around her, watching and waiting for her to throw the prize. "Okay. Here you go." She tossed the short branch down the snow-covered trail, then watched, feeling content as all four dogs charged after it. Life was good.

"Hey, Kate," Paul hollered from the back porch. "I got a call from Jack. There's a family that needs a doctor right away."

"Okay. I'll take care of the dogs."

Kate secured Buck, Jackpot, and Nita, then headed toward the cabin with Angel beside her. She stepped inside the house, eager to get into the air. "Where are we headed?"

"A homestead outside of Valdez."

"What's happened?"

"I'm not sure, except that a child is ill."

Kate gave a nod. "We'll need some general supplies and food. Can you take care of that while I get the plane ready?"

"I'm on it." Paul set his medical bag on the table and opened it. "Guess I won't be chopping wood today." He went to work inspecting his supplies.

Kate set a pail of oil on the stove to warm and hurried to the bedroom to pack some clothes. She hated the idea of a sick child, but flying with Paul and working with him was always exhilarating.

By the time she'd added the warmed oil to the engine, given the plane a thorough inspection, and had it flight ready, Paul had made his way down the trail. He loaded the supplies and his medical bag. Angel leaped aboard.

"I'll crank her," Paul said.

Kate doubled-checked the gauges. When the flywheel was going well, she started the engine.

Paul climbed in, latched the door behind him, then stashed the crank and took the passenger seat in front. "Low ceiling," he said, scanning the gray cloud cover.

"Looks like snow's on the way." Kate set up for takeoff and then moved down the runway. "You and Clint did a good job on the airstrip." She gradually picked up speed. The plane lifted off and Kate made a wide sweep away from home and turned south.

"Clint's a good hard worker and a fine neighbor." Paul gazed down the frozen Susitna River, then pulled out a map he'd drawn up. "Jack gave me the coordinates and explained where to find the homestead." He held out a chart along with some notes for Kate.

She studied it. "Shouldn't be too hard to find. Is there a landing strip?"

"Guess we'll find out when we get there. But since they live along Robe Lake there's a good chance they've cleared a place on the ice—no way in and out of there in the winter other than by plane. Unless they use dogs."

"We'll find them." With confidence, Kate headed southwest out of Cook Inlet and along Turnagain Arm.

"Lots of ice floes," Paul said, looking at the muddy ocean water below.

Kate followed the coast with its forests of spruce and hemlock reaching toward the water's edge, then she maneuvered through Portage Pass to avoid hidden peaks and treacherous winds in the mountain terrain. She moved up Portage Valley, breathing in the beauty of the glacial floes that wound their way through the mountains. The views slipping by below warmed Kate's heart. There was nothing like flying.

"I'm always impressed by the beauty of this territory," Paul said.

"Yeah. I don't think I'll ever get used to it. Anyway, I hope not." Kate smiled at Paul. Her life was pretty nearly perfect. She had the career she'd always wanted and now she got to share her life with the best man she'd ever known.

Kate flew over Valdez. "Okay, watch for the lake. It might be hard to spot because of the heavy snow. It'll blend into the terrain."

"Is that it?" Paul shouted over the noise of the engine.

"Could be. It's a lake all right."

Paul looked at the map, then his notes. "Jack said the house would be on the Valdez side of the lake." He scanned the forest that pressed in around the frozen, snow-covered lake. A cabin emerged from the forest, smoke trailing into the sky from a chimney.

"That's got to be it." Kate pushed the control wheel in and gradually descended. She dropped down over the lake for a closer look, hoping for a good place to set down.

Someone stepped out of the cabin and trudged out into the snow in front of the house. He waved his arms over his head.

"This is it." Kate made another pass over the area in front of the cabin to make sure it was clear of debris and hidden berms. Everything looked good. She set up close to shore, using the visible trees to give her some depth perception over the milky white lake.

The skis touched and Kate could feel them sink into the

deep snow. "They've had a lot of snowfall." She taxied at a good clip so she could maneuver the plane around so it faced the way she'd come in—lined up in the tracks she'd already laid down. It would make for an easier takeoff.

Paul climbed out of his seat and grabbed his bag, his mind already with the patient waiting for him. He hoped they weren't facing anything too serious. As soon as the plane came to a stop, he moved to the back and opened the door. Angel jumped out and romped through mounds of snow.

"Well, let's see what's going on," Paul said, tromping toward the cabin.

The man who'd waved at them was tall and thin and, like many men in the bush, sported a full beard. He stood with his hands in his pockets while he waited for Paul and Kate. When they reached him, he held out a hand. "Sure glad to see you. I'm Ken Baker." He shook Paul's hand, then Kate's.

"Paul Anderson and this is Kate, my wife and pilot."

"We're thankful you come all this way. My boy's real sick. Nothing we do seems to help." He headed toward the cabin steps.

"How long has he been sick?" Paul asked.

"Nearly three weeks. He had a real sore throat and a fever, then he got better for a few days. Figured he was over it. The rest of the kids got sick right along with him, but they healed up—no problem."

"That's good to hear," Paul said, thinking through the possibilities.

"Caleb's got a fever, his body aches somethin' awful, and there're strange markings on his arms and legs—kinda like bruises."

"Let's have a look at him," Paul said, concern spiking. "Does he have a rash?"

"Nope. None that I seen."

Paul followed Ken indoors, stopping in the kitchen.

"This is my wife, Gertrude," Ken said.

"Nice to meet you." The heavyset woman swiped a strand of blonde hair off her face and tried to tuck it into the twist of hair at the nap of her neck. Three children clustered around her, and stared at Paul and Kate. Paul guessed they didn't see outsiders often.

"We've been real worried," said Gertrude. "Thank you for coming."

"I'm glad to."

Paul and Kate followed Ken and Gertrude into a stuffy room packed with beds. A boy who looked to be about ten lay prostrate in one of the beds. His breathing was labored and he was obviously very ill.

Ken leaned over his son. "Caleb, this is the doctor. He's come to make you better."

By the looks of the boy, Paul hoped the youngster's father was right. He put on a smile and sat on the edge of the bed. "Hello, Caleb. I understand you're not feeling so good."

The boy mumbled, "No sir. I ain't."

Kate watched from the doorway with the rest of the children crowding around her to peek in. Paul rested the back of his hand on the boy's forehead, then opened his medical bag and took out a thermometer. Placing it in Caleb's mouth, he said, "Keep this under your tongue." He retrieved a stethoscope from the bag, placed it against the youngster's chest, and listened. Caleb's heart rate was unusually rapid. "Can you take a deep breath?"

Caleb did as instructed, but the effort seemed almost too much for him. Paul moved the stethoscope and repeated the request. He made no comment as he lifted the child's arm and pushed up his pajama sleeve, but he knew the child was seriously ill. Caleb closed his eyes and moaned.

"Did my touching your arm hurt?" Paul asked as he bent the boy's arm slightly.

"Uh-huh."

The elbow was red and swollen. And there were uneven blotches that looked like bruises on both arms. He examined his trunk and legs—more bruises. Along with the blotches nearly all his joints were swollen, red and hot. *Rheumatic fever!*

Paul gently lowered Caleb back onto the bed. "You rest, son." He stood and looked at Ken and Gertrude. "Can we talk in the other room?"

Gertrude went pale, then after dropping a kiss on Caleb's forehead, she followed Paul into the adjoining room. "Okay, off with you," she said to the other children. "You have chores to do." Without argument, they hustled to the doorway where they pulled on coats and hats, then like a flock of sheep hurried outdoors.

"What is it, doctor?" Ken asked.

"Rheumatic fever. He has all the classic symptoms."

A small gasp escaped Gertrude. "Will he be all right?"

"It'll take time, but he should recover. His heart's working hard right now—that's a worry. With this kind of ailment, heart damage is our greatest concern. He needs to be hospitalized."

"No!" Gertrude blurted.

Her answer was so abrupt and defiant, Paul was taken aback. "They have a first-rate hospital in Anchorage and will take good care of him there. And Kate can—"

"I said, no." Gertrude shook her head back and forth. "Hospitals are places where people go to die. I won't allow it." She shot a glance at Ken.

He furrowed his brows. "Maybe the doctor's right, Gertie."

Gertrude's eyes brimmed. "I can't." She shook her head. "No."

Ken turned to Paul. "We had another boy, who got real sick with a blood disease. He went to the hospital and . . . he never came home." The room turned quiet as a tomb. "Is there something we can do here . . . at home?" Ken finally asked.

Paul would have been more comfortable with Caleb in the hospital, but he doubted there'd be any way to convince his mother to let him go. "He can stay here, but I really think his best chance at a full recovery is at the hospital. They have skilled physicians, and nurses will watch over him around the clock."

Gertrude pressed a fist to her mouth and shook her head. "Just tell us what to do. We'll take care of him."

Paul could see there would be no convincing her. He let out a breath. "How about if I stay for a few days? I can monitor his condition and that way if he becomes critical we can transport him."

Gertrude squeezed her eyes closed and tipped her face upward. When she looked at Paul, she seemed less frightened. "You promise he'll only go if it's necessary?"

"I promise."

"I think that's wise," Ken said, obviously trying to be sensitive to his wife, while doing his best to protect his son.

"All right. I'll agree to that," she said, balling her hands into fists.

Paul turned to Kate. "Can you come back for me in a week or so? If need be, I'll radio you."

"I can stay . . . unless Jack needs me." She took Paul's hand and squeezed it. "I don't have anything better to do." She smiled at him. "I'll let Jack know where I am."

"What if a call comes in?"

"I'll check with Jack off and on during the day, and if he has a run for me I'll go and then come back."

"We have a small room off the kitchen where you can sleep," Gertrude said. "It's not much, but I think we can make you comfortable."

"That'll be fine," Paul said. "I'll have another look at Caleb and get him started on some medication. And I think we can make him more comfortable."

"He says his legs hurt real bad."

"That's not uncommon. I'll show you how to make a tent with the sheets so they don't lay on his legs. His fever was pretty high, but a sponge bath should help that. And I've got some medication for his pain." He headed toward the bedroom with Gertrude close behind him.

Kate returned to the plane. She'd call Jack, then put the plane to bed for the night. She climbed inside the cockpit and turned on the radio. "This is Pacemaker 221. Come in, Anchorage. Over."

"Pacemaker 221, this is Anchorage. You still in Valdez? Over."

"I am. Paul needs to stay for a few days."

"I need you back here."

Kate looked toward the cabin. She hadn't counted on leaving right away. Caleb was still so ill. "What do you have?"

"A prisoner transfer from Kotzebue to Anchorage."

"Are there any other planes available?"

"No. You're it."

"Okay. When do you need me?"

"Kotzebue is expecting a ride to show up this week. You have about four days."

Kate could make it up there in three, maybe less if the good weather held, and stay only one night before heading back. "Okay. I'll head out first thing tomorrow."

"I'll notify the trooper who will be traveling back with you."

Kate worried about leaving the boy. "Jack, there's a boy here who's gravely ill. He might need a ride to the hospital. Will there be a pilot available?"

"Alan should be back late tomorrow and after that we should be covered. Over."

"Okay. I'll tell Paul. Over and out."

When Kate told Paul that she'd be transporting a prisoner, she was not prepared for his reaction. He excused himself and Kate from the Bakers and steered Kate outside.

As soon as the door shut, he said, "I don't want you going."

"Paul, it's not the first time I've transferred a prisoner." Kate stepped off the porch. "I've never had a problem. A state trooper always travels with a prisoner. You have nothing to worry about."

Paul squared his jaw. "No. I won't allow it."

Paul had never forbidden Kate to take a flight. She was stunned. "Not allow? It's part of my job."

"There's no reason for you to take that kind of a risk. You don't know what this man has done or what he's capable of."

"We don't even know if it's a man."

Paul blew out a puff of air. "How many women prisoners have you seen recently?"

Kate ground her teeth. "That's not the point."

Paul shook his head and turned his back to her.

"If the prisoner has been accused of a violent crime, I'll strap on my revolver."

Paul turned and looked at her. "Do you think that firing a gun inside a plane is safe?"

"No. But if I had to, I would. You know I keep a revolver

with me. I have ever since I had trouble with those three hunters—remember? One of them opened the door during a flight and nearly fell out."

Paul stared at her stubbornly.

"You've never given a hoot about me carrying a gun. Why now?"

"It's not the gun."

Kate took a deep breath. This was ridiculous. Keeping her voice quiet and steady, she said, "I'm going. First thing in the morning."

Paul didn't respond right away. He walked toward the lake and stared at Kate's plane. Finally he turned and asked, "Have you been practicing with that gun?"

Kate hated to admit that she'd barely looked at it in months. "No." She kept her eyes locked on his.

"All right, then . . . if you insist on behaving foolishly, you and I are going to spend time on target practice."

Still half angry with each other, Kate and Paul trudged into the forest. Paul cleared snow off a downed tree and set up five bottles as targets. He paced off about thirty feet. "Have you even fired that gun before?"

"Mike showed me once, a long time ago." She felt foolish. What good was a gun if she didn't know how to use it?

"Do you have bullets?"

Kate took a box out of her coat pocket and loaded six into the long-barreled Colt single-shot. She snapped the cylinder shut. "I know how to load and fire it, but my aim is pretty awful."

The tension between them eased.

"We'll work on that. Square off your stance, like this." Paul faced the target and stood with his feet apart and parallel with his left foot back slightly. "You'll have to pull the hammer down each time you want to shoot—this is a single-shot revolver."

Kate nodded.

"Use the sight here on the top of the barrel, hold it with both hands to keep it steady, and lock your arms. Then sight it in the target, take a breath and hold it, then squeeze the trigger."

Kate grasped the revolver in both hands and took her stance. She felt nervous. She didn't like guns much. She held the revolver out in front of her. Using the sight, she aimed at the first bottle on the log.

"Pull back the hammer."

Kate did as he said, feeling her cheeks heat up. She'd nearly forgotten to cock it. She pulled the trigger and fired. The kick sent her hands up in front of her and made them tingle. The bottles remained standing. She blew out an exasperated breath.

"Try again."

Determined to hit her target, she held out the gun in front of her, pulled back the hammer, and with her hands steady, she squeezed the trigger. Again the bottles remained untouched. They seemed to stare at her, taunting. She dropped her arms. "I'm worthless with a gun."

"You've got four more shots in there. Don't give up. It's important, Kate."

"Okay." She clasped the revolver, and again held it out, making sure to keep her arms straight and tight. Sighting in the bottle, she gently pulled back on the trigger and fired. Her eyes opened wide in surprise when the bottle she'd been aiming at splintered, launching pieces of glass in all directions. "I got it! I got it!"

"Good job." Paul gave her back a friendly slap. "Okay, now finish off the rest of them. You'll have to reload. You only have three bullets left and four bottles."

"I'll need a whole lot more than three bullets." She gave him a wry smile.

She and Paul spent another thirty minutes practicing. By the time they finished, Kate felt almost proficient. It made her feel slightly more secure.

Before daylight, the following morning, Kate packed up and readied her plane for takeoff. Paul was busy with Caleb. He hadn't improved at all since the previous day, but he was no worse. When Kate was ready to leave, she wasn't sure she ought to go. What if the boy took a turn for the worse?

She made a stop in his room and told him she'd be back within a week and that she expected him to be feeling much better by then. He promised he'd try.

Paul followed her out to the plane.

With a glance at the cabin, Kate said, "Caleb's not looking good. Are you sure he won't need to go to the hospital?"

"He's holding his own. I doubt he'll get any worse. You take care of yourself. Don't get careless, Kate."

She wrapped her arms around his neck. "I'll be fine."

Paul's expression remained stern. "Even though there's a trooper with you, you've got to stay on your toes."

Kate smiled and kissed him. "Don't worry about me—you have a boy in there to think about." She gazed at clouds scuttling across a hazy sky. The first light of day touched them with pink. "Hope the weather holds out. I won't be gone long. With the longer days I'll be able to get in more flying hours."

Paul pulled her close. "I wish you weren't going."

Kate stepped back. "I know. I'll be careful. And I'll pray for you and poor Caleb. I hope he gets better soon."

"Rheumatic fever hangs on. Caleb will be sick for a long while." He glanced at the cabin. "I wish they'd agreed to hospitalization. I'll stay as long as he's in danger. By the time you get back we ought to know how he's going to fare."

"Okay." Kate stepped forward and hugged Paul again, realizing this would be the longest they'd be separated since they'd been married. "I'll miss you."

"I'll miss you too. Please be cautious."

"I will."

"And use your gun if you have to."

"You worry too much." She dropped one more kiss on his lips and then climbed into the plane.

Paul watched her taxi down the airstrip. Kate waved to him and lifted off, forcing her mind away from thoughts of how far she'd be from Paul, and instead turned her mind to Kotzebue.

Transporting prisoners always made her nervous. Most were jailed on petty charges, but some were violent and dangerous. Which would it be this time?

— 8 —

The sun glowed from the midst of a deep blue sky as Kate watched the small village of Candle slip by below. "We're nearly there, Angel." She gave the dog a pat. Kotzebue wasn't far now.

The trip had gone smoothly. The weather had held, there'd been no mechanical problems, and long April days had provided Kate with plenty of flying time. She'd reach Kotzebue long before dark, which meant there'd be time for a visit with the Turchiks. The following morning she'd be on her way back to Paul. She smiled, thinking of him and feeling the warmth of his embrace before she'd left him. She ran a finger over her lips, remembering his passionate kiss.

This trip would be better if he was with her. She'd rather be on a medical run than carrying a prisoner to Anchorage. She felt a stir of apprehension. Her only instructions were to show up at the jail. She wouldn't know what kind of crime had been committed or who she was transporting until she got to Kotzebue. And she guessed that Paul's fears had stirred some of her own.

Finally she spotted Kotzebue resting on a small peninsula along the edge of Kotzebue Sound. She felt as if she were home. The Turchiks were like family. Happiness bubbled up inside of her.

She hadn't always felt that way. She remembered her first visit to the region, which had seemed inhospitable and foreign. She'd nearly lost her way in the winter darkness and had even questioned why she'd foolishly taken on the challenge of flying the bush. Over time, the people and the territory had changed her. She'd come to see the splendor of the vast wilderness even when frigid temperatures kept it locked away from the world. The Arctic possessed a beauty unlike any other.

Kate set the Bellanca down on the airstrip south of the village. Nena stepped out of a cabin that squatted alongside the landing field. Bundled in a heavy parka, she shuffled toward the plane, her mukluks scuffing up a small ice cloud around her feet.

Angel woofed at Nena, leapt from the plane, and then she was off, her nose to the ground. Kate stepped out. Even though she knew to expect it, the cold hit her hard. She sucked in frigid air and coughed, then smiled as Nena approached. "I don't know if I'll ever adjust to the weather up here," she joked, pulling her friend into a tight hug. "Oh, it's good to see you."

Nena stepped back. "The weather—it is a nice day today." She grinned, her almond-shaped eyes nearly disappearing in her dark, weathered skin. She studied Kate. "I think being married is good for you. You look prettier than ever."

"You think so? I am happy. I love Paul and I love being married." Kate patted her arms, trying to dispel some of the cold. "You look wonderful. You're glowing."

"I am?" Nena smiled, her cheeks rounding. "It is the baby."

"A baby? You're having a baby?"

Nena nodded.

"How wonderful!"

Nena rested a hand on her abdomen. "It should be here by the end of summer." She grinned. "And you? You will also have a baby soon?"

Kate was taken aback by the question, but she should have expected it. Nena always spoke her mind. "Not yet. When God wills it." The conversation she had with her mother came charging back. Kate wanted a child, but didn't know what she'd do about her work if she had a baby.

Kate turned to the plane. "I'd better get this bird taken care of. I can't wait to see the children."

"They are excited to see you too."

Working together, the two women drained the oil, tied off the plane, and draped and secured a tarp over the engine. Then with their arms linked, they headed toward town. A cold breeze blew in from the frozen bay, creating glittering ice fog.

Kate pulled her hood closer around her face. "It's freezing."

Nena laughed. "Yes. But soon it will be spring."

"It can't be soon enough for me." Kate put her head down to keep out the cold and kept walking.

When they stepped into the Turchiks' combination home and general store, the children swamped Kate with greetings and hugs. Kate knelt and gathered them into her arms.

She looked at Peter, the oldest. "You are growing so fast. You're nearly a man."

A flush rose in the nine-year-old's cheeks. "My father said I can go with him next winter when he hunts for seal and walrus." He threw his shoulders back.

Kate picked up little Mary, who was nearly five. "And how about you? You're not a baby anymore. Do you want to go hunting too?"

Mary smiled and dimples appeared in both cheeks. "No. I do not hunt."

"Really?" Kate looked at Nena.

"It's not the custom for women to hunt."

"I want to go hunting," Nick piped up. He looked at his mother as if hoping for affirmation.

"One day. Now you are not old enough." Nick's smile turned into a pout, but Nena ignored it. She took off her parka and hung it on a hook made of walrus tusk.

The children engulfed Angel with hugs and kisses. They loved animals and especially Angel.

Kate could already see the bulge of Nena's growing child. An unexpected longing for one of her own welled up inside of her. How long would she have to wait? She hung her coat beside Nena's.

"I have tea. Would you like some?"

"That sounds good." Kate followed Nena into the kitchen and sat at a rustic table made of driftwood.

Nena filled two cups. "There is a celebration tonight. The men killed two walrus so it was decided we have a good reason for fun. That's where Joe is. He would have met the plane, but there is a fire to build and to keep burning so the meat will cook." She set a cup of tea on the table in front of Kate. "I made fish pie for the feast. You'll come?"

Kate took a sip of the strong tea. She knew to refuse the invitation would be seen as a snub. Her body longed for sleep, but she wasn't about to reject her friends or pass up an opportunity to experience a native celebration. Not to mention she'd never eaten roasted walrus. "I wouldn't miss it," she said, taking another drink. The tea felt warm in her empty stomach. "First I have to talk to the trooper. He has a prisoner to transport."

"I can take you." Nena drank down her tea, then called to Peter. He appeared from a back room. "You watch the children," she said. "We will be back soon." She and Kate pulled on their parkas and then headed down the street, toward a makeshift jail.

"Do you know what the prisoner did?"

"Yes. That George Ujarak—he is a very bad man."

"What did he do?"

"He said he came to hunt, but when he got to Arthur's house, he took his money and then he shot him. Poor Arthur. He never did nothing bad to no one. He was a good man."

So much for not being dangerous. "I'm sorry to hear that." Kate took in a deep breath and the cold air burned her lungs. "At least he's been caught and will pay for his crime."

"It would be better if he paid for it in Kotzebue," Nena said with more vehemence than Kate usually heard from her. "But there's no place for a trial here." She stopped and looked at Kate. "You be careful with George. Do not trust him."

"I'll be careful. But there's nothing to worry about." Kate wondered why, if she believed that, her stomach was doing flips. "The trooper will make sure he's secure. All I have to do is fly the plane."

Nena nodded, but it looked like she was holding back something. Finally she said, "I will pray for you." She stopped in front of a building that was only slightly larger than an outhouse. "This is it."

Kate made arrangements with trooper Ted Jacobs to meet at sunrise the following morning, then she and Nena returned home. Nena got the children into their boots and coats and then they all headed for the celebration.

Large hunks of meat hung on spits over a fire. Fat dripped and sizzled, flaring in the flames. Men and women had gathered in groups and were talking about hunting and fishing. The women spoke about weaving and children. Some of the villagers stood around a large skin blanket they gripped in their hands. They tossed a girl high into the air. Laughing, she reached her arms out and kicked her legs as she flew. When she came back down, she put her hands at her sides. The villagers tossed the girl back into the air. Kate laughed and cheered along with everyone else as the youngster flew higher and higher.

After feasting on rich walrus meat, breads, soups, and other delicious and not-so-delicious foods, the people gathered and sat before a group of men playing drums made from seal skins stretched tightly across large hoops. Men and women danced, stomping their feet and moving their bodies to the rhythm of the drums. The merriment carried Kate to a place where she nearly felt like one of the natives.

When the music stopped, three of the men told stories of ancient days and of hunting adventures. Children and adults alike listened, enraptured by the tales. Kate knew it was a privilege to be included.

Later that night when she climbed into bed, she was happy and content and barely gave the next day's flight a thought before falling to sleep.

The following morning, Kate was up early and at the airfield before daybreak. She wanted to get this flight over and return to Paul.

By the time Trooper Jacobs and the prisoner George Ujarak arrived, Kate had the plane ready to go. Right off, she noticed the difference in stature between the two men. Ted was short and stocky and much smaller than George. The difference made her uneasy.

"Morning," Ted said. "Looks like you're ready to go."

"I figured we ought to get an early start if we want to make Anchorage in two days." She glanced at the sky. "As long as the weather holds out, it shouldn't be a problem." She glanced at George, whose nearly black eyes were filled with contempt and his lips were tightly compressed. Fear spiked through her. She turned to Ted. "Let's load up and get out of here."

George's hands were shackled, but he had no difficulty climbing aboard the plane. Kate wished his feet were shackled as well. Maybe Ted would do that once he had the prisoner seated. George stopped at the door and looked down at Kate. His lips slid into a salacious grin and he flipped long black hair off his face. Kate felt a chill go through her. Nena was right—George was evil.

Ted poked George with a billy club. "Get in there."

The two men disappeared inside the plane, and Kate turned to Nena. "I hope next time I can stay longer." She gave her friend a hug.

"Maybe by then the summer will be here. We can pick berries."

"I ought to be back before summer. Paul's scheduled for a trip and I intend to be his pilot." She grinned.

Nena nodded. "Good." She glanced at the plane. "You be careful. I don't like that man, George."

"Me neither, but Trooper Jacobs seems competent."

Nena stepped back as Kate climbed aboard. With a wave she closed the door and latched it, then moved to the front of the plane and slid into her seat. She glanced over her shoulder at the trooper. "Ought to be a good flight."

He looked out the window. "I'll be glad to get back to Anchorage. Kotzebue's too cold for me." He chuckled, then glanced at George, who was staring out the window.

"Are you going to shackle his feet?" Kate asked.

"No. He's not going anywhere." He rested his hand on a holster at his side.

Kate nodded, but she didn't feel safe. She considered insisting on securing George's feet, but decided the trooper knew what he was doing and kept her thoughts to herself. Kate taxied onto the airstrip, facing into a gentle, steady wind, and then headed down the rustic runway. The plane shuddered and bumped across the ice and snow as it picked up speed. Once in the air, Kate made a wide turn flying over the ice pack and then headed south. With a glance over her shoulder at her unsavory passenger, she felt an urgency to get him out of her plane. She'd be relieved to reach Anchorage. Angel sat on the front seat, using Kate's pack as a headrest. Kate's revolver was in the pack. She'd meant to put on her holster but had forgotten in her hurry to get into the air. Still, she was glad that Paul had made her do some target practice.

"You make this trip often?" the trooper asked.

"Pretty regularly. There are always people and supplies to transport. Plus the doctor comes up to care for the villagers. Summer travel is busier and a lot easier. I'll be glad when the ice melts."

George had his arms clasped across his chest and he pressed his forehead against the window. He stared without blinking. Kate headed inland, where she'd negotiate the Mulato Hills and then follow the coast to Unalakleet. She ought to make McGrath before nightfall.

The sun was at its highest and filled the cockpit by the time Kate flew over Unalakleet. The warmth had lulled her passengers into sleep. She was feeling sleepy as well. When she reached to turn off the heat, sounds of a struggle came from behind her. Alarm shot through her and she turned to look. George was strangling the trooper with the chain that attached his handcuffs. Ted fought to get his fingers between the chain and his throat, but George pulled tighter, holding him against his broad chest. Ted reached for his gun.

"Stop!" Kate shouted, realizing George wouldn't listen to her. She reached for her pack, but Angel was lying on it. She shoved the dog aside. Angel leaped off the seat and stood between Kate and the men, her hackles raised and teeth bared.

The prisoner jerked hard on the chain and Ted went limp.

Was he dead? Kate's hands shook as she fumbled through her pack. Where was the revolver?

George grabbed Ted's gun, and standing hunched over in the crowded space, he pointed it at her. "Set the plane down."

With a deep-throated growl, Angel moved toward George. "Shut that dog up." He turned the gun on Angel.

No. Not Angel! Kate rested a hand on her dog. "It's all right, girl. Calm down." Trying to keep her hand from shaking, she stroked the dog. "There's no place to land here."

"South of town. I got a ride waiting." He snickered.

Kate stayed on course. If she landed, he'd almost certainly kill her.

"Do it!" he shouted. Then, his voice low and menacing, he added, "You wouldn't want your dog hurt, now do you?" He laughed.

'Okay. I'll land." Kate turned back toward Unalakleet. She had to do something. The plane dropped into an air pocket.

"Hey. No funny business." He pointed the gun at her. "You try anything and I'll shoot you."

"You won't do that. You need me to fly the plane." Kate figured he must not be very intelligent to think shooting her would help him. Maybe she could outmaneuver him.

"I don't have to kill you, just make you suffer a little." He laughed, then turned the gun on Angel. "Figure this dog is pretty important to you. It'd be easy to put a slug in her."

"I'm doing what you asked. We hit an air pocket. It happens all the time." Her mind churned with ideas. How could she get her gun without him shooting her or Angel? She glanced at her bag, then at the prisoner. He kept looking out a window, but she knew the moment she reached for the bag, he'd be on her. *A lot of good target practice did me.*

When Unalakleet came into view, he said, "Head east of town. There's a spot. You'll see it."

Kate made a wide swing around the town. If she could knock him off his feet, she might have time to get her pistol. She'd have only one chance. Her heart battered her ribs. She was gripping the control wheel, but loosened her hold to give her a better feel of the plane.

George was still standing and gazing out the window.

Lord, I need you . . . now. Kate pulled back sharply on the control wheel while increasing speed. The plane moved into a steep climb and she banked hard to the right.

— 9 —

George stumbled back and fell over one of the seats, a string of oaths flying from his mouth.

With a vicious growl, Angel jumped on him and ripped into his coat. With a big beefy arm, he knocked the dog into the back. Angel yelped and then didn't move. Kate felt sick. What had he done?

While bringing the plane back to level, she fumbled for her pistol, then pointed it at George. She pulled back the hammer. "Stay where you are," she shouted. Her insides quaked, but she managed to hold the gun steady.

He clambered to his feet and his eyes went to the trooper's gun that had fallen to the floor.

"Don't even think about it," Kate warned, her voice venomous. "If you move, I'll put a bullet between your eyes." She hoped she sounded convincing. One session of target practice didn't make her an expert shot, but he didn't know that.

George didn't move, but his lips stretched into an ugly sneer. "So, how do you think you'll get this crate on the ground and keep that gun pointed at me?"

Kate wasn't sure how she'd do that. She hadn't thought that far ahead. "Get up here and sit down," she ordered.

He moved gingerly toward the front. Kate knew he could

easily overpower her. Maybe she ought to wound him. But what if she missed and the bullet put a hole in the plane and hit something vital? She didn't want to take the risk. She needed another plan.

"Stop right there." With one hand on the control wheel and the gun in the other, she said, "Get the key for the cuffs out of the trooper's pocket."

George's eyes widened.

Kate tried to look tough. "Give me any reason and I'll shoot you."

George did as she told him. "I'm not going to hurt you. I just want a ride out of here," he said, digging through Ted's pockets. He came up with the key. "Set me down and I'll be on my way."

Kate ignored him. "Unlock the cuffs."

He unlocked them. "Look, you're dog's fine." Angel sat on her haunches in the back. "We're all fine. I figure this trooper here will wake up and he'll be fine too."

Kate hoped that was true, but she was almost certain it wasn't.

"And I promise, I'll just get off and move along. You'll never see me again."

"I'm supposed to trust you?"

"Sure. Why not? I got nothing against you. I just want to be free, that's all." A grin spread across his face.

Kate shook her head.

His grin slid away and a sneer replaced it.

"Clasp one cuff around your right wrist and the other around the bar on that seat." She nodded at the seat beside him.

George looked at the seat, then back at Kate. "No."

Kate pointed the gun at his knee. "It's that or a shattered kneecap—which would you prefer?"

100

He didn't move.

"I'm not giving you any more warnings. One. Two—"

"All right. All right." George moved to cuff his wrist, but instead he lunged at her.

Kate didn't want to chance a wild shot, so she turned the plane sharply to the right and headed into a dive. George lost his footing and fell forward, toward Kate. His head hit the interior wall and he fell to the floor, sprawled between the seats. He was close enough to reach Kate.

Struggling to pull out of the dive, Kate kept her gun pointed at him while watching their descent at the same time. The plane shuddered, and for a moment, Kate feared she'd asked too much of it. She quickly uncocked the hammer and, still holding onto the gun, moved her right forearm behind the wheel to get more control.

Gradually the nose came up and the engine evened out. George looked like he was unconscious. Kate hoped so. She didn't want to shoot anyone, not even George. If he was out, she needed to get on the ground fast, before he came around.

She circled Unalakleet and lined up with the airfield, hoping someone would be there to help. Still keeping an eye on George and on the controls, she came in with a hard landing. George didn't move. Neither did Ted.

As soon as she rolled to a stop, Kate approached George. With her gun pointed at him, she nudged him with the toe of her boot. He didn't respond. Afraid it was a trick and that he'd grab her at any moment, Kate quickly stepped over him. He remained still. She leaned over Trooper Jacobs and checked for a pulse. She knew he was gone—his color was bad, his lips blue. And there was no pulse.

Angel limped toward her. Kate buried her fingers in the dog's ruff. "Come on girl, let's get out of here." She stood and moved to the door and opened it. With a quick look at the two men, she climbed out of the plane.

Her adrenaline kicking in, she ran for the radio shack, praying someone would be there. She threw open the door and relief swept through her like a flood. A man stood over a barrel stove.

He turned toward her. "What in tarnation? You okay?"

"No. I need help. I've got a dead trooper and an injured prisoner on my plane." Kate was nearly shrieking.

The man wasted no time. He picked up his radio and called for help. His look steady, he said, "Name's Steven Marshal, ma'am. Why don't you have a seat."

"Kate Anderson," Kate said, but instead of sitting, she walked to the door and watched the plane. "I don't know how long that prisoner will remain unconscious. We need to truss him up."

Steven grabbed a handgun. "I'll take care of him." He glanced at Kate. "You said you have a dead trooper on board?"

"Yeah." Kate strode along beside him. "Ted Jacobs."

Steven's expression turned grim, but he kept up his pace. "Did you know him?"

"Yeah. He came through pretty regular. He was a good man." He squared his jaw, then asked, "How about the prisoner? Who is he? And what happened to him?"

"Name's George Ujarak. I was transporting him to Anchorage when he overtook Ted and killed him." Kate's breath caught in her throat. "I managed to knock him off his feet by going into a dive. He hit his head and the last time I saw him he was unconscious."

"We better get to him before he comes to."

When they reached the plane, Steven cautiously climbed the steps and peered inside. With his gun ready, he stepped in. Kate followed, her own gun in hand.

When she stepped into the plane, Steven was leaning over

Ted. He rested a hand on the dead man's shoulder, then moved to George, who was still sprawled out on the floor. Kate wondered if he was dead too.

With his pistol pointed at George's head, Steven nudged him with the toe of his boot. "Hey, you. Get up." He kicked him harder. "I said get up."

A moan came from George. He pushed up on one arm and looked over his shoulder. Blood seeped from a gash on his forehead.

Steven took a step back, keeping his gun aimed at George. "On your feet, you piece of filth."

George put a hand to his head. "I'm bleeding." The fight had gone out of him.

"Yeah. And if you don't do what I say, it's gonna get a lot worse."

George pushed to his knees, then grabbed hold of a seat and wobbled to his feet. Steven backed toward the door. Figuring he had everything in hand, Kate made her way down the steps to the ground. Her legs quaked. Angel leaned against her. Kate rested a hand on the dog's head, but kept her eyes on the door.

As Steven made his way down the steps and George appeared in the doorway, Kate said, "Watch him. He's tricky."

"He ain't gonna get away with nothin'. He'll hang, that's what he'll do." Steven's anger seethed. "Takin' someone's life is frowned upon here. He'll pay."

George stood in the doorway. He shielded his eyes with his hand. "My head hurts bad, real bad. I can barely see. I think I might've blinded myself."

"Good. Get down here."

Kate heard the sound of an engine and turned to see an old Ford pickup roll onto the landing strip. She'd never seen a car in this part of the country and figured they must have brought it in one piece at a time. Two men climbed out.

"Hey, Steven, you need some help?"

"Yeah. Get this man in cuffs and haul him off to jail. He's a prisoner and he killed Ted Jacobs."

Quaking inside, Kate sat on a log and watched while the men secured George and tied him in the back of the truck. She stared at Ted as they carried his body out of the plane. Kate had seen more than her share of death. She never got used to it. Every time she was reminded how tenuous life is. Sometimes there was no tomorrow.

"We'll take care of things from here," said the trooper who had been driving the truck.

Kate nodded. "Thanks for your help."

"I'll need you to fill out some papers."

"Sure. But I'm in a hurry—want to make McGrath today."

"Won't take long. And hey, Steven told me what you did. Good work." He gave her back a pat and walked with her to the truck.

After the paperwork was done, Steven dropped Kate at the airstrip. "You'll be notified about the trial."

Kate nodded. All she could think of was home. "Come on, Angel. Let's go."

Angel had recovered enough to take the steps with ease and disappeared into the plane. With a steadying breath, Kate climbed in to see Angel nosing around. There was blood splattered throughout the passenger section.

She grabbed Angel's collar to hold her back. "No, Angel, go sit!" She motioned toward the cockpit and Angel jumped up into her seat.

Kate pulled out a rag and wiped up what she could. The rest would have to wait until she got home and had time to give the plane a thorough cleaning.

She looked down at the bloodstained rag in her hands. Kate suddenly felt sick. She closed her eyes and leaned against the seat until the nausea passed, then she tossed the rag into a trash bag and climbed into the pilot's seat.

Kate was never so happy to see the Anchorage airport. She was tired, ready for normal and to be on her way home. First, she had to face Jack. She had no trooper and no prisoner and she hadn't radioed in. He'd want an explanation and she hadn't been ready to give it. She walked toward the shop, gearing up for the inquisition.

Jack worked at the bench and Alan was pouring himself a cup of coffee. Jack looked over his shoulder at her. "No passengers?"

Kate figured she'd keep things matter-of-fact. She signed in. "No. And I need a form for an in-flight incident."

Jack straightened and eyed her suspiciously. "Why? What happened?" He glanced out the window. "Where's that prisoner and trooper you're supposed to have with you?"

Kate took in a breath. "Trooper Jacobs is dead and the prisoner, George Ujarak, is in custody in Unalakleet." She faced him and braced her hands on her hips. She didn't want Jack to see how wobbly she felt.

He moved to the desk, pulled out a drawer, searched through some papers, and then slapped a form on the desk. "So, what happened?"

Kate grabbed a pencil out of a tin cup that was sitting on the desk and bent over the form. "The prisoner killed Ted Jacobs, the trooper, then tried to hijack the plane. I managed to knock him out with some fancy maneuvers and then set down at Unalakleet. Law enforcement took over there." She straightened.

Looking startled, Jack asked, "You all right?"

"I'm fine. I just need to get home."

Jack took in a deep breath. "Never knew anyone for getting

into trouble like you." He shook his head. "Glad you made it back in one piece." Without another word, he turned and went back to work.

Kate thought she heard concern in his voice. Maybe he did care. She finished filling out the form, then dropped the pencil back into the cup. "If you don't mind, I think I'll take a couple of days off."

Jack didn't look up. "Suit yourself."

"I'll be in Anchorage tonight and then head for Robe Lake first thing in the morning."

"No need. Paul called in for a flight this morning. He's home."

"And the boy?"

"Guess he's gonna make it."

Feeling as if she'd been drained of all her energy, Kate walked to her plane. She needed Paul. When she landed on the creek, Paul was waiting for her at the edge of the ice. He waved. All Kate could think of was his strong arms around her.

When her feet met the snow-covered creek, she wanted to run to him. Instead she made herself walk, and in as normal a voice as she could manage, she asked, "So, how is the little boy?"

"He's going to be fine." Paul stared at her. "Did something happen? Are you all right?"

"I am now." She stepped into Paul's arms. The tears came as she clung to him.

Paul smoothed her hair. "Whatever it is, it's all right, Katie. We can fix it. What happened?"

"You didn't hear about it on the Mukluk News?"

"Haven't had time to listen. What did I miss?" He held her away from him, concern etched into his face.

"Flying is a crazy business for crazy people. Maybe it's time for me to get out."

"What?" He held her away from him.

She shook her head and sniffed. Paul handed her a handkerchief and she blew her nose. "The prisoner I was supposed to transport killed the trooper assigned to transporting him."

"When? Where were you?"

"Flying the plane."

Paul blanched.

"He would have killed me, except I managed to knock him off his feet by throwing the plane into a dive. He hit his head and was knocked out." She sniffled into the hanky. "The authorities in Unalakleet took over after I landed there." She hated that she couldn't stop crying. "I was so scared."

"Katie." Paul pulled her back into his arms. "Thank God you're all right." He held her close for a long while.

Kate finally drew in a strengthening breath and stepped away from Paul. "I'm being a cry baby. I need to get my gear and put the plane to bed."

"We'll do it together."

Once they were indoors, Kate changed into clean clothes and, with a blanket wrapped around her, settled into a chair. Paul gave her a bowl of hot soup and pressed a gentle kiss to her forehead.

She caressed his cheek and gazed into his warm brown eyes. "I'm so lucky to have you."

He sat on the sofa across from her, his arms resting on his thighs, hands clasped in front of him. He didn't say anything for a long while, then he asked, "Did you mean it about quitting?"

Kate shrugged. "I don't know. Maybe."

"I think you should—settle down and have a family. We have more than enough to do around here to keep us busy. It would be good for you. Maybe you should take some time off to think about it."

Kate couldn't sort out her emotions. What did she want?

Maybe it was fear or just plain weariness talking to her. She was a pilot. How could she give up something that was part of her?

"I think I just got a little shook and it all came pouring out when I saw you." She spooned soup out of the bowl. "I'm better now. Everything will be fine." She slurped the soup from the spoon. "Life's not safe, not for anyone, especially not up here."

"Maybe you could take safer runs?"

Irritation chafed at Kate. She knew she was being irrational. Paul was just watching out for her. Still, no one, not even Paul, was going to tell her what she should or should not do. "So, I could be half a pilot?" she asked sarcastically.

"No. That's not what I meant."

"Well, if I take only the safe runs, that's what I'm doing. It's not fair to the other pilots—my leaving them with all the dangerous runs. What does that say about me? That I can't be counted on? That a woman's not up to the task?" She shook her head. "I can't do it."

"All it says is that you're reasonable."

"No." Kate stood, walked into the kitchen, and set her bowl down hard on the counter. "It was just my emotions speaking earlier—nothing more. I'm fine now."

"And what about me? I'm your husband. What I feel doesn't matter?"

"Of course it matters. But you wouldn't want me to do my job halfway." Kate folded her arms over her chest. "What happened was a fluke, nothing more."

"Until the next fluke comes along. One of these days it's a fluke that'll kill you."

"You knew what you were getting when you married me. We had an agreement—you said I could fly when and where I wanted—it would be up to me."

Paul threw up his hands. "I don't understand you. One minute you're saying maybe you ought to stop and the moment I say that might be a good idea, I become the bad guy. That's not fair, Kate."

"And your making me feel guilty because I want to fly isn't fair." She pulled on her boots, grabbed her coat, flung open the door, and stormed out.

Paul stepped onto the porch. "Kate. We have to talk about this."

She kept walking and didn't look back. There was nothing to talk about. They'd never agree.

— 10 —

Kate kept her eyes focused in front of her and started down the trail that led to Patrick and Sassa's. A tree branch caught her across the face. She brushed it aside and kept moving, barely noticing the sting. Snow squeaked beneath her boots and cold whipped her face, but she didn't care.

She turned onto a spur trail that led to the creek and her favorite thinking place. This time of year, the meandering creek was frozen and buried with snow, but she still found the spot calming. She entered the clearing, brushed snow off a log, and sat.

She envisioned what it would be like during the summer— the smell of wildflowers and greenery, birdsong and the buzz of insects. Warmth.

Kate stared across the icy creek, hoping for a glimpse of a fox or maybe even a moose. All she saw was bright white piles of snow, ice exposed by brisk winds, and frosted alder and birch. Her hands were freezing—she hadn't taken time to put on her gloves. She rubbed her palms together, then reached into her pockets and found a pair of fur-lined gloves.

She tugged them on, and then pulled the fox-lined hood of her parka tighter around her face.

She rested her arms on her thighs, frustration and confusion still brewing. Why had she gotten so angry? All Paul had done was to care about her and voice his opinion. Wasn't that what married people were supposed to do? Couples who loved each other should care enough to speak their mind, to support one another, and to listen. It's what she'd always believed, or thought she believed. Instead she was fighting for independence and refusing to rely on her husband's support and concern. She'd always been headstrong and couldn't count the number of times her willfulness had created friction between her and her mother . . . and now Paul.

What was wrong with her? She did have doubts, especially after what had happened on this run. And there was no denying the danger of being a bush pilot. But she couldn't give it up. She'd fought hard to gain a place as a respected pilot in the toughest terrain in the world. She wasn't about to quit because of one incident. Paul should have known that about her. Kate pressed her elbows on her legs and rested her chin in her hands. Maybe she was expecting too much from him.

Her thoughts wandered back to their wedding day. Life had seemed perfect. She hadn't been naïve enough to believe there would never be disagreements, but what had happened between them seemed bitter and harsh. There must be a way to remedy their differences without all the ugliness.

She closed her eyes and breathed in deeply through her nose. What did she want? She loved being Paul's wife and the solitude here on the homestead, but she also relished the challenges she faced in the cockpit of her Bellanca. She'd been convinced that there was a way to be a wife and a pilot. She'd imagined being out on a run facing the excitement and challenges of flying the Alaskan territory, and then returning to the homestead and to Paul where she could gather strength from the solitude and her husband's devotion. Had it been a pipe dream?

Her thoughts returned to Unalakleet and her stomach knotted as the scene in the plane wound through her mind. What if it happened again? It could. She knew it. Anything could happen in the bush—anything.

Kate scuffed the snow with the toe of her boot. Was she too stubborn and ambitious for her own good? Too full of her own needs to be the kind of wife Paul needed?

She gazed up at the gray ceiling that promised snow. "Lord, what do you want?" she whispered. If she refused to abide by her husband's wishes, was it the same as refusing to obey God? She'd heard the teachings about wives submitting to their husbands. When she'd taken her wedding vows, she'd agreed to obey Paul.

A long stem of grass poked out of the snow and Kate knelt to pluck it. It was withered, but somehow it had survived the cold and snow. A groan reverberated through Kate's soul. She didn't want to be like this weak stalk—surviving, but not thriving. Would being a submissive wife consume her own spirit?

And Paul's faith had withered. She knew that at one time he'd been a man of God, but now she wasn't sure how he felt about the Lord. If she submitted to him, she would be placing her life in the hands of a man who wasn't even sure he trusted God.

All the years her parents had been married, her mother had submitted to her father. It seemed easy for her. The only real contention between them was his flying. Her mother had been afraid something would happen—just as Paul feared for her. Yet, they'd been happy.

Kate wished she could talk to her mother. If only she lived

closer. Maybe Helen or Muriel could help. Kate considered flying into town.

Steps crackled through the snow from the trail behind her. Thinking it must be Paul, Kate fixed her gaze on the far side of the creek. She wasn't ready to talk to him.

"Ah, here you are," came Sassa's friendly voice.

Surprised, Kate turned to look at her neighbor. "Hi. What are you doing out here?"

The native woman smiled and held up a basket. "I brought you something."

"How did you know I was here?"

"I talked to Paul." A shadow of concern touched her eyes. "I thought you might be here." Her brown eyes were quiet and softened with compassion. "Are you hungry? I baked apple muffins this morning. I took some to your place—that's when I talked to Paul." A breeze kicked up and a pile of snow fell from a tree branch and plunked on the ground beside Sassa. She laughed and looked up into the limbs. "Nearly got me." She moved to Kate and handed her the basket with a single muffin in it. "I left the rest at the cabin with Paul."

Kate wasn't hungry, but she accepted the treat. "Thank you. Do you mind if I eat it later?"

"Oh sure. Whenever." Sassa sat beside Kate. "I love this spot. I come here sometimes too. It's a good thinking place."

Silence settled over the two women. The hush of a winter forest and its occasional clatter of bare limbs shifting in the breeze was the only sound.

"Paul told me what happened on your trip. I've been thanking God you are all right." She leaned closer, touching her arm to Kate's.

"I did all right until I got home and then I just kind of fell apart. I didn't even know I was that upset. But when I saw Paul, everything that had happened seemed to crash down on me—the trooper dying and that horrible man. All of a sudden I realized how close I'd come to dying."

"Sometimes that's what happens when we hold in our feelings—they come pouring out in a hurry." She grinned. "Heard you knocked out that prisoner, though."

"Actually, he fell when I forced the plane into a dive."

Sassa chuckled. "Smart thinking."

Kate smiled. "I guess it was." She stared at a hawk circling above the trees on the far bank. "When I broke down in Paul's arms, I told him that maybe I shouldn't fly. Right away he agreed." She grasped her hands tightly in her lap. "We had a fight. I'm not sure what to do."

Sassa grinned. "So, you got mad because he agreed with you?" She draped an arm around Kate and hugged her. "You two will figure it out."

"But we've only been married a couple of months. I didn't think newlyweds fought."

Sassa chuckled. "Is this your first argument?"

Kate nodded, then shrugged. "We've had some small disagreements but nothing like this."

Sassa smiled broadly. "You should see me and Patrick. We've come close to all-out brawls."

"But you've been married a long time." Kate glanced up the trail, as if someone would overhear her. "Does Patrick tell you what to do?"

Sassa laughed. "He tries." She shook her head slightly. "Not really, anyway not much. But we don't always see eye to eye."

"It seems like you're the one who makes the decisions."

"Sometimes I do. Me and Patrick kind of take turns, but usually we decide together."

"What about the Scripture in 1 Peter that says a wife is supposed to obey her husband?"

"There's so much more to being married than that one

Scripture." She placed her hands flat on her lap. "If Patrick and I have a big decision and can't agree, I let him decide. That works for us. But when you look at God's Word, you gotta study all the words before and after a Scripture and think about who God is talking to and why. You need to take into account all of God's Word. Like the Scripture that says a husband is supposed to love his wife like Jesus loved the church. Jesus gave everything, even his life."

Kate had never really thought about what that meant. "He did give everything, didn't he." A man was supposed to sacrifice everything for his wife?

"Sometimes I get bossy with Patrick. But he loves me just the way I am. He's a good, kind husband."

Kate was sure Paul loved her. Her eyes held Sassa's. "Paul doesn't want me to fly."

"Did he say that?"

"Not exactly. But I know it's true."

"What did he say?"

"That I should take safer runs and that he wished I'd stay home. He wants me to be like my mother—keep house and have babies." Kate's tone had turned disparaging.

Sassa narrowed her eyes. "Are you sure of that?"

Kate couldn't answer. She wasn't sure. She hadn't let him finish speaking before storming out of the house. Instead, she'd assumed he wanted what most everyone else seemed to expect from a woman. But Kate knew Paul wasn't like everyone else. Shame washed over her and she said softly, "No. I'm not sure."

"Don'tcha think you ought to be sure? And even if he does feel that way, it'd be natural for a man to want his wife safe and close by." She rested a hand on Kate's arm. "Is that a bad thing?"

"Of course not, but he understands how important my job is to me."

"He does, for sure. And it's because he loves you that he lets you fly, but he's just a man and so he gets afraid."

Reason seeped into Kate's frustration. Guilt, like that of a child caught in a lie, moved through her. She'd been so sharp with him, unfair.

Sassa patted Kate's arm and then stood. "You eat that muffin and you think about it. Then go talk to that fine husband of yours." She stood and shuffled back up the trail.

Paul sat at the table, greasing a pair of boots. He rubbed the leather hard. What did Kate want from him? Even when he agreed with her it wasn't enough. He dipped the rag into a tin of bear grease and, using a circular motion, worked the fat into the leather. Why had she run off like that? What did he do wrong? All he wanted was to help. Kate had been the one who was upset and she wasn't even certain she should keep flying. One minute she was ready to quit and the next she was fighting to stay in the air.

He shook his head. If he lived to be a hundred, he'd never understand women.

He heard someone pounding snow off their boots, and then the door opened. He didn't look up. He knew it was Kate. What could he say? Most likely whatever came out of his mouth would be wrong. He scooped more grease onto the rag and rubbed it into the boot. He could hear Kate hanging up her coat and then she walked to the stove.

"Do you want some coffee?" she asked.

"Sure." She sounded amiable. Maybe she was done being mad. He didn't want to fight. He chanced a glance at her. She had her back to him, but her stance seemed relaxed. She filled two cups and carried them to the table.

"Thanks," he said, setting down the greasy rag and picking

up the cup. He took a drink. It was overcooked from sitting on the stove too long. "Kind of bitter." He set down the cup and returned to his work.

"Would you like me to make a fresh pot?"

"Nah. It's fine."

Kate sat and silently drank her coffee, watching him.

Paul was determined not to start a conversation. It was up to her. He hadn't done anything wrong. He waited and picked up the other boot.

Kate finished her cup and stood, then she sat back down, her cup between her hands. "We need to talk."

Paul glanced at her, but kept polishing, pretending to be composed.

"I mean about what happened . . . I'm sorry for losing my temper. I don't even know why I got so mad." She tipped her cup on edge. Silence swelled. "If you're not ready to talk, I understand."

She went to get up, but Paul grabbed hold of her hand. "I'm ready." He looked at her, his heart longing to put an end to their controversy. He set down the boot. He loved her more than he could have imagined loving any woman. "So, what happened between us?"

"I don't know." Kate chewed on her lower lip. "I guess I was more upset than I thought. After what happened, I'd been holding in my feelings . . . By the time I got home it all just spilled out. I said things I really didn't mean. But it seemed like you jumped on the opportunity . . . as if you'd been waiting for a chance to get me out of my plane. I guess . . . ," she shrugged, "that sometimes it feels like you don't respect what I do and that you don't trust me to do a good job."

"I trust you. It's the plane and other people I don't trust. You're an unbelievable woman and a fantastic pilot. I'm so proud of you, Kate. But I love you . . . so much." Paul didn't want to say the words. He knew they weren't what she wanted to hear and he'd promised not to say them. But how could they solve their differences if he wasn't honest. He took her hands in his. "Kate, I'm afraid for you. I don't want you to die somewhere out in the wilderness—alone or at the hands of some crazed passenger." He studied her steady gaze but couldn't see what she was feeling. "I know I agreed when we got married that you could fly. And I told you I wouldn't interfere, but . . . isn't it reasonable for you to take safer runs?"

Kate looked at the table and their clasped hands. "I want to listen to you and to be an obedient wife—"

"I don't want an obedient wife." He grinned. "If I did, I wouldn't have married you."

Kate looked up at him and smiled.

"I want you to make wise decisions of your own choosing, but I want to be able to tell you how I feel. We're supposed to help each other, right?"

"Yes." Kate compressed her lips. "But I've never been a wife before. I want to do it right, but sometimes I don't know what that is. All I know for sure is that I love you." She closed her eyes for a moment. "There's something inside of me that fights back when anyone tries to tell me what to do—even when it's just a suggestion." She smiled softly. "Even my father had a hard time with me."

Paul squeezed her hands. "I understand that. You're strong and you know what you want. Being married isn't easy for anyone, and for us, it may be especially difficult. We're not exactly a run-of-the mill couple."

Kate took in a quaking breath. "I was just thinking that." Her expression resolute, she continued. "I can't take safe flights only. It's not fair to the other fellas, and it would ruin my credibility as a pilot." She wet her lips. "It's kind of like asking you, as a doctor, to take only patients you know won't die."

The truth of her statement cut straight to Paul's heart. He understood what it meant to lose a patient—he'd lost two of the most precious people in his life and it had been his fault. Kate still didn't know. He'd never found a way to tell her.

"What is it, Paul? I know there's something you're holding back from me. Please let me help."

This was his chance. Paul tried to form the words, but he couldn't open his mouth. He cleared his throat. It felt tight, as if someone were strangling him. "I . . . I can't talk about it. Not yet."

"Okay." Kate's tone sounded hurt. "Can we pray? About us and about whatever it is that is hurting you so much?"

"Pray?" Paul didn't do much praying these days. "Sure. But maybe you should do it. Me and God, well, we've kind of been out of touch lately."

"I can do it."

Still clasping hands, Kate and Paul bowed their heads. The room turned quiet, then Kate said, "Dear Father in heaven, thank you for Paul. He's a good man, better than I deserve. I know it was you who brought us together, but we need your help. We've got a lot to learn about being married and loving each other. Please show us the way. Help us to be patient and kind with one another. Show us how to resolve our differences. And Lord, please give Paul peace about my flying and heal the hurt he carries in his heart." Kate took a slow breath. "And Lord, if I'm not supposed to fly, please tell me. Help me to hear your voice and help me obey you."

Paul was startled at Kate's request. She was willing to give up what she loved most in life for him. He squeezed her hands and with a bit of hesitancy, said, "Thank you, God, for Kate. She's a wonderful wife. And she loves to fly. I need to learn to trust you. Help me."

— 11 —

Kate flipped a flapjack, and then checked the eggs to see if they were done. The two-way radio crackled to life. "Kate. This is Anchorage. Over."

Kate moved to the radio and sat down. "Hi, Jack. What you got for me? Over."

"There's been some trouble up at Poorman's Creek, outside of Talkeetna. Guess a fella's been shot. Likely a conflict between miners. They need a doc up there pronto."

"Do you have the exact location?"

"Yeah, but you'll have to come in to the airfield to pick up the chart on this one. The landing site's dicey and hard to spot from the air. Plus a trooper will be riding out with you. Over."

Kate's stomach dropped. "A trooper? What's going on up there?"

"Don't know for sure, but figured better safe than sorry. Over."

"We're on our way. Over and out."

More trouble. Kate's stomach churned as her mind threw her back to the last time she'd been on a flight with a trooper. She glanced at the griddle. Smoke rolled out from under the flapjack. She leaped to her feet, lifted the burned breakfast onto a plate, then hurried to the door. Stepping onto the porch, she called, "Hey Paul, we've got a run."

"Okay. I'll feed the dogs and then be in." He whistled for the dogs.

Kate returned to the kitchen, set the burned flapjacks aside for the dogs, and finished making breakfast. She heard his steps on the porch.

The door opened and Paul stepped inside. "What's up?"

"I got a call from Jack. There's trouble up by Talkeetna at Poorman's Creek." Kate held out a plate of unburned flapjacks that she'd buttered and drizzled with syrup. "You better get something in your stomach." She sat down and smeared apple butter on a flapjack, folded it in half, then picked it up and took a bite. "Jack said that someone was shot. It could be an accidental shooting, but he seemed to think it was some kind of clash between miners."

"Better eat fast." Paul took a large bite of his flapjacks. "Don't know why anyone would get into that business. It's dangerous and generally not profitable." He cut off another piece and swirled it through syrup on his plate. "Did he say how serious the injury is?"

"No."

Paul folded the last of one of the flapjacks into a stack and shoved it into his mouth. Leaving the rest on his plate, he said, "We better get moving."

"We have to stop at the airfield to pick up a map and a trooper. I hope he doesn't need to bring back a prisoner." Kate grimaced.

Paul set his plate in the sink. "I swear, things are getting more risky all the time. It's only been a few weeks since you had to testify about the incident in Unalakleet."

Kate set off on a defensive litany. "There's always been

conflict in the territory. This may be the twentieth century, but Alaska's still a wild place. And the trouble in Unalakleet was a couple of months ago. We haven't had any problems since then." She shrugged, trying to look unruffled. "Things like this happen. We'll be fine. I just hope the man who was shot is okay."

"Yeah, me too." Paul strode into the bedroom to get his medical bag. "Glad I restocked this. Gunshot wounds can get messy." He ushered Kate out the door and they headed for the creek with Angel trotting alongside them.

Once they were in the air, Kate followed the Susitna toward Cook Inlet. Heavy, dark clouds reminded her of the cretonne tapestry drapes that used to hang in her aunt's gloomy sitting room.

The conversation between the creek and Anchorage remained light, even though Kate was certain Paul was worried about what waited for them, just as she was. When they landed at the airfield, Kate noticed the trooper's car right off and the seriousness of the situation hit her. This could be bad. She kept the Bellanca's engine running and left Angel and Paul in the plane while she ran for the shop.

When she stepped inside, Jack looked at her from behind his desk. "It's about time."

"I can't get from the creek to here in ten minutes. You know that."

"You bet I do. And if I'd had another pilot around, I'd—"

"Yeah, I know . . . I'd still be sitting out on the creek." The last thing Kate needed was verbal warfare with Jack, so she asked, "Where's the map?"

Shoving a cigar between his teeth and biting down, Jack bent over a map on his desk. He plucked a pencil from over his ear.

Kate moved to the other side of the desk and the trooper

stood beside her. "I'm Matt Lawson," he said with a quiet smile. He had eyes the color of forget-me-nots.

"Kate Anderson." She shook the man's hand, remembering the last trooper she'd flown with. "Thank you for accompanying us."

"All in the line of duty, ma'am."

"Okay," Jack said, with the pencil pointed at the map. "Take the usual route, like you're headed for Talkeetna, but Poorman's Creek is west, so you'll shoot over right here." He put an X on the map. "And follow Peters Creek past Petersville. When the creek makes a wide turn toward the west, you go straight north." He drew a sharp line on the map. "You'll start seeing miners' cabins and sluice boxes along the creeks up there. Poorman's Creek is due north of the turn. It gets kind of tight in there with the hills and mountains, but there's a place to put down—you'll see it." He straightened and looked at Matt Lawson. "Understand you've been up that way a time or two."

"More times than I'd like. Miners get nervous, and pretty soon you've got trouble. They usually simmer down before things get out of hand, but once in a while we have to haul a man into the pokey. Sounds like this is one of those times. I figure someone's out there with a gun and a foul temper."

Oh brother, Kate thought. *Another crazed prisoner.* "Let's get moving." She grabbed the map and chart, tucked them under one arm and strode toward the door.

"Call in and let me know when you've got things under control," Jack said, unable to conceal his concern.

"Sure," Kate said, and walked out.

Kate had made a lot of runs to Talkeetna and was familiar with the route. But when she veered off at Peters Creek, it was new territory. The land was ribboned with streams and potted with lakes and ponds. "There's a lot of marshland out here."

"Yeah," Matt called from the seat behind her. "It's a rough hike in if you don't have a plane. Still, the miners keep coming—determined to strike it rich."

"What kind of luck do they have?" Paul asked.

"Some of them do okay. But once a fella sees that gold glittering in a pan, he gets the fever and he'll work until he's broken down. In the end, most go back to wherever they came from, poorer than when they arrived."

The small hamlet of Petersville slid by below and Kate continued to follow Peters Creek northward. Hills and mountains created erratic wind currents and the plane jumped and bounced its way along. Mount McKinley stood amidst the peaks, like a monarch overseeing his royal court.

"That's quite a mountain, ain't it," Matt said. "Never get tired of looking at it. If I was younger, I'd have a hand at climbing it."

"Why?" Paul asked. "I've treated more than one mountain climber. You'd just be looking for trouble."

"Don't know—it's a challenge—something that sets a man apart from the rest."

"Yeah, if they live," Kate said, looking back at him.

"A lot more bush pilots die every year than mountain climbers." Matt lifted a challenging eyebrow.

"There are a lot more pilots."

"Okay. You got me on that one." Matt chuckled.

Paul kept quiet, but he gave Kate a knowing glance. She didn't say anything. There were more important things to do, like find the landing field and the man who had been shot. She turned her focus to the wetlands below. They were hedged in by scrub spruce and birch. She spotted a moose standing along the edge of a pond. "Look down there," she hollered.

"This is good moose-hunting country," said Matt. "I brought out a big bull last season."

Kate saw a sluice box standing alongside a tiny creek that tumbled into Peters Creek. Then she saw another one and another. And there were small cabins tucked into the trees beyond the creek banks. A few of the sluice boxes had men working them. "Maybe one of these days I'll get myself a claim," Kate said with a teasing smile for Paul.

"Backbreaking work," Matt said. "We're coming up on Poorman's Creek. The landing site is just to the west of it. You'll see it any minute now."

Kate scanned the landscape. There didn't seem to be any place to set down. All she could see were forests and waterways interspersed by bogs. And then, all of a sudden, it was there. If she hadn't been looking, she would have mistaken it for a grassy bog. "That it?"

"Yep. There's not a lot of room so you gotta get down right away. Good thing there's not a lot of trees. Still had a couple of close shaves on this one."

Kate could see the landing strip was just long enough. And that trees didn't crowd the end of the runway. She didn't need a trooper telling her how to fly. "It's long enough. I've set down in tighter spots than this."

"No one's got time to put in a proper landing field. All they have on their minds is gold."

"Do you know where we're supposed to find the injured miner?" Paul asked, scanning the smattering of cabins below.

"Whoever made the call said they'd try to get to the landing strip." Matt gazed out the window. "Don't see anyone."

Kate noticed he had his hand resting on the gun at his side. Angel paced, as if she could feel the tension.

"Ma'am, it'd be good if you kept the dog in the plane along with yourself. Let me handle this. 'Course I'll need the doc."

Kate clenched her teeth. She didn't want Paul going out there without her. He needed someone to watch his back while he worked. "I know how to use a weapon. And you might need another hand."

The trooper peered at her. He squinted as if he were weighing the options. "Suit yourself, but don't get in the way."

Until that moment, Kate had liked Matt Lawson. Now, he was just like any other man who underestimated the abilities of a woman simply because she was female. "Don't worry. I won't be in the way," she said, disdain dripping from her voice.

Matt looked at her as if he had no clue why she'd be annoyed. Men.

"Okay, guys. I need you all in the back."

"Why in the back?" Paul asked.

"With all the mud and ruts, it'll help stabilize the landing." She looked at Paul. "Can you take Angel with you?"

"Sure." Paul climbed out of his seat, resting a hand on Kate's shoulder for a moment. "Okay, Angel. Come on, girl."

He led the dog to the back and sat down. Matt made his way toward the rear of the plane and squatted beside Paul.

Kate made another fly over, getting a better feel for the landing site. "This could get rough, grab hold of something," she called.

"Slow and easy," she told herself. Kate dropped down over the trees and leveled out. She needed to keep the tail low and get all three wheels down at once. The brush at the other end of the runway rushed toward her, but she didn't dare slow down too quickly or the plane could get bogged in the mud and the prop would end up in the muck. With only yards to spare, the plane slowed and Kate managed to get it turned back the way she'd come in.

Matt hurried forward and popped open the door. "Let's go. We can't give the thug, whoever he is, one extra minute."

Paul grabbed his bag. "You take care of the hooligan and I'll take care of the injured."

Matt stopped and stared at him. "If we want to get whoever's been shot, we'll have to work together." He jumped out before Paul could respond.

Angel leaped from the plane before Kate could stop her. She set off, nose to the ground. Paul climbed down and waited for Kate, then the two of them followed close behind Matt. Paul had his medical bag in one hand and a gun in the other. Kate had never seen him use a revolver before. It felt strange to see him with one. She'd tucked her revolver into her belt, but as she ran for the cover of the trees, she pulled it out.

The three of them stopped beneath a spruce. Paul gazed down at her. "Kate, I'd feel better if you stayed with the plane. You'll be safer there and we might need to get out in a hurry. I have no idea how badly injured my patient is."

"The engine's warm. I can get us off the ground in no time. And I'm not leaving you. Especially while you're working on someone who's been shot—you'll need me to watch for whoever did the shooting."

He let out a breath of frustration. "All right." He gave her a quick kiss.

Matt moved toward a brushy area and squatted. His pistol ready, he studied the terrain. Paul and Kate hunkered down beside him.

"No sign of anyone," Matt said. "Figure our culprit's hiding. We'll have to find the victim first. Maybe he can give us some information." He peered into the forest. "You two keep your eyes open and your heads down. And stay close."

With her heart thrumming against her ribs, Kate asked, "Which way's the camp?"

Angel stayed at her side, as if she knew Kate might need her.

"Down by the creek. You can hear it," Matt whispered. "We'll have to move in slow and see what's going on."

Staying low, Matt moved forward toward the sound of the stream.

Every nerve in Kate felt like it was vibrating. What was she doing out here, hiding in the forest with a gun in her hand? She didn't remember that being included in the pilot's handbook. She stayed behind Matt and Paul, watching the forest and praying someone didn't have a gun trained on them. When they came upon a rustic cabin, Matt motioned for them to stay put while he moved cautiously toward it.

When he reached the side of the shelter, he crept along one wall to the door. Leaning away from the entrance, he used the toe of his boot to push the door open. Holding his gun with both hands, he looked inside, then stepped through the doorway. Kate prayed. A moment later he emerged, then motioned for them to follow.

When Kate and Paul caught up to him, Kate asked, "What'd you find?"

"Nothin'. It was empty, doesn't look like anyone's been using it."

Angel trotted ahead, her nose to the ground, and Kate called her back. They moved along the edge of the creek until they reached another cabin. This one had smoke rising from a chimney. It was a little larger than the first. Again, Matt moved in while Paul and Kate held back and watched for signs of anyone sneaking around outside. Kate's mouth was so dry it felt like her tongue was glued to the roof of it. She knew this wasn't something she ever wanted to do again.

The trooper stepped inside the cabin and then motioned for Paul and Kate to join him. "You've got one dead and another needing help." His brows were furrowed. "I've got a madman to find." He headed toward the creek.

Paul moved into the cabin with Kate beside him. There was a man and a boy both lying on the floor in a pool of blood. Kate's heart leapt at the sight of them. It looked like the man had tried to protect the child, who couldn't be more than ten years old. Angel stayed with Kate.

Paul knelt beside them and felt for the man's pulse. "He's gone."

Kate moved to the door and crouched just inside while peering out. "What about the boy?" She glanced at Paul as he examined the child.

"He's alive." Paul carefully rolled him onto his side and stripped off his shirt.

Kate wondered how long he'd stay alive. There was a lot of blood. Who would shoot a child? "Is he going to be okay?"

"Don't know yet. He's lost a lot of blood, but it looks like the bullet went right through him—that's good." Paul examined the exit wound in his back, then laid him on the floor and put a stethoscope to his chest. "Lungs sound clear. We need to get him to the hospital."

"We can't leave 'til—"

A gun blast pierced the forest. A second followed the first.

Kate dug her hands into Angel's ruff and prayed, "Lord, let Matt be all right."

She waited and watched while Paul bandaged the youngster's wounds. Angel stepped onto the porch and stood at the foot of the steps. Kate could see movement among the trees. Was it Matt or someone else?

Holding her revolver in both hands, she aimed toward the sound. "Someone's coming," she whispered and pulled back the hammer of the gun. Her hands quaked. A branch snapped. If it was Matt, wouldn't he say something?

Matt emerged from the trees. "Hold on there. It's me."

Kate released the hammer, lowered the gun, and let out

her breath. She hadn't realized she'd been holding it. "Thank God it's you. When I heard the gunshots . . . "

Matt glanced back the way he'd come. "Well, we won't be transporting any prisoners today. Darn fool." He looked at the cabin. "How's the boy?"

"He needs a hospital."

Matt stepped past Kate and into the cabin. "Is he gonna make it?"

"He's lost a lot of blood, but I think he'll be all right. He needs more care than I can give him here." Paul gave a nod at the man lying on the floor. "Figure that's his father."

"I'll get him and you take the boy," Matt said.

"The man's dead."

"Yeah, well, he still deserves a ride back to Anchorage and a proper burial." Matt hefted him up off the floor. "Especially because of the boy. Let's get out of here."

"Of course." Paul gently lifted the child.

"What about the man you shot?" Kate asked.

"I'll have to come back for him."

The idea of leaving a dead man lying in the forest for the animals to scavenge made Kate's stomach lurch. She didn't say anything and hurried ahead. At the plane she grabbed a couple of blankets for the injured youngster and a bag used for carrying out game. They could lay the dead man on it.

With the two settled in the back, and Paul caring for the boy, Kate started the engine and they headed for Anchorage.

An ambulance transferred the child to the hospital. The man presumed to be his father was moved to the morgue. Kate and Paul filled out forms for the sheriff's department and answered a few questions, and then they headed toward home. For a long while they didn't speak. Kate's mind kept replaying the sight of the boy and his father lying in the cabin, blood all over them. Bile rose into her throat and she started to quake. The echo of the gunshots reverberated through her mind. What would have happened if the trooper had been the one killed? Her legs felt weak.

"You all right?" Paul asked.

"I'm fine. Why?"

"You look pale."

"I'm okay. Just a little queasy."

"Yeah, me too."

Kate nodded. She didn't tell him she'd been feeling queasy a lot recently. And that she'd missed her monthly. Now was not the time to talk about it. "Do you think that little boy will be all right?"

"Yeah. He'll be okay. But," Paul shook his head, "he lost his father over a piece of land and a gold rock."

"I wonder if he has a mother?"

"I hope so."

"What if he doesn't? What happens to him then?"

"Don't know. Maybe he has family."

Kate remembered how steady and skilled Paul had been. Love and admiration for him swelled inside of her. "He probably wouldn't be alive without you."

"Someone would have gone after him."

Kate reached out and squeezed Paul's arm. "I'm so proud of you."

Paul didn't reply for a long moment. He rested his hand on Kate's and stared out the window. "Seems like we're always running into trouble these days."

"It's my first shoot-out," Kate teased, trying to lighten the conversation. "I kind of felt like I was in one of those western movies."

Paul wasn't smiling.

More seriously, Kate added, "Everything turned out all right. We have a lot to be thankful for."

His voice grave, Paul said, "We're okay, but a little boy lost his father and he's got several painful weeks ahead of him." He compressed his lips. "Sometimes it seems like God just watches and lets the world go on while people do whatever they want. Like he's not here."

"He's here. And he cares, but we're not puppets. He doesn't pull our strings and make us do what he wants. People make choices." Kate searched her mind for the right words. "I don't know why that man died today, but the boy lived and so did we. And I'm thankful for that."

"Yeah, I guess you're right," Paul said, but his tone didn't sound agreeable. He squared his jaw, folded his arms over his chest, and stared straight ahead.

Kate wanted to cry. Something was wrong with Paul. He was so angry. And she knew it had something to do with why he'd come to Alaska. "What happened today was awful and we're both understandably upset. But why do you shut me out? Please tell me what's wrong."

He looked at her. "What do you think is wrong? An innocent man died. Isn't that reason enough to be upset?" He turned his gaze back to the window.

Kate felt sick inside. If only she could talk to her mother. She'd know how to help. Maybe she should speak to Helen. When Kate landed on the sandbar, she stayed in her seat and didn't turn off the engine. "I'm going back to Anchorage. I need to speak to Helen."

Paul stared at her, surprise and hurt in his eyes. "Okay. I've got plenty to keep me busy here."

He didn't kiss her or even touch her. He just grabbed his bag and climbed out of the plane. Angel trotted up to Kate, then climbed onto the front seat. Kate buried her hands in the dog's fur.

She watched Paul walk away and climb into the dory. Maybe she should stay. She wanted to be with him, to tell him she loved him and to make things right between them. She nearly shut down the engine. But she knew that before she could do any of that, she needed advice.

And while she was in town, she'd see a doctor. He could tell her if she and Paul were going to have a baby.

Staying in Anchorage had its advantages, such as grocery stores. Kate had managed to get everything she needed in no time at all. She clutched two bags of groceries against her chest as she stepped into the house. Angel squeezed past her and went to work investigating. Using her foot to close the door, Kate moved to the kitchen and set the bags on the shelf.

She turned and gazed into the front room while memories of Mike cascaded over her. For a moment, it felt as if her breath were being choked off. If only he were still alive. He'd been a true pal, someone who understood her in ways no one else did, not even Paul.

Paul was right. They ought to sell this house. Their home was on the creek, not here. But no matter how reasonable it seemed, Kate couldn't bring herself to part with the place. It was a piece of Mike. She couldn't simply dispose of it.

In spite of the cool June weather, Kate opened the kitchen window. The house smelled musty and felt chilly, so she started a fire in the kitchen stove. It didn't take long before she had a crackling fire going. The sound of it made the place feel more cheery. And the aroma of burning wood chased away the stale odor.

She put the groceries away, hung her coat in a closet by the front door, then turned and eyed the front room. It was tidy and looked clean, but she knew the floor needed to be swept, and the furniture encased with a thick layer of dust needed cleaning. It would have to wait until morning.

She walked into the bedroom and set her bag on a bed draped with a brightly colored quilt Helen had given her when she'd first moved into the house. She sat on the edge of the bed and opened the bedstead drawer. It was empty—like the house. Loneliness enveloped Kate. She thought of Paul and wondered what he was doing. Maybe she shouldn't have come.

Opening her knapsack, she took out a handkerchief and her Bible and placed them in the drawer. Now it was no longer empty. Her stomach rumbled with hunger. Scrambled eggs and toast sounded just right for dinner.

After the coffee was brewing, Kate went to work on her meal, clacking eggs into a bowl. She caught sight of a neighbor mowing his yard and breathed in the aroma of freshly cut grass. She decided that before she returned to the homestead she'd mow her own lawn.

Angel nuzzled Kate's hand. "Hey, girl. How you doing? Does it feel like home?" Kate knew the answer was no. The cabin was home. She scrubbed the dog's fur. They'd both be happier out at the creek. She'd acted too hastily. She should have waited, cooked dinner for her husband, and maybe they could have talked about what had happened.

She picked up the phone and called the airfield. "Jack. This is Kate. I was wondering if you could radio Paul for me. Can you tell him I'll be home late tomorrow?"

Jack agreed and Kate hung up, feeling slightly better. Her mind moved to the visit she'd arranged with Helen. When she'd stopped at the store, they'd agreed to meet the next day. She wished there were some way to get together tonight. She needed to talk to someone now. But she was tired and certain that, after a day's work at the store, so was Helen.

One thing she could do was to make an appointment with the doctor. The idea of seeing him made her heart skip. She picked up the receiver again and tapped the ringer. When an operator picked up, Kate asked, "Can you connect me with Dr. Malone's office, please?"

"Certainly. One moment, please."

Kate waited until a woman answered. "Hello. Dr. Malone's office. May I help you?"

"Yes. This is Kate Anderson and I was hoping I could see the doctor tomorrow."

"Let me check his schedule."

Kate could hear the shuffle of paper. Her stomach tightened. Until this moment, the possibility of having a child hadn't seemed real. She'd explained away her symptoms and wasn't even certain she was ready to be a mother. There were so many changes going on in her life. And she was busy. How would she keep up her flying schedule if she had a child to care for? Maybe she wasn't ready for a baby.

"Would 3:30 in the afternoon work for you?" the woman on the other end of the line asked.

"Yes. That would be fine."

"Good. Did you say your name was Kate Anderson?"

"Yes."

"Oh, I know you. You're the pilot."

"Yes. I am," Kate said, feeling a bubble of pride inside. She really *had* made a name for herself.

"Well, we'll see you tomorrow, then. Good-bye."

Kate hung up and stared at the phone. A baby—could it be possible? Her stomach turned. She didn't know how to be a mother. Would she be any good at it?

Stop worrying. I don't even know if I'm pregnant.

Right now she needed to eat. Tomorrow she'd think about mothering. After she had the eggs cooking, she placed two slices of bread in an electric toaster—an indulgence she'd made when she moved into the house. Toasting bread was so much simpler. Scrambling the eggs with a fork, she cooked them until the yolk was nearly hard and then slid them onto a plate alongside her toast.

She poured herself a cup of coffee, sat at the table and went to work on the eggs. Eating alone didn't feel right. She was used to sharing her meals with Paul. The house felt too large and too quiet. If she hadn't gone off in a huff, Paul might be here with her. And they could have visited the doctor together. That's how it should be.

Feeling melancholy, Kate propped an elbow on the table and rested her chin in her hand. She didn't feel like eating. Gloominess draped itself over her. "That's enough," she told herself. There was nothing to feel bad about. She'd had an adventure and lived through it. That was something to be thankful for. And a wife couldn't expect her husband to always be cheerful. She straightened and took a bite of the eggs.

After finishing her meal, Kate cleaned the dishes, added wood to the fire, and then dressed for bed. Fluffing her pillows, she settled beneath her covers, pulled the sheets and blankets up under her chin, and closed her eyes. She prayed for Paul, for the two of them, and about the possibility of their having a baby. She also asked that God show her what kind of wife he wanted her to be.

When she finished praying, a picture she'd seen of Charles Lindbergh in the newspaper flitted through her mind. It had been taken after his record-breaking flight from Long Island to Paris, France. He'd looked jubilant. What would it be like to accomplish something so amazing? He'd made the flight in thirty-three and a half hours. She doubted she'd ever do anything really spectacular like that. Especially if she was pregnant. Dreams like those would have to go.

She picked up a book from the bedstead that she'd purchased at the store. Helen had raved about it and had acted as if she'd swoon when she mentioned a character called Rhett Butler. Kate smiled at the notion and opened the book to chapter one.

The following morning, Kate woke with the book lying on the bed beside her and the lamp still on. She'd been more exhausted than she realized and hadn't even made it through the first chapter before falling asleep.

Kate dragged herself out of bed, feeling slightly ill. She decided to skip breakfast. After getting dressed, she worked on household chores. She started on the indoors first, then tackled the weeds in the flower beds along the front of the house. There wouldn't be time to mow the grass. She and Helen had agreed to meet for lunch.

The morning passed quickly and Kate realized almost too late that she'd left herself very little time to clean up before meeting Helen. She hurried indoors, showered, and changed, and then headed for Third Street, enjoying the June sunshine.

Maybe she'd been overly upset the previous day and made too much of Paul's mood. Still, it would be good to spend time with Helen.

When she stepped into the store, Helen peered at her from around the end of a row of shelves. "Good morning, young lady." She glanced at a large, black-framed wall clock. "I mean afternoon. Where has the time gone?" She untied her apron. "Albert," she called. "I'm going out. Can you mind the store?"

He walked from the back of the mercantile. "Anything for you, dear," he teased, then turned a smile on Kate." How are you today? You look a little tired."

138

"I am. Guess what happened yesterday wore me out."

"I'd expect so," Helen said. "We heard all about it. Why didn't you say something when you were here?"

Kate shrugged. "I don't know, just tired I guess. Have you heard anything about the little boy who was shot?"

"Yes, as a matter of fact we did," Albert said. "Jolene Snyder—you know, the one who works at the hospital in admitting. Well, she's a friend of ours and she told me he's doing real fine." He frowned. "Too bad about the boy's father, though." He rested a hand on Kate's arm. "We're thankful you and Paul are all right."

Kate blew out a breath. "Me too. It was pretty awful." She didn't want to talk about it, so she turned to Helen and asked, "Are you ready to go?"

"I am." Helen hung up her apron and pulled on a coat.

Kate moved toward the door. "Where would you like to eat?"

"If you don't mind, I thought my place. I've already made up some goodies and it's so much homier there."

"That sounds perfect."

Helen gave Albert a kiss. "I'll be back in a couple of hours."

"Take all the time you need." Albert brushed his thinning hair off his forehead. "It was good to see you, Kate."

"You too." Kate gave him a hug, then led the way out the door with Helen close behind.

Helen had prepared a salmon salad with hardboiled eggs in it and fresh bread. The two friends sat across the kitchen table from each other. "This looks delicious," Kate said, pushing her fork into the salmon mixture and spreading a little on a slice of bread.

Helen took a bite of salmon. "I made pound cake for dessert. I had berries left over from last summer and stirred some into the batter." She smiled and the creases at the corners of her eyes deepened. "It's so nice to have you here, but I'm thinking you've got a purpose."

Kate poked her fork into her salad. "I guess I do. But now that I think about it, I'm feeling kind of silly. I think after what happened yesterday, I was overly emotional."

"Well, since you're here, maybe you'd like to talk about it and we can decide if it's just emotions or something more."

Kate took a sip of tea. "When Paul and I were flying out to the creek yesterday, after we dropped off the trooper and the boy who had been shot, Paul acted angry. And as it turns out, he was—at God. You'd think he'd be mad at the man who did the shooting, but he blamed God for the death of the child's father."

"Really?"

"It's not the first time. Ever since we first met, he's reacted that way when there's a tragedy of some kind. We've discussed it, but he's never given me a reason why he feels the way he does. I know it has something to do with what happened in San Francisco. He's seemed so happy since we've been married that yesterday took me by surprise."

Helen pushed her plate to the side and folded her hands on the table in front of her. "Of course he's happy. He's a newlywed." She smiled, then asked, "What was it about yesterday that got his dander up?"

"He said something about the man dying and leaving a son without a father. He was angry that God would allow something like that to happen. When Mr. Clarkson was killed by my prop, he reacted the same way."

"Have you talked to him about San Francisco and why he moved here?"

"I've tried, but he won't discuss it."

"I can only guess at what is hurting him, but I'm confident God will heal his heart . . . at the proper time."

Kate nodded. "I wish there were something I could do to help. And . . . well, whatever it is, it affects our relationship. He's afraid something terrible is going to happen to me."

Helen steepled her fingers, then pressed her palms together. "Is that an unreasonable fear, considering your line of work and what's happened recently?"

"No . . . I suppose not. But when he married me, he knew that what I do can be dangerous. I don't think he does it on purpose, but he makes me feel guilty because I want to fly. Sometimes he acts as if I'm trying to make him miserable. I'd never do that, but I can't stop flying."

"He's asked you to quit?"

"Not exactly. But when the trooper was killed a couple of months ago, I kind of fell apart and . . . I said I wasn't sure I wanted to fly anymore. Paul was quick to let me know he thought it would be good if I quit. He wanted me to stay home and help him take care of the homestead—be a housewife."

Tears blurred Kate's vision. "I thought he knew me better than that." She wiped at her tears. "He wants me to quit, but he's not willing to just come out and say it. There's been tension between us that wasn't there before."

Helen leaned over the table and gave Kate a hug. "It'll be fine. You'll see."

"What do you think I should do?"

"I'm not one to speak about being 'just' a housewife. Albert and I have worked together at the store for years. We've shared the chores there and here at home. But, I'm not doing anything that puts my life in jeopardy." She took a sip of tea and then set the cup in its saucer. "But . . . if Albert asked me to stay home . . . I would. He wouldn't ask if it wasn't important to him. He always thinks about me first." A look of recollection crossed Helen's face. "Of course that's not how it was in the beginning. We were crazy in love, but he was headstrong and sometimes he was even a bit of a troublemaker."

"Albert?" Kate couldn't imagine the quiet man as anything other than gentle and thoughtful.

"Oh yes. He was a rascal. But I loved him. And the more I loved him, the more he loved me. Over time he gentled down. Being an example to our husbands is the best way to help them."

"If I keep flying, am I going against God's will? I mean, doesn't Scripture say women are supposed to obey their husbands?"

Helen thought for a moment. "It does say that, but Paul's not asking you to give up flying. He's just afraid, and understandably so. Maybe you two can come to some sort of compromise. What about taking safer runs, at least for a while? The other pilots will understand, won't they?"

"Maybe, but I'm afraid I'd lose their respect." Kate knew it was her pride speaking. "I guess we'll have to talk about it." She took another bite of fish. "And there might be another complication."

"Oh?"

Kate looked up and met Helen's gaze. "I think I might be pregnant."

Helen's blue eyes widened. "Oh! How wonderful!"

"I have an appointment with the doctor this afternoon." Kate glanced at the clock. "I'm not even sure how I feel about flying if I am pregnant. But I know what Paul will think. He's already lost a wife and a son. That's one of the reasons I didn't say anything to him. And I don't want him to be my doctor. I know he'll worry too much."

Helen compressed her lips, then looked at Kate with determination. "This is a matter for prayer." She reached for Kate's hands and the two women bowed their heads. "Dear Father in heaven, we thank you for the gift of love you've given to Paul and Kate. But new love can be complicated. We ask you to give them wisdom and a love for one another that overrides their differences. We lift up Paul to you. You know what tears at his heart. Place a balm upon his wound and give him a life filled with love and contentment, peace and faith. And Lord, if Kate is carrying a child, we thank you for the gift of life. May you keep your hand of protection on her little one. Amen."

Kate opened her eyes, feeling better and more at peace. "Thank you," she said. With a glance at the wall clock, she said, "I've got to go or I'll be late for my appointment."

Kate left Helen at the store and headed toward the doctor's office. It had been wise of her to come. Helen was a good friend. She always seemed to know just what to say. Kate felt more at ease about her and Paul. She was certain love was strong enough to overcome their differences. And she'd do whatever it was that God asked of her.

When she arrived at the doctor's office, she stopped and stared at the door. It was possible her life was about to change, dramatically. Taking a quieting breath, she gripped the doorknob, opened the door, and stepped inside.

The secretary was friendly and handed her a form to fill out. When she'd finished, Kate was led to an examination room where the nurse told her to remove her clothing and put on a cotton gown. She left the room. While Kate disrobed, her stress mounted. She'd never had any sort of female exam before. She wasn't quite sure what to expect.

She was sitting on the examination table when the doctor came in. Kate felt exposed.

Tall and slender, Dr. David Malone looked to be in his forties. He was friendly and his personality put Kate at ease. He went through the questions with her, then did an exam. It was humiliating but not as terrible as Kate had expected. When he finished, he asked her to get dressed and told her he'd return in a few minutes.

Her adrenaline pumping, Kate dressed, but had trouble

hooking her buttons because her hands quaked. What if she wasn't pregnant? What if something was wrong? Wouldn't the doctor have told her if she was pregnant? She managed to fasten the buttons on her shirt and was putting on her shoes when a knock sounded at the door.

— 13 —

Kate followed the Susitna inland to Bear Creek. She'd radioed Paul before leaving Anchorage to let him know she was on her way. She flew over the cabin, hoping to see him, but there was no sign of him. Certain Paul would hear the plane and meet her at the sandbar, she headed for the landing strip.

Her stomach quaked. She wasn't sure how to tell him. She'd never been in a situation like this before. How did you tell a man he was going to be a father?

She hadn't exactly been surprised at the doctor's announcement that she was pregnant, and yet awe and amazement had swept through her. She nearly skipped out of his office, her doubts and questions seeming to have vanished. She was going to be a mother!

After she'd finished her evening meal, she invited Helen and Muriel over for dessert. She wanted Paul to be the first to know, but she needed to tell someone. They'd both been ecstatic, accepting the announcement as if there were no concerns, just the joy of motherhood. If only it were that simple. Maybe it was supposed to be.

They'd stayed late, chatting and making plans. Muriel

thought it would be fun to have a party to celebrate and she thought it would be especially fun if the attendees brought gifts for the baby. Kate definitely didn't want to do anything like that. So Muriel said she'd sew some special garments for a newborn. Helen was already planning the colors for the yarn she'd use to knit a blanket. They were both full of tips on parenting. Their time together had made it real.

Now it was time to tell Paul. He'd said he wanted children, but Kate wasn't sure how he'd respond to the news. His baby boy had died, and this might remind him of what he'd lost.

When she approached the gravel sandbar, she spotted him. He was heading out in the dory. She'd been preoccupied and brought the plane down late. The wheels touched, bouncing on the gravel, and the end of the tiny island rushed toward her. With only yards remaining, the plane rolled to a stop. With a whispered prayer of thanks, Kate took off her leather helmet and shut down the engine. Angel was already at the door, her tail wagging. She was glad to be home.

When Kate opened the door, Angel leaped out and ran for Paul, who was beaching the boat. Kate tied down the plane.

Paul knelt and opened his arms to Angel, pulling her into a hug. "How you doing, girl?" He gave her a quick rubdown, then turned his attention on Kate. "Nice to have you back." A smile touched his lips. "But you cut the landing a bit close, don't you think?

Kate glanced at the plane. "Yeah. Guess my mind was on something else." How to tell him—that's where her mind had been and still was. She wanted it to be perfect. "I'm sorry I left angry. I'm glad to be home," she said, walking up to him. Their lips grazed and they gave each other half a hug. *He's still angry*, Kate thought.

Paul shoved his hands in his pockets and walked toward the boat. "So, how was your trip into town?"

"Good."

"Did you see Albert and Helen?"

"Uh-huh."

"How they doing?"

"They're good. And so are Muriel and Terrence. I guess Terrence has been doing a lot of fishing. Muriel wishes he'd stay home more." Kate offered Paul a small smile to see how it would be received.

"He's got to get the fish while they're running," he said and gave Kate a hand into the boat.

She sat on the middle bench while Paul pushed the dory off the rocks and leaped in. He dropped onto the seat in the back and started the motor, then turned the dory toward the creek.

"The mosquitoes aren't bad," Kate said, swiping at one. "They're usually thick by now."

"They'll show up. They always do." Paul kept his eyes on the shore. "Guess who did show up already."

"Who?"

"Jasper. The day you left, when I got up to the house he was sitting on his perch just like always."

"He waited until I was gone, huh."

Paul didn't reply at first, then with a grin, he said, "Guess he knew how lonely I'd be without you."

Kate breathed in a lungful of relief. Things were all right. "I'm sorry I left the way I did."

He steered toward the dock. "You had good reason. I was bad-tempered and antagonistic. I wouldn't have wanted to be with me either." He shut down the engine, glided alongside the dock, and when he came to a stop, he tied off the boat. "I don't know why I act like that."

"Everyone gets in a mood sometimes. I'm not exactly the most even-tempered woman in the territory."

Paul went to give her a hand out of the boat, but he hung on and pulled her to him. "I love you, Kate. I'm sorry."

She threw her arms around him. The boat wobbled and she fell backward, but Paul held her securely. She laughed and he laughed.

"We ought to get out of this boat," Kate said, stepping onto the dock. She was dying to tell him.

"I think we're meant just for each other." Paul climbed out of the dory and moved to Kate, pulling her close to him. "I've missed you." He kissed her, the way a man in love kisses a woman.

Kate melted into his arms. "I'm so glad to be here, together. The house in town was empty without you."

They separated and Paul slung an arm around her shoulders and they headed up the trail. "So, why *did* you go to town, besides my lousy mood?"

"I was upset and needed time to think. I wanted to talk to Helen. She's like a mother to me. I'm new at being a wife and I thought she might have some good advice for me."

"Did you have a nice visit?"

"Yes."

"And . . . what kind of advice did she give you?"

"The just-between-women kind." Kate smiled up at him and then leaned against him. "And . . . while I was in town I went to see the doctor."

Paul stopped. "Why? You're married to one." His brows creased with concern. "Are you all right? You've seemed a little under the weather lately."

"If you noticed, why didn't you say something?"

"I thought it might be nerves from all the trouble you've been drawn into lately." He narrowed his eyes. "So, why didn't you come to me?"

"I didn't want you getting your hopes up and with your past

and all . . ." Kate knew it was time to stop delaying. "I went in to see the doctor because . . . we're going to have a baby."

"You're pregnant?"

Kate nodded.

A broad smile emerged on Paul's face and he let out a whoop and pulled her into his arms. "I wish you'd told me sooner. When?"

"January." Paul's excitement only heightened her own. Kate laughed. "I'm still stunned. You're happy about it?"

Paul's eyes warmed, becoming more tender than usual. "I've never been happier." He held her against him, then tipped her face up and gently kissed her forehead. "I do wish you'd told me instead of going to another doctor, though."

"I know. But I think this will be better. You just have to be the father, not the doctor."

His lips lifted slightly. "I think I like that."

"I've been thinking . . . until the baby's born," Kate looked at her stomach and rested a hand on it, "I'll take safer runs and I won't work so hard. But it's just for a while. After the baby gets here, I'll have to figure out how to be a mother and work."

"Sounds good to me."

Paul circled his arm around Kate's waist, and the two continued up the path. "Let's tell Patrick and Sassa. They'll want to know."

"I can't wait to see Sassa's face when she hears the news."

"And I wish I could see your mother's face when she hears. We'll have to call them on our next trip into town."

Their hands clasped, they walked the trail that connected the two homesteads.

In the summer twilight, Paul and Kate snuggled down into bed and pulled the blankets up around them.

"That was fun. I knew Sassa would want to celebrate." Paul chuckled.

"She and Patrick are good people. I'm glad they're our neighbors." Kate rested her head on Paul's chest.

He caressed her back, his mind unwillingly going to Susan and his son. A twinge of sorrow pierced his heart. She'd be happy for him, he was sure of it.

"Lily might have found a match in Clint. They seem to like each other . . . a lot," Kate said.

"What do you think of him?"

"I like him. He treats her and the baby like they're special. He's a hard worker. Klaus would be happy with what he's done with the place." Kate blew out a soft breath. "It would be so wonderful for Lily if they got married. Clint would make a good husband and father to Teddy. Sassa would be over the moon about it. She'd have her daughter and grandson right here on the creek." Her voice sounding sad, Kate said, "I wish my parents lived close."

"Maybe one day," Paul said. "Once they hear about the baby, your father might be willing to give up the farm and move."

"I don't know about that. He loves his apple trees."

"As much as a grandson?"

Kate sat up. "A grandson? What if we have a girl?"

"All the more reason." His heart full, Paul pulled her back down beside him. "Boy or girl, it will be perfect." He kissed her. "We better get some sleep. With the long days, it seems the work never ends. And we might have a call for a flight. Plus you need your sleep."

"Yes, sir. I'm going to sleep right away, sir."

With Kate in his arms, Paul lay awake long after she'd fallen asleep. He couldn't settle down. His mind whirled with what the future might look like. He was going to be a father again and he couldn't keep from imagining what that would be like. He'd wanted it for so long, but never thought it would happen for him. At least not until Kate came into his life.

"Thank you, Lord," he whispered, feeling guilty over how angry he'd been with God just a few days before—and so many times. He'd blamed God for everything that went wrong, but he'd never really thanked him for all the good things he'd been given.

When he woke the following morning, his first thought was, *I'm going to be a father.* Instead of joy, anxiety grabbed hold of him. He didn't know how to be a father. What if he did it all wrong? And then he remembered his own father who had been kind and devoted to his children. He'd been a good example, which made Paul feel better.

He rolled over and looked at Kate, who was still asleep, with her cheek resting on her arm and her short hair all tousled. She was beautiful. He longed to reach out and touch her, but fought the impulse so she could sleep. He wondered if they'd have a boy or a girl.

Carefully and as quietly as possible, he climbed out of bed, pushed his feet into slippers, and headed for the kitchen. He switched on the two-way radio, just in case a call came in, then put coffee on to brew.

He considered making breakfast but decided to wait until Kate woke up so she could choose what she wanted. He glanced out the porch window to see if Jasper was on his perch. He wasn't there. Disappointment pricked him. The radio crackled to life and Jack's voice came over the speaker. "Anchorage airport to Paul Anderson. Come in. Over."

"Anchorage, this is Paul. How are you this fine morning? Over."

"All's good here. But I need a doctor up at a homestead outside the valley. There's a woman too sick to travel."

"What's the problem?"

"Her son called in and said she's got a bad cough and high fever."

"Kate will need the coordinates."

"Get her on the radio and I'll give them to her." Jack sounded surly.

Kate wandered into the front room, stretching her arms over her head. "What's going on?"

"Sounds like Jack got up on the wrong side of the bed. We've got a medical call, but he needs to tell you how to get there." He dropped a kiss on Kate's cheek as she passed him.

"Morning, Jack. So, where are we headed?"

"I'll need you to land at the airstrip on the north end of Palmer. A man will pick you up there and take you out to his homestead. Over."

"Gotcha. Over and out." Kate flipped off the radio.

"He could have told me that," Paul said.

"Yeah, but you know Jack. He has his own way of doing things." Kate looked at the coffeepot longingly. "No time for lounging around this morning. How long's the coffee been cooking?"

"Just put it on. We'll have to settle for water. It sounds like that woman needs a doctor right away. We better get dressed and be on our way."

They got ready and headed for the creek. Once they reached the plane, Kate released the ties. "We'll have to turn her around manually. I didn't leave enough room to make a wide turn."

"Okay," Paul said and moved to the back of the plane.

Kate took a wing and together they manipulated it so it was facing downriver. Kate and Angel climbed in while Paul cranked the flywheel.

The engine came to life and Paul took his place up front

beside Kate. "This should be a pretty easy trip. It's not far to Palmer from here."

"Maybe we'll be home by lunch." Kate smiled and then kissed him. "Forgot to say good morning."

"You hungry? I brought some bread and cheese."

"My stomach's growling, but I'm feeling kind of sick. I'm not sure whether to eat or not."

"Eating a little should help. It's normal for a pregnant woman to feel poorly first thing in the morning."

"That's me, a pregnant woman." Kate grinned. She accepted the slice of bread Paul offered, took a bite, then checked her gauges and revved the engine. "Everything looks good." She held the bread between her teeth and tugged on her flight helmet. Soon they were headed down the sandbar and lifted into the air. The skies were clear, the sun bright.

Kate was familiar with the landing site outside of Palmer and had no difficulty finding it. When she touched down, a young man of fifteen or so ran toward the plane. He met them as they climbed out.

"Hi. I'm Frank. You must be the doctor," he said to Paul.

"Paul Anderson. Nice to meet you." He grasped the young man's hand and shook it. "This is Kate, my wife and pilot."

"Heard of you," Frank said. "We better get a move on. My mom's real sick." He headed for a black pickup truck on the roadway alongside the airstrip. He was in a hurry and Kate and Paul nearly had to jog to keep up. Frank climbed in behind the wheel. Angel was loaded into the back, then Kate and Paul got in up front.

"You sure you know how to drive this thing?" Paul asked, nervous about the youngster's age.

Frank gave him an annoyed glance. "Been driving since I was ten. Don't need to worry 'bout me."

"Okay," Paul said, wishing he'd kept his mouth shut. "So, how far is it to your place?"

"Not all that far, but it'll take awhile. The road don't go all the way." He pulled onto a dirt road and headed north. He didn't slow down for ruts or holes and the truck bounced and danced its way along.

"What do we do when the road ends?" Kate asked.

"The teenager looked at her, but didn't answer right away. "Horses, ma'am. Got a stable for 'em at the end of the trail. They're waiting for us. But I wasn't counting on anyone but the doc coming along. So I only brought two of 'em down."

"Horses?" Kate couldn't keep the anxiety out of her voice. "I haven't ridden since I was a girl." She looked at Paul. "Do you ride?"

"Not exactly. I had an uncle once with a small farm who had horses. I remember riding a time or two at his place when I was a kid."

Kate lifted her brows. "This ought to be interesting."

"It ain't nothin'," Frank said. "The horses are gentle and our place is only a couple of miles up the trail. We figure on cutting in a road, but we just got moved in last year. First we've got to prove up the place so we can hang onto the land. Government's got requirements, you know."

"Yeah, I understand it's a lot of work." Paul folded his arms over his chest and tried to envision himself riding. It wasn't a pretty picture.

They traveled another twenty minutes on the crumbling road, then pulled off into a wide place. Just inside the tree line stood a small barn with a corral. Frank ground to a stop, jumped out of the truck, and slammed the door, then ran for the barn.

Paul and Kate followed. Angel seemed happy to be on an adventure. By the time Paul and Kate reached the barn door,

Frank was already on his way out leading two horses, both saddled and ready to go. They were large animals and still had their winter coats. "If you want to go, Mrs. Anderson, you'll have to ride behind the doc here."

"I'd like to go along," she said, but she sounded a little unsure.

Paul was ready to question the decision when Frank said, "Okay then." He kept the reins of a dark brown gelding and handed off a dirty white mare to Paul. He pulled himself up into the saddle and waited.

Paul stood beside the filthy horse, trying to convince himself that one day this would be a fun story to tell his son or daughter. He wasn't sure how to mount and hang onto his medical bag at the same time.

"I'll take that bag for you," Frank said.

Paul handed it up and the teen hooked it over his saddle horn.

Paul placed his foot into the stirrup and pushed up while pulling on the saddle horn. He gave it a little too much muscle and nearly toppled over the other side.

Frank laughed.

"It's been awhile," Paul said, getting his balance and settling into the saddle. He held out a hand to Kate, doubting the wisdom of her riding in her condition. He kept quiet about his misgivings, knowing that trying to convince her to stay put would be futile. "Put your foot in the stirrup and I'll haul you up."

Even as tall as Kate was, she had trouble reaching the stirrup. It took a couple of tries, but she managed to get her foot in and braced, then grabbed hold of Paul's hand. He pulled her up and she swung a leg around behind him and over the horse's rump. She was getting settled when the mare gave a little hop and a buck. Kate grabbed hold of Paul and nearly dragged him off.

"You gotta watch her," said Frank. "She's touchy around the loins."

"Where?" Kate asked.

Frank rode his horse up close to them and pointed at the area just behind her belly. He turned his mount toward the trail and cantered off.

Paul did his best to follow and wished the boy would slow down. He held the reins with one hand and gripped the saddle horn with the other. "You okay?" he hollered to Kate.

"Yeah. As long as you stay on, I'll be fine." Kate tightened her grip around his waist and leaned against his back.

"At least I don't have to steer—this horse knows exactly where it's going."

With Angel loping alongside them, the riders followed a muddy trail into a lush forest of birch, alder, aspen, and cottonwood. There was a smattering of fir and an occasional spruce. The trail wound up and around boulders, and Paul nearly tumbled over the mare's head when she plunged down a steep embankment and splashed through a stream.

"Hang on tight," he called as they headed up the other side.

When Paul thought his legs wouldn't grip a minute longer, they broke into a clearing where a small cabin and a barn with a corral huddled. A cache and a shed stood just beyond the house. Chickens clucked and scattered as the horses trotted up to the front of the cabin.

Frank leaped down. "Well, this is it."

Paul could hear pride in his voice.

The front door opened and a weary-looking man with a long gray beard stepped onto the porch. "Thank God. I didn't know what to do. I was wondering if anyone was gonna come." He clapped his son on the shoulder. "Good job." He turned to Paul and held out his hand. "I'm Jake Andrews."

"Paul Anderson. And this is Kate Anderson, my wife."

"Good to meet you. Come in. Agnes is in the back bedroom." He walked inside, stepping over a long-haired black dog who barely bothered to look up. "Agnes, the doc's here. Everything's going to be fine now."

The house smelled of liniment and tobacco smoke and was stifling hot. Paul had grown to expect that. Most people believed they were supposed to keep a sick person warm, which was fine as long as they weren't running a fever.

He followed Jake to the back room where he found a tiny woman buried in a pile of blankets. She barely opened her eyes to look at him, then she coughed—a deep rumbling sound came from deep in her lungs.

"Hello, Mrs. Andrews. I'm Dr. Anderson."

She didn't acknowledge him. She was occupied with managing her next breath. The blue tint to her lips attested to her lack of success. This woman was extremely ill.

Paul opened his medical bag and lifted out a thermometer and set it on the bedstead. "How long she been sick?"

"A good week anyway. She's usually strong as a horse, never gets sick. But this time she just seemed to get worse and worse. She gonna be all right, Doc?"

Paul lifted Mrs. Andrews' gray braid and gently draped it over one shoulder. He placed his stethoscope to her chest. He listened to her heart, which was beating rapidly. Most likely from the fever. "Can you take a breath for me, Mrs. Andrews?" She breathed in and Paul heard a rushing sound and then an ominous crackling. He moved the stethoscope. "Again?" She managed another breath and Paul heard the same sounds. It wasn't good.

He placed the thermometer in her mouth and waited a few minutes while removing the blankets, exposing Mrs. Andrews thin frame hidden beneath a heavy nightgown. "Frank, can you get me a bowl of tepid water?"

"Sure." The boy hurried out of the room.

Paul removed the thermometer. Mrs. Andrews' fever was 104 degrees. He shook down the thermometer and returned it to his medical bag. "She needs to be cooled down. Her fever's high."

"How do we do that?" Jake asked.

"First of all, keep the house cooler, just warm enough so she won't catch a chill, and keep the blankets off."

"But I . . . I'm freezing," Mrs. Andrews managed to whisper, grasping her thin arms across her chest.

"You're going to feel cold, but it will help bring down the fever. Once the fever's under control you'll feel better."

Jake sat in a chair next to the bed and took his wife's hand. "So, what is it, Doc? What's wrong with her?"

Paul put his stethoscope back in his bag. "Pneumonia. She needs to be in the hospital. Do you have any way down to the road that doesn't require riding a horse?"

"If the snow was on the ground, I could use the sled, but it's a little late for that. And you seen that trail—it's not good for nothin'."

Paul searched his mind for a way to get the woman out. It was too far to use a litter. And riding a horse was out of the question. He looked at the ailing woman. If she stayed here, she could well die. Had she considered what it might cost her when she joined her husband in this isolated place? Paul took out a small tin can. He couldn't rescue everyone. "I want you to give her one of these three times a day. They should help clear up this lung infection, but it can cause stomach upset, so don't be surprised by that. And make sure she drinks plenty of water. Try to get her to eat a little. That might help."

Jake took the tin. "What is that stuff?"

"It's a new sulfa drug. It's showing great promise." Paul smiled. "Do you have aspirin?"

"Yeah. Agnes is careful to keep some in the house."

"While she's running a fever, I want you to make sure she takes two every four hours. And keep her cooled off."

Frank showed up with a pan of water and a washcloth. Paul sat on the side of the bed and dipped the cloth in the water and gently washed her face and neck, then rolled up the sleeves of her nightdress and cooled her arms.

"I'm freezing," Agnes said through chattering teeth. Gooseflesh popped up all over her skin.

"I know. I'm sorry, but this will help." Paul made sure his voice was calm and soothing. He looked over at her husband. "Call in if she doesn't improve in a few days. Or if she gets worse."

Paul stood and handed the pan of water to Jake. "I'd feel better if she were in the hospital."

"There's no way to get her there. I got nothin' 'cept the back of a horse." Jake's face showed his anguish and frustration. "First thing, I'm puttin' in a road. Don't care what it takes."

Agnes coughed and coughed again. Finally, she sat up and sucked in oxygen, then spit into a rag. The sputum was the color of rust. Exhausted, she lay back down.

Paul moved toward the door. "We'll need a ride back to the road and into Palmer."

Frank stepped up. "I'll take ya."

Jake took a jar out of a cabinet and fished out a dollar bill and some change. "I wish I could pay ya more. I know you came a long way." He pressed the money into Paul's hand. "Thank you."

Paul knew the family had little to spare, but he'd learned not to refuse. Most people in the bush were principled and didn't expect something for nothing.

He pushed the money into his pants pocket. "Thank you."

With one more reminder that Agnes take her medicine,

Paul and Kate headed back down the trail to the waiting truck, and Kate's plane.

That night as Paul and Kate sat down to a dinner of bacon and fried potatoes with gravy, Kate reached across the table and smoothed his brow. "You're tired."

"I am. And that ride up and back down that trail wasn't easy on my backside or my back. It's aching."

Kate smiled softly. "You were wonderful with Mr. and Mrs. Andrews. I hope she gets well. Do you think she'll be all right?"

"The sulfa pills should help." He shrugged. "I think she'll recover. With the new drugs there are fewer deaths from pneumonia." He took a bite of potatoes and chewed slowly. He was almost too tired to eat. "It probably wasn't a good idea for you to ride up that trail today, not in your condition."

"I know. I thought about it." Kate picked up her coffee and took a drink. "I won't do anything like that again, at least not until after the baby is born. But after that, I'm thinking we ought to get a horse. It could be fun."

"Oh yeah—fun." Paul chuckled, then more seriously said, "Kate, while you're pregnant you can do most everything you've always done, with a few precautions. And I think we ought to move into town a month before it's due, otherwise we might not be able to get there when you go into labor.

Kate rested a hand on her abdomen. "Sassa already mentioned that she thought it is important for a child to be born at home. I'll have a time convincing her otherwise."

"Don't you worry about Sassa. I'll talk to her."

"It is a touching idea, that a child begin its life in its own home."

"Yes, but not as safe." He stood and leaned over the table to kiss her. "I love you. And that baby of ours. I'm not taking any chances. I'm going to take good care of the two of you. I promise."

He remembered a similar promise he'd made years before. He'd let his wife down. The memory of how it ended sent a wave of guilt over him. But things would be different this time. He'd make sure of it.

— 14 —

Kate finished washing the evening dishes and then joined Paul, who was sitting on the sofa, reading. "It's getting dark so early."

Paul set his book in his lap. "Winter's nearly here."

"I love winter, except for the darkness. 'Course this year we'll have the baby, which will make up for the short days." She smiled up at Paul.

He rested a hand on Kate's stomach. His eyes widened. "It moved."

"It's a busy child."

"Just like its mother."

"I'm resting today," Kate said, tucking her legs in under her. She looked at the book Paul held. "What are you reading?"

He held up the book. "*Of Mice and Men* by John Steinbeck. It's good, but I've got a feeling it's going to have one of those gut-wrenching endings. You know John Steinbeck. He always touches on the dark side of life."

Kate leaned against him. "I'd rather think about the joys of life." She rested her hand on her stomach and smiled. "We got a lot done this week. The last of the vegetables are canned.

It was so nice of Lily to come over and help." She smiled up at Paul. "She talked a lot about Clint. I think she's in love."

"He's a fine man," Paul said. "Those two are a good match."

"I hope they get married."

Paul set his book on the table and draped his arm around Kate. "It feels good to have most of the winter preparations done. I finished splitting the wood. I'm pretty sure we've got enough to last us through the winter. And the smokehouse is jammed with salmon."

"I hope the smell doesn't call in the bears," Kate said.

"I don't think we need to worry. The smokehouse is sturdy. I made sure of that." He rested his cheek against Kate's hair. "Good fishing season, one of the best I've seen since I moved here. We have more than enough to see us through the winter. That, with a successful hunting season—I'd say we're pretty well set. It'll be a good year for us."

"I guess the lull in flights worked out." Kate stood and moved to the kitchen where she picked up a dish towel and refolded it. She stared into the sink. "A lot of my flights went to other pilots."

"Because we're living out here?"

"Jack never said anything, but that's my best guess." She turned and looked at Paul. "I wouldn't want to be anywhere else. I love it here."

"Me too. But . . . town would make more sense." Paul's voice lacked conviction.

"It's all right. I'm supposed to be resting every day anyway. You did say it's good for me. And getting in and out of the plane is more and more difficult." Kate patted her stomach. "I'm fat."

"You're not fat. You're pregnant. And you're beautiful."

"Oh yeah—real beautiful," Kate said with a smirk. Still,

she loved that he had said it. She thought he actually believed it. "The lot in town is small. What would we do about outbuildings and gardening? Where would you put the dogs?" She returned to the sofa and sat beside him.

"People who live in town buy more and grow less. That's what my family did when I was growing up."

"But I love our garden." Kate didn't know why she was disputing Paul. Living in town did make more sense. And lots of people lived without gardens and smokehouses.

Paul rested his chin on her head. "Yeah, I love it too."

"You said we were going to make a run into town soon to stock up on a few items before the snow flies. When did you want to go?"

"How about tomorrow?"

"I'd like that. I've been missing Muriel and Helen." She sat up straighter. "Can we take the boat instead of the plane?"

A gust of wind rattled the windows. Paul glanced over his shoulder and out the window. "You sure you want to do that? It's cold."

"It's not that bad. And if the sun is out, it will help. This time of year it's so beautiful. I think it would be fun to take the dory. It's been too long since I've seen Cook Inlet from sea level." She smiled. "The fall colors would make for a nice change of scenery."

"Okay. As long as the weather's good." Paul pressed a kiss to her cheek. "We can stay over one night, which would make for an easier day coming and going."

Kate nestled against him. "I'd like that. And I'll pray for good weather."

Paul gave her a crooked smile. "I swear God listens to you, so I figure we'll be taking the boat."

When Kate woke, faint morning light filtered in through the window. She climbed out of bed and crossed the room to have a look outside. The forest and outbuildings were outlined against the dawn. Last night's wind had stilled and the glow of morning showed pink in a sky smattered with clouds. "Thank you, Lord."

Wearing a smile, Kate returned to the bed and sat beside Paul, who was still sleeping. "Hey, lazybones. It's time to get up."

Paul rolled onto his back and opened one eye, then the other. He stared at Kate. "What a sight to behold first thing in the morning."

Kate laughed. "Is that a compliment or a criticism? I know how I look when I wake up."

He rested a hand on her thigh. "You're beautiful, always."

"You're a romantic in disguise, aren't you?"

"Maybe." He grinned.

Putting on what she hoped was a smug expression, Kate said, "The wind stopped and there are only a few clouds. I guess God heard my prayer."

"I'm not surprised." Paul placed a hand on Kate's rounded abdomen. "How are my two favorite people this morning?"

"Good. And this one," Kate put her hand over Paul's, "slept last night, which means so did I." She stood. "Get up. If we're taking the boat, we've got to get moving." She headed into the kitchen and put on a pot of coffee, then went to work preparing a breakfast of oatmeal with sugar and molasses.

After they'd finished eating, Kate packed extra clothing while Paul prepared the dory for their trip, made arrangements for the dogs, and carried food that Kate had prepared down to the boat. By the time he returned, she was ready to go.

Angel stood at the door, her tail waving. "Sorry, girl. Not

this time. There won't be enough room for you on the way back." She looked at Paul. "Did you talk to Patrick?"

"No. He was still sleeping. But Lily was up. She said that she and Clint would see to Angel while we're gone."

"Good." Kate gave the dog an extra pat and stepped outside, with Paul behind her. She could hear Angel whining at the door, then heard the sound of her toenails on the window glass. She'd jumped up on the sofa to watch them. "It feels strange leaving Angel behind. I'm so used to having her with me."

Paul glanced back at the house. "I figure she feels the same way."

The air felt brisk but not wintery. "I love this time of year." Kate breathed in the exuberance of the forest splashed with red, yellow, and orange. "It looks like God's taken out his paintbrush and had a party."

"Yeah, that's because he knows what's coming," Paul said dryly. "Winter."

"Come on now, where's that romantic spirit I saw this morning?"

"It went into hiding," Paul said with a half grin.

Undaunted, Kate continued, "It's the perfect time to make a slow trip to Anchorage. The world is beautiful."

"It might look good, but a dory isn't the most comfortable transportation. You sure you'll be all right?"

"I'll be fine. I've been feeling good all along—no aches or pains . . . hardly."

"All right. If you're sure."

When they reached the boat, Paul gave Kate a hand in, then untied the rope from the mooring and settled in the back beside the motor. It took only one yank on the starter and the engine puttered to life. He pushed away from the dock and turned the rudder so they were headed toward the Susitna River.

Soon the river would freeze. This would be the last boat trip until spring. When they entered the bay, it seemed bigger than Kate had remembered. She gazed out toward the sea, then at the shoreline, which looked like a collage of color. Mountains rose up on the far side of the bay like hazy blue and white crowns.

"It's unbelievably gorgeous," Kate said. "I'm glad we brought the boat instead of the plane."

The swell was calm and rocked the dory gently like a mother rocks a cradle. Kate looked back at Mount Susitna. "You know, even though I nearly died at the foot of that mountain, it still feels special to me. It's not like most of the peaks in the territory. She's quiet and gentle. I'd love to make a fishing trip to one of the mountain lakes before they freeze."

"Sounds like a good idea, but I've got some medical runs coming up."

Something bumped the boat. "What was that?" Kate asked, staring into the water.

"Probably a log. Better keep a look out." Paul stood and studied the waves. "Ah, there's our culprit." He smiled broadly. "Whales. We're in the middle of a pod of belugas."

"There's one!" Kate pointed at what looked like a white ghost drifting past the boat just beneath the surface.

A few yards ahead of them, one of the eye-catching mammals surfaced, then dove back into the sea with its white tail hesitating for a moment before disappearing beneath the swells.

"Until I came here I'd never heard of a white whale," Kate said. "I think they're fantastic."

Paul and Kate watched and waited, hoping they'd see another one, but the whales were gone. "They must be on a mission," Paul said. "No dillydallying for them."

The rest of the trip was uneventful, except for a couple

of sea lions sunning themselves on a buoy. Paul turned the boat toward them, hoping to get a closer look. Barking at the intruders, the animals looked like they would stand their ground, but when Paul got closer, they dove into the sea.

Kate felt a swell of happiness. "I love Alaska. You never know what you're going to see. Except that it will either be unusual or delightful."

"Or scary as all get-out." A gentle expression rested on Paul's face. "It gets under your skin, all right. When I first came here, I didn't know if I'd ever feel at home. Now I don't think I could be happy anywhere else."

"I know this is the place for me. I don't ever want to leave." Kate gazed at the town of Anchorage perched on the hills above Ship Creek. "Are you still set on our moving into town a month before the baby comes?"

"Yes. It's the safest thing to do. What if you went into labor and the weather was bad and we couldn't get in?"

"I guess I'd have the baby at home. Sassa told me she'd help."

"I don't care what she said." Paul sounded angry. "I want our child born in a hospital."

"Okay. But you have to admit it would be nice to bring the baby into the world out on the creek."

"Kate, you never know what might happen during a delivery." Paul's tone was grim. "We're not taking any chances."

Kate wished he'd tell her why he felt so strongly about their baby being born in a hospital. Lots of babies were born in their own homes. Every time she'd tried to broach the subject of why he felt the way he did, he'd shut down. She was pretty certain it had something to do with what had happened to his wife and son. He was haunted by it and would never be free of it until he brought the secret into the light.

By the time they approached Anchorage, Kate's back ached.

She was glad to see the docks. Although the trip had started out wonderfully, it had been more difficult than Kate had anticipated. She decided she was too far along for adventures.

Paul gave her a hand out of the boat. "You hungry?"

"Starved. Seems I'm always hungry." She chuckled. "Let's go to the general store first and see if Helen and Albert are working. Maybe we can have lunch together."

"Sounds good to me." He took her hand. "But . . . maybe we ought to drop off our bags at the house first, then go over to the store."

"That's a good idea."

Paul draped a knapsack over one shoulder and carried the travel case. He and Kate strolled up the road away from the bay. Kate was grateful to be out of the boat. Walking felt good.

"We'll have to get a fire going in the house before we go to the store. It's really cold." She glanced at the bags. "Why don't you let me carry one of those?"

"No. I've got them." His tone was unyielding.

Kate still hadn't gotten used to his protectiveness. She hated being doted on, but with Paul there was no way around it. "It's cold. Colder than I expected," she said, pulling up her hood.

When they approached the house, Kate was surprised to see smoke trailing out of the stovepipe in the roof. "There's a fire going. I wonder who did that? No one knew we were coming."

Paul shrugged. "I don't know, but I'm grateful." He walked up the steps and opened the door for Kate. She stepped in and was greeted with shouts of "Surprise!" from Helen, Albert, Muriel and Terrence, and the fellas from the airfield, including Jack.

"What? What is this?" she asked.

Muriel hugged her. "It's a party, for you." She smiled broadly.

"But how did you know?" Kate turned to Paul.

"I radioed when I was at Patrick's," he said, a glint of mischief in his eyes.

Muriel grinned. "I've been planning for weeks."

"A party for what? It's not my birthday."

"No. But it's nearly your baby's birthday," Helen said.

Muriel took Kate's hands. "We thought it would be fun to celebrate and to get you some things that you'll need once it arrives."

Kate put her hands to her cheeks. "I had no idea. Thank you." She turned and looked at Paul. "You knew all along?"

He laughed. "Yep."

It was a good party. Everyone had a fine time, even Jack. Kate received all sorts of gifts for the baby—blankets, diapers, and clothing. And then Paul brought out a cradle.

"What in the world?"

"He made it himself," Helen said.

"When? Where?"

"Out in the shop. You're gone a lot, you know. And it's not hard to get a package picked up and delivered when you know the right people."

Kate knelt beside the wooden cradle and imagined her baby lying in it. "Oh Paul, it's beautiful." Tears moistened her eyes. "I didn't even know you knew how to make something like this."

"Patrick helped me."

Kate stood and faced him. "You're amazing. Thank you." She kissed him.

"When Helen told me about Muriel's idea for this party, I thought it would be a good time to give it to you."

"I have nearly everything I'm going to need." She looked around the room. "Thank you all so much." When she looked at Sidney, she caught him blinking back tears. He loved children. She hoped that someday he'd decide marriage was for him.

The following day, Paul and Kate purchased the remaining items they'd need, along with some goods for the upcoming winter. Most of it Kate would return for in her plane, leaving some for their short stay when the baby was born.

They set out for home beneath sunny skies. Anchorage gradually faded into an obscure coastline. They seemed to be traveling more quickly than usual. Kate thought it must be because she was anxious to get home, but then the engine quit and they continued to travel rapidly westward.

"Oh brother," Paul said. "Now's not a good time for you to get temperamental."

"Why are we moving so fast if the engine's not running?" Kate asked.

"It's the tide change. In this area the currents can be powerful. We need to get the engine started."

Kate felt a pulse of fear. "Can you restart it?"

"It shouldn't be a problem."

He stood and grabbed hold of the starter rope and pulled. The engine sputtered but didn't catch. He hauled on the rope again. Still nothing. Kate was beginning to think they'd have to row their way home.

Finally, he pulled and the engine caught, but Paul lost his balance. He tumbled backward, over the side and into the water. Before he could grab hold of the boat, the current caught him and swept him away from the dory.

"No! Paul!" Kate had heard of bore tides and knew she had no time to waste. She scrambled to the back of the boat and cranked the engine up as fast as it would go. It wasn't fast enough. She kept her eyes on Paul, and although the boat was also being dragged in the current, he was moving faster and was being carried farther and farther away. The water was too cold. If she didn't get to him soon, he'd drown.

"Paul! Hang on," she yelled. She closed the distance—not far now. She was almost certain the current was slowing. When she got close enough, she could see that Paul was struggling to stay afloat. *Lord, please don't let him die. Please.*

He slapped at the water, his arms almost useless. Kate pulled up alongside of him and let the engine idle as she reached over the side and caught his hand.

"I . . . I can barely move," he uttered, his voice weak. He struggled to get a grip on the boat and climb over the side, but fell back into the water. With strength Kate didn't know she possessed, she hauled him into the dory and into her arms. Clinging to him, she sobbed.

"I thought I was a goner," Paul managed to say through chattering teeth. "The water's so cold hypothermia set in fast. I couldn't move."

"Let's get you out of these clothes and into something dry." Kate helped him strip off his wet clothing and then rummaged through his bag and pulled out a warm flannel shirt and dry pair of pants. Paul was shaking so badly he couldn't dress himself. Kate helped him, then wrapped him in a couple of wool blankets. "It's a good thing we bought these."

He was still trembling so badly, Kate felt desperate to warm him up. She unbuttoned her coat and pulled Paul against her, offering her own body warmth. The cold of his body was shocking and soon Kate was shivering too.

"I was so afraid I'd lost you," she said.

They sat on the bottom of the boat for a long while, holding each other. Paul's shivering quieted. "Like I said earlier, Alaska can be scary." He chuckled.

Kate smiled. "The baby's happy. He's kicking really hard.

Here, feel." She took Paul's hand and placed it on her stomach. "Can you feel him?"

Paul's eyes warmed. "So, you've decided we're having a boy?"

"What?"

"You called it a him."

"I did, didn't I?" They both laughed.

Paul rested his cheek against Kate's abdomen. "Nothing's going to happen to me. We're in this together, the three of us—forever."

— 15 —

Kate pulled on her boots and laced them, then grabbed her coat from its hook and put it on. The house was clean and the baking done. She needed something to do. She stepped onto the porch, and then shoved her hands into her gloves. Jasper's perch was empty. He'd been gone for several weeks. He'd never taken to Kate, but now that he was gone, she missed him.

Pulling the door closed, she gazed at a white world, savoring the hush of the year's first heavy snowfall. She took in a breath of contentment. She was happy. With only two months left until the baby was due, she was home most days, filling in on flights only when needed. And for reasons she didn't completely understand, most days that was fine with her. She thought it must have something to do with her woman's need to settle in and prepare for the birth.

Feeling like an overblown balloon, she made her way down the porch steps and headed toward the shop. Opening the door, she stepped inside. Paul was working on his traps, making sure they were ready to be set out. He looked up.

"Hi. How you doing?" he asked.

"Good. The baby's busy this morning. Must be happy."

Paul kissed her. "Just like its mother."

"I am." She turned her attention to the traps on the workbench. "Just thought I'd come and say hi. The house is clean, bread is in the oven, and the stew is on." She laughed. "Listen to me. I sound like Helen, all domestic."

"Don't worry. It's temporary." Paul smiled. "I know you. Soon you'll be off on all sorts of new adventures." He pulled her into his arms.

"It's hard to imagine right now. I'm having more trouble than ever getting in and out of the plane." She rested a cheek against Paul's chest. "I don't mind being a homebody for now, though." She gave him a squeeze and then sat on a stool beside the workbench. "But I have been thinking about after the baby is born. I'm not sure how I'm going to work and be a mother."

"Maybe we should talk to Albert and Helen. They did it."

"They own a store. You're a bush doctor and I'm a pilot— it's not quite the same thing."

"True." Paul leaned against the bench and folded his arms over his chest. "I suppose we'll figure it out as we go. We can share responsibilities and the baby will have to enjoy flying."

Kate closed her eyes. "What about the danger we'd be putting him or her in? Every time I go up, I know something bad can happen, but I choose to take a risk. Is it fair to the baby?"

Paul's expression turned pensive. "I've been thinking about that. And I don't have a definite answer." He blew out a breath. "I take the same risk. And when you were little, you went up with your father." He scratched at a day's growth of beard. "Everything in life requires risk. I don't want you to be unhappy and I don't want our child to grow up being afraid of adventure. I do think that if you're making a run you know could be risky, then you'd be wise to leave the baby with me or Sassa or Lily. And if you're in town you can count on help from Muriel and Helen."

Kate was surprised. He'd had such a hard time accepting the dangers of flying.

"All we can do is take every precaution—"

"And leave the rest up to God," Kate interjected, knowing Paul was trying, but it wouldn't be easy on him.

"Just living out here is dangerous. I plan to take our son or daughter fishing and hunting. And I'll teach him or her to drive the sled." He paused, then added, "I figure nothing in life is safe."

Kate thought he sounded like he was trying to convince himself. "We'll figure it out."

Paul picked up one of the traps. "Some of these need replacing. While the weather's clear, I want to make a trip to Susitna Station and get a few traps. The dogs are ready for a run anyway. It'll be good for them."

"That sounds like fun. I can pack us something to eat and I'll make coffee to take along."

Paul eyed her warily. "I don't know, Kate. It's quite a ways and with you being so far along . . ."

"I'm fine. I've been feeling good. And I'll ride on the sled. What harm is there in that?" She stood. "I'd really like to go."

Paul gave her a slow smile. "Okay. But you've got to ride the whole time, no trudging through the snow or driving the team."

Kate looked down at herself. "Do I look like I'd enjoying running behind a sled, even if I could?" She laughed and headed for the shed door. "I'll get everything ready. When do you want to leave?"

"How long until that bread's done?"

"It was nearly ready to come out of the oven when I left the house."

"Okay then. You take care of that and our lunch and I'll get the sled and the dogs ready to go."

"Do you mind if Angel comes along?"

"It's fine as long as she doesn't try to play with the other dogs."

"That's not a problem. Once the team's in the harness all they think about is working anyway." Kate hurried back to the house, excited about having a little adventure.

When Kate stepped onto the porch, the dogs were harnessed, barking and ready to go. She sat on the sled and Paul made sure she was bundled up beneath blankets and a fur robe.

"Okay. That's enough. Pretty soon I won't be able to breathe," Kate said with a laugh.

"When the wind hits you, you'll be grateful. The temperature's dropping. It's down to 18 degrees. And once we get moving it'll feel even colder."

Kate looked up at him and smiled. "Let's go."

Paul bent down and kissed her, then stepped behind the sled and got a good grip on the lines, stood on the boards, and called, "Hike up!" Nita, who was in the lead, charged forward. Buck and Jackpot pulled hard, following close behind her. Paul looked up at the gray skies and felt a twinge of apprehension. With the temperature dropping and the clouds moving in, it could mean a storm. He looked at Kate tucked in and eager. She should probably stay home. But he knew better than to say anything now. There would be no way to convince her to stay.

Angel ran alongside the dogs, then veered off and happily investigated any and all points of interest as the sled moved across the frozen creek, over the Susitna, and up the bank on the far side. The snow was dry so they made good time as they slushed along the bank above the river.

Wanting to keep the dogs' load light, Paul ran behind as much as possible.

"You doing all right?" he asked Kate.

"Fine. I love this!" She pulled the blankets more tightly up under her chin.

"Let me know if you want to stop." His lungs burning, Paul stepped onto the boards and rode for a while.

Angel had tired of exploring and now ran alongside the dogs. Occasionally she tried to engage one of them in a game. Jackpot and Buck ignored her, but Nita snarled and snapped at her a couple of times.

"Angel! No!" Kate hollered more than once. Finally, she lifted her hand and called over her shoulder. "Paul. Stop."

"Whoa," he hollered and the dogs reluctantly pulled up. "You need a break?"

"No. I was just thinking that maybe I ought to have Angel ride with me. I don't like her taunting the dogs."

"That'll add sixty-five, seventy pounds to the load. But if you think you can get her to stay put, go ahead."

"Come on, Angel," Kate said and Angel leaped up onto her lap, crowding Kate's belly. "Lay down."

The dog found a spot on top of Kate's legs. Panting, she rested her head on her front paws and Paul set off again. Angel stayed put for a little while, but she was soon restless and wanted off. When Susitna Station came into view, Paul was grateful. He and the dogs needed a rest and he'd feel better once Kate was indoors warming up. It felt like the temperature was plunging. Angel leaped off Kate's lap and ran ahead. She knew the town and the general store where Charlie Agnak usually had a treat for her.

"Whoa!" Paul called as they moved into the village.

The dogs stopped and stood panting. They watched Paul, waiting for a drink and something to eat. Paul dug under a

178

pile of wool blankets for water bottles he'd filled with hot water before leaving. He poured the water into bowls for the dogs while Kate took dried fish out of a bag and gave a hunk to each dog. Angel trotted back for her share.

When Paul and Kate stepped inside the store, Charlie was in his usual spot in a chair close to his barrel stove. He looked up in surprise. "Didn't hear no plane." He took a bite of jerky.

Paul stripped off his gloves. "We brought the sled."

"In this weather?" He looked at Kate. "In your condition? An Indian lady maybe, but you—not good."

"You think the weather's going to turn bad?" Kate asked.

"Yep. And real soon too. You warm up, then you get home." He poured two cups of coffee and handed one to Kate and the other to Paul. Paul didn't much care for Charlie's coffee, but he accepted it anyway and took a sip of the bitter brew. "Drink up," he told Kate. "It'll warm your insides." He grinned when she tasted the coffee. "It's good for you."

She lifted an eyebrow just slightly at Paul, then took a real drink. "I'm riding," she told Charlie. "And Paul's got me bundled up tight."

Charlie nodded, and then turned to Paul. "So, what you need?"

"Just a few legholds. You have any left?"

"Yeah. I got some." Charlie hobbled toward the back wall, hunched over the way he always was. Paul wondered what the old native had done to his back. He'd never asked. Charlie didn't seem to be in pain and Paul figured if he wanted a doctor's opinion, Charlie would have asked.

"These are all I got left," Charlie said, stopping in front of a half-dozen traps hanging on the wall.

Paul lifted down four of them. "These'll do." He followed Charlie to the front of the store.

"You need anything else?"

Paul glanced at Kate, who was standing by the stove still trying to down the coffee. Something sweet would help clear away the bitterness. "You have any candy?"

"Sure. Always got candy. It's right down there." He nodded at a shelf just behind Paul.

"Kate, would you like some?" Paul perused the sweets.

Kate set her cup on a small table near the fire box and joined him. "Sounds good."

There were Tootsie Pops, Chick-O-Sticks, Licorice Snaps, Sugar Babies, and Snickers bars. "Not a lot of choice," Paul said.

"I love Chick-O-Sticks." She picked up a box and opened it. She popped one in her mouth and closed up the box. Paul selected two Snickers bars, two boxes of Sugar Babies, and some Licorice Snaps. He winked at Kate. "Doesn't hurt to stock up."

He set the candy on the counter beside the traps and then paid Charlie, who put the money in a box in a drawer.

"You better head home," Charlie said. "I'm tellin' ya. A storm's coming. I always know."

"We're on our way," Paul said, wishing Kate had stayed home. He strode toward the door with the legholds draped over one shoulder. "Thanks, Charlie."

"Bye, Charlie," Kate said, slipping out the door in front of Paul.

The dogs stood and whined, their tails wagging. Paul stashed their water bowls away, packed the legholds on the sled, and helped tuck Kate beneath the blankets. The air was frigid and a light snow fell. They'd better hurry. Charlie had lived here all his life. If he said a storm was coming, it was.

Paul stood behind the sled. "Hike up!" he called, and the dogs set off down the trail the way they'd come. Angel trotted alongside. For a while, she seemed content to tag along, but it didn't take long before she was pestering Nita. The wind picked up and the snow fell harder. Soon Paul and Kate were fighting their way through an angry blizzard. Kate bundled deeper beneath her blankets. Paul pulled his hood closed so that the only part of his face exposed was his eyes. He chastened himself for bringing Kate.

They were moving along the Susitna when Angel's persistent nipping set off Nita's temper. She'd had enough and laid into the younger dog. Angel broke free of Nita's hold and plunged down the bank. Nita charged after her.

"Whoa! Whoa!" Paul hollered, but Nita was beyond hearing. The other dogs followed, towing the sled down the slope. It cut across sideways and tipped, throwing Kate, the blankets, and the supplies into the snow. The drag of the sled finally forced the dogs to stop.

"Kate! Are you all right?" Paul crouched beside her.

She pushed up on one arm and peered at him through the swirl of white. "I think so."

Paul gave her a hand and helped her stand.

"I'm okay," she said, brushing snow off the front of her coat and pants. "Darn that Angel. She's definitely not a mushing dog. From now on she stays home."

Paul was already working to right the sled. Kate got down beside him and pushed. Together they tipped it back on its runners. Beginning with Nita, Paul worked his way through the traces, untangling the harnesses and lines. Kate repacked the supplies and blankets.

"I'll wait until you get the sled on the trail before I get back on."

Paul got the dogs moving and Kate hoofed it up the embankment, alongside him. When they were back on the path, Kate went to climb on the sled, but stopped and sat on the edge for a few moments.

"What is it?" Paul asked.

"I don't know. Pain." Her expression was concentrated. Finally she straightened and took a deep breath. "It's gone." She settled on the sled.

"When we get home, you're going straight to bed. This whole thing has been too much for you."

Kate nodded and pulled the blankets around her. Paul tucked them snuggly, then leashed Angel and hurried to the back of the sled, feeling an urgency to get Kate home. He yelled at the dogs to hike up, and then he ran behind, one hand gripping Angel's leash and the other on the sled. He moved his gaze from the trail ahead and then back to Kate. More than once it looked like she clutched her stomach. He prayed she wasn't having contractions. It was too early.

When Kate pulled her legs up and rolled to her side, Paul stopped the sled and moved around to her. "Are you all right?"

"No. I'm still having pains."

"Is it a steady pain? Or does it come and go?"

"It comes and goes."

"How often do you think?"

Kate shrugged. "I don't know—every few minutes."

Paul reached beneath the blankets and Kate's coat so he could rest his hand on her stomach. He waited a few moments and then he felt the alarming tightening of muscles. Kate blew out a breath and closed her eyes.

"Is it bad?"

She nodded.

"Try to relax. I'll get you home." She was almost certainly in labor. If the baby was born now it would die. *Not again. Please, not again.*

He hurried the dogs and ran until he could barely suck oxygen into his lungs. If the baby was born out in this storm, there'd be no hope of survival.

When they approached the junction where the Susitna River and Bear Creek met, Paul felt momentary relief. They'd made it. He let the dogs have their head. They knew the way home. When they pulled into the yard, Paul lifted Kate and carried her into the cabin where he gently laid her on the bed. "How are you feeling?"

"Not good. The pains are getting worse and closer together." Kate's eyes filled with tears, pleading for Paul to help her. "If the baby is born now, will it die?"

Paul couldn't answer her. Instead he said, "We need to stop the labor. You stay down. Whiskey sometimes helps." He hurried into the kitchen and took a bottle of whiskey from the cupboard and poured a small amount into a glass. Returning to Kate, he handed her the glass. "Drink this down."

Kate drank it, grimacing. "Oh, that's awful."

"Yeah, but it may help. Sassa might know a native remedy. Will you be all right while I go and get her?"

"Yes. I'll change into my nightgown." Kate managed a small smile. "Go. I'll be all right until you get back. But, please hurry."

Paul started to leave the room, then stopped and returned to Kate. He took her face in his hands. "Everything is going to be all right. I promise." He pressed a kiss to her forehead, then hurried out of the house. He ran to the Warrens'.

Paul didn't bother knocking on the door. He walked in. "Sassa! Sassa!" He looked about the room. The boys were gathered around a board game on the living room floor and Patrick sat at the kitchen table. "Is Sassa here?"

Patrick pushed to his feet. "Sure. She's upstairs. What is it?" The boys crowded around Paul.

"It's Kate."

Sassa hurried down the stairs. "What's wrong?"

"Kate. She's in labor . . ."

Sassa's brown eyes widened. "It's too soon."

Lily stood on the stairs behind her mother. "What can we do? Is there anything we can do?"

Paul looked at Sassa. "Do you know of a remedy that will stop her labor?"

"Sometimes the root bark from the highbush cranberry can stop labor. It's good for cramping. I have some." She grabbed a bottle from the cupboard, then put on her parka. "We have to get her into bed with her feet higher than her head." She opened the door. "Lily, bring the birthing blanket and some clean washcloths."

Lily nodded and watched as Paul and Sassa hurried out.

When Paul walked into the bedroom, Kate lay on the bed, looking frightened. He crossed the room and sat beside her. "Are the contractions any better?"

"No. I think they're worse. Will the baby be all right?"

He met her eyes. "Sassa's making an herbal tea for you."

"That's not what I asked."

Paul took in a breath and let it out slowly. How was it that he was again so close to losing a child and maybe his wife? Once wasn't enough? Bitterness hardened his heart, but his words were quiet and gentle. "We'll do everything we can."

"And we'll pray," Sassa said, walking into the room. "I've been talking to the Father all the way here." She smiled. "The tea is brewing." She took a pillow off the bed and placed it under Kate's feet. "Do you have more?"

"There's one in the closet," Paul said.

"Well, get it. And any others you have."

Paul took the pillow out of the closet and handed it to Sassa, then he strode into the front room and grabbed a blanket. He rolled it up and placed it on top of the two pillows. Kate handed Sassa the pillow she'd been using for her head, then lay down and put her feet on the stack of pillows and closed her eyes.

"It is important to keep the feet higher than your head," Sassa said, then left the room. She returned a few minutes later with a cup of hot liquid. "Here, drink this. It will help."

Kate pushed up on one elbow and took the cup. She smelled the brew, then took a sip and grimaced. "It's bitter. What is it?"

"A special tea. It might help your baby wait for another day to meet the world."

Kate managed to drink the entire cup, then lay back down.

Paul prayed the remedies would help. All they could do now was wait. But if the baby arrived tonight, could he save it?

The baby came—still and silent. She took not a breath nor made a single cry.

Paul did all he could to stir life into his little girl, but nothing he did helped. She was born meant for heaven.

The day was cloudy and frigid when Paul walked to the shed to build a coffin. He took great care to make every cut clean. He sanded the wood smooth and matched up each angle perfectly. When it was finished, Kate placed the baby blanket inside that Helen had made. Paul gently laid their swaddled daughter on the blanket and then stepped back and pulled Kate to his side. The new parents gazed at their little girl. She was tiny, but perfect. Paul picked up the lid of the coffin, carefully set it in place, and nailed it shut.

They chose a place behind the house among a grove of trees for Emily's resting place. During the summer, it was a quiet glen in the midst of the lush forest. Patrick and Clint had dug a small grave and now Kate stood among friends while Paul placed the tiny coffin in the frozen earth.

Kate didn't want to look, but she couldn't take her eyes off the casket. Her child lay inside. How was it possible?

Her little girl would never know the love of her parents,

the smell of summer lilies, or the warmth of her mother's arms. And Kate would never see Emily smile, never hear her laugh, or feel her pudgy arms about her neck and the drop of a wet kiss on her cheek. Tears rolled down her face. So many dreams lost. Why?

Paul took his place beside Kate and tucked her arm into his. They didn't look at each other. Paul's eyes held a depth of sorrow Kate knew reflected her own. She didn't want to see it.

Patrick stepped to the front of the group, removed his hat, and tucked it under one arm. He opened a large black Bible and read, "'To everything there is a season, and a time for every purpose under heaven. A time to be born, and a time to die; a time to plant, and a time to pluck that which is planted; a time to kill, and a time to heal; a time to break down, and a time to build up; a time to weep, and a time to laugh; a time to mourn, and a time to dance; a time to cast away stones, and a time to gather stones together; a time to embrace, and a time to refrain from embracing; a time to get, and a time to lose; a time to keep, and a time to cast away; a time to rend, and a time to sew; a time to keep silence, and a time to speak; a time to love, and a time to hate; a time of war, and a time of peace.'"

He closed the Bible and looked at the handful of people with eyes filled with sorrow. He turned his gaze to the new grave with its little coffin. "Lord, we know life and death is not in our power to decide. Only you can make such a weighty decision. And we trust it to you. We thank you for little Emily. Even though she never breathed of this earth, she has given her parents many hours of joy. And she is in your kingdom now where she waits for a reunion. We praise you for your promises and for the hope that we have in you." He glanced at Paul and Kate.

Kate felt as if her heart were being ripped from her chest.

She leaned heavily on Paul, afraid she couldn't stand under the weight of grief. The sorrow cut her heart so deeply she wondered how it could keep beating.

Patrick continued, "Your Word says you will bind up the brokenhearted. We trust you and ask that you place a healing balm upon our hearts. We thank you for your everlasting presence and the gift of your love. As you take little Emily into your arms and hold her close, we ask that you bless us with the peace that surpasses all understanding. Amen."

Kate wanted to be the one holding Emily. Why had God selfishly taken her?

It wasn't God. She had insisted on going with Paul.

Patrick placed his hat on his head and looked at Paul and Kate, his brows furrowed, eyes awash with tears. He picked up a shovel and handed it to Kate.

She stepped forward, and stared at the coffin. She didn't want to put dirt over her little girl. And then strength flowed through her as she remembered, *For dust you are and to dust you shall return.* She pushed the spade into the mound of earth, scooped up a small amount, and tossed it on top of the wooden box. She gave Paul the shovel and he added another scoop of soil. He returned the spade to Patrick. Paul and Kate watched as Patrick and Clint covered the grave and pounded a marker into the ground.

"You two take all the time you want," Patrick said. "Me, Sassa, and the kids will be at the house."

Sassa, eyes awash with tears, pulled Kate into her arms. She held her for a long moment, then turned and took Patrick's arm. The children walked quietly in front of their parents toward the trail that led to their house. Sassa sniffled into a handkerchief.

Clint set his hat on his head and with a nod toward Paul and Kate he stepped back. Lily handed Teddy to him, then moved to her friends. She hugged Paul and then Kate. Tears spilled onto her cheeks. "I'm so sorry. So sorry." She joined Clint. With Teddy bundled up close to him, Clint grasped Lily's hand and they walked away.

Snow started to fall. White crystals froze on the fresh mound of earth. Soon the grave would be buried, the marker no longer visible. Kate couldn't bear the thought. She ought to go, but how could she leave her little Emily alone beneath the earth?

Paul placed an arm around Kate and she looked up at him. He stared at the grave, his chin quivering, tears running unchecked down his cheeks. Kate grabbed him about the waist and buried her face in his coat. Sobs rose from deep inside. It wasn't fair. It wasn't right.

When she was cried out, Paul said, "It's time to go. Do you think you can make it?"

She nodded and, with their arms intertwined, they walked away.

The time at Patrick and Sassa's dragged. Kate felt like a shadow—not fully present. Sassa offered a meal of meat, bread, and cheese. Kate tried to eat, but her throat wouldn't allow her to swallow. Lily was saying something about summer plans, but Kate couldn't focus on the conversation.

Paul stood with the men. They talked about hunting, trapping, and their latest adventures. Paul acted like he was listening, but every few minutes, he'd look at Kate. Their eyes would meet and they knew—they would never be the same.

Kate was thankful when Paul suggested they leave. They walked home in silence, Kate's mind trapped in a loop of memories—the birth, lifeless little Emily, a casket instead of a cradle, the burial. Kate tried to shut it off, but it continued to wind through her thoughts again and again.

Snow blew sideways in a sharp wind that howled across

the creek. Kate thought it strange that she didn't feel the cold. When they reached the cabin, Paul helped her up the steps and inside, then went to care for the dogs. She looked around the house. The storm bellowed outside. Inside it was cold and quiet, like a tomb. Kate slumped to the sofa—Emily couldn't hear the storm.

She sat, not knowing what to do. There should be a baby needing a meal or a changing. Kate should be admiring her little one—cradling it against her shoulder. But there was none of that, only emptiness. The baby that had been her constant companion for months—kicking, squirming, and hiccupping, waking her in the middle of the night—now she was gone. Kate's womb and her arms were empty.

Kate sat for a while and finally picked up a book that Paul had been reading. She opened it and stared at a page without seeing it. Finally, she closed it and set it on the occasional table. With a heavy sigh she headed for the bedroom and undressed. She was tired. Only yesterday, she'd given birth. She donned her nightgown, then climbed into bed and pulled the blankets up under her chin and rolled onto her side. Sleep. She craved sleep.

Kate closed her eyes, but her mind carried her to the grave. She heard the sound of the door opening, accompanied by the howl and chill of the wind as it swept into the house. She could hear Paul stoke the fire and the aroma of burning wood drifted on the air. Angel walked into the room and stood beside the bed. With a whine she rested her chin on the edge of the mattress. When Kate didn't reach for her, she nuzzled Kate's hand.

"Not now, girl."

Angel watched Kate, then finally lay down on the floor beside the bed.

Kate stared at the wall as daylight faded away in the window. When Paul came in, he moved carefully and quietly. Kate felt the bed give as he climbed in beside her, careful not to touch her.

"I'm awake," she said quietly, keeping her back to him.

"I thought you'd be sleeping."

"Can't." She felt Paul leave the bed and heard him open his medical bag.

He returned to the bedside. "Here take this." He held out a spoon of some sort of liquid. "It will help."

Kate took the bitter elixir. What did it matter?

He draped an arm over her and pulled her close. They lay like that for a long time, neither of them speaking, but Kate felt stronger because of him.

"I'm sorry," Paul said. "I let you down. I shouldn't have allowed you to come with me and . . ." His words were choked off.

Kate clasped his hand. "It wasn't your fault. I wanted to go. I insisted." She was angry with herself. "I had to have my way."

"I knew better. And when the baby came, I should have been able to save it. I didn't know how."

"There was nothing you could do."

"You don't understand."

Kate could hear the words stick in his throat. "It's not your fault," she said, rolling over and facing him. When she saw the anguish in his eyes, she wished she'd kept her back to him.

"I have a knack for killing people—not doing the right thing, not knowing enough."

"That's not true. You're a wonderful, kind man and you're a good doctor. The baby just came too early. She was too small."

Paul stared at her. "I killed my wife and my son."

Kate didn't know how to reply to his statement. She'd

wanted to know what had happened in San Francisco. Now was the time, but she was empty with nothing to give. Now she didn't want to know. "What happened?" she asked reluctantly.

Paul closed his eyes. When he opened them, he looked past Kate, as if he were seeing something. "I knew Susan was ill. I told her to go to the hospital, but she said she was fine, and I let her have her way. I should have insisted she go. Instead I did nothing to save her." His eyes pooled with tears. "A good doctor, a good man would have been firm and resolute."

"What happened?"

"She hadn't been feeling well—terrible headaches, pain in her abdomen, dizziness, and swelling in her hands and feet. I knew the signs. I'd seen it before. I should have done something."

Kate thought her pain couldn't be worse, but now she felt the weight of Paul's piled on top of what she already carried—this terrible heartache he bore all these years. Her tears were now for him. She rested a hand on his.

"I . . . I came home . . . after working my shift at the hospital. And I found her on the hallway floor. She was still alive, but she couldn't move or speak." He stopped and looked as if he were there again, seeing his wife like that for the first time. "I picked her up and carried her to the car and drove as fast as I dared to the hospital." He stopped and took in a shuddering breath. "She never recovered. We tried to save the baby, but it was too late."

Kate closed her eyes and prayed that God would renew her husband's broken heart. She took his face in her hands, her eyes brimming. "You did all you could. You couldn't do more. It was your love that allowed Susan to do what she wanted. You understood that she felt secure at home. You were being the gentleman you are." Kate wished there were something more she could say or do that would wipe away his sorrow.

She pressed her forehead against his. "Sometimes us women
. . . we think we know everything by what we feel in our gut.
And sometimes we're wrong. You aren't responsible for what
happened to Susan."

"Better to be a doctor than a gentleman." Paul closed his
eyes and a sob bubbled up from inside. And then it was as if
the floodgates of anguish were opened as one sob followed
another.

Kate wrapped her arms around him and pulled him close.
Lord, help him. He's a good man. Help us.

———————

Paul made Kate stay in bed for a week, but after that, one
day melded into the next as they did their best to return to
a normal routine. No matter what they did, nothing was as
it should be. Instead of taking runs, they remained close to
home, staying busy with chores. Paul had noticed that Kate
placed a hand on her abdomen from time to time. She didn't
say anything, but he knew she longed for her child. He wished
there were a way to get that day back, to make a wiser choice.
And he longed for just one day when he didn't think about
what had happened to Kate and to Susan.

One morning he left the cache with fresh bait. Knowing
he'd be home for a few weeks, he'd decided to put out a trapline. It was time to check it. He didn't really care whether he
caught anything or not, but it kept him busy. And he wasn't
even sure he wanted to go back to working as a doctor. He
didn't want to be part of someone else's heartache. He had
enough of his own.

He started toward the sled when he saw Kate. She knelt
over the grave and cleared away freshly fallen snow. His heart
squeezed. After every snowfall, she made sure to brush away
the snow. He'd be glad for spring, but even as the thought

came to him, he knew she'd still tend their daughter's resting place, making sure it was clear of weeds and keeping fresh flowers on it. She wouldn't forget.

He cleaned off the sled, then unleashed the dogs. Buck seemed most anxious to go, so Paul placed him in front.

By the time he had all three dogs harnessed, Kate joined him. "I hope you have better luck today," she said, watching the dogs pace and whine. "They're ready for a run." She looked back at the cabin. "I wish Angel had been trained to pull a sled. I think she'd like it."

Paul smiled. "Nah. I think she was meant to fly. I doubt she'd take to a harness." He pulled his hood up. "I won't be gone long. With just one line and all three dogs we'll move along quickly. I'll be back in time for dinner."

"Good. I'm cooking up a couple of grouse, along with spuds and peas. Thought maybe I'd make biscuits too. You'll be hungry by the time you get back."

"You can count on it." He kissed her. "I'll be thinking about you," he said, wishing that when he returned they'd have something to talk about besides the mundane. They never discussed their future or the next run or Kate's job. Life felt aimless.

She rested a hand on his arm. "Be careful."

"I will." He stepped on the boards and called, "Hike up."

The dogs lunged forward and headed down the trail leading southeast away from the cabin. He looked over his shoulder. Kate stood watching him. When they were first married, he'd longed for the thrill that came with each day. Back then, life had seemed like one grand adventure. How quickly it had changed.

He tried to keep his mind on the task at hand, reading the terrain and the depth of the snow and guiding the dogs. They'd had a heavy snowfall the last few days, which most likely buried his traps. The air was cold but not as frigid as it had been. He glanced at the sky where a patch of blue appeared in the cloud cover.

Buck, who was generally obedient and steady, wasn't listening to his commands. Paul had to correct him several times. He decided to place Nita up front. While he was moving Buck into the second position, the dog lunged toward Jackpot and tore into him. Jackpot responded and the two dogs ripped at each other.

"No! Enough!" Paul shouted, yanking the dogs apart. He dragged Buck back into position. "What's wrong with you today?" Paul asked, but he knew. Buck was the dog Paul felt closest to and when Paul was out of sorts so was Buck. "Sorry, boy. I know it's not your fault. Things will be better soon."

With the dogs back in place, they set off. Paul had only a handful of traps left to check. He hadn't stopped to eat and he was hungry, so he hurried, knowing Kate was preparing dinner.

When he reached the next trap, he called the dogs to a halt. Getting down on his knees, he pulled the trap out from beneath spruce boughs. It was still set and had a chunk of meat in it. He removed the moose meat and tossed it to Nita, who gobbled it down. Taking a chunk of salmon, Paul set it in the trap and moved it back into place beneath the boughs. He pulled the jaws apart, but he was in too big a hurry, and when he tried to set the spring, the trap snapped shut on his hand, biting through his gloves and into the flesh of his hand.

"Ahhh!" Paul clenched his teeth. Pain radiated through his hand.

He pried the trap open and pulled its teeth out of his skin and his glove. He could feel blood flowing, so he quickly removed his glove and clamped his other hand down tightly on the wounds.

"Dang it." He hurried to the sled and dug into his pack for a cloth. He took a quick look at the lacerations, but there was too much blood to see how bad the damage was. He wrapped the injury tightly and held it for several minutes. When he thought the bleeding might have stopped, he removed the wrapping, cleaned the hand with snow, then examined it. The teeth had bit deeply into the soft part of his palm. He wiggled his fingers and bent them. No broken bones. That was good. It had started bleeding again, so he rewrapped it. His hand pulsed with pain.

Paul looked up the trail and tried to decide whether to go on or return home. He wasn't of much use this way, so he headed back to the cabin.

When he pulled into the yard, Kate stepped onto the porch. "Do you need help with pelts?"

"No. I didn't catch anything, except my hand." He lifted his bandaged, bloody appendage.

Kate hurried down the steps and ran across the yard. "Are you all right?" She gently took his hand in hers. "What happened?"

"Got careless and a trap bit me. I'll be fine, just need to get it cleaned and bandaged. Good thing it's my left hand."

"I'll put the dogs up and feed them," Kate said.

"You sure you're up to it?"

"I'm completely fit," Kate said. "And a lot better off than you are."

"Okay," Paul agreed reluctantly and trudged toward the house. Once indoors, he hung up his coat and then moved to the sink. He washed both hands with soap and water, washing the wound thoroughly. Gritting his teeth against the pain, he scrubbed it until he was convinced it was clean. He took a closer look. The puncture wounds were deep and would likely become infected. No telling what kind of bacteria festered

196

on the teeth of a leghold trap. He put cold water and soap in a bowl, then added hot water from the kettle, then moved to the table and sat with his hand soaking.

A few minutes later, Kate walked in and sat at the table beside him. "Is it bad?"

"Nah. It'll be fine."

"Let me have a look."

"So, you're the doctor now," Paul teased.

Kate gave him a disgruntled look.

Paul held up the hand and allowed her to examine it. "It looks nasty. It'll need some antiseptic."

"Yeah, I figured that out," Paul said sarcastically. "Can you get my bag?"

Kate retrieved Paul's medical bag from the bedroom. He took out a bottle of Listerine. "Can you open it for me?"

Kate unscrewed the lid. "Hold out your hand," she said.

Paul did as instructed, this time without any barbed remarks. Kate poured the liquid antiseptic slowly while Paul rotated his hand under the flow of medication.

"Okay. That's good," he said. He dabbed at the moisture, then allowed Kate to bandage the injury. His hand throbbed, but he kept that to himself.

"Do you need anything else?" Kate asked, pouring the water down the drain while Paul returned the supplies to his bag and closed it.

"Dinner. That's what I need. I'm starved."

The following day, Paul finished up the trapline, and returned with one fox and one marten. His hand ached, so when Kate volunteered to help him skin out the animals, he gladly accepted. Once indoors, with Kate's assistance, he changed the bandages. His hand was swollen and red. The pain was worse than the day before.

"It doesn't look too good," Kate said.

"It's not unusual. But it probably wouldn't be a bad idea to wash it again with Listerine. I'm waiting on an order for more sulpha powder."

Once the hand had been doctored and rebandaged, Paul moved to his chair in the front room. Kate offered him coffee.

"No thanks. Not tonight. I think I'll go to bed early."

Kate sat on the sofa. "Thanksgiving is in another two weeks. I was wondering what you wanted to do."

Paul shrugged. "Whatever you want is fine with me."

"If I could, I'd go to my parents' place. Mom has a way of making every holiday special." Kate let out a sigh. "But since we can't do that, I think I'd like to spend it here, just the two of us."

"Sure. We'll have a nice meal together. I've got a goose out in the cache." Paul rested his bad hand in the other and winced at the movement.

"Are you sure your hand is all right?"

"It's sore. But that's to be expected." Paul didn't want to worry her. She had enough to think about. But if his hand was worse tomorrow, he could be in real trouble. "I think I'll hit the sack. I'm tired." He moved across the room, kissed Kate good night, and walked into the bedroom. Since the baby, they seemed to go to bed separately most of the time.

When Paul woke the following morning, the first thing he was aware of was the throbbing in his hand. His head ached and he didn't feel well. Kate was still asleep, so he got up quietly and went into the kitchen. He sat at the table and unwrapped the bandage. His hand felt warm to the touch and was more swollen and red than the previous day. The punctures oozed pus.

Kate walked into the room and peered over his shoulder. "Oh Paul, that looks awful. You need to see a doctor."

"I am a doctor."

"You know what I mean. I think you need to go to the hospital."

Paul blew out a sharp breath. "Yeah. It needs to be lanced and cleaned. I'd rather not have to do that to myself."

They quickly packed up and headed for the plane. Once in the air, Kate seemed to perk up.

"You almost look happy," Paul said.

"I feel better. I should have gotten off the ground sooner." She leaned over and kissed him. "I'm sorry the reason we're flying is because of your injury, but I'm glad to be in the air again."

Paul held up his hand. "If you feel better, it's worth it."

After landing in Anchorage, Sidney gave Paul and Kate a ride to the house. "Good thing I was at the airfield. Don't think Jack would've left—too afraid of missing a trip." Sidney grinned, then almost apologetically he added, "Money's tight for everyone." He pulled up in front of the house.

Paul started to climb out.

"You stay put," Kate said. "I'll take care of everything." She carried the knapsack inside, closed Angel indoors, then hurried back to the car. "Let's get the doctor to a doctor," she said and Sidney headed for the hospital.

Just as Paul had thought, the wound needed to be lanced and cleaned. The doctor on call was pretty sure it would be fine, but asked that Paul return in a few days to have it checked. "No reason to take any chances," he said, cutting off the last piece of tape and pressing it down on the bandage.

Sidney dropped Paul and Kate at the house and drove away. Just as they stepped inside, the telephone rang. Kate answered it.

"Hello." She listened, then said, "Just a moment," and turned to Paul. "It's for you. From San Francisco."

Paul moved to the telephone. Before he spoke, he took a deep breath. "Hello. This is Paul Anderson."

"Paul, is that you?"

Paul recognized his brother's voice. "Robert. Yeah. It's me, all right."

"How are you doing?"

"I'm fine. How'd you know to call me here?"

"I got the number from a fella at the general store. Said he thought you were out at the creek, but I figured it was worth a try to call anyway."

"Is everything all right?"

Robert was silent for a long moment, then he said, "It's Mother. She's very ill."

"What's wrong?"

"Her heart is failing. She's been sick a long time. I didn't want to bother you with it, but now the doctor says she's dying—it could be days or weeks. I thought you'd want to know . . . maybe come home."

The room felt like it had tilted. Paul grabbed ahold of the counter. "They're sure?"

"Yes. You know Mother. She's keeping a stiff upper lip and all, but she's not looking good."

"I've got some things here—"

"It's been too long, Paul. Mother needs to see you. We all do."

Paul didn't know what to do. He couldn't leave Kate, but how could he not go home? "I'll talk to Kate and get back to you."

"Okay, but don't take too long."

"I won't." Paul hung up and turned to Kate.

"What do you need to talk to me about?"

"My mother's dying. Her heart is failing. But with everything that's happened . . ."

"Paul, you have to go. It's your mother."

— 17 —

Tucking his ticket into his coat pocket, Paul opened the door of the depot for Kate and followed her out. In an effort to keep an optimistic tone, he said, "Good thing we called right away. I got the last seat available. Seems everyone's heading south before winter." His smile couldn't erase the heartache he felt. He hated to leave Kate. It was the worst time possible.

"Yeah, good thing," Kate said, as a cutting burst of wind swirled bits of ice and snow inside the covered platform. She tucked an arm into Paul's and leaned against him.

Paul circled an arm around her shoulders and pulled her close. "I don't have to go."

"Yes you do." Kate met his eyes. "Once your mother is gone, you won't have another chance. I'll be here when you get home."

"But—"

Kate pressed her gloved fingers against his lips. "I have Helen and Muriel here in town and Sassa and Lily at the homestead. I won't be alone."

Paul nodded and tried to blink back his tears. He knew she was right, but leaving her felt wrong.

"Paul . . . maybe this is just what you need . . . to heal the hurt you carry inside." She kissed him gently. "I think it's providence that the ship sails tomorrow. It would be terrible if you'd had to wait." Kate watched the snow fall. "No telling how long this weather will keep planes on the ground."

"Hope the tracks stay clear so I don't miss the boat," Paul said, relenting to the inevitable, his mind turning to his mother.

"Maybe the weather will improve as you head south."

"There's a good chance. My stomach will be happier. It doesn't appreciate rough seas." He chuckled, but the sound of it was hollow. "I'll be glad to get into Seattle."

"Does your train leave the same day?"

"The day after. I was told to be at the train depot by 7:00 a.m. on the eighteenth. I should make San Francisco late on the twentieth."

Kate wrapped her arms around his waist and held him tightly. "I'll be thinking about you on Thanksgiving." She couldn't disguise her melancholy.

"This was supposed to be our first Thanksgiving together." Paul rested his chin on the top of her head. The idea of their being apart during the holiday made his stomach ache.

"I know. But it'll be nice for you to be with your family."

"It's been a long time . . . with my mother so ill, I doubt anyone will be in a holiday mood."

"Of course. But what a blessing that you'll have each other." Kate's cheery voice sounded phony. She gave him another squeeze.

Paul knew better. He had run out on them. "I doubt Audrey will be happy to see me."

"Audrey?"

"My youngest sister." He let out a sigh. "She always says what she thinks and usually doesn't consider how it sounds."

"Why wouldn't she be happy to see you?"

"I left when she needed me. She and Susan were very close."

"Oh dear. But she must understand."

"I hope so." He forced a smile. "She's not so bad really. She has a good heart. But she'll give me a piece of her mind."

"Certainly no one holds you responsible for Susan's death."

"Guess I'll find out."

"The only one who needs to forgive you is you. You're the one holding on to the guilt. Until you can let go, you'll be miserable." Kate looked up at him. "I know all too well. Even when I understood that God had forgiven me for Alison's death, I wasn't able to forgive myself."

Paul cleared his throat. "I know what you're saying. I appreciate it . . . but it's not just something a person decides to do. I can't seem to get it from my brain to my heart."

"Paul, you have to let God in. He'll do it *for* you." Another gust of wind and ice blew in under the roof. Kate shivered. "I wish I could have flown you down."

"I'd have liked that. But there's no reason to take the risk. And I don't know how long I'll have to stay. I'd hate for you to fly back by yourself."

Kate stepped in front of him and planted her hands on her hips. "I made my very first trip north by myself."

"Yes, and if I remember correctly it was summer." Paul grinned. "I expect the weather was a bit balmier." He tweaked her nose. "I'd worry about you every moment. And to tell you the truth, I've got enough on my mind." He stuck his hands in his pockets.

"I know. I wish life was easier." Kate's eyes swamped with tears. "We've lost so much." She rested her hands on his arms. "Sometimes it feels like everything is about pain and loss."

Paul pulled Kate to him and held her against his chest. She pressed her forehead against his coat and clung to him.

For a long while neither of them spoke. Paul looked down the tracks. The train was late. "I pray I make it in time . . . before my mother dies. I have so much to tell her." He took a ragged breath. "Today, six days on the ship and then another two on the train—it's a long time."

The sharp blast of a train whistle carried on the wind. "That must be it," Paul said.

Kate glanced up the track, then handed him a basket of food. "Don't forget this. You'll get hungry." Her smile was tremulous. "Helen added some cookies and sweet bread."

"Thank her for me."

Kate stared at Paul, as if she were trying to memorize his face.

"The days will go quickly," Paul reassured her. "I'll be back before you know it."

Kate nodded, but Paul thought he saw doubt in her eyes. "Of course. It's just that you've never been so far away."

Paul had not been home to California since Kate had known him. What if he fell into step with his old life? Would he want to stay? He'd had a life there—a home, a career, a family. Panic struck a rhythm in Kate's chest. What if he realized he'd made a mistake by leaving California? What if he decided San Francisco was home?

Paul looped an arm around Kate's waist and the two of them watched the train pull into the station amidst a cloud of steam and rasping steel as the wheels ground to a stop. The doors were opened and people disembarked. All of a sudden the station was crowded with passengers. People greeted one another while others said farewells.

"I'll be back as soon as I can." Paul held Kate's face in his hands. "I promise." He kissed her. "I'll be thinking of you every day."

Kate placed her hands over his. "Me too."

Paul pulled her into an embrace. "You'll be with me and . . . the baby too." He pressed his cheek against hers.

Kate clung to him, then stepped away. "I'll be fine."

"Promise me you won't spend Thanksgiving alone."

"I promise. I have lots of friends." She took his bandaged hand, and gently dropped a kiss on it. "You take care of this hand. Have the ship's doctor see to it."

"I will."

"Board! All aboard!" a porter shouted.

"I love you," Paul said.

"I love you." Kate kissed him. "Go. It's time."

Paul walked to the train and climbed aboard. At the top of the steps he turned and looked back, then disappeared inside. Kate watched for him, and when he sat in a seat next to the window, she waved. He waved back at her, then the two gazed at each other. For reasons Kate didn't understand, this felt like a final good-bye. What was wrong with her?

When the train moved slowly south, Kate wanted to run after it, to stop it, to tell Paul to stay. She felt silly. It wouldn't be that long and she'd see him again.

The recent bout of cold weather had frozen the creek solid enough to land on, but the landing strip would need work. Kate made a pass over the frozen stream. It looked good, although there was some windblown snow. Angel stood on the seat and whined. She was glad to be home.

Kate brought the aircraft in cautiously, watching for small berms that might catch the tip of a ski. She made a clean landing.

Smoke rose from the cabin's chimney. Someone must have sent word that she was on her way. Her eyes misted. She'd been blessed with good friends. But just seeing the cabin brought back painful memories that snagged her frayed heart.

Kate climbed out of the plane, secured it, drained the oil, and then tarped it. The snow had stopped and the wind was quiet, but one thing she knew about Alaska was the weather changed like a drifting wind. The Pacemaker needed to be prepared for whatever came along.

Kate grabbed her pack and the mail she'd brought for Clint and Sassa, then trudged across the frozen creek and up the trail to the house. The dogs were barking. Angel took off ahead of Kate to say her hellos.

When Kate stepped into the yard, she gave the place a quick inspection. Everything seemed in order. She set her bag and the mail on the porch, then joined Angel and greeted the dogs. Their tails flew with excitement. Kate noticed the water in their dishes wasn't frozen, so someone must have recently fed and watered them. She smiled and again counted herself blessed. She gave each dog a warm hello, then let them off their leads. They ran and jumped and tousled in the snow. Kate watched, thinking they were like children. She'd let them have their freedom for a while and then return them to their leads.

She headed for the house, and when she lifted her bag and the mail, she heard a familiar cawing sound. "Jasper! You're back!" She wanted to reach out and stroke the raven's shiny black feathers but knew he wouldn't tolerate it. She'd have to write Paul and let him know the bird had returned. He'd be glad. "Welcome home, you rascal," she said as she moved to the door. The bird looked at her with his small black eyes. Kate opened the door and stepped inside.

The first thing she noticed was the smell of coffee and freshly baked pastries. Tears sprang to her eyes. Tears were always close. No doubt Sassa and Lily were behind the goodies. A basket and a plate with bread and a block of cheese wrapped in waxed paper sat on the table. Beside it was a note. Kate picked it up. "Welcome home. Thought you might be hungry." There was no signature. There was no need for one.

Kate lifted a plaid kitchen towel off the basket, which held fresh muffins—berry and apple. She draped the towel back over, then moved to the bedroom and set her bag on the bed. The room was quiet and cool—empty. How long would it be before Paul returned? And where was the cradle that belonged beside her bed?

Before her emotions overran her, she returned to the kitchen and poured herself a cup of coffee. It was good and strong, just what she needed. She sat at the table and gazed out the window. She was tired, too tired. Her eyes went to the glen where her baby lay. Tomorrow, she'd clear away the snow.

After finishing off the coffee, Kate moved to the door and headed for the cache to retrieve dried fish for each of the dogs. She dropped the food in their plates and then called them. The brush crackled, announcing their return, and a moment later they broke free of the forest. Buck was in the lead and he slammed into Kate.

"Hey, be careful," Kate said, petting him.

Catching the smell of food, he pounced on his meal just as the other dogs trotted into the clearing, tongues lolling. They ignored Kate and went straight for their bowls. Angel held back, knowing better than to challenge any one of her canine friends over a meal.

Kate secured them to their leads, then moved to the house. Angel pranced along beside her, knowing her meal was waiting. Kate grabbed a chunk of fish off the edge of the porch and moved inside the cabin, where she placed it in Angel's bowl. The dog quickly went to work on the food.

Kate hung her parka on the hook inside the door, clicked on the radio, and moved to the overstuffed chair in the living room and dropped into it. She gazed around the room. It was too empty. She needed Paul. She needed her baby girl. Kate dropped her head against the back of the chair and closed her eyes, trying to suppress the rising ache inside.

She didn't know how long she sat there, but soon dusk settled over the landscape and the house turned cool. Kate pushed out of the chair, lit the lanterns, and added wood to the stove. Her empty stomach rumbled, reminding her she hadn't eaten since breakfast. After refilling her coffee cup, she took a plate down from the cupboard and a knife from a drawer and sat at the table. She sliced off a piece of bread and a wedge of cheese and ate. She'd thank Sassa and Lily in the morning.

Angel lay with her head over Kate's feet, seeming to know her mistress needed to feel her closeness. The clock hanging from the wall whispered the time with each pass of the pendulum. The fire crackled.

Paul should have made it to Seward by now, if there hadn't been a delay. The ship was scheduled to leave at 8:00 a.m. the next morning. The thought of him sailing off made her long for him more. Maybe she should have gone with him. *No. His first meeting with his family, after all this time, should be between them alone. I don't belong there.* They needed time to reconnect and to settle questions and grievances. And of course his mother needed him. Kate would only be in the way.

She finished her dinner, then washed the knife and plate, dried them, and returned the dishes to the cupboard and the knife to its place in the drawer. With that done, she turned and looked at the empty room. If only Lily or Sassa would stop by. She glanced at the dark window. Of course they wouldn't. It was late and they'd want her to rest. She considered reading but doubted she had enough energy even for something that simple. Bed was where she needed to be.

The radio crackled and Jack's voice came at her out of the stillness. "This is Anchorage Airport. Come in, Kate. Over."

Kate hurried to the table and sat down in front of the radio, clicking on the speaker. "This is Kate. What can I do for you, Jack? Over."

"We have an emergency. A couple of fellas didn't return from a moose hunt. We're sending out search planes first thing in the morning. We'll need as many eyes as we can get. Over."

"I'll be there. Over."

"Good. See you tomorrow. Over and out."

Kate clicked off the radio. She felt better, knowing she had something to do with the next day. She'd dreaded having too much time to fill.

A quick trip to the Warrens' and she'd arranged for the care of the dogs. There was little time for chatting, so she was soon home again where she packed a bag for the morning, set the oil pot beside the stove, and headed for bed.

Kate lay in the dark, her mind unwilling to rest. All she could think of was Paul. She prayed for him. She knew he was still grieving for their little girl and now . . . his mother. It was too much, even for a resilient man like Paul. Sorrow sat heavy in the pit of her stomach and kept her awake most of the night. She was thankful when it was time to get up.

She climbed out of bed and put the pail of oil on the stove, along with the coffeepot. After dressing, she made herself some toast and drank warm, weak coffee, then using a flashlight to find her way, she headed for the plane. Angel trotted alongside her, seeming eager to be on the move.

The air was chill and a sharp breeze whisked Kate's hair into a frenzy as she readied the plane in the dark. She cranked the flywheel and climbed aboard, thankful to shut out the wind. She wanted to get in the air. Angel took her place in the front passenger seat, and Kate settled behind the control wheel and fired up the engine. Just as she spotted a crease of light along the horizon, she taxied down the airfield and lifted off.

When she reached Anchorage, Kate could see that an all-out search was in process. The airfield was empty of planes, all except Alan's. Cars were lined up in front of the shop. Leaving the engine running and Angel in her seat, Kate ran across the field to the office.

"I got here as fast as I could," she blurted when she stepped inside.

Alan stood at the workbench, a young man beside him. He looked like your average Joe, nothing to write home about—medium build with a mop of unruly brown hair that fell into his eyes. He brushed it aside, revealing eyes that held humor and expectation.

Alan straightened. "I'm just about ready to head out. I'd like you to meet my friend, Donald Harrison. He's a pilot too."

"Nice to meet you, Donald." Kate held out her hand and shook his.

"Good to meet you."

"Hey Jack," Alan said. "Since we're in need of pilots right now, how about giving Donald a chance. He's just up from Sacramento."

Jack eyed the young man suspiciously. "You got your own plane?"

"Yes sir. I sure do." Donald smiled, revealing overly large teeth that stuck out slightly in front.

"What kind of experience you got?"

"Well, sir, I've been flying for a few years. About five years ago, I took lessons and went out and got myself a plane.

Since then I've had odd jobs, but mostly I've been hauling passengers and cargo between Sacramento and Los Angeles."

"What makes you think you can fly in Alaska? It's nothing like the namby-pamby kind of stuff you've been doing."

Donald looked at the floor and stuck his thumbs into his front pants pockets. He glanced at Alan and then Kate and finally settled his gaze on Jack. "Figure it'll take me awhile to get the hang of things up here, but I'm a good pilot. You'll see, if you'll just give me a chance to prove myself. I'll take any runs you got, not passengers, just freight. And when you think I'm ready, I'll do any kind of flying you want."

Jack mumbled something about greenhorns, then picked a dead stogie out of the ashtray and stuck it between his lips. The room was silent. Jack lit the cigar and took several quick, small puffs. When the end of the cigar glowed red, he removed it from his mouth and studied it for a moment. "You on the level?"

Donald's skin turned slightly pink. "Yes sir," he said.

"Don't ever show up here half-swacked. You do and you're out."

Donald lifted his hands up. "No sir. I won't. I swear. I never touch liquor."

Jack pushed to his feet. "All right. I'll give you a chance. But don't disappoint me."

Donald smiled broadly. He stepped toward Jack with his hand extended.

Jack shook it. "Well, get out there. We have missing men."

"I was thinking he'd fly with me today, since he doesn't know the territory," Alan said. "And I can use an extra pair of eyes."

"Okay. Sure."

The two pilots headed out, the wind breezing in as they opened the door.

He looked up from a graph on his desk. "Glad to see you," he said, surprising Kate with his respectful tone. "Sidney and Kenny are already out lookin' and now Alan and what's his name. There's a pilot from Merrill Field too." He leaned over the graph. "There are two men out there. They were hunting in the Copper River Basin and were last seen ten days ago. They were supposed to return three days ago, but there's been no sign of them and no word. The families are in a tailspin." He turned to the map. "Right now I have pilots searching these areas." He pointed at sections on the map. "I need you to take the south end."

Kate leaned over and studied the map. Paul's ship should be leaving port about now. She tried to focus and felt guilty that her mind was on him instead of the missing hunters. "Okay. I'm on it." She took the charted map and headed for the door. "I'll radio in if I see anything."

Jack studied Kate. There was no hint of his usual antagonism or frustration. Finally, with a nod, he turned his attention back to the charts spread across his desk.

Kate and the other pilots searched for five days, but finally bad weather grounded them. There was little to no hope that the men had survived. Most likely the families would have to wait until spring thaw to discover what had become of them. Or they might never know.

While Kate signed out and prepared to catch a ride to her house with Sidney, Jack leaned back in his chair. "Good work, Kate."

Had she heard him right? Jack had never thanked her or offered encouragement of any kind. What was he up to? "I wish we'd found those guys. I hate to think of them out there, maybe still alive and suffering."

"They're not suffering. By now, they're long gone." Jack's jaw was tightly squared. Then he looked at Kate. "I've been hard on you. 'Course a lot of it you deserved." He tried to smile, but couldn't quite pull it off. "I just want to say that I'm . . . well, I'm sorry about what happened . . . with the baby." He folded his arms over his chest, clearly uncomfortable in the role of comforter.

Kate wasn't sure how to respond. This was so unlike Jack. She managed to say, "I appreciate that."

"Yeah. I can't imagine how it would be." A gust of wind blew down the chimney and smoke roiled out of the stove. "Dang it! Need to replace that piece of rust. Barely keeps this place warm." He pushed out of his chair and strode toward the stove.

The rare moment had passed. "I'll see ya," Kate said and stepped outside.

The temperatures had held steadily in the teens and wind blew snow sideways. Kate bundled inside her coat and ran toward Sidney's car.

Sliding in, she said, "Thanks for the ride."

"No problem." Looking weary, he scrubbed at several days' growth of beard. "Hate to think that those fellas are still out there. I pray they stumbled onto a cabin. Maybe we'll have a nice surprise one of these days and find out they survived."

He leaned over the steering wheel and scraped ice from the inside of the windshield. "The heater in this old rig barely keeps ya warm." He glanced at Kate. "You hear from Paul?"

"No. The ship's probably a day out of Seattle, so I doubt I'll hear anything until he makes San Francisco."

"Hope the trip wasn't too rough."

"Me too. And I hope his mother doesn't pass away before he gets there. It's been a long time since he was home."

"A shame. A pure shame. Man's gotta stay connected with family. Learned that the hard way." Sidney pulled onto the street. "Wish I'd had more time with my father before his stroke."

213

"You're out in Kenai all the time these days."

"Yeah. Now that he's gone. But I've got a lot of family out there." He shrugged. "So, how bad is Paul's mother?"

"Bad. Robert, Paul's brother, said she won't survive for long. I was hoping to meet her one day."

Sidney settled compassionate eyes on Kate. "And how are you?"

"Okay. Work has been good for me. Gives me less time to think."

"Good." Sidney nodded, looking as if he was fishing around in his mind for something more to say. Finally, he asked, "So, do you have plans for Thanksgiving?"

Kate hadn't given the holiday any thought. "I don't know. I'll be on the homestead. The Warrens will probably invite me over."

"Nice folks." He grinned. "That Sassa, she's full of sass." He laughed.

"She is," Kate said, trying to sound cheerful. But the idea of spending Thanksgiving with Sassa wasn't appealing at the moment. In truth, she didn't feel like celebrating anything. And she didn't feel thankful.

She and Paul had planned an intimate celebration, just the two of them and their unborn child. It would have been their first Thanksgiving as husband and wife. She rested a hand on her flat stomach. Paul was gone. She was lonely. And her womb was empty.

— 18 —

Paul gazed at the fog-shrouded bay as the train clacked its way across the lower deck of the Bay Bridge. He'd never been across the immense bridge before. It hadn't been built when he left San Francisco. In the distance skyscrapers, like tall, sturdy trees, stood amidst an eddy of fog.

His stomach twisted at the realization that he'd soon be greeting his family—people he'd cut out of his life seven years ago. Robert had promised to meet him, but Paul didn't know if any of the others would be with him. He expected a difficult reunion.

As the train moved into the city, memories bombarded him. This had once been home. As a youngster, life had been one big adventure. There was always something to do, somewhere to go. And after he'd married Susan, they'd explored the city together, enjoying the wide array of distractions. It had seemed an idyllic life . . . until the day Paul was reminded how unstable and treacherous even a perfect life could be.

A longing for his cabin and its solitude filled him like a hunger that could not be satisfied. He needed to be there, not in this place filled with pictures that glinted at him from the past.

The blast of the train whistle startled him and dragged Paul back to the present. He felt as if a weight had been placed on his chest, and he was sweating. He took a handkerchief from his coat pocket and wiped his brow. His hand still ached, but only slightly, thanks to the ship's doctor.

With a detached heart, he tried to concentrate on the city. It was just the place he'd come from, bigger and more congested than he remembered.

"Third and Townsend Depot. Five minutes," called a porter.

Paul's heart raced. He should have stayed in touch with his family. Guilt like a bore tide swept over him. How could his family forgive seven years?

He buttoned up his overcoat and put on his hat. It would be cold and miserably wet outdoors.

Was Robert waiting? Through the tragedy, Paul's departure, and the years that followed, his older brother had remained a steady presence, if only by the written word. He'd offered encouragement and grace. He'd asked for nothing. Paul was certain that wouldn't change now, but as to the rest of the family . . . If his youngest sister, Audrey, was with Robert today, she'd give Paul a tongue-lashing. Carolyn would be more reserved, but unable to disguise her hurt and disappointment. She and Susan had been fast friends. His brother Sean had been young, with his mind on girls and his new life as a student at San Francisco State College when Paul had left. Paul doubted he had cared.

His mind drifted to his mother. She'd always been strong as steel. When Susan died, she was the one who'd held the family together. Her faith never wavered. Paul wondered how she was holding up under her present difficult circumstances. He'd known that she'd eventually die, but not yet. He couldn't imagine the world without her in it.

As a doctor, he'd seen people in the final stages of heart

failure. It was not an easy death. Someone as good as his mother shouldn't suffer. He didn't know how he'd react when he saw her. Would he be able to put on a brave front?

He feared he'd see disappointment in her eyes. She hadn't deserved his long absence. All those years ago, it had seemed the only thing for him to do, and over time he'd never been able to confront his failure. He hadn't been thinking of anything but his own needs.

The train slowed as it approached the station, couplers chattering and steam hissing. Paul searched the platform for Robert. He spotted him right off. Robert was taller than most everyone else, and he stood erect with his shoulders back, watching the cars roll past. He looked a good deal like Paul, except he was larger in girth and height. Paul barely managed to suppress a groan when he saw Audrey standing beside him. She wore a smart white hat with a red bow that matched the color of her dress, which peeked out from the bottom of her belted trench coat. Blonde curls framed her face and her blue eyes searched the train. Paul stepped away from the window. He didn't want her to see him, not yet.

He waited until all the passengers had disembarked, then made his way down the narrow aisle to the door. Robert and Audrey were standing alongside the train, searching for him in the crowd of people. When Robert spotted him, his face lit up and he waved. Taking long strides, he headed straight for Paul.

Robert grasped Paul's hand and pulled him into a tight embrace. Emotions of love and gratitude sprang to life inside Paul. The two men held on to one another, then stepped back.

"Well, it's about time. I was beginning to think I'd never see you again." Robert clapped Paul on the upper arm. "You look good." His brown eyes shimmered with pleasure. "Oh Lord, it's good to see you." His eyes wandered to Paul's bandaged left hand. "What'd you do to yourself?"

"I tangled with a trap, but it's fine now." Paul gazed at Robert. "You look in top shape." He felt a swell of love for his brother. With less enthusiasm, he turned to Audrey.

She smiled up at him from beneath the brim of her stylish hat, and then threw her arms around his neck and hugged him. "Oh, I've missed you." She held on tight for a few moments, then stepped back. The smile had been replaced by pursed lips. "Why in heaven's name have you been up in that godforsaken wilderness all this time? You went off with barely a word and left us wondering and praying." She folded her arms over her chest. "And Mother. She never said an unkind word, but we all knew she was worried sick about you. And she needed you. She loved Susan too."

"I know. I'm sorry. I have no excuses."

"I'll be candid, I had a hard time forgiving you, mostly because of Mother." Audrey continued to glare at him for another moment, then her expression softened. "Well, you're home now." She hugged him again. "I'm glad you're here."

Robert rested a hand on Paul's back and looked back toward the train. "No Kate? We hoped we'd get to meet her."

"Not this trip."

"Of course, not in her condition," Robert said.

"Actually . . . Kate lost the baby a few weeks ago."

"Oh." Audrey's exclamation slipped from her lips. The brightness in her blue eyes dimmed. "I'm so sorry. How awful."

Paul didn't want to talk about the baby. It only reminded him that Kate was home, facing the loss on her own. If not for his foolhardiness, she'd still be eagerly awaiting the arrival of their little girl.

"Well, brother, Mother's waiting. Let's get your bags."

"How is she?"

"Looking forward to seeing you."

"No. I mean—"

"You know Mother. She's strong as steel . . . but with each day that passes she becomes physically weaker. She spends most days in bed. She could go at any time." Robert's eyes dimmed. "I think she's been waiting for you."

The trip home felt as if Paul was walking through memories. As they moved through the Financial District with its impressive French Renaissance architecture, he remembered trips into that part of town to do business with his father or with Robert. Union Square, with its Dewey Monument, was a place he'd spent a good deal of time. Susan had a penchant for fashion and one of her favorite places to shop was at O'Connor, Moffatt & Co. Sometimes he'd join her, and while she did her shopping, he'd visit with other men in the courtyard who were also waiting for their wives. Often, after Susan had completed her shopping, the two of them would share a picnic lunch on the lawns outside the plaza. It was fun to sit and chat outdoors and watch people come and go. His heart squeezed at the memory.

When his brother turned onto Franklin Street, Paul's mouth went dry. Was the entire family waiting for him? The car passed a parade of Victorian homes and then they reached the one where he'd grown up. It was a three-story house with a basement. He suddenly recalled a joke he and his brothers had pulled on his sisters. They'd convinced them that monsters lived in the basement. He smiled. Audrey had refused to set foot in the basement for two years, until their father insisted she face her fears.

He studied the house. It looked bigger than he remembered, perhaps because the cabin he'd grown accustomed to was so small. The house was painted an olive green and had rows of narrow windows with white panes that gazed down on the street. Bay windows with lace curtains rounded out the southwest corner of the house on all three floors. The yard was well tended, shrubs neatly trimmed and the gardens free of weeds. The trees were bare and smartly pruned. Broad brick steps led to a landing and windowed front doors. Paul's stomach tightened.

Robert pulled to the side of the street. Before he could get out and open Audrey's door, she'd climbed out on her own and was hurrying up the front steps.

Robert grabbed Paul's bag out of the trunk. "Figured you'd want to stay with Mother."

"Of course." Paul headed up the steps and walked into a tiled vestibule. A large crystal chandelier lit the interior entrance and a mahogany table with a mirror over it stood along one wall. Paul glanced in the mirror as he moved past to hang his coat on the coatrack.

Audrey waited at the foot of the stairs. "Mother's in her room."

Paul gave a nod. His stomach felt queasy.

Robert followed Paul inside. "I'll put these in your room." He hefted the suitcases slightly.

"I can do that."

"No need," Robert said.

Paul removed his coat and hung it on the rack. The house felt overly warm. With the cool damp weather, he was certain fires burned in the hearths in the parlor and the front room, as well as the kitchen and the occupied bedrooms. "Warm," he said.

"You can't be serious." Audrey hugged herself. "It's freezing. You're simply used to the Arctic cold."

"I don't live in the Arctic."

"Well, wherever it is you live. I know it's much colder there than here and it's buried in snow."

She was still peeved with him and rightly so. Paul made no mention of her snippy tone. "True. It is cold and we do have snow, but the summers are warm. It's beautiful there. I'd like to show it to you." He stared at her and felt a challenge coming from her. It reminded him of when they were children. "You're mad at me for not coming home and I understand that, but you never came north either."

Audrey puckered out her lower lip. "My understanding was that you didn't want visitors." She looked at Robert. "Isn't that right?"

Robert cleared his throat. "Perhaps it would be better if we didn't discuss this right now."

"Fine. But I am right." Audrey removed a hat pin, lifted off her trendy hat, and placed it on a shelf above the coatrack. "I doubt I'd like it. I'm not fond of the country."

Although Paul wanted to defend his home, he bit his tongue. An argument would serve no good purpose. And one rarely won a disagreement with Audrey.

He moved to the stairway and placed a hand on the mahogany banister. "Mother's still in the same room?"

"Yes. Go on up. I'm sure she's waiting for you." Robert took the steps, a bag in each hand.

Paul sucked in a breath of courage and headed up, afraid of what he'd find. His mother had always been vigorous. He didn't want to see her sickly and dying. He took each step with resolve. When he reached the top of the stairway, he stopped. Everything looked just as it had. The occasional table with a crystal vase brimming with flowers stood in the alcove at the top of the staircase. His mother had always kept flowers in the house. He headed down the hallway adorned with a vividly colored Oriental rug.

When he reached her room, which was the last one at the end of the corridor, he stopped and stared at her bedroom door. He remembered how she'd insisted on this particular room because it offered the best view of San Francisco Bay.

He opened the door, doing his best to be quiet in case she was asleep. The room was furnished with dark mahogany and a four-poster canopy bed sat like a centerpiece. His mother had always loved the bed. It had been a gift from his father. She sat among plump pillows, her gray hair braided and draped over one shoulder. Her white dressing gown looked as if it had been starched. She'd always been a small woman, but now she looked tiny in the large bed.

Her bright blue eyes had dimmed and her complexion was pallid. She smiled and held out a hand to him. "I can barely believe what I see. Come here and give me a kiss."

Paul obeyed and bent and kissed his mother's cheek. Her skin felt dry and paper thin. Shaking slightly, she placed her hands on his face, and then kissed both of his cheeks. "God has blessed me."

Although frail, she retained her inner strength and beauty. He sat on the bed and gently grasped her hand. "It's good to be here."

"It took you long enough," she said, her speech sounding as if it were barely managing to squeeze past her voice box. "I was beginning to think you'd never come home and I'd have to die without you." She gave him a playful smile. "Stand up and let me have a look at you."

Paul stood and held his arms away from his sides. Being scrutinized made him feel uncomfortable.

"Dear me. What's happened to your hand?"

"It's nothing. A little cut that's healing well."

She studied him, her eyes touched by pleasure. "You've become a strapping young man. Nearly as big as Robert." She pressed her palms together. "It would seem Alaska has been good for you." She narrowed her eyes. "But you should have come home sooner and more often."

"You're right. I should have. I'm sorry, but I thought you understood . . . the why."

She puffed out a breath between shriveled lips. "I suppose I do. But the time comes when we must move on. It should not take something as drastic as my death to bring you home."

"I'm truly sorry. I see now how wrong I've been. But I did think about you and the rest of the family often. I missed you. I just couldn't come back and face what had happened."

"It was a long time ago." She caressed his cheek, her eyes holding his. "You're still carrying around all that hurt, aren't you?"

Paul straightened. "Not so much now. I got married."

"Yes. Robert told me. I'm happy for you. And I heard there's going to be a baby."

Paul cleared his throat. "Was. We lost the baby—a girl . . . just a few weeks ago." An ache tightened his throat. He missed Kate.

"Oh, Paul. I'm truly sorry." She closed her eyes, and it looked like she was praying. When she opened them, she said, "Your little one is with the Father." She glanced at the door. "Did you bring your bride with you?"

"No. She wasn't up to the trip." Paul knew that wasn't entirely true, although the journey would have been arduous for Kate. The whole truth was, he needed to come alone. He needed to face this place and his family on his own.

"I'm sorry to hear that. I'd hoped to meet your young lady. She must be very special to have captured your heart." She grasped Paul's hand.

"There's no one like Kate. She's a pilot and flies all over the Alaskan territory."

"Yes. I recall hearing that. And Robert said you're working as a bush doctor now." His mother smiled gently. "I'm so proud of you." She took a quaking breath, which set off a spasm of coughing. She pointed at a glass of water on the bedstead.

Paul handed it to her, and with trembling hands, she sipped. "That's better." She returned the glass to Paul. "Maybe we can talk more later. I'm a bit worn out."

"Okay. I'll get settled and see you for dinner?"

"That would be splendid."

"I'll bring our meals up." Paul bent over her and kissed her forehead, struggling to hold back his tears. "I'll see you later." When he stepped into the hallway, Robert and Audrey were waiting for him.

"How does she seem to you?" Audrey asked. "I mean from a doctor's perspective."

"Understandably weak and fatigued, but her mind is just as sharp as ever. And she seems in good spirits."

"She's sleeping more and more," Robert said.

"With a condition like this, that is to be expected. Her heart is failing and is unable to pump an adequate supply of blood to keep her strong."

"So, you agree with the doctors?" Audrey's eyes teared.

"Robert said she has the best in the city. And from what I've seen, she appears to be failing." He rested a hand on the closed door. "If you don't mind, we've planned to share our evening meal together in her room."

"No. Of course we don't mind. However, Sean and Carolyn will be here. Carolyn's bringing her children." Robert glanced down the hallway. "I know she's hoping to spend time with both you and Mother."

"I'll see to it that she has plenty of time for both. I'm looking forward to seeing her and her family," Paul said, although he wasn't, not completely. He knew there would be questions, and although Carolyn was not as confrontational as Audrey, she had a way of letting her feelings be known. "If you'll excuse me, I could do with a nap before dinner."

"Certainly," Robert said. "I've got work at the office. And before returning, I'll swing by and pick up Mary and the children. Ever since hearing you'd be coming, Rebecca and John have talked of nothing else." He smiled.

"I've missed them. They're nearly grown, what are they—eleven now?"

"In February."

"Did you hear, Mother's decided to come down and share Thanksgiving dinner with us?" Audrey asked. She glanced at Paul. "I'm afraid it'll be too much for her."

"If she wants to have dinner with us, then so be it," Robert said.

"She's a determined woman," Paul said, then shoved his hands into his pockets and walked down the hallway toward his room, convinced that this would be the last holiday he'd share with his mother.

Paul spent the next few days becoming reacquainted with family, getting to know his four nieces and one nephew, and catching up on all that had taken place since he'd escaped to Alaska. Young John was the most inquisitive of them all and the two hit it off immediately.

Audrey had no serious beau and stated quite openly that she wasn't at all certain she would ever marry. She was dead set against placing herself under any man's authority. Paul thought she and Kate would get along well together. Sean made very few appearances. From what Paul could gather, he had a busy social life and with the holidays approaching intended to make an appearance at as many gatherings as possible. He'd been friendly with Paul, but had more on his mind than family. Carolyn had taken on the task of making sure all the details for the holiday were attended to, and she and Audrey spent countless hours in the kitchen baking.

Mary, Robert's wife, was friendly and outgoing, but she

had much more in common with Audrey. The two never seemed to tire of discussing the latest in local art and theater.

Carolyn said very little to Paul about his absence, and it had taken her time to warm up to him, although her husband, Charles, was friendly and seemed to genuinely enjoy Paul's company. It wasn't until a late-night chat in the kitchen that Carolyn finally talked freely and with genuine enthusiasm laughed over fun recollections.

Paul spent a great deal of his time with his mother, but managed to see a few friends about town. His closest friend and former colleague, Walter Henley, was unavailable due to an influenza outbreak. They made plans for after the Thanksgiving holiday.

Used to the seclusion and solitude of the homestead, Paul sought time alone at the beach as often as possible. He'd find a log, sit and watch fishing vessels and sailboats. He longed to sail again. It had been one of his and Susan's favorite activities. Watching a sleek vessel dance across the waves, pushed along by a brisk wind, brought back memories of outings they'd taken. She felt close.

The sailboat disappeared into a mist and Paul's mind wandered to Kate. He envisioned her amber eyes and her hearty laughter. He longed to be with her. But he couldn't leave, not now. He'd tried to contact her by telephone, but she hadn't been home. Out on a run, no doubt. He'd write her when he got back to the house.

Thanksgiving arrived with a flood of activity. The house was filled with the delectable smells of roasting meat, sweet rolls, and pies. It resounded with laughter and family conversation. How strange it seemed that as his mother lay dying, the family celebrated. It didn't seem right. But even now his mother's spirit filled the house. She'd always overflowed with cheer and even in these last days she possessed an essence of incomprehensible joy.

Finally it was time. The table was set and the food prepared and set out. Paul and Robert hurried up the stairway to their mother's room.

Paul knocked. "Dinner's ready."

Carolyn opened the door. "Mother's ready. But she'll need help getting downstairs."

The head of the Anderson household sat in a cushioned high-back chair, her gnarled hands clasped in her lap. Her silver hair was coiffed and Paul guessed that she'd taken time for a bit of rouge and lipstick. She wore one of her favorite dresses, a lavender gown with butterfly sleeves.

"Mother, you look beautiful," Robert said.

"Of course I don't, but I thought it fitting I wear my best." She smiled. "And it smells as if my two daughters have outdone themselves." She lifted a hand. "I could do with a little help."

Paul and Robert moved to either side of the chair. Each held her arms and lifted her to her feet. She tottered slightly and Paul grasped her more tightly. He could smell the delicate fragrance of roses. She was wearing her favorite perfume.

His mother straightened. "I'm ready." Taking a step and leaning heavily upon her sons, she made her way down the stairs, making an entrance into the dining room.

"Oh Mother, you look stunning," Audrey said.

Sean hurried around to the end of the table and pulled out a chair for his mother. She sat carefully and Sean pushed the chair up to the table. She closed her eyes for a moment and breathed deeply, then she gazed at her family. "How wonderful to be here with all of you." She settled her eyes on Paul. "Would you mind giving thanks?"

"Certainly," Paul said, stumbling over the word. He was

the last one who should pray. And everyone at the table knew that, but as he looked at his family, they wore expectant expressions, not critical ones. Audrey and Carolyn both seemed close to tears. Paul bowed his head, his mind blank. What should he say? He'd been angry with God for so long.

And then seemingly from nowhere a flood of thankfulness washed through him. "Our heavenly Father," he began. "I cannot begin to express how lucky I am to be a part of this family. Thank you for their love and acceptance, their forgiveness. They have welcomed me back into the fold and have blessed my life. My sisters have labored over this meal. I ask that you bless the work of their hands. And strengthen our mother who is at the heart of this family. Amen."

He looked up to find Carolyn dabbing at her eyes and his mother smiling broadly, her eyes brimming with tears. "Thank you, Paul. Now Robert, would you carve the turkey for us?"

The meal was perfection—family recipes handed down through the years—sweet potatoes, mashed potatoes, gravy, cornbread stuffing, and corn casserole along with cranberry gelatin and the lightest of sweet rolls. Paul was glad he was there, but wondered about Kate. What was she doing on this day? She'd said something about spending it with the Warrens.

He noticed his mother ate very little, but her eyes were alight with pleasure as she listened to her children and grandchildren reminisce with story after story. It was a day to treasure. She went up to bed early, and Paul sat at her bedside, wondering how much longer she would remain with them. She wore a smile in her sleep, but her color was off, her lips tinged blue. The celebration had taken a toll. Paul decided to remain at her side through the night, just in case she might need him.

She blinked open her eyes and looked at him. "I'm so thankful you're here. I prayed and God brought you home."

Alaska had been home for so long, but at this moment the house where he'd been loved and nurtured felt like home. "I'm sorry it took me so long to get here."

She raised her hand to quiet him. "It doesn't matter now. What matters is that you're unhappy. I can see it in your eyes."

Her voice was so quiet, Paul could barely hear. He leaned closer. "I'm fine, Mother. I have a good life, good friends, and a wife I cherish. I want you to meet Kate. You'll love her."

"I see the love you feel each time you speak of her. I'm sorry I won't have the opportunity to meet her."

"Don't talk like that. You may have many more years."

His mother was silent for a moment, then she said, "We have no time for pretending. I'm dying . . . soon." Paul started to speak, but she shushed him. "Listen to me. You must find a way to forgive yourself. If you don't, your self-loathing will destroy you. I wish you could see what I see—a fine, honorable man. God has given you so many gifts, and he didn't intend for you to hide yourself away where your gifts are hidden, they're meant to be shared."

"But I'm working . . . as a doctor."

"That is a gift, but it's not the one I'm speaking of. It's you, your heart and kindness and deep affection for family that you've hidden from the ones who love you."

"After what happened, I couldn't stay. You know that. Susan was everywhere. It felt as if I couldn't breathe because of her presence and her absence." Without warning, the impact of her loss swept over Paul, as if she had just died. "Why, Mother? I don't understand why God let her die."

"Susan was here as long as she was meant to be. Her days were numbered before she was even born."

Paul shook his head. "Her life was cut short because of me. Just because God knew doesn't mean he wanted her to die. We were meant to have a life together—I can't forgive him for snatching her away from me. I can't forgive myself for not stepping in." He sat on the chair, unable to hold back his tears. "If I had done what I should have, she and my son would still be here."

His mother reached out and took his hand. "Oh my dear son, I wish I knew all the answers. I don't. But I do know that you didn't kill your wife. You did all you could."

Paul's chest felt as if it would explode. "I love Kate, but I still miss Susan."

"Love once born never leaves us." She stopped and took a small breath. "Soon I'll see sweet Susan and my grandson." She smiled. "And my granddaughter. Oh, to hold them . . ." Her eyes brimmed with tears. "I want to tell Susan that you're well."

Paul wished he could assure his mother that he was happy and content, but there was still a dark place inside of him that threatened to destroy everyone he loved, including Kate. He pressed his mother's hand to his cheek. "I don't want you to go."

"I know." She struggled for her next breath. "But I'm ready. Soon I'll see your father and so many others. And I'll stand before the Lord. I can't even begin to imagine the wonder of it." She stopped and seemed to rest, then opened her eyes. "There's something more I must say."

Her voice was weakening. Paul could barely understand her.

"We are born, we live, and we die. The time goes by quickly, like a morning mist swept away by the warmth of the sun. Don't throw away the moments." She rested her hand on his, her skin frail and paper thin. "Tell your Kate hello from me."

— 19 —

Paul remained at his mother's side through the night. His brothers and sisters sat with him much of the time. He felt like he was part of a death watch as her breathing became more labored. Robert's wife, Mary, made sure there was coffee and tea, and sometime around midnight she baked a pound cake, sliced it, and set it out, but no one ate any of it.

Carolyn sat beside Paul and leaned over her mother, holding her hand. "Mama, it's all right if you want to go now. We'll be all right." Her eyes glistened. "You'd be so proud of Charles. He's watching over the children and even managed to get them into bed. He's reading *Gulliver's Travels* to them." Her words sounded like they had been choked off and she pressed her mother's hand to her cheek. "I love you, Mama." She gently set her mother's hand on the cushions, glanced at Paul, and rushed out of the room.

When Esther Anderson breathed her last, morning light defined the outside edges of the draperies. Paul had hoped she would awaken, even if just for a moment, but she never did. He caressed her hand. There was no need to tell anyone right away. Just a few more moments alone would be all right.

He gazed at her. She looked peaceful, the lines of her face

had softened and her lips were lifted in a quiet smile. Wisps of gray hair curled around her face, reminding him of a halo. As much death as he'd seen, it always took his breath from him. One moment a person was part of the world and the next they were gone—from flesh to spirit in an instant. He leaned his forehead against the bed and cried.

Hearing a sound at the door, he stood and wiped his eyes. Robert opened the door and stepped inside. Audrey walked in behind him.

"Is she gone?" Robert asked.

Paul nodded. He couldn't speak.

Audrey rushed to the bed. "Mama. Oh Mama." She draped herself over her mother and sobbed.

As Paul walked toward the door, Robert grasped his arm and Paul rested his hand on his. "I'll tell the others," Paul said and walked out, wishing Kate were with him.

After everyone had been told, Paul went to the phone and called the house in Anchorage. "I'm sorry, sir, but there's no answer," the operator said.

Paul could barely manage his disappointment. "Can you dial another number for me?"

"Certainly."

Paul gave her the name and number of the airfield, then waited while she made the connection.

Jack answered and the operator said, "I have your party for you, sir."

"Paul. Long time since we heard from you," Jack said.

"I was wondering if Kate was around."

"Nope. She's out on a run today. She'll be back late."

"Can you have her call me, here at my mother's house?"

"Sure thing," Jack said. "Everything all right there?"

"Yeah. Everything's fine." Paul wasn't about to talk to Jack about what had happened. "Thank you," he said and hung up.

Audrey spent the day sobbing into a handkerchief, while Carolyn took on the tasks of final arrangements. There was a lot to attend to, but Audrey said she couldn't bear to even think of it. Sean, looking morose, managed to be too busy. Robert had court hearings that couldn't be delayed. So preparations for the funeral were left to Paul and Carolyn. She put in a call to the mortician. Within the hour, two men showed up and their mother's body was taken.

Carolyn managed to get Audrey to take care of laundering the bedclothes while she and Paul made a visit to the mortuary. They met with the mortician to fill out paperwork, choose a casket, and order a headstone. The place of burial had long since been chosen and paid for. Their mother would lie beside their father.

Paul had taken his cue from Carolyn and had remained stoic throughout the process. She'd never openly shown her emotions. When Paul dropped her at the house, she had a list of tasks that needed her attention. Paul gratefully retreated to the beach. When he reached a place to pull off, he sat in the car and stared at the open water. A brisk breeze kicked up whitecaps and seagulls dipped and soared on the wind currents. Paul wondered what it would feel like to be one of those gulls—with nothing to think about except the moment.

With a heavy sigh, he left the car and walked onto the beach. Hands tucked inside his coat pockets, he ambled along the rocky shore. Small waves lapped at the beach, carrying white foam onto the sand. Wind caught at his hair and made his eyes water.

He'd hoped for solace, but there was none. He'd never known a world without his mother in it. It didn't seem right. Even when he lived far from home, he found comfort knowing she was here. He bent over and picked up a broken shell, remembering all the trips to the beach his family had taken together. Searching for undamaged shells had been one of his mother's favorite pastimes. She'd exclaim over each and every one, cleaning off dirt and sand, and then showing it off to the children before adding it to her collection.

Tears burned his eyes. Why had he waited so long to return? He'd been a fool. With ferocity, he cast the shell back into the ocean. His frustration and grief exploded in one word. "No!" A sob escaped and he sank to his knees. His mother had needed him. Susan had needed him. Kate had needed him. And he'd let them all down.

Now, he needed Kate. He longed for her loving arms and the warmth of her body, her strength and her faith that was so much like his mother's—steady and immovable. Kate would know what to say.

A rain squall washed in from the sea and drove Paul off the beach and to the shelter of his car. He didn't want to go back to the house. But what if Kate called him? He had to be there. In his mind he made plans to leave. The sooner he got back to Alaska, the better.

He remembered the day he'd left San Francisco after Susan died. He'd run. He'd left his family when they needed him. His stomach lurched, and for a moment he thought he might get sick. Was he about to let them down again?

Paul awakened the morning of his mother's funeral and moved to the window. Fog had moved in during the night and blanketed the city. He glanced at the clock—nine. He'd better get showered and dressed.

After a simple breakfast, it was time to leave for the church. Paul stepped out the front door and into sunshine. He lifted his face to its warmth, then looked at green lawns and holly wreaths. He'd almost forgotten Christmas was only weeks away. It seemed strange to have spring weather at this time of year. Taking in a lungful of fresh air, he walked to the car and opened the door for Audrey, who slid onto the backseat. Sean sat up front. No one spoke.

Carolyn, with the help of her husband, got their children into their Buick sedan. They followed Paul when he pulled onto the street.

The church barely had enough seating for all who had come to pay their respects. Esther Anderson had been admired and loved by many. Paul sat between Robert and Audrey in the front pew. If only Kate were with him. He needed her. They'd talked the previous day, but only for a few minutes. She was on her way back to the airfield. She'd offered him all the solace she could, long distance. It hadn't been enough.

The scent of lemon oil and wood polish mingled with the fragrance of flowers stung his nose. Paul's mind wandered to his home on Bear Creek. He longed to be where the scent of spruce and pine filled the air and the quiet of a snow-laden forest calmed his spirit.

Reverend Tyson had been Esther Anderson's pastor for more than thirty years. When he stepped to a wooden podium in the front of the church, Paul could see the sorrow that lay behind his eyes. He swiped graying hair off his forehead, laid his hands on an open Bible lying on the podium, and gazed out at the people who had gathered to say farewell. He smiled kindly. "Thank you for being here. Esther had many friends. We'll miss her."

Paul didn't hear any more. His mind was caught up in memories of his mother and father, brothers and sisters. They'd shared so many good times.

The minister moved to a high-backed chair and sat. Robert walked to the lectern. He'd been chosen to speak for the family. He looked calm, but Paul could see perspiration shimmer on his upper lip and on his forehead. He stood for a moment and looked out over the sanctuary and the people gathered there, then his eyes rested on the casket at the front. Paul had tried to avoid looking at it. He didn't want to think about his mother lying in a box. It still didn't seem possible.

Robert began with stories of his mother and father and how they had parented in unity. He told tales about himself and his brothers and sisters and the mischief they'd often gotten into. He explained that their mother was a no-nonsense kind of woman who also distributed grace liberally.

Paul remembered her steadfast faith and love. Even after his absence she'd accepted him back with loving arms. Gratitude washed over him. *Thank you for her, Lord.*

After the service, Paul and his brothers and three additional friends carried the coffin to a hearse that waited in front of the church, then family climbed into cars and followed the vehicle through the streets of San Francisco to the cemetery. The coffin was set in place and then family and friends gathered around. Sunshine warmed the grasses. The trees were bare, but they didn't look stark. He gazed at his father's headstone. *They're together now.* Paul tried to still his quivering chin.

After the funeral service, people gathered at the house on Franklin Street. Carolyn had refused the help of caterers and had done up the dining table and serving table beautifully, using the family's finest tablecloths and best silver. She'd arranged brightly colored flowers in crystal vases and set them out. And she'd prepared a simple meal with the help from women in the church. Everything was perfect. Paul stood beside her and placed an arm around her, giving her a gentle squeeze. "Mom would have loved this."

She looked up at him, her eyelashes wet with tears, and then leaned against him. "Thank you." She rested against him for a moment, then said, "I'd better see to our guests." She hurried off.

Conversations eddied around Paul, but they sounded hollow to him. He wasn't sure what he should do or say. He was approached again and again with condolences. Each time, he answered with what he hoped was a proper response, but the whole time he wondered why people put themselves through all of this. It seemed meaningless. He supposed it was a way of letting go. All he wanted was time alone.

He walked into the parlor, thankful to find it empty. He stood at the window and stared out at the lawns. His nephew John wandered into the room. He didn't say anything as he roamed about, looking at family photographs.

Finally, the youngster stopped and stood beside Paul and gazed out of the window. "Grandmother loved her gardens. But this spring she won't be here to tend to them." He was quiet for a long while, then he asked, "Do you know what heaven's like?"

"No. Not really. Except that it's a place where there is no pain or suffering and that everyone who lives there is happy. The Bible talks about how beautiful it is, like nothing we've ever seen."

"So, do you think Grandma's happy?"

"Absolutely," Paul said, though he wasn't certain of that. He wasn't certain of anything just now. "She's with Grandpa. You know how much they loved each other."

Tears spilled onto the boy's cheeks. "I miss her. Why did she have to die?"

Paul circled an arm around John and pulled him close. "I don't know, but she had a long life."

The two stood like that for a few minutes longer and then John stepped away. "Thank you, Uncle Paul," he said and then walked out of the room.

An ache tightened in Paul's chest as he watched the boy leave. Why was life filled with so much sorrow? If Kate were here, she'd help make sense of it all.

Someone cleared their throat and Paul turned to see his friend and old colleague Walter Henley standing in the doorway.

"Do you mind a little company?" Walter asked.

"Of course not. Come in."

"I'm sorry about your mother. She was a fine woman."

"Yes. She was." Paul reached for Walter's hand. "It's good to see you, friend. It's been too long." The two embraced and patted each other on the back. "Come and sit down." Paul moved toward a settee. "You're looking . . . worn out. And a little thicker around the middle." He gave his friend a teasing smile.

Walter patted his stomach. "My wife's a good cook." He folded his tall frame onto a cushioned chair across from Paul. "And as to being worn out, I am. Can't keep up with all the people who are sick with the flu. And I'm getting old."

"You're not so old. You only have a few gray hairs." Paul studied Walter for a moment. "I like the gray in your beard. You look distinguished."

Walter stroked the tidy beard. "So, what have you been up to in the great Alaskan wilderness? I heard you're working as a doctor."

"That's right. And I like it. I fly into the bush, from village to village, plus I stop at some of the mining camps and homesteaders' places. It's always interesting. Out there, you never know what you're going to be faced with. One night I did an appendectomy on a kitchen table."

Walter shook his head. "You always were one for adventure. We could sure use someone like you at the hospital, especially now with the influenza outbreak. I can barely keep up with my regular patients—I'm spending too much time at the hospital." He leveled serious eyes on Paul. "I really could use an extra hand."

"I wouldn't know what to do anymore. It's been so long."

"You'd get the hang of it in no time. Even with this flu, it's probably easier than what you do in Alaska."

"Why the shortage of doctors?"

"You know—attrition, plus the city's population is growing. And whenever there's an outbreak of any kind, we have trouble keeping up. When I left the hospital last night, the hallways had patients lined up on cots. There aren't enough beds."

"I'd like to help, but I'll be heading home soon . . . after the reading of the will. Kate's waiting for me." Paul felt a prick of guilt. He should stay . . . but Kate needed him. He needed her.

Walter nodded. "I understand. How is that wife of yours? I'd like to meet her. She sounds rather remarkable."

"She is." Paul didn't want Walter to know about the baby. There'd be questions and the circumstances were too similar to what had happened with Susan. It'd be like digging into a festered wound.

"So, is she still flying?"

"Oh yes. Can't keep her on the ground. She's a good pilot. We make a lot of runs together."

Walter leaned back and crossed one leg over the other. "I was serious about needing a doctor to help, but I could also use you . . . long term. And there's plenty of work for pilots in the area. I'm sure Kate could find a job with one of the local outfits."

Paul wasn't sure what to say. The idea of moving down had crossed his mind. That way he'd be close to his family and still be able to work as a doctor. And Kate could fly.

"Kate and I are happy in Alaska," he said. "It suits us. And we're needed there. Aren't many doctors and there are never enough good pilots." Even as he spoke, he imagined what life for him and Kate would be like in San Francisco. "Maybe you should give up city living and lend a hand in the wilderness?"

Walter laughed. "Me? You've got to be kidding. Don't get me wrong. I'd love a little adventure, but to actually move? My Julia would never stand for it."

Carolyn stepped into the doorway. "Paul. I'm sorry to disturb you, but some of our guests are leaving . . ."

"I'll be right there."

He pushed to his feet and watched Carolyn walk away.

"Will you have time to join me and the wife for a meal before you leave town? Julia's a fine cook."

"I'd like that. I'll see what I can do."

"Good. I'll be in touch."

The two men walked toward the door. Paul's mind lingered on the what-ifs of living and working in San Francisco. Maybe he should talk to Kate about it.

Attorney Arthur Barkley sat at the head of the dining room table while Paul and his brothers and sisters silently waited for him to begin. He opened a briefcase and took out a packet of papers, adjusted his wire-rimmed glasses, and peered over the top of them at the family. "I was distressed to hear about your mother's passing. My condolences."

There was a murmur of appreciation.

"Your mother and I met last on January 21 of this year. She wanted to make some adjustments to the will. The majority is exactly as she and your father agreed upon before his death."

He cleared his throat and read through the designations made to the Anderson children. There were specific items listed for individuals. Paul was the recipient of one of his father's rifles. The business and financial assets were equally distributed among the siblings, leaving them all well-off.

There was one unexpected announcement—the house. Esther Anderson had made her wishes clear. The house was to go to Paul.

"She asked me to convey to you that she'd rather the house not be sold," Mr. Barkley said. "It was her wish that you live here. However, if that is not to your liking, it can be given to one of the other children. And if no one wishes to live in the home, it can be put up for sale along with its contents. The proceeds are then to be evenly distributed among you."

Silence descended over the room. Mr. Barkley placed the papers inside his briefcase and closed it. "I'll make sure that you each receive a copy of the will." He stood. "If you choose to sell the house, I'll be happy to assist and will oversee the distribution of funds."

"Thank you," Robert said, and walked Mr. Barkley to the door. When he returned to the dining room, no one said a word. Silence felt like a heavy shroud.

It was Audrey who spoke first. She pressed fingers to a fevered brow. "I'm glad she gave the house to you, Paul."

"But you've been living here." Paul didn't know what to say. Why would his mother have given it to him?

"I have, but Mother knew that I intend to move into an apartment of my own. My job at the paper provides ample income. And now with my inheritance I'll have no difficulty whatsoever."

"I don't plan to live here," Paul finally managed to say. "Kate and I have a home in Alaska and responsibilities to the people there."

Carolyn looked at her husband, Charles. "This is a lovely

house, but I'd much prefer to remain where we are. The children are settled there."

Charles patted her hand. "I agree."

"And the same goes for me and Mary," Robert said, placing an arm around his wife.

"I love our home," Mary said. "It has the loveliest view of the bay." She folded her hands in front of her on the table, her lips compressed.

Paul turned to Sean.

"Don't look at me. I don't want the thing. I've got my own house, and I can't be bothered to look after this place. It's too big for just me."

All eyes moved back to Paul.

Audrey spoke. "Mother wanted you to have it. You must stay." She coughed and pulled a handkerchief out of her dress sleeve to cover her mouth. "You're the practical choice. We all know how much she longed for your return."

"I can't stay here." Paul felt guilt work its way through his insides. "Audrey, I think you should remain here. After all, it's home to you."

She shook her head no, then pressed a hand to her temples and rubbed them.

"Are you all right, Audrey?" Carolyn asked.

"Yes. But I have the most horrid headache and a sore throat."

Paul studied her. She didn't look at all well, and if the high color in her cheeks were any indication, she had a fever. "Maybe you should lie down."

"No. I'll be fine." She sat straighter in her chair.

Carolyn's husband, Charles, spoke up. "I wasn't born into this family, but Esther always made me feel as if I were. There's been what feels like a chasm here since you left, Paul. I'm thinking that your mother understood that this house needs you." He hurried on before Paul could speak. "It would be idyllic, close to the hospital. And since you and Kate have only just started your lives together, I expect there will be children. This place offers ample room for a growing family."

Audrey pressed her perfectly manicured hands together. "I think it's an ideal solution. It would be fabulous to have you and Kate close by. We'd be a family again. And I'd love to become better acquainted with her. She sounds absolutely fascinating." Audrey leaned forward. "I could write a story about her piloting adventures for the paper."

Paul looked at the faces around the table. He felt cornered and confused. "I have a life in Alaska, good friends, and my medical practice."

"You call flying into villages a practice?" Audrey challenged.

"I don't suppose you'd see it that way, but I'm needed. And to a pilot, there's nothing to match flying in Alaska." Paul knew Kate loved the challenge of the north, but he also wondered if she could be happy here in San Francisco. There would certainly be a need for good pilots. And here, she would be safer.

— 20 —

A loud popping sound startled Kate awake. It was still dark, but she left the warmth of her bed and gazed out of the window. She couldn't see anything except ice fog. She decided that what she'd heard was the sound of a tree branch breaking under the weight of ice that had built up. Chilled, she returned to bed, pulled the blankets up under her chin, and snuggled down, hoping for more sleep. No such luck—her mind was awake.

She wondered what time it was and tried to read the clock. With a sigh, she turned on the bedstead lamp, squinting against the brightness of the light. It was 6:45, too early to get up and too late to go back to sleep. She dropped onto her back and rested her arms over her face.

Paul had left a message at the airfield the night before, and Kate had intended to call him when she got to the house. However, after building a fire, feeding Angel, making herself a meal, and then falling asleep on the sofa, it was too late to call.

She'd gone to bed frustrated with herself and hadn't dropped off to sleep until after midnight. She needed to call him. Throwing off her covers, she dropped her feet to the floor and hurried across the cold floorboards to the bathroom.

Still half asleep, she stared into the mirror, wishing she could call, but knowing it was too early. She splashed her face with water and felt more awake.

Returning to the bedroom, she took another glance out the window. Fog swirled in the outdoor light of a neighbor's house. Ice clung to a cottonwood tree like ivy hugging a rock hedge. She wondered how cold it was. Below zero for sure. She pushed her feet into slippers and pulled on a bathrobe. Coffee. She needed coffee.

Kate flicked on the front room light. Angel nuzzled her hand, then trotted to the front door.

"Stay close," Kate said, letting her outside, quickly closing the door against the frigid air.

Her arms prickled from the cold as she shuffled to the kitchen stove. She crumpled newspaper and shoved it into the firebox, added kindling, and then lit the paper. A tiny flame licked at the newsprint and flared to life. Flames traveled along the edges of the kindling and smoke curled up into the room. Kate placed chunks of wood in the fire, and then closed the firebox lid, her mind on Paul. Why had he called?

Accompanied by the crackling and popping sound of burning wood, Kate made coffee and set it on the stove, then built a fire in the parlor. She wished there were some way to coax more heat from the stove faster. Lifting a quilt off the sofa, she draped it around her shoulders and pulled it closed in front.

A whine came from the other side of the front door. "Oh, poor Angel. I forgot you." She hurried to the door and opened it. The dog pushed her way inside and Kate gave her cold coat a good rub, shivering as she did. "I'm sorry, girl."

With the quilt snugged around her, Kate sat in a rocker near the parlor stove. Paul's mother's funeral had been two days ago. She'd hoped for a call from him that day, but it hadn't come. Most likely he'd been busy with all the tasks that went along with a funeral. Still, she'd made sure to stay by the phone that day, but he didn't call before she had to leave. She glanced at the mantle clock. Seven thirty was still too early to call.

The aroma of percolating coffee made the house feel warmer. Kate closed her eyes and dozed. When she awakened, her eyes went directly to the clock. Only ten minutes had passed. She willed the hands to move more quickly. She had a mail run today. If she didn't get ahold of Paul before she left, she'd have to wait the entire day before she could try again.

Deciding she might as well eat, Kate removed the quilt and laid it over the sofa, then went to the kitchen to prepare breakfast. While she worked, she watched the clock. She'd wait until eight o'clock.

The coffee was ready, so she poured a cup, then flipped her French toast. Sipping her coffee, she waited, then took a peek at the underside of the toast—still not ready. She glanced at the clock. Only fifteen minutes had passed. What if Paul had called to tell her when he was coming home? Without warning, tears surfaced. She blinked them back and checked the toast again, but couldn't see through the blur of tears. She swiped them away and, deciding she didn't care how cooked the toast was, she slid it onto a dish and moved the skillet off the heat. After setting her food and coffee on the table, she returned to the kitchen for silverware, butter, and syrup.

Kate sat and gazed around the house. It was empty. She was alone. There was no Paul and no baby. She took an unsteady breath. What if there were no more babies? She pressed a hand to her flat stomach. She would have been only weeks away from delivery.

Kate forced her attention back to her meal and, forgoing the butter, drizzled syrup over the French toast. She took a bite and chewed, but could barely swallow past the tightness in her throat. *Stop thinking about it. There's nothing that can be done.*

She leaned back in her chair and took a couple of deep breaths, then lifting her cup, she sipped her coffee and turned her thoughts to a safer issue—Lily and Clint. They were sweet on each other. She wondered if they'd get married. She hoped so. They were perfect for each other and Clint would be an excellent father to Teddy.

She finished her meal and glanced at the clock—7:55. She'd wait. Kate set the dishes in the sink and rinsed them. It was time. She went to the telephone, and after giving Paul's number to the operator, she listened for his voice on the other end. Finally she heard, "I have your party. One moment please."

"Hello." It was Paul. "Kate?" He sounded tired.

"Yes. It's me. How are you?"

"I'm fine, just missing you."

Kate smiled. His words warmed the worry in her heart. "I miss you too. I would have called yesterday, but by the time I got home it was too late. You sound worn-out."

"I'm all right. I've had some long nights and there's been a lot going on here. How are you? I've been worried about you."

"I'm fine," Kate said, then knowing Paul would need more convincing, she added, "Really." She tried to sound cheerful. "Do you know when you'll be home?" There was a long pause on the other end of the line. Kate's heart thumped with anxiety. "Paul?"

Finally, he said, "I don't know yet."

"Oh. How was the service?"

"It was nice. Mother had a lot of friends and I think every one of them attended. I couldn't call until yesterday, but you weren't home."

"I'm sorry. I was on a run. I think about you all the time. Is your family well?"

"Yes, all except Audrey. She has influenza. There's an outbreak of it here."

"Oh dear. Is she all right?"

"She's pretty sick. And all of a sudden I'm the best doctor in the city. She won't deal with anyone but me. I'm keeping an eye on her."

"And you, how are you?"

"I'm okay. Tired. But I'm glad the funeral is over. Mother was ready to go . . . it's difficult. But Mother and I had some good conversations, and I'm rebuilding relationships with my family. I'm glad I came."

"Then I'm glad too. But I'm so sad about your mother." She'd thought about what it would be like to lose her mother and couldn't imagine life without her.

"And about coming home . . . well, there's a lot that needs to be done here before I can leave." He sounded like he was trying to be matter-of-fact.

Kate's heart sank. "Oh? What kind of things?"

"The attorney who's handling Mother's affairs met with the family yesterday. Mother gave her house to me. She doesn't want it sold. I've tried to convince Audrey to stay, but she refuses." His voice sounded hesitant. "I'm praying about it."

Alarm burst through Kate. "Are you thinking of living there?"

"No. Of course not. We have a house . . . well, a cabin. And we have the place in Anchorage too."

"And neither one them is anywhere nearly as nice as your mother's home."

"It is nice and has a certain charm, but so does our cabin. Though I must admit the two places couldn't be more different." He chuckled. "If Audrey won't live at Mother's, we'll have to get it ready for sale."

Kate's heart sank. She needed Paul. "Of course. What about Christmas? It's our first together."

"I was thinking you could come down. We'd spend the holidays here in San Francisco. You'd be able to meet my family and we'd be together."

Kate had imagined their first Christmas would be spent on the creek with their friends, not in a big city where she'd be among strangers. She hated the idea. "Is it possible for you to be home before Christmas?"

"If you can't come down, I'll fly up."

Kate felt relief and then guilt over her selfishness. "That's a lot of air travel for this time of year. It can be treacherous. I'd rather you stayed than put yourself at risk."

"I wish you'd consider taking a steamer down. I'd love you to meet my family and see my home."

Home? This is your home. "I'll think about it." Kate couldn't dredge up any enthusiasm.

"Another thing," Paul said. "I was asked by an old colleague of mine, Walter Henley, to return to work at the hospital and to join him in his private practice. I told him no, but with the outbreak of influenza I feel obligated to help, at least for a few weeks. The hospital and Walter are both short-staffed. And the hospital doesn't have room for all the patients. Walter said there were people sleeping on cots in the hallways."

Kate's stomach dropped. He *was* being sucked back into his old life. "That sounds horrible."

"It is. Will you be all right if I stay? Just until things settle down here."

And when will that be? Kate seethed. "It's up to you, not me," she said, biting off her words.

"I'll think about it and let you know." A long pause hung between them. "Well, I better go. This call is going to cost a pretty penny."

"Okay." Kate didn't want to say good-bye.

"I love you."

"I love you too."

"And what about Christmas? Will you come down?"

"Of course," Kate said, but she couldn't imagine it. "I'll see about making arrangements."

"I can hardly wait! There's so much I want to show you. Have you ever been to San Francisco?"

"No." Kate felt depressed.

"All the more fun, then. Bye, Katie."

"Bye." Kate hung the speaker in its cradle and sank into a chair. Paul wasn't coming back.

— 21 —

When Donald first went to work at the airfield, he took the easiest runs. He was friendly and laid-back—Kate liked him. He didn't look anything like Mike, but he approached life the same way Mike had, as if each day was just another adventure. Sometimes he could be overconfident, which worried Kate. Too much confidence could get a pilot into trouble.

Kate heard the sound of a plane approaching the field and looked out the window just in time to see Donald's Fairchild come in. The rear end whipped to one side and he lost control and headed toward the hangar bay. "No!"

Jack leaped to his feet. "What?" He swung open the door. "He's going to hit the hangar!" Jack let loose a string of profanity as he ran toward the field and watched Donald clip the side of the building and then roll to a stop. He stormed across the field toward the plane.

Kate hurried after him.

When Donald climbed out of his plane, Jack laid into him. "What in tarnation do you think you're doing?"

"I got hit by a crosswind and—"

"The winds aren't bad. In all my years I've never seen a pilot lose control over a little bit of wind like we got today."

"It came out of nowhere."

"You're fired. I knew you weren't ready for this job. Now, take your plane and get off my field!"

Donald's mouth dropped open. "But—"

"Git!" Jack headed toward the hangar. "And you'll pay for the damage to my building."

Kate followed Jack. "Hey, Jack. Give him another chance." She glanced back at Donald. "Everyone makes a mistake now and then. And sometimes the winds can gust pretty hard through here."

Jack stopped and glared at her. "And why should I give him a break? Novices cost me money—they're either too afraid to take a full load just in case they can't make a clean takeoff or they overload and end up in the drink somewhere. Today *he* nearly cost me a hangar."

"If every novice was fired because they made a mistake, there wouldn't be any pilots," Kate said, remembering how she'd felt when she first came to Alaska. "And you need pilots. All you've got is me, Sidney, who's out in Kenai a lot of the time, Alan, and Kenny. And if anyone needs to be fired, it's Kenny. He's not exactly the best pilot around." She glanced at Donald. "Sure, Donald's got a lot to learn, but he's doing all right. Give him another chance. One day you'll be glad you did."

Jack folded his arms over his chest and stared at the young man, then at the hangar. He looked back at Donald. "All right. One more chance. But that's it. If he makes one more mistake, he's out of here."

Kate smiled. "Thanks." She glanced over her shoulder at Donald and gave him the thumbs-up, then hurried toward her plane.

She took her mail run that day and then headed for the cabin. She'd spent too much time in town. Maybe the peace of the homestead would help bring her life back into focus. She didn't know if Paul wanted to stay in San Francisco. He hadn't said he did. She was probably just overly emotional because of everything that had happened. But what if Paul did want to stay? Could she live there and be happy? *It's not about where you live, it's about who you live with*, she told herself, but she wasn't sure she believed it.

When she flew over the landing strip, Clint and Lily were working on it. They both waved and then hurried to get off the ice and out of her way.

Kate made a pass over the frozen creek, double-checking for berms or debris. It looked clear. She set down and Lily and Clint ran to meet her.

Lily threw her arms around Kate. "I was wondering when you'd be back."

"I've been working and it's easier to stay in town, especially with Paul gone."

Angel trotted off with her nose to the ground, and when she heard the barking of the dogs, she tore across the creek and up the bank. Kate found herself wishing she were like Angel, oblivious to the disappointments and sorrows of life and happy just to be home.

"She's in high spirits," Clint said, wearing his usual large smile.

"I think she's been missing this place." Kate looked at the cabin. "I know I have."

"You hear from Paul?"

"Yes. His mother passed away."

"I'm so sorry," Lily said.

Kate gave a nod. "It'll be awhile before Paul can come home. There are a lot of things to do with his mother's estate." Kate set to work tying down the plane and Clint and Lily chipped in to help.

"You should have radioed to let us know you were coming," Lily said. "We could have gotten the cabin warmed up for you."

"I didn't want to bother anyone."

By the time Kate had the oil drained out of the plane, Lily and Clint had it tied down and were ready to secure the tarp. Kate gave them a hand.

"I'd offer you a cup of coffee," she said, "but it'll take awhile."

"How 'bout let's get a fire going in your cabin and while it warms up you can come to my house. You must be hungry and Mama made bread. It's still warm." Lily smiled.

"I love fresh bread, just out of the oven. Thanks." Kate already felt better. It was good to be among friends.

When Kate, Lily, and Clint approached the house, Sassa stepped onto the porch. She planted her hands on her hips and smiled. "How good to see you. Come in." She gave Kate a hug and bundled her inside. "We've missed you. And when is that Paul coming home?"

Kate shrugged and tried not to let Sassa see her apprehension. "I don't know exactly. His mother died and he will likely have to help get the house ready to sell. Plus he's going to go to work at the hospital for a while."

"I'm so sorry about his mother," Sassa said. "But it's time for him to come home . . . and be with his wife."

"He wants me to go down for Christmas."

"What you need to do is go get him and bring him back here." Sassa folded her arms over her chest. "Patrick needs to have a talk with him."

"Please don't say anything. He's been away from his family for such a long time. I'm sure he feels he's got to stay . . . at least for a while."

Silence swelled and filled the room. Finally, Lily said, "Mama, would you mind if I sliced some of the bread you made?"

"No. And I have fresh butter too." Sassa trundled into the kitchen and returned with a loaf of bread and a knife. "Would you like some hot chocolate? I've got extra. I made some for the boys."

"That sounds delicious. I've had a long day. There was a lot of mail. I guess with Christmas coming . . ." At the reminder that her Christmas was ruined, disappointment washed over Kate like the rapids of the Susitna.

After sharing a meal of buttered bread and hot chocolate, Kate pushed away from the table. "I better get home. The dogs need tending and I was hoping to pack down some of the deep snow around the cache before dark. I'd hate to have an animal get in there."

"I'll walk back with you," Lily said.

"Me too." Clint stood. "The bread was good, Mrs. Warren. Thank you."

"You're welcome, Clint. Come by anytime." Sassa smiled at the handsome native man.

Kate held back a chuckle. Obviously Sassa was hoping that Clint would become part of the family.

"Thank you so much for the food and your company," Kate said, giving Sassa a hug before leaving.

Sassa settled kind eyes on Kate. "I'm always here . . . if you need me."

Kate walked the path with Lily and Clint. When they came to the spur trail that led to Clint's cabin, they stopped.

"See ya tomorrow," he told Lily, then gave her a quick kiss on the lips. He offered both women a wave before trekking off toward his house.

"He's awfully handsome," Kate said quietly, watching the tall man walk away.

"He is." Lily looked flushed.

Kate turned and continued along the path, Lily beside her. "Are you two serious about each other?"

"We are." Lily looked at Kate, her face shining. "He's wonderful. I'm in love with him. And he loves me too."

"Do you think you'll get married?"

"He hasn't asked yet, but I think he will." Lily lifted her brows. "I'm waiting."

"I like him. And I think you two are just right for each other."

"I remember thinking there would never be anyone for me." Lily's eyes teared. "Teddy couldn't have a better father than Clint."

When they reached the cabin, Kate was surprised to see Jasper sitting on his perch by the back door. "Well, hello, Jasper. It's good to see you." The bird tipped his head to one side, blinked his small black eyes once, and then stared at her. It was good to have him home. Kate felt as if a piece of Paul had returned. She reached out to touch the bird, but he flew off.

Kate heard Jack's voice coming over the radio inside. She hurried indoors. Clicking on the speaker she said, "This is Kate. Over."

"Kate. I have a run for you. Kotzebue needs medical supplies for a flu outbreak. Over."

"Is it serious? What kind of flu?"

"Fevers. Coughs. Pneumonia. It's bad. They could sure use Paul. Wish he was here."

Me too, Kate thought. "He's still with his family."

"Well, tell him to hurry up and get his backside home. Over."

"I'll tell him. And I'll see you first thing tomorrow morning."

"I'll have everything ready to go. Oh yeah, you'll have a passenger—James Brinks. Over."

"Good." Kate liked the idea of sharing the flight with James. He was a nice man even if he did trade in reindeer antlers as aphrodisiacs. "See you tomorrow. Over and out."

Kate's thoughts went to Nena and her family. She hoped they weren't sick.

She studied solid clouds that looked like a gray blanket. "I hope the snow holds off. If the skies clear, moonlight will give me more flying time."

The following morning, Kate woke before daylight. The temperature was -5 degrees. She'd have to clear the wings and fuselage of ice before taking off. Coffee cooked while she packed a knapsack and heated the oil for the Bellanca. When she headed down to the plane, she looked at the sky. The stars were turning faint in a deep blue canopy. The sun would be up soon.

"Thank you, Lord," she said as she walked the trail, snow squeaking beneath her boots. Angel trotted along beside her, eager to be on her way.

By the time a crease of light arced across the horizon, Kate had the plane ready to go. Angel was inside resting on the front passenger seat. Kate checked the gauges. Everything looked good. She revved the engine, headed down the snow-covered ice, and lifted into the air. It was urgent that she get to Kotzebue. She hoped the medicine would help. If only Paul were here.

When she landed in Anchorage, Jack ran out to meet the plane. He handed up a box. "This is the medicine along with instructions on how to use it. Something I never heard of, but it's supposed to help. The doctor at the hospital called it colloidal silver. Said it was a good drug."

Kate set the box on the backseat. "Thanks. I'll do my best."

"I tried to get a doctor or a nurse to fly up with you, but the doc said they didn't have anyone they could spare."

Kate nodded. "Where's—" she started to say, then spotted a tall lanky man walking toward the plane. When he approached, Kate shouted, "Good morning, Mr. Brinks."

"Morning. Nice to see you."

"Climb on in." She stood aside while he made his way up the ladder and disappeared inside. "I'll be back in a few days," she told Jack.

Jack gave her what almost looked like a salute and Kate returned the gesture. She wondered what was going on with him. Lately he'd been treating her like she was just one of the guys.

Kate climbed in, pulled the door shut, and latched it. As she moved up front, she gave Angel a pat. Settling into her seat, Kate asked, "Isn't it late in the season for your trip to Kotzebue?"

"Yeah. I had some business that got stalled, but my supplier says he's got a shipment for me."

"You sure you want to go? There's a lot of sick people up there."

"I heard. But I'm not worried. I never get sick." He glanced out the window at the sky. "And God's given us fine weather. I'd say that's a good sign, wouldn't you?"

"Hope it holds." Kate lined up for takeoff.

For winter flying, the weather couldn't have been more perfect. The skies were clear, no headwind, and the temperature warmed into the high teens. Kate made good time. When she set down in McGrath, remnants of daylight still glowed in the sky. Mr. Brinks helped Kate put the plane to bed and then they headed for the roadhouse.

After sharing a meal with him, Kate went to her room while he joined a conversation with another man over a beer. She hoped for a good night's sleep. Tomorrow would be a long day. If the weather remained clear, she planned to make a run all the way to Kotzebue. It would mean flying by moonlight part of the way. She remembered her first night-flying experience in the far north. She'd nearly panicked in the darkness but spotted a point of light in the frozen wilderness and followed it to the village of Kotzebue.

The next day, with a white world below and a moonlit sky above, Kate made Kotzebue. Joe greeted her warmly.

"Welcome." He patted Kate's arm, then turned to Mr. Brinks. "Alex said you'd be here. He's got lots of antlers for you." He grinned.

"Good." Mr. Brinks slung his pack over one shoulder.

"Mr. Brinks," Kate said, "I was thinking about staying a couple of days. Would that be all right with you? I thought I might be able to help with the flu epidemic."

"Sure. I've got friends, and last time I spoke to them, they were in good health." He smiled. "So, I'll see you at daylight in two days?"

"Daylight." Kate watched him trudge toward town, then with Joe's help she drained the oil, tied down the plane, and tarped it.

"Nena's excited to see you."

"I've been wanting to see her too. I've been worried, hoping you and your family weren't sick."

"We're all right, so far."

Kate hadn't told Nena about the baby. She hated to talk about what had happened. There were always questions, which stirred up memories of that night and what was supposed to be.

When Kate walked into the Turchiks' home, the children were lying on the floor playing a game of cards. They looked up, smiles brightening their golden round faces. They leaped to their feet and ran to her. Kate gave them all hugs, and then the children surrounded Angel patting and stroking her.

Nena set aside a piece of fabric she'd been sewing. "Kate. So glad you are here."

"Me too. When I heard about the epidemic, I was worried about all of you."

"No sickness here. We are thanking God." She smiled, and then her eyes moved to Kate's abdomen and her forehead creased with concern. "Did you have your baby?"

Kate swallowed hard. "Yes. But she came early, too early. We buried her in a grove of trees behind our house."

Nena's eyes flooded with tears. "I am so sorry. So sorry." She pulled Kate into her arms and held her, gently rocking her back and forth.

Kate rested her cheek on Nena's shoulder, feeling as if her own mother were holding her. Finally she straightened but held onto Nena's arms. "It was a girl. Paul tried hard to save her, but she was too small." A baby's squall came from one of the back rooms. Kate's throat constricted for a moment, then she asked, "How is your little one?"

"Good. She's good." Nena shuffled into the back of the house and appeared a few moments later with an infant bundled in a blanket and cradled against her shoulder. She held her out so Kate could see her. "This is our Katie."

"You named her Katie?" Kate could barely see through a blur of tears. There were no words.

"If you hadn't saved my life, this baby would never have been born. So when me and Joe see that it is a girl, we know her name is Katie." She held the child out to Kate.

Taking the infant into her arms, Kate couldn't stop her tears. She held the baby close, drinking in the smell of her and embracing every little mewling sound.

"One day, you and Paul will have another baby," Nena said. "Me and Joe, we lost a baby, a little boy."

"You did? You've never said anything."

"He was perfect, but God took him to heaven. After that, he gave us Peter and Nick and Mary and now our Katie." She stood close and pulled both Kate and the baby into her arms. "You'll be a mama one day. I know it."

Kate wanted to believe her, but what about Paul? She handed Katie back to her mother. "Paul's in San Francisco."

"San Francisco? Is that far away?"

"Yes. Very far away."

"Why is he there?"

"His mother died. It's where he grew up. When he left, I thought he would come home soon, but he's still there and he's going to work in a hospital in the city. He said it was just for a little while, but . . ." Kate shrugged. "I think he loves it there."

"No. He loves Alaska. He loves you."

"I hope so."

"He'll come back. He belongs here."

Nena wasn't the first to say that, but Kate knew that once San Francisco had been his home. How did he feel now that he'd returned?

— 22 —

A breeze ruffled Paul's hair as he stepped off the cable car. The scent of sea air, baked goods, and coffee wafted through the streets. The bell of the cable car sounded sweet amidst the dissonance of congested automobiles. In the distance the deep blue bay glistened in the morning sunlight.

He felt almost lighthearted. It was one of those perfect days that swept away gloom. He wished he could share this with Kate and wondered what she was doing at this very moment. More than likely she was flying, seeing to the needs of Alaskans. Concern, like that of a father who'd lost sight of his child in a crowd, reached for him. He reminded himself that Kate was no child and he was not her father.

Paul walked toward St. Francis Hospital, knowing that fog and clouds could be counted on to creep back into the city and blot out the sun and its warmth. He stopped and stared at the four-story block building, which was divided into three wards. This was where his career as a doctor had begun. As an intern, he'd walked through the doors those many years ago, insecure and uncertain he'd chosen the right career. Time

262

and experience had given him confidence . . . until the day when he'd made the gravest of all errors.

Today he felt like the intern again, anxious and wondering if he belonged here. How had he allowed Walter to talk him into returning, even if it was just for a few weeks? He'd come back to San Francisco to see his mother and to say farewell to her, not to work at the hospital or reestablish himself in the city. Even with so many sick with influenza, he knew he ought to be on a ship heading home to Kate. But he felt stuck—Audrey was still sick and she was relying on him. Walter needed his help. But Kate needed him too.

As he approached the hospital doors, his anxiety and anticipation mounted. He didn't know what to expect. All he knew was, he was supposed to meet Walter here.

He walked up steps to the main entrance. Lattice-paneled double doors led into a foyer. He reached for the handle, hesitated, fighting the sensation that he didn't belong. He wondered what his mother would have thought of his returning to work at the hospital.

He opened the door and stepped into a tiled lobby. There he was greeted by familiar green walls, the antiseptic odor and subdued character of the hospital. Throwing back his shoulders and straightening his spine, he walked toward a desk where a woman sat at a typewriter.

She looked up at him and smiled. "May I be of assistance?"

"Yes. I'm Paul Anderson and I'm supposed to meet Dr. Walter Henley."

"Oh yes. Dr. Henley told us to expect you." She glanced at a corridor to the left. "I believe he's in the doctors' lounge."

"It's been awhile."

"Right through those doors," She nodded to the left. "Turn down the first corridor to the right and the lounge is on the left."

"Thank you." Paul made his way down the corridor, passing a nurse along the way. She looked familiar, but he only nodded and kept moving. When he reached the lounge, it was empty, which was okay. He needed time to collect himself.

The door swung open behind him and Walter walked in. He wore a broad smile and his pale blue eyes were bright with pleasure, making him look younger than his fifty years. He extended a hand. "Wonderful to see you. I'm grateful for your help." He swung open a narrow closet door in a row of closets. "While you're working here, you can keep your things in this locker." He stepped back, revealing a place for hanging clothing, with a shelf on top for personal items. He fished out a white coat hanging inside and handed it to Paul. "I guessed at the size. Hope it fits."

Paul shrugged out of his overcoat and hung it up in the locker, then put on the white jacket. He held out his arms. "Feels about right."

"And I thought you might need this." Walter lifted a stethoscope out of his jacket pocket and offered it to Paul.

He took it and draped it around his neck. "Now I feel at home," he said with a smile. And he did—the white coat and the stethoscope made him feel like he belonged.

Walter clapped him on the back. "Glad to hear that."

Paul set a lunch pail on the shelf. "Carolyn." He grinned. "I think she's decided I need mothering." The thought that he no longer had a mother broke over Paul like a wave crashing against the shore. "I guess maybe I do," he barely managed to say.

"I'm sorry, Paul. She was a fine woman."

"She was indeed."

"So, you ready to go to work? I thought you might like to make rounds with me later today."

"I'd like that." He sucked in a breath.

Walter reached out and gently squeezed Paul's shoulder. "Relax. You'll do fine."

Paul raised his brows in a way that said he wasn't sure he believed Walter. "The last time I was here—"

"I know. It was a bad day, a terrible day. But this is a new beginning." He headed for the door. "I'll introduce you around. We've got a lot of new doctors and nurses."

The introductions were easy enough, except for a doctor called Craig Alden. His mood seemed intense as he gazed out from beneath heavy dark brows. When he shook Paul's hand, he said a clipped, "Glad to have you." Then he returned to his scrutiny of a chart he'd been going through.

Walter steered Paul down the corridor and away from Dr. Alden. "Don't worry about him. He's all work and no play." He rested a hand on Paul's back. "He's a fine doctor, though."

"That's good to know."

After rounds, Walter said, "I'll need you in the emergency medicine department today. The waiting room is filled to overflowing with sick people. You're a godsend. Tomorrow, I'll need help with my private practice. I'm spending so many hours here I can't get to my regular patients. Will that work for you?"

"Sure. I've done a lot of emergency work the last several months."

"Good. I'll see you later, then."

With a wave, Walter ambled down the corridor and disappeared through a doorway. Paul remained where he was, as if rooted in place. Now what? He imagined his cabin on the homestead, and a longing for the simple, quiet life he had there enveloped him. He and Kate were happy. A craving for her became so intense it hurt. Maybe she'd come for Christmas.

"Doctor! Please! I need a doctor," someone shouted.

The brittle voice snapped Paul back to the present. He ran down the hallway. When he entered a waiting room, he immediately found the source of the frantic shouting. In the midst of a sea of coughing, sniffling, and fevered patients a man sat in a chair with a bandaged hand clutched to his chest. A thin woman with her hair all askew and grasping her coat at the neckline stood beside him. A pretty young nurse was trying to straighten the man's arm so she could look at his hand.

The woman with the wild hair shrieked, "He just nearly cut off his finger with an axe." She caught sight of Paul. "Help him!"

As Paul hurried across the room toward her, he noticed a pink lace nightgown sticking out from beneath her coat. He placed a hand on the woman's shoulder. "Everything's going to be fine. We'll take care of him." He made sure to keep his voice calm. He turned to the suffering man. "Sir, I'd like to have a look at your hand. But we'll need to go into an examination room."

The gentleman looked up, his hand still clutched to his chest. "Whatever you say, doc."

Paul helped him to his feet. "Right this way." He glanced back at the nurse. "Has he been signed in?"

"No. They just got here."

"Ma'am, can you fill out a little paperwork for us while I have a look at his hand?"

Seeming slightly calmer, she asked, "Where do I go?" She clasped her hands against her abdomen.

"Just down there." Paul pointed at a desk where a clerk sat, watching the commotion. "She'll have some questions for you, and when you've filled out the paperwork, a nurse will bring you back." He gave her a reassuring smile. "Your husband's going to be fine."

She let out a wheezy breath and seemed to deflate. "George, will you be all right without me?"

Her husband nodded. "You go ahead, Edith."

Edith walked toward the clerk. Paul steered George to a treatment room. "Here we are. Now, sir, can you lie down for me?"

The nurse rolled a table with instruments alongside the examination table. "It's nice to see you again, Dr. Anderson." She smiled. Something about her looked familiar.

Paul stared at her. "Patty?"

"Uh-huh." Her smile broadened and two dimples appeared, one in each cheek.

"I thought I knew you. You've grown up."

"I was just out of nursing school when I came to work here." She tossed blonde hair off her shoulder.

Paul turned to his patient and unwound the bloodied cloth that had been wrapped around his hand.

"I heard you were in Alaska," Patty said. "What are you doing back here?" Her pale cheeks turned pink. "I'm sorry. That came out wrong. I'm glad you're here, I'm just wondering why. You don't have to tell me, of course. It's none of my business," she prattled.

Paul finished with the wrappings and dropped them into a bowl Patty held out for him. "My mother was sick so I came down. She passed last week. I'm working here temporarily, just to help out."

"I'm terribly sorry to hear about your mother."

"She lived a good long life."

"You two done getting reacquainted? Or do I need to call another doctor?" George held up his bloodied hand.

"Sorry, sir." Paul examined the hand. "I'll need something to clean away this dried blood."

Almost before he could finish speaking, Patty handed him a wash basin with sudsy water, along with a cloth that had been soaking in it.

"Thank you." He washed away the blood from the fringes of the injury. "I'm sorry. This is going to hurt."

As he cleaned the nearly severed finger, George sucked air in through clenched teeth and let out a quiet moan.

"Whoever wrapped this did a good job. The bleeding's pretty much stopped."

"That was my wife, Edith. She did real good, until we got here. She's like that. When you need her, she's steady as a rock, but once the crisis is over, she falls apart."

Paul smiled. "A lot of people are that way." With the damaged finger clean, he examined it more thoroughly. George's index finger was sliced clear down into the bone, between the knuckles and the hand. Paul manipulated it to see if it was broken.

George yowled. "What're you trying to do? Rip it the rest of the way off?"

"Just checking to see if it's broken. I'll need an X-ray to make a determination. The cut's deep, and since it was an axe blade that did the damage, we'd better get a thorough look."

Paul sent George off to get an X-ray done, then moved on to the next patient—a boy with a high fever and cough, like most of the patients waiting . . .

As the day wore on, his confidence grew. Paul eased into the rhythm of hospital life and his role as a doctor. Moving from patient to patient was similar to the kind of doctoring he did in Alaska. He liked it and here he had everything he needed for each procedure, the assistance of a trained nurse, and sterilized equipment.

It was close to two o'clock when there was a break in patients. Paul could scarcely believe the day was nearly over. He was hungry and went to the cafeteria to get a drink to go with his lunch.

Walter was already there, seated at a table. He waved to Paul and said, "The soup's real good today—bean."

Soup sounded good, so Paul decided he'd eat in the cafeteria and save his packed lunch for the following day. He chose a cheese sandwich and a root beer to go along with his soup. He carried his lunch tray to the table where Walter sat. "Mind if I join you?"

"I'd be offended if you didn't." Walter leaned back and lit a cigarette. "So, how's the day been for you?"

"Good. But I'm not sure I've ever seen so many sick people. And some of them are really sick. I've had at least four cases of pneumonia so far today."

"It's a bad bug. And with each week there seem to be more who are sick." He took a drag off his cigarette. "Patty's working with you?"

"Yes. She's a big help. Knows what she's doing."

"When I told her you'd be here today, she was thrilled, maybe too much so." Walter drew his lips into a tight smile. "I don't think she knows you're married."

"What difference does that make? I barely know her."

"As I recall, when she was a very young student nurse, she was quite taken with you. And she's never married. She may see you as the latest most eligible doctor in this place." He took a drag off his cigarette and blew the smoke toward the ceiling. "My guess is she sees you as an attractive catch."

"Nah. I doubt that."

Walter shrugged. "I'll bet I'm right." He grinned.

Paul took a bite of his sandwich and the sharp flavor of cheddar swept his mind back to the first meal he'd shared with Kate. It was the night she'd gotten them thrown out of the restaurant in Anchorage over the way a native couple had been treated. Paul smiled. She was really something. With no dinner, she'd made them cheese sandwiches. His heart swelled at the memory.

"So, do you think you might be interested in staying around for a while? I could use someone like you in my practice and even without this epidemic the hospital is shorthanded."

Paul didn't answer right away. Now that he was here, he

wasn't sure what he felt. He'd run away to Alaska to escape. Now the reason no longer existed. He recognized that the guilt and anger wasn't in this place, it was in his heart. No matter where he went, he took it with him. He gazed out the window at the city rolling across the hillsides, reminding him of heavy timbered forests. "I have a homestead in Alaska. I don't think Kate wants to leave. And the people who live in the bush need a doctor."

Walter nodded. "I understand. But you're a good doctor and this hospital is one of the finest in the country. At St. Francis you'll be challenged—every kind of injury and disease comes through here. And we have the best technology available. Your skills will be tested and tried. They'll be expanded."

Paul took a drink of his root beer. The idea of working here was enticing. Maybe Kate wouldn't mind so much. They already had a house if they wanted it.

Kate sorted mail, her mind preoccupied with Paul. When would he come home? She didn't understand why he had to stay so long. He had two brothers and two sisters who could see to the tasks of his mother's estate. And why was he working at the hospital? Did he want to stay? Had he decided San Francisco was his home and not Alaska?

She felt as if he'd deserted her. During one of the most difficult times in her life, he'd left her to tend to his family. She understood the original urgent need, but now it was the hospital. Did they need him more than she did? It was time for him to come home. She couldn't decide if she was more angry or hurt, but tears stung as she tried hard to blink them away. She didn't want the guys to see her crying.

The sound of the shop door being opened and then closed summoned her curiosity. Alan said something she couldn't quite distinguish. Wiping away the tears, she moved to the door. Angel lay beside the woodstove, clearly more interested in a nap than a conversation between pilots.

"I've got a run up to Kotzebue," Sidney told Alan. "Can't take anything else."

"What about Donald?" Alan asked.

"I'm ready," Donald said. "Talkeetna's not so far, and if Jack'll give me a map, I can find the landing strip.

Kate stepped into the room. "I don't know. It's locked in by mountains and the weather during the winter is pretty unpredictable. And by the looks of things today, I'd say a more experienced pilot would be better."

"You ought to know by now that this territory's nothing like what you'd been flying down south." Sidney grinned. "In fact, you sure you don't want to skedaddle on home? You look a little wet behind the ears."

"I'm not leaving." Donald stared hard at Sidney. "I'm ready to fly this territory." He glanced at Kate. "She can vouch for me. She knows I've been doing okay."

"You mean since you hit the hangar?" Kate smiled.

Donald's face turned red and he stuck out his chin. "It could've happened to anyone."

"All right. All right," Alan said. "I'll take the run to Talkeetna and Donald can come with me." He strode toward the door. "Let's get a move on."

When they walked out, Jack stopped working and stared at the door. He sat and leaned back, picking up his cigar again and clamping it between his teeth. "I'll bet he doesn't make it a month before he turns tail and runs south." He grinned, his gaze moving to Sidney and then Kate.

She lifted her eyebrows, not sure how to respond. It didn't sound like Donald had much experience. She had to agree with Jack—he'd probably pack it in after a while.

A few days later, Jack had errands to run in town and he left Kate and Donald at the shop. Donald gazed out the window. Snow came down softly and the temperature was dropping. "I think I'm ready to make a run to Fairbanks or maybe even Nome. And I'd really like to get a look at the Southeast."

"This time of year, getting back and forth to those places is real dangerous," Kate said, stroking Angel's heavy coat. The dog leaned against her. "Be patient. Allow yourself time to learn."

"I'll never make any money the way I'm going. I spend most of my time sitting in here and feeding the fire." He took a sinker from a box that had been sitting in the shop for at least three days. He dunked the stale donut in his coffee and took a bite.

"When I first came, I had a lot more experience than you, and all Sidney would let me do is the mail run. He owned the airfield back then. I was frustrated, like you, but it was good practice, which I needed. Flying this territory isn't like any other place that I know of. It's big and full of trouble. A pilot never knows what they're going to come up against. I've had some close calls. Probably should have died a few times." She reached out to him and gave his arm a pat. "Be patient. You've only been here two weeks. That's nothing."

The door opened and Jack stepped inside. "Okay, who wants to make a trip to Palmer?"

Knowing how much Donald wanted more flights, Kate said, "Give it to Donald. I'll wait and see if something else comes in."

Later that morning, Kate wished she'd taken the run. There were no other trips that day. Disappointed, she headed for home. The house was quiet as usual. Kate tidied up, made herself a late lunch, and then sat down to write to Paul. There wasn't a lot to say, nothing much had been going on. All she could think of was how much she missed him and wanted him to come home. But she couldn't fill the pages with that. She rested her cheek on her hand. Hoping he'd be home for Christmas, she hadn't made a reservation to travel south. Besides, she'd decided that if he didn't come home, she'd fly down. The weather could be unpredictable, but it was unpredictable everywhere in Alaska. And surprising him would be fun. She looked back at the paper and started writing, telling him about her latest runs, the dogs, and the homestead. Maybe the reminders would bring him home sooner.

When she returned to the airfield, the phone jangled just as she walked into the shop. It was a call from a passenger looking for a ride to Fairbanks. "Figure this is yours," Jack said. "No one else is here."

Just as Kate spoke, Alan flew in.

"When do I need to be ready?" Kate asked.

"Your riders are on their way." Jack glanced outside. "It's late. You'll have to stay over."

"No problem."

There were no more mishaps the next couple of days. On the third day, Kate and Donald were in the shop when a call came in from a homestead north of Palmer. "Ol' Jacob Collins needs a lift into town. Kate, can you give him a ride after you finish your mail run?"

She'd hoped to spend a little time at the cabin during the day. There were chores that needed to be done and she had planned on a visit with her neighbors. "Maybe Donald wants to take it."

"You know how that landing strip can be up there. It gets dicey in the gorge. Never know what the winds are going to do."

Kate looked at Donald.

The young man got to his feet. "I can do it. I've handled every run you've given me—no problem."

"If the wind catches you up there, you can get in a heck of a lot of trouble real fast." Jack studied Donald. "Guess you gotta learn sooner or later." He leaned over his desk and rolled out a map. "Get over here and I'll show you what you need to do."

Happily, Kate completed packing her mailbags. Donald helped her load them.

"Hey, thanks for not saying anything . . . back there."

"Experience is the best teacher. And it's not that tough a landing. Just keep the winds in mind. They can come through the gorge there in a rage."

"I'll remember." Donald chucked the mailbags into the back of Kate's plane. "See you later," he said and strode toward his plane.

Kate got Angel loaded up and she took off shortly after Donald. There was a lot of mail because of the upcoming Christmas holidays, but she still managed to make her deliveries, do a few chores around the homestead and get in a quick visit with Sassa and Lily. She made it into the airfield just at dark. Angel leaped out of the plane and galloped to the office door.

Icy winds whipped at Kate as she trudged toward the shop. When she stepped inside, Sidney, Alan, and Jack were all there. "Feels like we've got a storm coming in. Any reports on the weather?"

Instead of an answer, the men stared at her, their expressions sullen.

"What's up?"

Jack leaned on the desk. "Donald . . . he crashed."

Kate's stomach plummeted. "Is he all right?" She glanced at the door. She hadn't seen his plane, but its absence hadn't registered with her.

"No. He's not," Alan said, his tone icy.

274

"Evidently the wind caught him when he was making his approach—slammed him into the rock face east of the homestead." Sidney took a drag off his cigarette. "He probably died instantly."

"Me and Jack went up and retrieved his body," Alan said. "Why didn't you just take that run, like Jack asked you?"

"I . . . I thought he'd want it. He's been asking for more time in the air."

"He wasn't ready for that one. And you knew it." Alan glared at Kate.

"How could I know that? I haven't even flown with him."

"All right, you two," Sidney said, his tone conciliatory.

Alan ignored Sidney. "If you'd done like Jack said, this wouldn't have happened."

"You're the one who asked Jack to give him a job. Didn't you know how green he was?" Kate knew she was being cruel. But she wasn't about to take the blame for what happened. She stepped closer to Alan and met his gaze. She could see hurt and guilt in his eyes. Shame and sadness enveloped her. He'd been so young. "I guess someone should have gone with him. I'm sorry, Alan. I didn't mean what I said. And you're right. I should have gone. I'm sorry."

Alan walked to the door. He opened it and stood there, then he turned and glared at Kate. "Maybe it's time you acted like a wife and joined your husband." He stepped out, slamming the door behind him.

Kate stared after him. Maybe he was right. Maybe it was time for her to be a wife . . . if Paul still wanted her. He had his old life back, the one before he'd known her.

— 23 —

Peering through a hole she'd scraped in the ice on her windshield, Kate turned her car onto the street and headed for the airfield. She hoped Alan wasn't there. At Donald's funeral, she'd expected him to be solemn and tearful, but he'd refused to speak to her, and if looks could kill . . . well, her life would be over.

She understood. If she'd been more interested in Donald's safety rather than her own needs that day, he wouldn't have died. But she also knew that in a pilot's life, danger and the threat of death were part of the job. Frustration welled up inside Kate. She was tired of blame. She'd carried the blame for Alison's death for years. Then her despair over the early birth and death of her daughter was intensified because she knew it had been her choice that brought on early labor. And now Donald?

Guilt made her chest feel tight. She longed for the comfort of Paul's arms. If only he were home. She'd expected him back long before now. His explanation about why he had to stay was reasonable, but she wanted him to be unreasonable—for her. And the longer he remained in San Francisco, the more she feared he wouldn't return.

She'd sought solace in God's Word, but it was fleeting. And she couldn't find peace in prayer. After the funeral, she'd gone to Muriel's. She needed to talk to someone. But the baby was sick with croup and Muriel was worried and worn out. Kate didn't want to burden her further, so she stayed only a short while, then returned to her empty house.

She was confused. Paul loved her, she was certain of it. At least he had before he'd gone to San Francisco. What if being home had nurtured the memories he had of Susan? And maybe being with his family had convinced him that he belonged in San Francisco? Kate felt sick. She needed to see him.

Maybe there wouldn't be any runs today. She wanted to be home at the creek, tucked away in the cabin where she could feel cozy and secure.

The temperatures were frigid and a gray sky threatened snow. By the time she'd reached the airfield, the interior of her car still wasn't warm. She pulled to a stop in front of the shop, dropped the gearshift into first, and shut off the engine. The only plane on the field other than Jack's was Alan's. Kate let out a groan.

She sat in the car for a few minutes. She wasn't ready to talk to him. Angel nudged her hand and Kate scratched the underside of her neck. "So, you ready for another day?"

Kate forced herself to open the car door and step out. An icy wind caught hold of her hood. She shivered. Angel leaped out and ran for the shop door. Kate walked through fresh snow, and when she stepped inside the shop heat was the first thing she felt. She headed toward the stove, but didn't see Alan. She glanced at Jack, who was filling a cup with coffee. "Morning. You have anything for me?"

Jack set the coffeepot back on the cookstove. "I was just getting ready to call you." He took a drink of the coffee. "I need you to make a run up to Palmer with me."

Disappointment swept over Kate. "What's up?"

"I've got a passenger who needs a ride up, and I've got to fly a plane down for a friend of mine. I'll need you to fly my bird back for me."

"Who's going to man the shop?"

"Alan's on his way in. He's down in the dumps and said he'd fill in for me while I'm out." His eyes slid to Angel. "I don't know about taking the dog."

"She won't be a problem and this time of year she's not shedding."

Jack lifted his eyebrows in a mocking way, then said with a resigned voice, "All right."

Kate hadn't flown with Jack in a long while. She'd never much liked it. His surly personality seemed even more extreme in close quarters. Maybe today wouldn't be so bad. Recently he'd been almost cordial. "Sure. I'll go along. I can always use the money."

"Good." Jack took another drink from the cup and then set the mug on his desk. He pulled on his parka and dug into the pockets for his gloves. "Give me a hand with the plane."

Jack's Stinson was faster than her Pacemaker, but it was also smaller—a four seater with little storage space. Yet Kate couldn't deny that it was a good plane. It was reliable, plus fast and maneuverable, which made it easier to get in and out of tight spots. Kate helped Jack pull off the tarp. While he poured in warm oil and fueled up the plane, Kate scraped ice from the windows and made sure the fuselage, tail, and wings were ice free.

About the time the plane was warmed up and ready to go, a pickup pulled onto the field. The driver climbed out and walked around to the bed. He lifted out a suitcase. Another man, much larger than the first, heaved himself out of the truck. He took the suitcase and lumbered toward the plane.

Kate guessed he weighed more than three hundred pounds. She wondered if he'd fit through the plane door and into a seat.

Jack eyed him, but said nothing. When he approached, Jack said, "You must be Eugene Phelps." He held out a hand in greeting.

"That I am," he said, shaking Jack's hand.

"I'm Jack Rydell."

Eugene's gaze fell on Kate. "You headed for Palmer, too?"

"No. I'm helping out Jack."

"She's one of my pilots." Kate thought she heard a tone of pride in Jack's voice.

"Nice to meet you, Kate," Eugene said, clasping her hand with fingers that looked like sausages. He smiled and his flushed cheeks rounded. His two chins became three.

"We better be on our way, otherwise the daylight won't hold out long enough for us to get back." Jack stood at the bottom of the steps. "Everything's ready to go." He took the suitcase and climbed inside.

Kate waited with Angel. Eugene stood at the bottom of the steps, rubbed his clean-shaven chin, and studied the door. She guessed he was trying to figure out just how he was going to fit his bulk through it. Kate was more concerned about how the plane would handle with Eugene's extra weight—there was no way to distribute it.

Eugene lugged himself up the steps, hesitated at the door, then managed to squeeze through. He sat in one of the two rear seats. Angel leaped inside. Kate climbed in and closed the door, then squeezed past him to get to the front passenger seat. Angel sat in the other passenger seat in back. Maybe her weight would help offset some of Eugene's.

Jack glanced back and smirked, then leaned closer to Kate and said, "Good thing this is a short flight." He taxied as close to the end of the runway as possible and lined up for takeoff. He'd need all the space he could get to make sure the plane was airborne in time to clear the trees.

Jack revved the engine and then opened the throttle as he sped down the airstrip. The plane rolled toward the end of the runway. For a moment it looked like they might not get off the ground soon enough. Jack pulled back on the stick and the skis lifted, though the Stinson felt sluggish.

"Eugene," Jack hollered. "Move closer to the middle aisle and lean forward." The big man's face reddened. Wearing a humiliated expression, he did as he was asked. Kate could swear the tops of the trees tickled the plane's belly as they cruised over them, but they'd made it and headed north.

In the turns, the plane was slightly less responsive than usual, but Jack seemed at ease. He never said much when he flew and today was no exception. Kate wondered what he was thinking. The plane made a sudden dip slightly left. Kate looked back to see that Eugene, who had been nodding off, had fallen against the window and was fast asleep.

She turned to face the front, gave Jack a sidelong look, then folded her arms over her chest. Sinking down into her seat, she leaned her head back and closed her eyes. As always, her thoughts turned to Paul. She hadn't heard from him in four days. No phone call. No letter. She wondered what he was doing. Christmas was only two weeks away. Would he make it home? He'd have to decide soon. It was already nearly too late to travel by ship. It was possible that if he didn't sail, he could take a passenger flight, but those were spotty this time of year. She decided that when she got back to Anchorage, she'd call him. The idea of them not being on the homestead for Christmas made her stomach ache. Her hope was slipping away that their first Christmas, as husband and wife, would be spent celebrating together at the creek.

Again, trepidation trudged through her mind and her heart. Had he changed? She couldn't imagine him other than strong and steady and gentle-hearted. No matter where he lived, that's the kind of man he was.

She felt a sudden flare of anger toward his family. Had they convinced him to stay in San Francisco and work for the hospital? Maybe Audrey didn't really need him. What if they'd convinced him his time in Alaska had been a mistake—that she was a mistake?

She tried to envision life in a city like San Francisco. If she and Paul lived in a place like that, they wouldn't be the same couple. Alaska was part of who they were.

She gazed down at the forest below. Alders and cottonwoods stood naked and frozen, their bare branches mounded with shavings of white. Wind whipped flurries of snow, almost like a white fog, about the plane. In spite of the low visibility Kate felt at ease. Jack had always bragged about his skill as a pilot. Kate hated to admit it, but it was true—he was good. And he'd made this trip more times than anyone she knew.

When they reached Palmer, the snow was coming down hard. Jack remained calm and confident. Kate hoped the weather would clear so she wouldn't have to stay over in Palmer. She wanted to go home to the cabin.

"Hey, Eugene. Wake up!" Jack yelled. "I need you to move toward the center of the plane." Jack didn't bother to look back to see if Eugene had followed orders. He kept his full attention on his job, his eyes on the landing strip, now buried in fresh snow.

Eugene scooted toward the aisle and the plane dipped slightly to the right. Jack made a quick correction and at the same time a crosswind hit them. The runway was coming up fast. Jack skillfully touched the pedals, kept a light hand on the stick, and the bird came back into balance. The skis touched down smoothly and then they were on the ground. Jack hadn't shown the slightest sign of stress.

He grinned. "That was fun."

Maybe he *was* the best pilot around. Kate was impressed. "Good job," she said.

"What did you expect?" Jack was still in possession of his usual bravado. "I've done this a thousand times. Easy as pie."

He taxied toward the end of the runway, stopping close to a small building. The place looked deserted. There'd be no hot coffee or fire to keep them warm.

Jack shut down the engine and then headed for the back of the plane. He squeezed past Eugene and opened the door. Icy wind and snow swirled inside. He grabbed Eugene's bag and climbed out, then waited while the big man worked to get free of the plane and made his way down the steps. Even in the cold, he was sweating. Angel waited for Kate, then climbed out ahead of her.

Eugene looked about. "I was expecting a ride." A few moments later, a Ford sedan slid around a corner at the end of the field and headed toward the cluster of travelers. Eugene waved, then turned to Jack and reached into his pocket. He took out a wallet and opened it, then counted out several bills and handed them to Jack. "Thank you."

"Anytime." Jack tucked the money into his front pants pocket.

Eugene gave Kate a little wave, opened the back door of the sedan, and threw in his suitcase, then climbed into the front passenger seat. Tires spinning, rear end fishtailing, the car moved away and disappeared in the blowing snow.

Jack gazed around. "Hmm." He walked toward a hangar and disappeared inside. A few moments later, he reappeared. "Plane's here, but no Eddie. Something must have held him up. He's usually pretty reliable."

"So, what now?" Kate asked. "Obviously there's no one in the shop. And I'm not about to stand out here and freeze to death." She pulled her hood closer around her face.

"He'll show up. Until then, how about you and I get something to eat."

"Sounds good to me." Squinting, she looked up into the falling snow. "Do you think this storm's going to let up?"

Jack shrugged. "How should I know?" He headed toward the edge of town, which lay only a few blocks away.

When they reached the café, Kate tapped the toe of her boots against the porch to knock off snow. Jack held the door for her. She stepped inside, thankful to be out of the weather. Angel managed to slip in ahead of Jack. Kate pushed back her hood, savoring the warmth of the room and the smell of coffee and cooking meat.

"What are you two doing out in this kind of weather?" Ruth, the owner of the café, asked.

"Had a passenger to deliver and a plane to pick up," Jack said.

"Only you would be crazy enough to fly in a snowstorm."

"It wasn't snowing when we left Anchorage," Jack said as he moved to a small table plastered with bright green paint with wooden chairs to match. He sat down and Kate took a chair across from him. Angel lay beside her.

Ruth grabbed two mugs and a pot of coffee. She set the cups in front of Jack and Kate. "Good to see you, Kate." She smiled, creases from lots of smiles deepening at the edges of her blue eyes.

"Seems I'm in here at least every few weeks these days."

"And where's that handsome husband of yours?"

"San Francisco . . . his mother died."

"Ah sweetie, I'm sorry. You tell Paul for me."

"I will." *If I ever see him*, she thought.

Ruth filled the two mugs. "Figure you'd want coffee on a day like this." She glanced out the window. "You'll probably need a couple of rooms over at the hotel. Don't look like you'll be flying back to Anchorage today."

"What's your special, Ruthie?" Jack sat back in his chair and studied the woman, a touch of humor in his eyes.

Kate wasn't sure she'd ever seen that look on Jack's face before. If she didn't know better, she'd say he was sweet on Ruth.

"Don't call me Ruthie. My name's Ruth."

"I think Ruthie sounds a lot sweeter. Gotta make up for your prickles somehow."

Ruth ignored the remark, but a smile tugged at the corners of her lips. She pulled a pencil and a pad out of her apron pocket. "So, what would you like? And there's no special, just the usual."

Jack took a toothpick out of a container on the table and stuck it between his teeth. "How 'bout liver and onions. You make the best around. Just make sure you get a thick slab of liver."

"You know how I make them. It'll be just how you like it." She turned to Kate. "And how about you, honey?"

"I'd like a toasted cheese sandwich and some potato chips."

"You want a Coke to go with that?"

"No thanks. Coffee's fine. But I would like a little cream with the coffee."

"I'll get that for you." She winked at Jack before walking away, then headed for the counter.

Kate could barely keep from chuckling as she watched a smile emerge on Jack's face. He *was* sweet on her. More interesting than that was Ruth seemed to like Jack.

Kate leaned on the table and said under her breath, "Seems you've been keeping a secret hidden away up here in the valley."

Jack looked as if he didn't know what she was talking

about. "Secret? What secret?" He pushed against the table, straightening his arms and his spine.

"Don't worry. I won't say a thing." Kate grinned and leaned back in her chair. "But what happened to Linda?"

"She was a little too sweet for my taste." A devilish grin touched Jack's lips. "Now, a woman like Ruth . . . well, she's something special."

Ruth returned with the cream. She set a small pitcher down in front of Kate. "Fresh today. Gertrude brought it in." Ruth shook her head. "Can't imagine milking those filthy cows morning and night, especially during the winter. My hat's off to the farmers around here. It's a hard life." She tucked her shoulder-length blonde hair behind her ears. "I'm happy right where I am. Don't mind cooking, and being here I get to see folks coming and going."

"You're not busy today." Jack gazed toward the kitchen. "And where's your help?"

"Sent Sally home. Nearly left myself. Didn't think I'd have any customers. People tend to hide out when the weather gets bad." She walked toward the kitchen. "I'll have your meals in two shakes."

Jack watched her go, admiration in his eyes. When she disappeared into the kitchen he turned back to his coffee and took a drink, then stared out the window. "Storm's getting worse." His lips tightened into a line. "Figure Ruthie's probably right. We'll have to check in at the hotel. Won't make any money this way."

Kate added cream to her coffee. She didn't want to be here either. She'd planned on being tucked away, warm and safe at the cabin.

Jack set his cup on the table. He stared at the dark brew for a long moment and then cleared his throat. "Been wanting to talk to you." He pressed a hand over the top of the cup.

Jack only talked to her when something was wrong. This couldn't be good. Her stomach tightened and she set her cup on the table. "What about?"

"A couple of things, actually." Jack slid his lower jaw to one side. "First off, I wanted you to know that I don't think you had anything to do with Donald's dying. He made his own choice. And Alan never let on how wet behind the ears Donald was. I wouldn't have hired him if I'd known." He shook his head in disgust. "These young bucks come up here, thinking they're invincible. Next thing you know they're dead." He took a drink of coffee. "I don't want you carrying around a load of guilt that doesn't belong to you."

That was the last thing Kate had expected to hear. Ever since she'd gone to work at the airport, anything that went wrong, Jack seemed to find a way to blame her for it. "Well . . . thanks, Jack. I appreciate your saying that. But I wish I'd taken that flight. Instead, all I could think about was getting home." She let out a breath. "At the very least I should have gone with him."

"Like I said, none of us knew how green he was. If we had, everyone would have made runs with him to make sure he knew what he was doing." Jack scrubbed his short-shaven beard.

Kate had never seen him like this. She wondered what had come over him. A crash came from the kitchen. "I hope that's not our dinner."

"You need any help back there, Ruthie?" Jack called.

She peeked out the door. "No. Don't need no help."

Jack pushed his empty coffee cup aside and clasped his hands on the table in front of him. "And the other thing is . . ." He pushed his tongue into his cheek. "I'm sorry."

Kate wondered if she'd heard right. "Sorry? About what?"

"I been hard on you . . . from the very beginning. I'm not

exactly the easiest guy to get along with no matter who you are, I know that." He tightened the grip he had on his hands. "But I was harder on you. Figured I'd chase you off easy, but you wouldn't give up." He dared a glance at her, then looked back at his hands. "When you showed up, I didn't think any woman belonged in a plane, especially not in this territory. And then you turned out to be good. Made me madder than the dickens. Don't know why exactly, but doggone it, a woman pilot shouldn't be better than a guy."

Kate was stupefied.

He glanced toward the kitchen doorway. "When you left after Mike died, I figured we'd never see you again, that you were just a fragile female like I thought. And then you came back, more determined than ever. And you kept right on flying. It was back then that I started wondering if I'd been unfair. After the baby . . . you showed up for work. I never figured that would happen."

Kate tightened her hold on her coffee cup. Jack was making it sound like all of it had been easy for her. What would he think if he knew how close she'd come to never flying again?

"You showed me I was wrong. You're as good and maybe even better than any one of us guys." He licked his lips. "Well, I just needed you to know that."

"I nearly didn't come back after Mike died," Kate said. "I'm not brave or anything like that. I just love to fly. Guess that just makes me stupid." She half smiled. "Like all the rest of you pilots."

Jack chuckled. "You got that right." He sat straighter in his chair. "Don't get any ideas about me being soft on you. I'm not. I'm the same mean cuss I've always been."

"I know," Kate said, but she felt warm inside. If Jack had come around to see her as a pilot, that meant she'd done what she'd set out to do—prove women could be as good as men when it came to flying. She'd earned her place among the Alaskan pilots. "Thanks for telling me. It means a lot. And I don't think you're as mean as you put on. But I won't tell anyone." She grinned, but knew that in another moment things would go back to the way they'd been before. That was all right. She knew the truth.

"So, where's that husband of yours? Does he plan on coming back?"

Kate didn't want to talk about Paul, especially when she didn't know what was going on with him. "After his mother died, the family wanted him to help with the estate. And there's a flu outbreak in San Francisco, so he's working at the hospital, helping out. He'll be gone for a while."

"I thought he had a lot of family. Can't they take care of things like the estate? And he's got a new wife up here and a whole lot of people counting on him. And San Francisco's got plenty of doctors."

Kate shrugged.

"You tell that man to get himself back up here," he snarled. "I mean it. He needs to get his rear home." His voice softened. "If you have to, go get him."

— 24 —

The weather was clear and cold when Kate flew into
Anchorage. Her thoughts on Paul, she scrambled out
of the plane and hurried toward the shop. Maybe he'd
called.

Angel squeezed through the door in front of Kate. Alan was
the only one in the shop. Ill at ease, Kate said a quiet hello,
signed in, and then asked, "Any telephone messages for me?"

"Nope." He dunked a sinker into his cup of coffee and
took a bite.

Kate felt as if the oxygen had been sucked out of her lungs.
Why hadn't he called? Busy or not, he could make time for a
simple phone call. Hurt twisted into anger. She'd call him.

Putting aside her ire, Kate approached Alan, who sat behind the desk, his feet propped on an open drawer and his face
hidden behind a comic book. He didn't look up. Kate cleared
her throat and he peered around the edge of the comic. "I
need to say something . . . about Donald . . . You were right.
I should have gone with him. Saying I'm sorry won't change
anything, but I am . . . sorry."

Alan put the comic book down. "It's not your fault. Like
you said, I'm the one who got him the job in the first place.

I knew he had a lot to learn. Just figured I'd have more time to work with him. I apologize for taking my hurt and guilt out on you."

Kate leaned on the table. "All of us should have made time to help him."

"Yeah, I guess so, but the fact is he chose to go. Every one of us knows when we take a run we might not come back. He knew it, but he wanted to fly and he was willing to take the risk."

Kate straightened. "He was just like the rest of us."

"Yep." Alan nodded.

Kate moved toward the door. "Jack should be here anytime. I'm heading out to the creek. I'll see you in a few days." She opened the door. "God willing."

She stepped outside, pulled the door shut and walked to her car. While it warmed up, she scraped ice off the windows. Disappointment, like a heavy weight, settled over her shoulders. She couldn't think of any good reason why Paul hadn't called.

By the time Kate reached the house, she'd changed her mind about calling him. If he wanted to talk to her, he would've called. She packed a bag and then headed back to the airfield. Once at the cabin, she'd feel better.

Kate flew up the Susitna and as she neared Bear Creek she could feel tight muscles relax. She was nearly home. When she flew over the cabin, feelings of elation and sadness mingled. It would feel like home if Paul were here.

Christmas was less than two weeks away. If he were coming home, he was nearly out of time. Maybe he planned to surprise her. Kate wanted to believe the fantasy, but she knew better. Paul wasn't the spontaneous type.

She flew over the landing strip to check for ruts and debris. All looked well, so she banked the plane and lined up for the landing. When her skis touched down, they bounced over small ridges in the ice. Angel hopped out of her seat and trotted to the door. Kate shut down the engine and climbed into the back. "Okay, you're free," she said, opening the door. Angel leaped out and ran toward the cabin where Kate could hear the other dogs barking. Angel had a homecoming. If only she did too.

Kate gazed across the frozen creek toward the shoreline. Mostly hidden by trees, the cabin was barely visible. She remembered how homecomings used to be. Smoke would trail from the chimney and Paul would greet her at the creek edge, pulling her into an embrace and kissing her. They'd walk up the path together and she'd be welcomed into a warm home with the aroma of roasting meat or stew. Kate chased away the image. Today he wasn't here.

After she'd secured the plane and drained the oil, Kate grabbed her knapsack and headed across the frozen creek toward the trail. Ice crunched beneath her boots. When she walked into the clearing behind the house, the dogs barked a greeting. She should pay the Warren boys. With Paul's absence, they'd done a lot of extra work with the dogs and deserved to be paid.

Angel tussled with Jackpot and Buck lunged on his lead, straining toward Kate. Nita sat on her haunches, tail whacking the snow-covered ground. Kate walked up to her and rested a hand on the dog's head. "Good to see you, girl." Nita stood and rubbed against Kate's leg. Kate moved to Buck. "Stay down," she said. He was too big and might knock her on her backside. After giving him a thorough rubdown, she knelt and put her arms around his neck. Overcome by emotion, she buried her face in his thick ruff.

"Oh, I've missed you," Kate said, feeling as if she were speaking to Paul. She wiped away tears, told herself to stop being silly and stood.

She freed the three dogs so they could run. All four romped down the trail. Kate smiled. Even without Paul, it was good to be home.

She gazed at the headstone in the clearing and remembered. Her heart ached. Being home would never again be fully satisfying. Someone would always be missing. The snow had been cleared away. Either Sassa or Lily deserved her thanks.

With a heavy sigh, Kate headed indoors. First off, she lit a fire in the stove, then put on a pot of coffee. A quick glance through the cupboards told her she should have stopped at the mercantile in Anchorage. She hadn't been thinking about food. There was enough to cobble together some dinner, but tomorrow she'd have to do some baking and raid the cache.

A knock sounded at the back door. It was Sassa and she was wearing a big smile.

"Hi," Kate said, opening the door. "How nice to have a visitor."

"I heard your plane and thought you might want some company. I brought you fresh biscuits with dried highbush cranberries in them."

"They sound delicious. And your timing is perfect. I was just rummaging through my cupboards and had decided I need to do some baking." She accepted the basket from Sassa. "Will you share one with me along with a cup of coffee?"

"Oh sure." Sassa walked indoors and looked around. "So, Paul's not with you?"

"No. He's still in San Francisco."

Sassa raised an eyebrow, but said nothing more about his absence. Sitting at the table, she clasped her hands in front of her. "How are you?"

"I'm fine—strong as ever." Kate set the biscuits on the table, took butter out of the cupboard, and placed it beside the biscuits. "Sorry. It's frozen. Maybe it'll soften a little as the room warms up." She sat. "It'll be a few more minutes before the coffee's ready." She rested her arms on the table. "How's the family?"

"Good. Lily and Clint are getting married." Sassa's smile returned.

"I knew they would. When is the wedding?"

"In three days. She'll tell you all about it. I don't think she wanted me to say anything, but . . . how could I keep it a secret?" Sassa laughed. "Good news needs to be shared."

"I'm happy for them. It's wonderful news."

"It is. We weren't meant to be alone." Sassa gazed at her folded hands. "What about you and Paul? Why is he still gone?"

Kate nearly groaned. Instead she tried to make light of Sassa's inquiry. "If I had a penny for every time I've been asked that question." She made an effort to smile. "Paul's helping with the estate and he's working at the hospital because there is a flu outbreak in the city."

Sassa compressed her lips and the line of her jaw tightened. "I don't understand any of that. He has a family here."

Kate didn't want Sassa to be angry with Paul. It only made her feel worse. "He'll be back as soon as he can. I'm sure of it."

Sassa pushed herself out of her chair and walked to the window. With her arms folded across her chest, she gazed outside. "It's too soon . . . since your child died. There is no good reason for him to be gone, not now." Her voice was hard.

"He had to go. His mother was deathly ill."

"Yes." She turned and looked at Kate. "But now she is gone and that is over." Creases furrowed her brow. "Paul has never disappointed me . . . until now." She looked intently at Kate. "This is not right. You go get your husband and bring him home."

Kate wanted him here, but she wasn't about to drag him

back. He had to want to be here. "I . . . I . . ." She let out a huff and then turned her back to Sassa. "I'm beginning to think he wants to stay in San Francisco."

"No. Not Paul." Sassa put an arm around Kate's shoulders.

Kate glanced at her. "If he does, I'll have to live there too."

"Did he say that he wants to stay?"

"No. But he hasn't called me in four days, and the last time I talked to him, he sounded content there, as if he were home."

Sassa held up a hand. "First, phone calls cost a lot. And you suppose too much. Our minds can play tricks on us." She smiled softly. "You and Paul belong here. Maybe he needs reminding. You go and help him remember."

"I'm considering it."

"Okay. But don't wait too long."

When Kate went to bed that night, she was unable to sleep. She couldn't decide if she ought to go to San Francisco or not. And if Paul wanted to live there, how would she convince him to return to Alaska? Should she?

She tried to imagine what it would be like and what she would say. When she'd talked to him on the telephone, he hadn't seemed to understand how she felt. Instead of promising to come home, he'd invited her to spend Christmas with him and his family.

Kate finally fell asleep, but there was no peace in slumber. Instead she dreamed a terrible dream. Paul was in a boat way out in the sea. Watching from a much larger boat, Kate knew something terrible was going to happen.

Paul's boat was too small and the wind blew harder and harder and the waves got bigger and bigger. His vessel started to sink. He cried out for help and Kate rowed and rowed. But no matter how hard she rowed, she never got any closer. She watched Paul's boat sink, engulfed by dark waters. For a time, Paul managed to stay afloat. Kate tried to get to him, but he succumbed and disappeared beneath the waves.

When she woke, Kate was shaking. At first it felt real, not like a dream. She climbed out of bed and stood for a moment, still quaking. She filled her lungs with air, then went to the kitchen and splashed her face with cold water. The dream was still close.

She filled a glass with water, then went to the front room where she huddled in a blanket on Paul's chair. If only he were here where she knew he was safe. Had the dream been a sign? Did he need her? Did God still speak to people in dreams?

She had to go after him.

Kate spent the remainder of the night in the chair. She slept, but mostly she waited for daylight. If she was going to San Francisco, there were preparations she needed to make.

Before sunrise, she climbed out of the chair, stoked the fire, and put on coffee. Then she got dressed and pulled on her boots, lacing them up tightly. She took down her parka and put it on, then filled a mug with coffee. Needing brisk air to refresh her mind, she stepped out onto the porch. Sunlight blushed pink in the morning sky. Angel hurried past Kate and ran straight to the other dogs. They greeted one another, whining and tussling, their chains clanking.

It was cold, but Kate didn't mind. Piles of white mounded against the cache and the toolshed. A squawk startled her and she turned to see Jasper sitting on his perch.

"So, you're back." Kate liked that. In ways she couldn't understand, the bird and Paul were connected in some manner. Having Jasper here made Paul feel closer. Although she knew better, Kate tugged off a glove and reached out to stroke the raven's shiny black head. She was surprised that he didn't peck at her. Instead he remained still and allowed her to touch him. Up until this moment, Jasper had never allowed anyone to touch him, except Paul. Kate's heart warmed as she stroked the bird's head and then ran her finger tips over the feathers on his back. They felt silky.

Why was he allowing this? Was it a sign? Kate had never been one to look for signs, but would she be foolish to ignore them? First, several people had told her to get Paul, then the dream, and now Jasper. Surely it was more than coincidence.

Her voice low and warm she said, "It's good to finally get to know you. I wish I could take you with me. I think Paul would like to see you." She could hardly wait to tell him that Jasper had allowed her to pet him.

Kate set her mug on the railing, then scraped snow off the top step and sat down. She needed to plan. If she was going to leave, it had to be soon. She wanted to be in San Francisco before Christmas. The idea of surprising Paul tantalized her. Yet fear prodded her. What if he didn't respond the way she hoped? Of course he would. He'd invited her, hadn't he? She didn't much like the idea of spending Christmas with people she didn't know. It was possible they saw her as a threat, someone who would take Paul away from them.

"Hello there," Lily called as she walked into the yard.

Kate stood. "Hi."

Lily moved to the bottom of the steps. "What are you doing out here?"

Kate sucked in a deep breath. "I'm enjoying the sunshine, but the cold's about to chase me indoors." She glanced at the thermometer. It had dropped to 10 degrees.

"It's nice to have you home. How long are you going to be here?"

Kate hadn't solidified her plans yet, so she simply said, "Probably a few days. I'm sure Jack will have work for me soon."

Lily nodded.

Kate looked out at the headstone that marked her little girl's grave. "Who took care of the grave while I was gone?"

"I did. Well, me and Clint. I thought you'd feel better knowing she wasn't being ignored."

"That was thoughtful. Thank you. I have fresh coffee and biscuits your mother brought over yesterday. Would you like some?"

"I was hoping you'd ask." Lily followed Kate indoors and she sat at the table while Kate filled a cup with coffee and set the biscuits on the table.

"I'm thinking about writing to Teddy's father."

"I thought you already had."

"I did, but he didn't answer. Maybe he didn't get it. Or maybe he wasn't ready to be a father. But Clint and I've been talking and we think he deserves another chance. It seems right to let him know how Teddy's doing. And let him know that if he wants, he can come and see him." Lily picked up a biscuit, broke off a piece, and popped it in her mouth.

Kate set Lily's coffee on the table. "I thought you didn't want to have anything to do with him."

"After talking to Clint about it . . . and since we're getting married"—a smile momentarily emerged on Lily's face—"it seems like the right thing to do."

"Your mother told me about you and Clint. I'm happy for you. She said you're getting married right away."

"Two days. There's no reason to wait. The minister is coming from Susitna Station."

"I think it's wonderful. You two belong together."

"I'd love it if you'd stand up with me."

"Oh." Kate knew it would mean putting off her trip, but how could she say no? "I'd be honored."

"Thank you." Lily took a drink of coffee. "I can barely wait to be Clint's wife. He's a wonderful man."

"What should I wear?" Kate asked.

"It's just in Mama's living room. Do you have a dress you wear to church?"

"I do."

"I'm sure that will be just right." With a smile on her lips, Lily closed her eyes. "I can't imagine being married." She wrapped her arms around her torso. "Two more days feels like forever." She leaned toward Kate and said softly, "I just wish Paul were here. Do you know when he'll be back?"

"No. But I'm going to find out."

— 25 —

Paul pushed away from the table and carried his breakfast dishes to the counter. "That was good. Thank you, Carolyn."

She set the dishes in the sink and turned on the water. "It's the least I can do."

"You're here every day, working. Then you go home and take care of your own family."

She smiled at him over her shoulder. "I'm glad to do it."

Paul gave her a sideways hug. "What do you need me to do today?"

Carolyn added soap flakes to the water. "I thought you were working for Dr. Henley."

"Not until this afternoon."

Carolyn turned toward Paul and leaned a hip against the counter. "I've been thinking about Kate. Christmas is nearly here. I can't imagine if Charles and I had spent our first Christmas apart. And worse, Kate just lost a child." Her tone somber, she added, "Maybe it's time you went home."

"But—"

"You've got to stop listening to Audrey. I love her dearly, but she is a bit self-centered. Just because she wants you here

doesn't mean you should stay. She will be fine without you."
She smiled tenderly. "Nothing would make me happier than
having you close by, but I'm not so sure that's what's best for
you . . . or for Kate."

Paul was having trouble deciding what he ought to do. He
missed Kate and knew that soon he had to close the distance
between them. He was happy in San Francisco. Life here was
stimulating. He enjoyed working with Walter, and having the
first-rate facilities of St. Francis at his disposal was something
every doctor wanted. Walter had promised him opportunities
to take part in breakthrough surgeries. He didn't have any
of that in Alaska. And leaving made him feel as if he were
shirking his family duties, again. He had a chance to make
up for some of the lost years.

"I wish I'd returned sooner . . . at least for Mother's sake."
He pushed his fingers through his hair. "I'm not sure what
to do. While I was in Alaska, I felt at peace—I loved it, but
here I have my family and my medical practice."

"You were working as a doctor in Alaska. And you have
family there too." Carolyn's voice was sharp. "Or have you
forgotten?" She turned the water faucets off.

"Of course I haven't. I think about Kate all the time."

"Do you think that does her a bit of good? Speaking as
a woman, I'd prefer to have my husband's arms around me
more than his thoughts."

"I asked her to come down for Christmas. And I was wondering how she'd feel about living here. We could buy a place
outside the city. And she could still fly."

Doubt touched Carolyn's brown eyes. "I understood why
you left after Susan died. And I know you feel as if you deserted your family. But we were fine. You were the one who
needed us. I'm sorry I didn't stay in touch more. I relied on
Robert's reports too much."

Paul leaned against the counter. "I knew you cared. I'm the one who withdrew." An ache tightened in his throat. "You've all been so good to me. And Mom . . . I'm grateful I got to spend time with her."

Carolyn rested a hand on his arm. "We are glad you're here, but do you know that when you talk about Alaska, something in your face changes—it comes to life, especially when you talk about the adventures you and Kate shared. Every time you mention her, it's like the sun comes out."

"Really?" Paul liked that. "I wish she was here. I doubt she'll fly down this time of year. It's too dangerous even for Kate. If she's going to make it in time for Christmas, though, she's nearly out of time to get a steamer. I haven't been able to get through to her. I've called the airfield but no one answers. And she hasn't been at the house. She's probably working or out at the cabin."

"I'll keep you both in my prayers." Rolling up her sleeves, she said, "I'd better get these dishes taken care of."

"So, what do you want me to do?"

"Some of Mother's things still need going through. Her office hasn't been touched."

"I can take care of that."

"Can you go through her desk and sort out what needs to be saved and what needs to be thrown away? There are boxes in the garage."

"Sure." Paul gave Carolyn a hug before heading out of the house.

When he stepped inside the office, the richness of the room enveloped him in warmth. His mother had made it a sanctuary of sorts. All the wood furniture was rich mahogany and there was an elegant suite of chairs and a davenport upholstered with taupe and rose angora mohair. Two walls were filled from floor to ceiling by bookcases crowded with books of every kind. As a boy, Paul had spent hours lounging on the window seat reading.

He placed the boxes by the desk, then walked to the bookshelf and took down a copy of Dickens' *A Christmas Carol*. He blew dust from the cover and opened it, thumbing through the pages. One Christmas season he'd read the book to his nieces and nephews. He smiled at the memory of the children's visits and how they'd always insisted on his reading more of the story to them. He replaced the book on the shelf. Sorting through all of them would have to be a family task that they did together.

He walked to the window and opened heavy brocade curtains. Light flooded the room. He moved to the desk and sat in a leather chair. His mother's presence seemed to linger here. With a heavy sigh, he started with the top of the desk. He set a burnished gold lamp with a hand-painted glazed panel in one of two boxes, added a box of stationery, and then picked up his mother's fountain pen. She'd been meticulous in her writing, never leaving smudges, and she had a florid script.

He placed the pen alongside the stationery, then added a large dictionary to the box. Scrap paper and odds and ends were tossed into a box for disposal. He had to tug on the center drawer to get it open. It was tidy and had few contents— another pen, envelopes, a book of poetry, and a photograph of him and Susan. He gazed at the young couple staring back at him. He barely recognized himself, but Susan was just as he remembered, with her shiny blonde hair and sweet smile. Instead of the gut-wrenching ache he'd grown accustomed to, he felt the happiness they'd shared. He slid the picture into his breast pocket.

Paul tackled the topside drawer next. It had an assortment of items—business cards, a copy of the book *Jane Eyre*, more photos, and a variety of office supplies. He reached into the back of the drawer and his fingers found the corner of an envelope wedged between the drawer and the desk. He tugged and it came loose.

It was still sealed. Paul turned it over, expecting it to be something his mother had overlooked and never mailed. His eyes went to the return address and his stomach dropped. It was from Susan. His gaze moved to the postage date—two days before her death. Staring at the envelope, he leaned on the desk. His mother must have misplaced it. Otherwise she'd certainly have opened it.

Wondering why Susan had written to his mother, Paul slid the envelope into his inside vest pocket. His hand trembled. He wasn't ready to read it.

While Paul finished sorting through his mother's things, his mind lingered on the letter. When he'd finished, he carried out the box of trash. "Carolyn," he called.

She appeared at the top of the stairs. "Have you finished?"

"I did. I left a box of usable items on the desk and I'll dump these things in the garbage. Then I'll be on my way."

"Thank you for taking care of that. Make sure to get your lunch before you leave. It's on the kitchen counter."

"Thank you." Paul rested his hand on his chest. He could feel the letter in his shirt pocket. He headed for the kitchen, picked up his lunch pail, and headed for the front door. Maybe he should read it before he started work? No. He'd have to be on his way to the next patient and he'd rather have time to consider its contents. He lifted his coat off the stand in the entryway, pulled it on, and left the house.

He stopped at Walter's office and picked up a list of names and addresses of patients who needed to see a doctor that day, and then he set off. Walter made weekly visits to the first man on the list, Dale Brown. He was elderly and bedridden with arthritis. The house smelled of liniment and cigarettes.

While Paul did his examination, Mr. Brown smoked and talked politics. He hated anything to do with the New Deal and with President Roosevelt.

Paul listened, encouraged him to do some exercises, gave him some pain medication, and moved on to the next home, which was located in a poor neighborhood. The house needed painting and the roof was covered with green fuzz. Paul stood in front of the porch steps, wondering if they were safe. They looked in need of repair. Seeing no other way to enter the house, he cautiously made his way up the rickety steps and knocked on the front door. A woman with mousy brown hair and pronounced cheekbones answered. She was excessively thin. "Yes? May I help you?"

"I'm Dr. Anderson. Are you Mrs. Erickson?"

"Yes."

"I'm here to see your son John."

"Where's Dr. Henley?"

"He's tied up at the hospital and asked me to help out today."

The woman eyed him suspiciously.

"If you'd like, I can have Dr. Henley see John another day."

"No. I want someone to look at him right away. He's not well." She stepped aside and opened the door wider.

Paul moved into a front room, with wooden floors and very few furnishings. A boy lay on a threadbare davenport.

Mrs. Erickson moved to her son. "This is John. He's twelve."

Paul would have guessed the lad to be closer to eight. "Mind if I sit?" John shook his head and Paul sat on the sofa beside him. "So, you haven't been feeling well lately."

"No sir."

"Can you describe the trouble?"

"Not sleeping too good."

"And he's restless, won't hold still when he is asleep," his mother said. "Sometimes his sheets are wet, from him sweating. I check him for fever, but he don't feel hot."

Paul listened to the youngster's heart and lungs, nodding as Mrs. Erickson talked. "How about his appetite?"

"He barely eats. Says he's not hungry."

Paul noticed the boy's stomach was distended. "He may have rickets. Does he get enough milk?" Paul knew the answer before Mrs. Erickson could respond.

"I do the best I can." She tipped her chin up slightly. "His father's workin' the docks, but he don't make much."

"I understand." Paul wished there were a way to help. He let out a slow breath. "He's got to get plenty of good cow's milk. And some extra butter plus as many eggs as you can manage." The creases in Mrs. Erickson's brow deepened. "And he needs lots of sunshine and fresh air."

She nodded, but despair was in her eyes.

Poverty. I hate it. Paul stood. "If you can do that, John should be all right."

"I'll try."

Paul closed his medical bag. He knew there wasn't enough money in this home for the kind of food the boy needed. He fished two ten-dollar bills from his wallet and held them out to her. The woman's eyes widened. "I want you to use this to get some of the food he needs."

She accepted the gift and in a small voice said, "Thank you."

"I'll tell Dr. Henley my findings. I'm sure he'll be back in another week or so to check on John." He briefly rested a hand on the boy's head.

Mrs. Erickson clutched the money to her chest. "The Lord bless you."

When Paul left, his mood was low. The money he'd given

wouldn't go far. But at least there were doctors here to help. He made his way back to the car and climbed in. His thoughts went to Alaska and to his patients there. What were they doing without a doctor?

He had two more stops to make, but the letter in his pocket didn't want to be ignored any longer. Maybe it was a good time for lunch.

Paul parked along the edge of the beach. He opened his lunch pail. As usual, Carolyn had made sure he had plenty. He removed the waxed paper from a roast beef sandwich and took a bite. He wasn't very hungry so he chewed slowly. The letter was on his mind. He returned the sandwich to the pail, closed the lid, and stepped out of the car.

He gazed at the sandy beach, the wind whipping his hair. It was cold, but he didn't care, and he started down the shoreline, heading for a large chunk of driftwood. When he reached it, he sat down and gazed out at the wind-whipped bay. Whitecaps flecked the blue waters like small snow-covered mountain peaks.

Finally, he reached into his pocket and took out the envelope. Every nerve in his body vibrated. He stared at the date. Susan hadn't known she would die in only two days.

He slid a finger beneath the seal. It came up easily; time had eroded the adhesive. There were two pages. The wind grabbed at the paper and nearly ripped it from his hands. He turned his back to the blustering air and read. When he saw Susan's writing, his heart wrenched. Unlike his mother, Susan's script was simple and unadorned. And there were smudges on the page.

"My dearest Esther," she began. "How I've missed you. I feel as if I've been locked away for months rather than weeks."

She hadn't said a word to Paul about being frustrated at her condition, which confined her to the house and to rest. Susan had never been one to complain. Paul returned to the letter. She went on to share some of what had been going on at home and that, aside from a headache now and again and swelling in her legs and feet, she felt quite well and she thought Paul worried too much.

The final days of her life swept toward him from the past—days of worry and anticipation. They were about to become parents. He remembered how Susan often rested her hand on her rounded stomach and how she'd talk to their son as if he were already in her arms. He'd tried to convince her to spend the final weeks of her confinement in the hospital, but she'd refused.

Susan continued, "I so wish you'd come for a visit. I'm not allowed to go out at all. I miss my family and friends. And Paul insists there will be no trips out until the baby arrives. And when that day comes I'm certain he will speed to the hospital in a frenzy, doctor or not."

Paul smiled. She was right. He would have.

"I'm concerned about him," she wrote. "He worries to the extreme. I doubt he gets much sleep for all of his anxiety. He watches over me with such care. There's never been a more devoted husband. I love him for his attentiveness, but I wish he would rest in the Lord more. After all, I belong to God. I trust him with me and my child."

Paul stopped reading, tears building behind his eyes. He had watched over her. He'd done everything he could to protect her. And Susan was right, he'd forgotten that God's hand was upon her. He felt a lightening of the burden he'd carried in his heart.

He wiped away tears and returned to the letter. "The waiting is dreadful. I'm so looking forward to pushing the pram down the street with my child in it. I do hope it's a boy. I'm sure he'll look just like his father and have the same sweet disposition.

"I wish you'd speak to Paul. He continues to insist that I stay at the hospital until our child is born. I've never told anyone, but I loathe hospitals. They smell of medicine and disease. And the horrid green paint they have on the walls is enough to make a person ill. Everyone is in a hurry, rushing from place to place wearing worry on their faces. It's a very unpleasant place."

She'd never told him how much she detested the hospital. Paul wiped his face with his hand. Or had she and he hadn't been listening?

She continued, "I don't know how Paul can manage working there. It's so full of pain and suffering."

That might be true, but it was also a place of healing, and he got to be part of that. He wished she would have seen that part of hospital life.

He returned to reading. "I truly want to have our child at home. It is warm and comforting here, the perfect place for a life to begin. I see no reason to go to the hospital at all. However, I can't persuade Paul to change his mind. Perhaps a word from you could make the difference. I know he's only thinking of my welfare, but I'm not afraid. I absolutely trust God. Our child and I are in his care. And should something go wrong . . . then it is his will. I have no doubts about his sovereignty."

Paul shook his head. He'd never had her faith. From the first day they'd met, she'd revealed it to him. They'd talked and talked and she'd openly shared her love for God without hesitation. All these years, he'd longed for the kind of faith she possessed and for the peace she carried within her. Now, she was in the presence of her Lord. Is that what God had intended all along?

Paul tried to imagine Susan and their son with God in heaven, living out an eternity of peace and joy. In all these years, he'd never considered their happiness. She'd been so young. It hadn't seemed fair. Didn't she have a right to a long life?

Paul could hear her speaking of God's will. How many times had he heard her lay a decision or a problem at the Lord's feet, always trusting, always believing for his best?

If what she believed was true, then she was where God wanted her. Paul had assumed that what had happened had been his doing because he hadn't insisted more strongly that Susan stay at the hospital.

As if blinders were being removed from his eyes, Paul could see. He'd done all he could. The rest was not up to him. He didn't possess the power to save her.

A sob rose from deep inside. He pressed the letter against his chest and dropped to his knees. As if a floodgate had been opened, tears flowed. He knelt on the deserted beach for a long time as seven years of sorrow were released. Finally, with the weight removed, he took a deep breath and looked toward the sky. A swirl of white clouds danced upon the wind.

It hadn't been his fault.

And now he knew what to do.

— 26 —

I wish you didn't have to leave so soon," Lily told Kate. She leaned against Clint.

"I'd like to stay, but I've got to get my plane ready." Kate hugged Lily. "I'm so happy for you." She looked up at Clint. "I expect you to take good care of my friend here. She's a special lady."

Clint smiled down at his bride and gave her a squeeze. "I promise."

Sassa held Teddy on one hip. "You'll look after each other. That's how it works between husbands and wives." Her brown eyes were bright with happiness.

Kate's pleasure slipped away. What was happening between her and Paul? It didn't feel like they were looking after each other. "I better go."

"Where are you off to now?" Sassa asked.

"I'm doing what you told me to—I'm getting my husband. Anyway, I hope that's what happens. I'm afraid he won't want to come back."

"He'll come. Don't you worry." Sassa gave Kate a hug with her free arm.

"Do you think you should fly down this time of year?" Lily asked.

"No. You take a ship," Sassa said. "The weather in the south is dangerous."

"I can't wait for a ship. Who knows how long it will take to book a cabin. And it's a day to Seward and then another six to Seattle. Plus two more on a train or bus." Kate shook her head. "It will take too long. We'll miss our first Christmas together."

"You're worried about Christmas? What about your life?" Sassa compressed her lips and shook her head.

"You don't have to worry. I've flown in every kind of weather, all over this territory. I've seen the worst Alaska has to offer. I'll be fine."

"Do not forget that you've also nearly died." Sassa softened her determined expression. "You go. But if the weather is bad, stay right where you are."

"I will."

"Promise."

Kate chuckled. "I promise." But even as she assured Sassa, Kate knew she'd push the limits. She felt an urgency that would be hard to restrain. "If I'm going to make Anchorage before dark, I'd better get moving. I already asked the boys if they'd watch over the dogs and they agreed." She smiled. "I promised to bring them something back from San Francisco."

Lily hugged Kate again. "I'll be praying for you and for Paul."

Sassa pulled Kate into her arms and held her tightly. "You come back, okay?"

"I will," Kate said, but she knew if Paul wanted a life in San Francisco, that's where she would stay.

It didn't take Kate long to ready the plane and load her bag along with extra water and fuel. After that, she fed and watered the dogs, gave them each a hug as if she might never see them again, and then headed for the creek.

The engine's roar filling her ears, Kate watched as the wind sifted fine snow over the surface of the ice. She sank her hand into Angel's deep ruff. "Ready, girl?" The dog whined and Kate started down the airstrip. The skies were clear, the air brittle as she lifted off the ground. She prayed the clear weather would hold.

Paul didn't know she was coming. She was sure that if he did, he'd try to talk her out of making the journey on her own, so she'd decided it would be better to just show up.

After a long night in Anchorage, the morning dawned clear and cold, a promising beginning. After a hurried breakfast, Kate headed for the airport. Jack and Sidney were the only ones in the shop when she walked in.

"Good morning," she said, hoping her excitement and trepidation weren't too obvious.

"Morning. No runs yet," Jack said, as he continued to read through a form.

"That's all right. I'm going to be gone for a couple of weeks."

Jack's head popped up. "What? Gone? But I need you here."

Trying to sound upbeat, Kate said, "I'm spending Christmas in California."

"You're leaving now?" Jack lifted his brows.

"Uh-huh. I know I should have let you know sooner, but I didn't even know until a couple of days ago. And you weren't here last night."

Jack scowled and leaned back in his chair, arms crossed over his chest. "You could have radioed."

"You'll be fine without me."

Sidney took a toothpick out of his mouth and tossed it

into the kindling box beside the stove. "I heard the weather's bad down south. Maybe you ought to hold off until it clears."

"I can't. Besides, it could change before I get there. If I'm lucky, I'll ride this clear weather all the way south."

Jack shook his head. "Knew you were a fool woman the first time I met you. But risking your life over a man?"

Kate wondered what had happened to the admiration he'd felt when they'd been in Palmer. "That man is my husband. And I'm not risking my life any more than when I fly for you." Kate knew better. This trip was different. She had very little flying experience in Southeast Alaska. The weather could be hideous and unpredictable. "I've got my maps and my plane's in top condition."

"Suit yourself," Jack said. "But pilots who leave their bosses in the lurch can't be trusted. So if someone comes along . . . well, I just might give them your spot."

Kate knew it was an empty threat. "Do as you like." She narrowed her eyes. "Whatever happened to your advice about bringing Paul home?" She grinned. "How'd you expect me to do it?"

"Yeah . . . well," he glanced at Sidney and cleared his throat. "I don't remember much about that."

"Today's the day." She strode to the door. "Oh. If Paul calls, tell him I'm on a run." Puzzlement crossed Jack's face, but Kate was done explaining and walked out.

She headed south. And she did ride the edge of high pressure coming from the north. With any luck she'd avoid the southern storms.

By the time she reached Juneau, the system was falling apart. Light clouds stretched across the sky, caught by upper airstreams. She'd done well, catching a tailwind and flying the calm airstreams, but all that was about to change. To the west, threatening clouds billowed above a dark sea.

The next morning the winds were strong and clouds hid the sky, but there was no snow or rain. Kate figured she'd make a stab at reaching Ketchikan. She dressed, skipped breakfast, and headed for the airport.

When she checked in at the airfield, the fellow manning the office said, "If it was me, I wouldn't go. Don't be a fool. That storm's coming in fast."

Kate stood at the door and looked at the sky. She knew it would be rough, but she'd seen worse. "I figure I'll be all right . . . at least as far as Ketchikan."

The man shook his head and shrugged. "Do as you like."

Once in the air, there were no quiet currents. Turbulence bucked Kate's plane, lifting her atop a mountain of air and then driving her downward. Snow splattered the windows, growing heavier as she pushed on. The storm allowed Kate only glimpses of the sea below and the heavy green forests that grew along the coastline. Had she made a terrible mistake? Would she die trying to reach Paul? Maybe she was a fool. She glanced at Angel, who lay curled up on the seat, sleeping. Kate remembered the story of Jesus and how he'd slept in the midst of a tempest. He'd trusted. *Lord, keep us in your hands,* she prayed and knew she wasn't alone. They'd be all right.

When she caught sight of Ketchikan, Kate heaved a sigh of relief, but getting down wasn't going to be easy. Winds buffeted her plane, tossing her about like a kite caught in a willful breeze. Snow was mixed with rain, visibility was still poor. Like a dance, her feet worked the pedals, her hands the control wheel. As she approached the ground, her speed dropped and she eased the control wheel forward, then felt the wheels touch. She bounced twice, but finally the plane rolled solidly on the ground. When it stopped, Kate rested her head on the control wheel. She'd made it.

She checked into a roadhouse, had a simple meal of soup and bread, and went to her room. Lying in bed, she imagined Paul beside her. She could nearly feel the warmth of his body, hear his steady breathing. She ached for him and prayed the weather would improve so she could continue south.

The following morning, she woke to a quiet world. Had the storm passed? She threw off her blankets and hurried to the window. The sky was gray, but the winds were quiet and there was no snow or rain falling. She smiled. She would be moving on.

After a breakfast of eggs and biscuits, she gathered her belongings and headed for the airstrip. She could make Seattle today, rest one night, and be in San Francisco the next day. And then in Paul's arms.

A low gray ceiling held Kate off the coast for most of the day. The terrain was too rugged to risk losing her way in the clouds and fog. By the time Kate spotted the emerald green islands of Puget Sound, daylight was fading. When the Seattle skyline came into view, she let out a whoop. She'd made it. Tomorrow she'd be in San Francisco.

Kate stepped out of the plane and into a warm drizzle. The air felt humid. She walked toward the terminal, Angel at her side. "So, girl, where do you think we'll stay tonight?" She checked in, got the name of an affordable hotel, and called a cab. She didn't have to wait long. Seattle had plenty of taxies. Big cities were nothing like Anchorage. Here there was abundance. In Alaska a person learned to make do. Kate preferred making do.

When she went to climb into the cab, the driver said, "No dogs!"

Kate kept a hand on Angel's collar. "I can't leave her here."

"No dogs." He squared his jaw and stared straight ahead.

"Look. I'll pay extra for her." She held out a quarter.

"One dollar."

Kate sucked in a frustrated breath. "Fine." She dug into her pocket and pulled out a dollar bill and handed it to the man. "Come on, girl." She climbed in and Angel followed, lying beside her on the seat.

At the hotel, Kate had the same argument with the clerk, which ended with the same solution. Once in her room, Kate showered, changed into a nightdress, and climbed into bed. She felt as if she was bundled inside a blanket of exhaustion, but she couldn't sleep. Her thoughts were on Paul. What would he do when he saw her? Would he be happy? What if he wasn't?

Of course he will be. He loves me.

Fatigue finally overcame her worries and she slept until morning sunlight slanted in a window. She opened her eyes and squinted into the light, then reached her arms over her head in a stretch. Excitement rolled through her. Today was the day!

Fully awake, she sat up and dropped her legs over the side of the bed. She'd skipped dinner the previous night and was starved.

Kate was more meticulous about her appearance, taking extra care with her hair and makeup. She also dabbed on *Evening in Paris* perfume. Paul would like that.

She left Angel in the room and went for breakfast in the hotel restaurant, where she laid out her map and studied it while she waited for her meal. The journey should be easy. All she had to do was follow US 99 south. She had it clearly marked, and where she turned southwest toward San Francisco, she'd placed a large black X.

As the waitress approached with her oatmeal and coffee, Kate rolled up the map.

"Where you headed?" asked the waitress.

"San Francisco."

"That's a mighty long way."

"Not so far. I'm flying."

The waitress smiled. "I always wanted to fly on one of those passenger planes. It must be exciting."

"It is," Kate said, not wanting to take time to explain that she was flying her own plane.

"Have a good trip." The woman moved on to customers at the next table.

Anxious to be on her way, Kate downed her oatmeal in a hurry, paid her bill, and returned to her room to retrieve her bag and Angel. The airport was close, so she walked, feeling more energized than she had since the baby died and Paul had left. With each step, her anticipation grew. She'd see him today!

Grateful for good weather, Kate flew south, her heart full as she took in the beauty of the rugged Cascade Mountains buried in heavy snow. Mount Rainier rose above the peaks as if she were standing guard. Yakima was on the other side of the mountains—so close. Kate decided she'd see her family on the trip back, if there was a trip back.

The Oregon countryside, with its open farms and forests, reminded her of a giant patchwork quilt. The Siskiyou Mountains of Southern Oregon seemed small compared with those in Alaska, but their wind currents were treacherous and took Kate by surprise. In a matter of moments her plane was tossed heavenward, and then dropped toward rugged white peaks. Kate brought the plane under control and vowed to respect *every* mountain range.

Beyond the peaks and hills of Northern California, the land seemed to reach out forever. Farmlands lay fallow and grasslands were a vivid green. The Sierra Mountains to the east looked blue, purple, and white, a feast of color and texture.

Kate contemplated what she should say to Paul. He'd asked

her to take a steamer, not fly. He'd likely be angry with her. And what would she do if he didn't want her here at all? He'd been less than communicative, calling infrequently, and there'd been only two letters. Of course telephone calls were expensive and Paul was a practical man.

When she was about a hundred miles north of San Francisco, Kate cut away from the highway and flew southwest. The countryside was mostly empty, with a few ranches and farms. It was possible Paul would want to live in San Francisco, so Kate tried to imagine life in a big city. It was difficult to see herself in a busy, congested world, but she figured God would enable her to do what was necessary. She wondered if anyone would hire a woman pilot.

When Kate approached the San Mateo airport, she radioed for clearance. She was instructed to wait while two larger aircraft landed. She circled the city. It was bigger than she'd imagined. How could a person live in such a place? Stacked along steep hillsides, buildings and homes crowded each other. Streets were congested with cars. And where was Paul in this huge city?

Finally, given the okay to land, she brought the plane in without mishap and taxied toward a hangar reserved for transient aircraft. A large, friendly looking man named Roger helped secure the plane and then checked it in.

"So, you flew all the way from Alaska on your own, huh." He shook his head and let out a low whistle. "Never heard anything like that. Even Amelia Earhart had a navigator."

"She made longer flights," Kate said, but she enjoyed the admiration.

Roger rested a hand on a wing. "Nice bird. I'll take good care of her for you." He walked along the side of her plane, running his hand down the fuselage. "How long you think you'll be in town?"

"Through Christmas. After that . . . I don't know."

He tipped his hat. "Okay. I'll see you after Christmas then. Enjoy your stay."

"Thank you." Kate slung her knapsack over one shoulder, hefted her bag, and headed toward the terminal. She patted her pocket where she'd tucked a piece of paper with Paul's address on it. Her heart hammered. Would he be home? What would she say?

Keeping a steady hold on Angel's leash, Kate walked out of the terminal. She hoped the noise and congestion wouldn't be too much for the dog. Angel was alert, but didn't seem distressed. *She's doing better than me*, Kate thought, wishing her heart would slow down.

A taxi zipped past her, then stopped in a hurry. Kate headed toward the bright yellow car. The rear door opened, and the man who was getting out looked so much like Paul that it took Kate's breath away. When he looked up, she felt as if her heart would stop. It really was him!

She dropped her bag. Angel barked and lunged on the leash. "Paul?"

Before she could take a step, he'd closed the distance between them and pulled her into his arms and held her tightly. "Kate. What are you doing here?" He held her at arm's length. "I didn't know you were coming." He laughed, then hugged her again.

She felt as if her legs would give out and wrapped her arms about his neck. "I wanted to surprise you. How did you know?"

"I didn't." He looked down at her. "I was on my way north . . . to see you. I'm catching a flight in an hour." His eyes widened. "We nearly missed each other."

"You never called and I didn't know if you were coming home."

"I did call—again and again. No one answered at the air-field and you weren't at the house. When I talked to Albert, he said he thought you were out at the cabin. Two days ago I tried again and Jack said you were on a run."

"I . . . I was afraid you didn't want me—that you'd found a new life here. I'm so sorry."

Paul smiled and there was a light in his eyes that Kate had never seen. "I did find a new life."

Kate took a step back, fear rolling through her.

Paul took her hands in his. They were warm and strong. "I'm happy, Kate. Truly happy. I found a letter from Susan."

A small gasp escaped Kate and alarm surged. Susan? A gust of wind caught her hair and blew it across her eyes.

Paul gently brushed it off her forehead. "Before she died, Susan wrote a letter to my mother. In that letter I saw her heart, and I understand better now about her death. It wasn't my fault. All these years I've been playing God. I can't begin to comprehend the ways of God, but I know he allowed Susan and our son to leave my life. I don't understand why, but maybe it's not for me to know."

A gush of air left Kate's lungs. It's what she had prayed for. He was free. "Oh Paul. I'm so happy. I've been so afraid for you, for us."

"You don't have to be afraid anymore." He pulled her close. "I've dreamed of holding you. I haven't stopped thinking about you, not for a minute."

"I thought you wanted to stay here in San Francisco. If you do, I'll stay too. It doesn't matter where we live as long as we're together."

Paul looked down at her, his brown eyes smiling. "I thought about it . . . for a minute. But you and I belong in Alaska. We have a mission there, a life waiting for us."

Kate nestled against him. "Oh how I love you." She

wrapped her arms about him, holding him as tightly as she could manage.

Paul rested his chin on her head. "I'm done playing God." He tipped her face up and gazed at her, his lips lifted in a lop-sided smile. "I'm no good at it anyway." Tenderness warmed his eyes and he pressed his lips to Kate's. "You belong to God. I'll do my best to care for you and help you see reason, but you're his."

Kate's heart was full. "I am, but I'm also yours." She pressed in closer.

Paul took her face in his hands and he pressed his lips to her forehead and then nuzzled her neck. She shivered beneath his touch. He sought her lips again, kissing gently, caressing . . . loving.

There in the midst of the city they were one, aware only of each other. "I was afraid I'd lost you," Kate said.

"Never," Paul whispered.

Acknowledgments

As a writer, I've learned to rely on God to provide resources and people who come alongside and supply knowledge and insight so the stories I tell will be genuine and spirited. He's never let me down. When I went to work on *Joy Takes Flight*, I did my part and God did his, and the plot, characters, and scenes in this book came to life. I believe with my whole heart that God brought together a team of writers, editors, and knowledgeable people to make this story soar.

Again, graciously, Gayle Ranney stepped up and provided her expertise as both a pilot and an Alaskan. She was able to fill in the gaps for me and help me plant Kate in the seat of her Bellanca Pacemaker in a way that would take readers along with Kate on her adventures. Thank you, Gayle. I am forever grateful.

Once more, my family provided details about Alaska that only Alaskans can know. I owe much to my brother Bruce, who patiently answered my questions and went above and beyond to provide extra material "just in case." He's lived the dream of experiencing the true Alaska. My dear sister Myrn gave me additional details that helped flesh out scenes. And my mother Elsa's love of her home state, her experiences, and her insights flow throughout the pages of this story. I love you, Mom.

In addition, God has blessed me with the greatest critique group. Ann Shorey, Judy Gann, and Sarah Sundin provided their friendship, writing expertise, insights, and devotion to the written word to help me create this story. I am forever grateful to you all, my writing comrades.

Sadly, Kelli Standish of PulsePoint Design will be moving forward to a new calling and I am forced to say farewell to her exceptional skills, original thinking, and energy and passion for creating the very best content and personality for my website. Your gifts helped to introduce my work to new readers. Thank you. I'm going to miss you.

It has been a privilege to work with the Revell team. To my editors, Lonnie Hull DuPont and Barb Barnes—you're top rate. To the editors working in the background, thank you for your sharp eye and dedication to quality work. I owe a great deal to Michele Misiak. It's been good to have a teammate who has worked hard to herald my work. Cheryl Van Andel, you and your team create fabulous covers. I've loved every one, and *Joy Takes Flight* is no exception. Although we are cautioned not to judge a book by its cover, a great cover helps. And you create stunning covers.

Wendy Lawton, you're more than an agent. You are a friend and a partner who stands beside me as I make my way through the weeds of this writing world. It is comforting to have you at my side. Thank you for all you do.

Bonnie Leon dabbled in writing for many years but never set it in a place of priority until an accident in 1991 left her unable to work at her job. She is now the author of several historical fiction series, including the Sydney Cove series, Queensland Chronicles, the Matanuska series, the Sowers Trilogy, the Northern Lights series, and now the Alaskan Skies series. She also stays busy teaching women's Bible studies, speaking, and teaching at writing seminars and women's gatherings. Bonnie and her husband, Greg, live in southern Oregon. They have three grown children and five grandchildren.

Visit Bonnie's website at www.bonnieleon.com.

Meet Bonnie at
WWW.BONNIELEON.COM

Sign up for her newsletter, read her blog,
and learn interesting facts!

BECOME A FAN ON

f Bonnie Leon

and

f Bonnie Leon's Fan Page

"Vivid writing. Bonnie Leon immerses the reader in the time period, the setting, and deep into the hearts of the characters. I didn't want to leave them behind when I closed the book."

—Lena Nelson Dooley, author of
Love Finds You in Golden, New Mexico

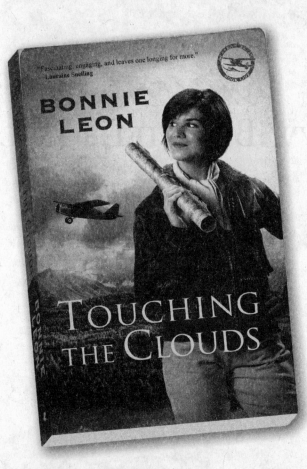

An adventurous young female pilot with a pioneering spirit makes a new start in 1930s Alaska Territory.

Revell
a division of Baker Publishing Group
www.RevellBooks.com

Available Wherever Books Are Sold

"This story is a winner—I loved it! Leon
has done a masterful job of bringing Alaska
and its people to vibrant life."

—Ann Shorey, author of
the *At Home in Beldon Grove* series

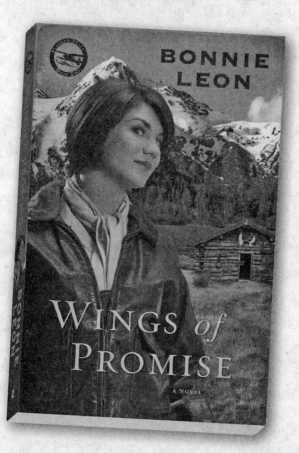

Full of high-flying adventure and tender personal moments,
Wings of Promise will sweep you away to the Alaskan skies.

"You'll disappear into another place and time and be both encouraged and enriched for having taken the journey."

—Jane Kirkpatrick, bestselling author

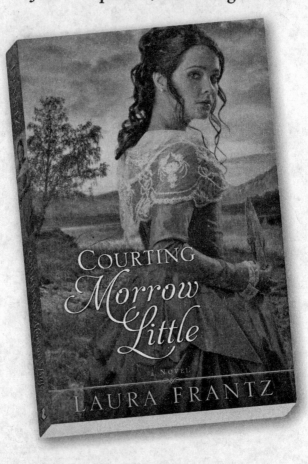

This sweeping tale of romance and forgiveness will envelop readers as it takes them from a Kentucky fort through the vast wilderness of the West.

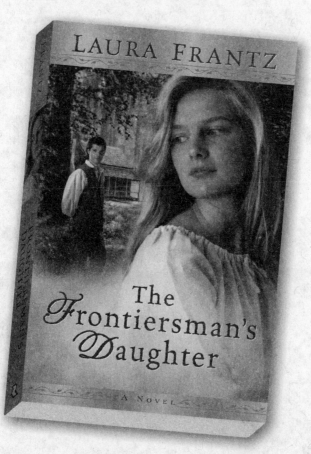

Find yourself immersed in this powerful story of love, faith, and forgiveness.

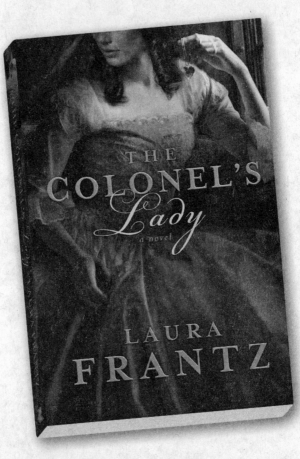

In 1779, a search for her father brings Roxanna to the Kentucky frontier—but instead she discovers a young colonel, a dark secret . . . and a compelling reason to stay.